THIS BOOK BE
MRS. MARION
OF:- 1st FLOOR
THE CO
WATERLOO Rd,
HAINFORD,
NORWICH,
NORFOLK.
NR10 3AX.

IN HONOUR BOUND

IN HONOUR BOUND

Christine Webber

CENTURY
LONDON MELBOURNE AUCKLAND JOHANNESBURG

Grateful acknowledgement is given for permission to quote from the song, 'Fool, if you think it's over', words and music by Chris Rea, copyright Magnet Music Ltd

Grateful acknowledgement is given for permission to quote from the song 'Autumn Leaves' which is used by permission of Peter Maurice Music Pub Co Ltd, London WC2H OLD

First published in Great Britain in 1987 by
Century Hutchinson Ltd
Brookmount House, 62–65 Chandos Place
London WC2N 4NW

Century Hutchinson Publishing Group Australia Pty Ltd
16–22 Church Street, Hawthorn, Melbourne, Victoria 3122

Century Hutchinson Group New Zealand Limited
PO Box 40–086, Glenfield, Auckland 10, New Zealand

Century Hutchinson Group South Africa (Pty) Limited
PO Box 337, Bergvlei 2012, South Africa

British Library Cataloguing in Publication Data

Webber, Christine
In honour bound.
I. Title
823'.914[F] PR6073.E1/

ISBN 0–7126–1691–8

Printed in Great Britain by
Anchor Brendon, Tiptree, Essex

To Jack Dominian for his invaluable help

Chapter One

'So are you primarily interested in surgery or show business?' From somewhere on the floor she heard a sharp intake of breath. There was a long pause which, had the interview not been live, might have been mistaken for a freeze-frame. The eventual answer did nothing to raise the temperature.

'Miss Bartlett, I sympathise with your desire to appear probing rather than merely decorative, but surely this trashy, tabloid approach is unnecessary?'

In the box above the studio the director, Mark, squirmed uneasily in his swivel chair. 'Oh-oh. How long to off-air?'

'Two and a half minutes,' came the reply.

'What the hell's happening down there? I know Aziz is a colourful character, but no one faults him medically as far as I know. Is Helen on to something, or is she just bitching? And why? Why would she do that?' Mark's questions hung as heavily in the air as the smoke from three lighted cigarettes and one cigar. He depressed the key that would effect contact with his presenter. 'Helen, you don't need me to tell you this isn't going well. I suggest you wind up early and do a longer end link.'

She was off-camera to the viewers, but on one of the monitors above him he saw her nod, though he was unsure whether it was as a consequence of his instruction or at something the interviewee had said.

'My point is this, Mr Aziz. Heart transplants are glamorous – people up and down the country support your efforts by running football matches, coffee mornings and so on, while less headline-grabbing branches of medicine are dying on their feet.'

'My dear lady, I have a skill which God gave me, and I have developed that through hard work, research and simply *doing*. I can give life to people, and I am not going to apologise just because it offends your particular type of social conscience.'

The PA and vision-mixer in production control were flustered now; they could see that the surgeon was countering Helen's questions with answers calculated to suggest she was hysterical and superficial. 'What a pig!' Sandy, the PA, was incensed. The vision-mixer, who was engrossed in cutting between the two protagonists, nodded her agreement.

The editor, puffing nervously in the corner, said nothing.

Helen was winding up. Those watching from the box knew that she was rattled, but technique was taking over. She sounded in command as she said they would have to leave many questions unanswered.

'Cut to camera two,' instructed Mark in the box.

'Twenty seconds to captions,' said Sandy.

'And that's it for tonight.' Helen smiled in close-up. 'Tomorrow our consumer feature asks, "Is knicker elastic as elastic as it once was?" We have our cookery spot, viewers letters and, of course, the summing up of the stories of the day. Who knows what they may bring?' She grinned. 'See you then. Have a good evening.'

The director had spun in the music. The caption was up. 'Five seconds to off-air,' said Sandy. 'Four, three, two, one – off-air!'

'Thanks very much, everybody,' said Mark. The editor was already collecting his papers together. A semblance of normality returned.

On the floor the surgeon unclipped the microphone from his tie with a deftness of movement that indicated television was not unfamiliar to him. He gave Helen a withering look. 'I can't say this has been a pleasure, Miss Bartlett,' he said, then he turned on his heel and left.

She sat slumped in the position she had adopted the moment the cameras were off her. A good programme was exhausting but exhilarating, a bad one utterly draining.

The sound man unmiked her. He wondered if he should say something. Helen was popular and, though her position removed her to some extent from the rank and file, she was generally regarded as one of the chaps. He risked it. 'Don't worry, love. He's a pompous ass, and that's what your viewers will think.'

Helen looked at the immaculate dark figure disappearing through the heavy double doors. She turned back sadly and shook her head. 'I blew it, Alan. I really ballsed it up.'

'Can I strike this chair?' It was one of the stage crew, unmoved by the recent drama and anxious only to leave for home.

'What? Oh . . . yes. Sorry.' She gathered up her scripts and walked slowly from the studio.

The hospitality room was buzzing. The post-mortem was already in progress. 'He was infuriating,' said Mark. 'Typical bloody Arab playboy. She was right in a way . . .' He tailed off. The editor had left, reluctant to face the viewers' phone calls, but the controller was there, and the head of stills, and the general manager, and the company secretary.

'She handled the end beautifully, I will say that. She lifted it by doing that menu of tomorrow's lightweights, but it was hardly Helen at her best,' said the controller. 'By the way,' he went on, 'did anyone offer Aziz a drink?'

No one knew.

'Is Helen coming up?' asked Bunny. He had been with the company for years as head of stills and a newspaper man before that. Presenters come and go, but he had always maintained that Helen was one of the best.

'Paul,' he said to the controller, 'why don't you go and find her? Tell her it wasn't so bad.'

'I can't do that, Bunny,' he replied. 'I'm going to the club in a minute. I'll talk to her if she turns up there. She'll probably bounce back tomorrow, but my guess is she won't want to face any of us tonight.'

His guess was right. Helen had already been sought out by Laura, a reporter and close friend. They needed a drink but decided against the hospitality suite and the club; instead they made for a hotel a few minutes' walk down the road. The girls had a good relationship and instinctively fell into a routine that was almost unconsciously re-enacted every time either of them had a bad day. The wounded party sat down in a corner while the other played the combined role of host and agony aunt.

It was a dark and sparsely populated room. Helen was glad of its gloominess. Her head was in her hands. She sighed deeply, and one tiny tear trickled, unheeded, down her cheek, leaving a faint flaw in the otherwise impeccable make-up. 'Oh, God, Laura!' she said at last.

'Do you want to talk about it?'

Helen sighed. 'I don't know what to say. I don't really know what happened.' Her left hand pushed back her hair impatiently as her right reached for the large gin-and-tonic.

'Look,' said Laura, 'I know we've said it before, and it doesn't help at the time, but the virtue of live television is that once it's over, it's forgotten. You're back on tomorrow. You'll be great and few people will remember today. Certainly nobody sitting at home is agonising over it as you are.'

'I know, I know . . . Oh, God,' Helen said again as she remembered. 'Let's talk about you instead.' So they did.

Laura was younger and taller; she had superb, wavy auburn hair and was involved long-term, and mostly happily, with a lover, which Helen was not. Like Helen, though, she took the job very seriously and knew exactly what her friend was going through. 'Helen,' she said finally, 'why don't you come back and have supper with Ian and me? He's in the business. He'll understand if you want to talk, and he'll understand if you don't.'

'No, I can't,' said Helen with a start. 'Heavens, what time is it?'

'Quarter to eight. Why?'

'I'm going to a dinner party and it's the last thing I want to do.'

'Can't you scrub it?'

'No, I can't. They're the sort of people who do the table properly. It would upset the numbers. He's a dentist in Harley Street. The've got a son who's a cameraman or something. I met them at a party. They asked me to dinner – well, you know why. People like us. I'm not being unkind, but it's 'er-off-the-telly and all that.' In spite of herself Helen smiled.

Laura smiled too, knowingly.

'Anyway,' said Helen, 'apparently they always watch the medical spot and seem to like it, though I expect tonight was the exception. Oh, God!' she said again.

Laura got up and kissed her friend on the cheek. 'It's probably a good thing. Leave the car, then you can have a good drink. What time do you have to be there?'

'Eight thirty,' said Helen. 'It's all right. You go. I'll go back to the studios, do the face and put on the posh frock. You know us – back in the old routine.'

They parted. Helen was beginning to feel a little better. Laura was looking forward to seeing Ian but she was troubled by the day. Helen was a good friend, and her behaviour tonight had not been typical.

Pockets of people within the company were, at that very moment voicing Laura's thought. The controller had reached the social club, where he made it a policy never to talk business. His deputy was already there, and although their habit was to seek out drinking partners from other sections of the company to, as they put it, keep their fingers on the pulse, Paul made straight for his colleague. He also broke his golden rule.

'Did you see *Reporting at Six* tonight, Brian?'

'Yup!'

'Well?'

'Well what?'

'You know – Helen.'

'She just bit off more than she could chew.' Brian was not quite as enamoured of their golden girl as most other people seemed to be.

'I think that's unfair. She may be attractive, but she's handled some quite harrowing stuff in her time.'

'I'm not knocking her.'

Paul privately thought that he was. 'You don't think we're pushing her too hard, do you?'

'Helen pushes herself,' said Brian. 'She's the one who agrees to all the personal appearances. She doesn't have to do them. She's the one who's always dreaming up new features, not us. I know it's a cliché, but she is your archetypal workaholic.'

'All right, then,' – Paul warmed to his theme – 'is she pushing herself too hard? It's true she never stops, but let's be honest, we do make use of that.'

'She's trying to prove something, that's all.'

'What?'

'It's obvious.' Brian expanded. 'She landed the job against tough, experienced competition. So she had that, plus what seemed to the rest of us to be an idyllically happy marriage. Two years ago husband walks out, bored with being Mr Thatcher, and if you look back, you'll see that ever since then she's worked like a maniac.'

'Well, I just hope she's not cracking up, that's all.'

'Now who's knocking her? You and I can make a mistake and very few people know it. This is her first major boob and the whole world sees it. Maybe she's pre-menstrual or something.'

Paul nodded. They were pleased they had found a plausible excuse. They emptied their glasses, ordered more drinks and proceeded to talk golf.

Back in the make-up room, Helen had made good the damage to her face; the veil was perfect, but her eyes betrayed the anxiety beneath it. She looked coldly at her image in the large mirror, which was surrounded by brightly lit light bulbs. 'Not so clever after all, are you?' she said out loud.

But a decision following a whole day of decision-making had yet to be made. She had told Laura she would go to the dinner party. Had she meant it, or had she said it simply to stop her friend worrying and to prevent any prolonged exchange? She wanted – needed – to dissolve, but she would not do it in company.

Her public self strode to the fore. She determined to go and to make a great effort. The dinner party in itself was of little consequence, but it would serve as a dress rehearsal for tomorrow. No one must be allowed to glimpse or guess at her inner disintegration. She walked to her dressing-room, having decided already to wear her favourite pale-pink Chanel suit. It was appropriately sedate, but feminine, and she felt good in it.

There was a knock on the door.

'Your taxi's here, Helen.' It was the duty security man.

'Thanks, George,' she said as she emerged. 'Have a good evening.'

'I don't suppose it will be as good as yours, luv,' he said.

If only he knew, she thought, as she was climbing into the cab.

'Evening, Miss Bartlett,' said the driver. He loved to pick people up from the studios. It gave him something to tell his missus when he got home. Helen assumed he had been on duty and had missed the programme. The guests at the dinner party, on the other hand, might well have made a point of watching it prior to meeting her. She checked her face in her compact mirror just for reassurance as the taxi sped through the streets of central London towards the gentler, more gracious environs of St John's Wood.

They arrived. She paid the driver and tipped him more than necessary before running up the steps to the front door. The Harrisons, it seemed, lived on the fourth floor. Betty Harrison answered the intercom, and Helen waited for the click of the lock, then pushed open the heavy door to find herself in a blue, deeply carpeted hall. She struggled with the lift gates and broke a nail in the process. Tears stung her eyes, and she took several deep breaths before pressing the button that would propel her to the site of her three-hour ordeal. She had made a quick calculation in the taxi of how long a meal with good wines would last and how soon she might escape.

Betty opened the gates at the top and kissed her warmly on both cheeks. 'My dear, how nice of you to come – but, before we go in, I must tell you something. It's my fault, and I did think you would have so much in common and it would all be so perfect . . .'

'Helen!' boomed Reginald from the doorway. 'How's

my girl? Looking as luscious as ever, eh? Pity I'm not twenty years younger.'

'Thirty,' said his wife drily.

Unable to avoid his insistent hand on her shoulder, Helen was hustled into the flat. 'Now, let me introduce you to everyone,' the voice went on. 'I'm sure this lady is a familiar face.' He was enjoying himself as he addressed the assembled gathering. 'This is my son, Herbert, and his wife, Dorothy.' Helen smiled politely. 'My partner, Cyril, and his wife, Sally – second wife, actually, lucky dog! Got time off for good behaviour and all that.' He chuckled at the joke which Cyril and Sally no longer found funny, if they ever had. 'And this – ' Reginald gestured towards the distinguished-looking, dark-haired man in the corner who was diligently studying a painting.

He turned. 'We've met, actually.'

It was Aziz.

There was absolute silence for a moment. Like the pause in the studio, it seemed to extend for ever. Helen closed her eyes and bit her lip hard. The pain was real but so, unfortunately, was he, for when she re-opened her eyes the surgeon was still before her, stubborn, solid and supercilious.

Six of the eight people present were aware of the events earlier that evening. Reginald and his son Herbert were not. They had arrived together only shortly before Helen. Reginald, who enjoyed these gatherings, had taken charge immediately, and his wife had not found the moment to tell him of the programme. Herbert's wife had not known that Helen Bartlett was to be there, so had not thought to mention it.

'Excellent,' said Reginald.

'What is?' asked his wife sharply.

Reginald looked surprised for a moment at her tone. 'That these two young people know each other, of course. Come along, my dear, let's get you a drink. I expect you've had a long day.'

Helen allowed herself to be led to the drinks table, where she was poured an enormous gin-and-tonic. She smiled at Reginald with new fondness; he had rescued her. He talked at her, pleased to have such an appreciative audience, and she used the one-sided conversation to regain her composure.

After five minutes or so her resolve, liberally laced with gin, was taking effect. She chatted brightly to Reginald on some new dental implanting technique she had read about. She had previously decided to act a part, but now that Aziz was here it was to be an Oscar-winning performance. Anger was replacing the hurt and shock. She remembered why she had asked her questions and felt more justified that she had done so by the minute.

Reginald broke away to supervise the seating plan, and Helen allowed herself a glance at the enemy. He was being well taken care of by Dorothy and Sally.

'You're here,' Reginald's voice broke her train of thought, 'on my left, Helen. We'll put Cyril beside you, Dorothy there, Herbert at the other end, Betty next to him, Sam in the middle, Sally next to me. Am I lucky or am I lucky?' he finished, looking lecherously at Helen on one side and Sally on the other.

Aziz was rather close for comfort but not impossibly so, Helen decided. She wondered what his connection was with the Harrisons and why Reginald had referred to him as Sam. It seemed an unlikely name for an Egyptian.

The octagonal plates indicated that the meal was going to conform to the *nouvelle cuisine* vogue. Betty Harrison was a spry sixty-year-old who clearly belonged to the breed of wives who keep abreast of new developments that relate to the home, love their husbands despite (or maybe because of) their chauvinism, delight in their children and grandchildren and read fiction rather than facts.

The salmon mousse was delicious – and the perfect formula for two of the guests who were not particularly hungry. Reginald was proud of his knowledge of wines and, if the array of glasses at every place was anything to go by, there was to be a lot of it. He explained each one as he poured it, and Helen asked what she hoped were intelligent questions. She was not a wine buff but her motto, 'you're safe with Sancerre', seemed to serve her well enough when she entertained.

Helen was too far away from the Harrisons' son to speak to him, but Cyril, on her left, explained that he was not the one in television but the one in dentistry and that they all, Aziz included, had rooms in the same large house in Harley Street. She asked quietly about the surgeon.

'Funny sort of fellow,' said Cyril. 'Very quiet, very well-bred, totally absorbed in his career. Some might say publicity-seeking, but I don't know. Doesn't mix much. Occasionally see him with some blonde or other, but he never brings them to anything. Bit surprised to see him here, actually. He tends not to accept invitations that are purely social.'

Helen encouraged Cyril to keep talking and, by giving him her whole attention, she could mostly avoid looking at the Egyptian. She noticed, though, that he was pleasantly attentive to the ladies on each side of him and indulgent of Reginald's pleasure in producing bottle after bottle of interesting wine while imbibing very little of it himself.

Helen had no such inhibitions. She knew she was drinking too much, but she knew too that her stories about the background of television were going down well, especially with those drinking as much as she.

The food came and went. A trio of tiny pink lamb cutlets. Next a salad or cheese and, later, zabaglione, which Helen declined, though Aziz did not. They left the table, and Helen wondered fleetingly whether the ladies would be encouraged to disappear altogether while the men indulged in men's talk and drank port or brandy. But no.

To her horror, as they adjourned to the lounge, she found herself next to Aziz. She felt sure he was as disquieted as she, but to refuse to sit by him would have spoiled her act of bravado. She broke the ice. 'How long have you been in this country, Mr Aziz?'

He looked surprised. 'I came to school here.'

They fell silent but realised individually and gratefully that everyone else was chatting away noisily. He looked at her dispassionately, almost disinterestedly, she thought.

'Why do you dislike me so much, Miss Bartlett?' He spoke softly.

It was Helen's turn to look surprised. 'I don't even know you.'

'What was all that about different branches of medicine and my depriving them?'

Earlier she would have sounded off extravagantly about one of her hobby-horses, but she recognised his attempt to diffuse the situation; moreover, she was mellowing with wine and the lateness of the hour. Suddenly she felt extraordinarily tired and unsure. It was an effort to explain, but she did so calmly.

'I receive letters all the time from people waiting and hoping for a cure for ghastly afflictions like cystic fibrosis. Old folk write to me when they're crippled with arthritis and have to endure pain for years before they get near the operating table for a replacement hip. A woman wrote yesterday who is bleeding continuously. She won't even see the consultant gynaecologist for four months. All I meant was, people fund-raise like mad for up-front medicine like open-heart surgery, and there's a scanner appeal in practically every county now because cancer continuously grabs the headlines. I'm not saying that's bad. All I am saying is that there's a hell of a lot of suffering in other areas that mostly gets forgotten.'

He looked at her more kindly. 'I see. I don't know much about you, Miss Bartlett. I had no idea you really cared.'

His gentleness caught her off-guard. She looked at him, feeling strangely vulnerable. 'Do you know, I think I ought to go. I'm awfully tired,' she said.

'You're not driving.' It was a statement rather than a question.

'No, I'll get a taxi.'

'I'll drive you.'

'No!' She surprised herself by her vehemence. Instantly she regretted it. 'I'm just not very good company.'

'Miss Bartlett, you've probably done enough talking for one evening. I'll drive you – in silence, if you like.'

She disliked him again. He was obviously mocking her.

They said their goodbyes together, much to Betty Harrison's surprise. It was raining, but his car, a silver

Mercedes convertible, was parked efficiently right outside. How perfectly predictable. He opened the passenger door, helped her in, reached for the seatbelt and handed it to her before shutting her inside. He was treating her like a weak and fragile female; it was an unfamiliar sensation.

'Where to, madam?'

'Holland Park, please.'

'Ah, that's good. Having made this noble gesture, I wondered if you lived miles and miles from me. As it happens, you don't.'

'Where do you live then?'

'Near Kew Bridge, so you're on my way.'

'Oh, good! I wouldn't want to be a nuisance.' She was sarcastic now. She was also dejected and exhausted. She sat numbly, watching his hands.

Naturally, he drove expertly and, true to his promise, did not talk until he needed to ask for directions. They motored slowly down the quiet avenue and came to rest on a bed of wet, slippery autumn leaves. He got out and walked around to help her. He took her arm.

'Thank you,' she said.

'Miss Bartlett, I'm not sure, but I think I may owe you an apology.'

She was almost too weary to reply, but not quite. 'If you're not sure, you don't,' she snapped. 'I'll tell you something, though,' she went on. 'I'm sorry. I'm sorry about lots of things. I'm especially sorry today ever happened.' Her voice was rising. She suspected she sounded hysterical, which, of course, would confirm his worst suspicions. She made the final effort that day to be reasonable. 'Thank you for driving me home, Mr Aziz.' And she was gone.

He sat for a while in his car. He selected a cassette of Brahms's *Requiem*. He listened to the pianissimo orchestral opening and, as the first strains of the chorus singing 'Selig sind' sounded all around him, he lit up his first cigarette of the day. He hardly drank, hardly smoked. His life was orderly and successful, but, as he sat in that leafy lane, something was troubling him. He brushed his hair back impatiently with his left hand. It had been a hell of a day. Damn the woman! He started up the engine and drove off at speed.

Helen was in bed, unaware of the scene outside. She was shedding the tears that had been threatening all evening. Uncharacteristically, she had not removed her make-up, and dark, damp streaks of mascara stained the cream lace pillow as she sobbed noisily into the stillness. What is happening to me? she wondered. I have everything most people would give their eye teeth for. But the more she tried to count her blessings, the more the tears flowed. Damn the man! she thought. It's all his fault. She switched off the bedside lamp. The sobs gradually subsided, and she slept.

Chapter Two

A milk float stopped in the street below. Helen heard the ratchet-like sound of a handbrake, the tinkling of bottles on a stone step and a hum as the vehicle restarted. She listened as the process was repeated several times with a gradual diminuendo. She was undeniably awake. Her head ached. Her eyes were heavy and her mouth dry. She had rarely felt less enthusiastic about a forthcoming day. She quickly ran over the events of the previous evening and blushed as she recalled the parting from Aziz. She decided, however, not to dwell on her embarrassment but to concentrate her mind on the task of getting through Friday.

It was her raging thirst that finally prompted her move from the womb-like warmth of her bed. She padded into her all-white kitchen in search of mineral water and orange juice. She peered at the kitchen clock, blinking against the glare of the sun streaming through the blinds; it was still only seven-thirty. My god, she thought, for she certainly ought to have slept longer in preparation for the challenge ahead. She guessed she must look dreadful but was not overly anxious to confirm her belief. She poured another glass of mixed water and orange juice. Her feet felt chilled on the white tiled floor, but she endured the discomfort while she swallowed handfuls of pills. Three primrose-oil capsules to soak up the alcohol, two vitamin B tablets for nerves and to keep grey hairs at bay, three vitamin C pills to prevent colds and to counteract the harmful effects of the odd cigarette, two ginseng pills (though for what she was suddenly unsure), five yeast tablets for good skin and three vitamin E capsules to halt the ageing process and maintain her sex drive.

'And that's a bloody waste of time,' she said aloud.

A plan, that was what was needed: a plan of action for today. She picked up a pencil and sucked the end of it till her priorities became clear.

1. 7.45 Do Jane Fonda workout.
2. 8.15 Switch on heated rollers. Get in bath.
3. 8.30 Put in rollers.
4. 8.35 Make up face.
5. 9.00 Listen to news.
6. 9.10 Skim through papers.
7. 9.30 Ring for taxi. Take rollers out.
8. 9.50 Leave.
9. 10.00 Arrive.
10. 10.30 Meeting.
11. Do letters on migraine.
12. Lunch – canteen.
13. Read biog. on Polish pianist, due in next Tuesday.
14. Get made up.
15. Do prog.
16. Drink with Laura.
17. Come home – early.

She underlined it twice at the bottom. She could cope with that.

Back in her L-shaped bedroom she popped the Jane Fonda cassette into her video machine and positioned herself so she could see both the television and her own image in the full-length mirror that ran down the side wall. If they could see you now, she thought, as she took in, for the first time, the ravages of the night before.

She bent and stretched with the class before her. Their contrived, almost brutal, good health was even more irksome than usual. Exercising was not her favourite activity, but as she flexed and reached out, feeling her lungs expand right to their base, she had to admit to feeling recharged.

As a rule Helen went to the studios without bothering about her hair or make-up. The daytime was for preparation, picking up on the news and features of the moment, arranging items and answering letters and phone calls. Glamour had no part in it. Come four-thirty, however, she would spend an hour in the make-up room prior to the programme and emerge transformed into the front person the viewers expected to see. Today was different, though. She sensed that if she looked good, she would be better equipped to deal with the criticism she was expecting.

Lying in the bath, she allowed herself a sneaking analysis of her state of mind. It was like levering open a jack-in-the-box in the hope of seeing the surprise without its springing out and taking over. She wondered, as the substance of a recent magazine article popped into her mind, if she might be suffering from 'burn-out', but until yesterday her work load, daunting though it might seem to others, had posed no problems to her performance.

Her fair skin was rosy after the bath, and she appraised her body in the mirror as she towelled herself dry. She sighed. She was in good shape for a woman of thirty-five, though it was hardly a matter for congratulation since no one nowadays saw her undressed. She stared at her mirror image and cupped a breast in each hand. She squeezed gently. It was comforting. A vague feeling of desire was stirring, desire for good sex and the release it brings rather than for anyone past or present. She allowed her hands to wander over her body. She stroked her inner thighs before her right hand sought her pubic hair. She yielded to her sudden need to touch and fondle and found herself already wet. Her nipples were erect; a faint flush was spreading from them into her neck. A string of orgasms might prove marvellous therapy, but firmly, if perversely, she chose not to find out.

By the time the taxi arrived, Helen felt she would pass muster. That was the easy part; now she must act as reasonably as she looked.

'Morning. Morning. Morning . . .' She greeted everyone in her familiarly buoyant style as she wandered through the already untidy and smoke-filled newsroom to her office through the double doors at the far end. There was a mound of fresh letters on her permanently untidy desk; perhaps a coffee injection would spur her on to deal with them. She walked purposefully back through the newsroom to the canteen beyond. People seemed to be looking at her strangely, but she pushed the observation behind her, hoping that, if only she could behave normally today, they would forget.

'Shall we start some of the mail before the meeting, Sue?' Her secretary was in a group of youngsters discussing the weekend ahead. She looked puzzled, for Helen did not generally want to know about the day's post until eleven o'clock at the earliest. She raised her eyebrows at the others before picking up her pencil and shorthand pad and following Helen to her office.

Several dozen letters later, which comprised the usual press releases, inquiries about recent features, requests for photographs and invitations to open bazaars, Helen reluctantly called a halt. Sue left to type the replies, delighted to escape. Helen generally took the letters at a more leisurely pace, brought them both coffee and asked about her boyfriend. Not today, though. She was being efficient in the extreme. But Helen knew it was one thing to conjure up Super-woman for her secretary and quite another to convince her colleagues at the ten-thirty meeting.

She had long maintained that the morning gathering should begin with an assessment of the previous day's performance. She had campaigned for a run-down of all the dissatisfactions with it and for answers to be given. She had lost that battle, and now that the only glaring mistake of the last programme had been hers, she was glad to have conceded the fight. No one mentioned her interview as they focused on the day ahead. It was to be a typical Friday, with the usual 'end-of-the-week' items, except for the fact that a women's action group had brought out a paper on sexual harassment at work and Helen was to conduct a live interview with one of the authors of the report.

'She'll be deadly earnest I expect,' said Derek the editor, 'but do what you can Helen, you know, lift it a bit. It's probably very worthy but it'll bore most of the viewers rigid.'

On any other day Helen might have disagreed and stood up for the plight of the working woman but this did not seem a propitious moment.

'News is twelve minutes,' the editor went on, 'that might change; there's not much about.'

'Where do you want me?' Helen turned to Mark.

'Stand in front of the desks for the opening,' the PA and the lighting man took note of his directions, 'go to the upper desk for the rest of part one and all of part two and we'll have you in the soft set with a sofa and pot plants for part three.'

So far, so good, Helen thought, as she returned to the sanctuary of her own office. Immediately the phone rang. She held her breath: it was Paul, the controller.

'Helen, I hate to bother you, but I've got Kurt Dempsey from the New York office coming in for lunch, and I wondered if you were free to cheer it up a bit.'

She was grateful, realizing this was Paul's way of reassuring her that, despite yesterday's calamity, she was still a valuable commodity. The gesture gave her confidence to deal with the next hurdle.

Sue called on the internal phone. 'Derek wants to see you in his office in five minutes.'

'Tell him that's fine,' Helen said with a calmness she did not feel.

Derek was the editor, her immediate boss. He was in a difficult position, which Helen recognised. He had to weigh up all the stories of the day, five days a week, fifty-two weeks of the year. He had to try to please everyone, which was an impossible task. He got his backside kicked if the programme failed to make the top ten; he had to keep hordes of temperamental egocentrics within bounds; and he had to answer to the monitoring of the watchdog committee. If they wanted to know how often Birmingham, Brighton or Buckingham had been mentioned in the past six months, he must supply the figures. Each day he had to maintain a balance between a good geographical spread of coverage and the production of the best news and features on offer. It was the worst job in the company.

Helen went to the lavatory to renew her lipstick before facing him.

'Hello Derek.'

'Sit down, will you?' he said without looking up.

His secretary arrived with coffee. There was silence till she left them.

'I'd like you to look at the recording of last night's programme,' he said finally.

'Derek, I know why, but I promise you, I remember everything I said. It's not necessary.'

'OK. Well, what happened?'

She shrugged her shoulders. 'I pitched it wrong. I think I was right – Aziz regularly appears in the gossip columns. I do feel he cares at least as much about his image as he does about his patients. And heart surgery does get a good press . . .'

'Off the record, I agree. But it looked like a private row. Frankly, it was embarrassing.'

To her horror Helen felt her eyes fill with tears. 'I'm sorry.'

Derek was sorry too and discomfited. Helen had never wept before him, even in the early days when she was learning the job. 'I didn't mean to upset you, Helen. We do overload you, I know, but it's your fault. You positively welcome it, and you've seemed, up till now anyway, absolutely impregnable.'

Through her tears she attempted to smile. 'Can I ask you something?'

'Certainly.'

'Please forget about yesterday and . . . this. It won't happen again.'

'I don't think it will, but I have been wondering if it wouldn't be a good idea for you to take a break. I checked the diary – you haven't had any leave for over a year.'

'I'll think about it,' she said defensively, 'but first I have to lay the ghost of yesterday.'

He nodded. She sensed he would like to continue but

would not waylay her if she interpreted his silence as meaning the conversation was at an end. So she left.

Derek sat for a moment before summoning his secretary. He liked Helen, though he did not find it easy to say so. In any case, she seemed on very good terms with several people senior to him, which was disquieting. In his less charitable moments he wondered if she might be having an affair with one of them, but he had never been able to substantiate his suspicions. She was good, no doubt about that, but it fell to him to temper her energy with realism. She was enthusiastic. She was committed. But, like most gifted people, she was volatile and *he* had to cope with that – no one else, least of all his superiors on the floor above, in their comfortably plush offices.

It was with a degree of relief that Helen tackled yet another cup of coffee in the quiet of her own room. She was shaking, though whether from her unusually high intake of caffeine or her state of mind she could not be sure. She felt humiliated that she had cried, but Derek had let her off more gently than she believed she deserved.

The prospect of today's programme frightened her much more than usual in the light of yesterday's fiasco, so the fact that she was required as the lunchtime cabaret was a diversion rather than a chore.

'Ah, Helen,' said Paul as she arrived in the boardroom, 'you know Kurt, don't you?'

Helen flashed the smile that warmed the hearts of lonely viewers daily. 'Yes, of course. Kurt, how are you? I haven't seen you since I was in New York.'

'I don't think you realise, Paul,' Kurt said expansively, 'how nearly you lost this lady in the States. Everywhere I took her they fell at her feet. I really think if she'd pushed for it, she could have landed herself a very lucrative contract.'

I can put up with plenty of this, she thought, though she answered modestly, 'Oh, I couldn't leave here. They've taught me everything I know.'

The game was in progress and each of them understood the rules. Kurt flattered her, which was certainly affirming; she indulged in a spot of arch grovelling, which the company appreciated; and Paul glowed with the suggested compliment that he was not only a wise man for having picked Helen in the first place but also an astute one for managing to retain her services. Still, there was no harm in it, for the basic sentiments were honest, if a trifle exaggerated.

'And when she said that bit about being touched up by the filing cabinet I thought I was going to wet myself!' Laura was laughing so much, even now, that the tears were streaming down her cheeks.

The girls were holding a much happier inquest on the show than they had the night before.

'How did you keep a straight face?'

'With immense difficulty.' Helen grinned. 'But, having blotted my copy book yesterday, I had to behave tonight.'

'What was her name again?'

'Freda Armstrong.'

This time it was Helen who went into peals of laughter.

The butt of their humour was the spokesperson on sexual harassment, and the reason for it was that she was so unattractive, she should have welcomed any harassment that came her way.

'Why do they do it?' asked Helen more seriously. 'It makes me angry, actually. Some women have a bloody awful time at work but no one will rate that report while they field such an unsuitable candidate. Why couldn't they have sent an attractive woman to do the interview?' She giggled again, remembering the unfortunate, fat Freda with her brogue shoes, divided skirt, severely short haircut and well-scrubbed face.

'Helen . . .' Laura paused, determined to find the moment to have her say. 'You know, we've all been telling you for ages that your galloping lifestyle is bound to catch up with you one day. Maybe yesterday was the day. I'm only saying this because we're friends: don't you think it's time you went away for a bit? OK, when you and Barry split up it was probably therapeutic to throw yourself into the job, but enough's enough.'

'Derek said much the same thing this morning, but I'm

not mad about going away on my own – I'd sooner be working.'

'What about the devoted David?' Laura was referring to the most recent of Helen's escorts.

'I'm not seeing him any more. I know he's wealthy, well-connected and unattached, but he's also terminally boring. Do you know, last time we went out I found it was infectious. If I said, "This trout is really lovely, David," once, I must have said it ten times. He didn't even notice. Oh, and talking of men – you'll never guess what happened last night.'

'No, I won't. Tell me.'

'Aziz was there.'

Laura's mouth dropped open. 'Did you speak to him?'

'Not much – till the end. I suddenly got ever so tired. You know me – one minute I'm tap-dancing on the tables and the next I'm in a heap in the corner. He offered to take me home.'

'I hope you refused.'

'I did, but he said he wouldn't bother me. He wouldn't even speak, so it seemed less trouble to accept.'

'Well, that was stylish anyway.'

'Hmm, he's that all right. Silver convertible Merc. – well, you'd expect that. But also, I don't know . . . courteous, I think. Yes, very courteous.'

'Are you seeing him again?'

'Certainly not,' replied Helen hotly, 'especially after his closing statement: "Miss Bartlett, I'm not sure, but I think I may owe you an apology." ' It was a wickedly accurate impersonation.

'How insufferable.'

Yes, insufferable is the word, thought Helen, as she drove home. Still, the crisis had passed and the weekend was to be busy with two charity functions and many miles of driving between them. It was how her life was. Mercifully, there would be no time to think.

Chapter Three

'Who were they from?' It was Sharon on the newsroom switchboard. She had taken the message from reception that there was a large bouquet for Helen.

'Oh, a past interviewee,' said Helen. 'Where's Laura?'

'I think she's in the cutting-rooms,' Sharon replied. 'Shall I try to find her for you?'

'If you don't mind. I'll be in my office.'

Helen had taken delivery of the flowers – a massive arrangement – and had left them in the wash basin in her dressing-room. She had removed the accompanying card, however, a task she performed swiftly, almost guiltily, as though, despite being alone, she were afraid of being found out. Now safely back in her office she re-read it.

It was Monday. The weekend had been tiring but rewarding. She had been on safe ground until this moment. The phone rang. It was Laura.

'Hi! Anything wrong?'

'You'll never guess what's happened,' said Helen. 'Oh, damn, there's the other phone. Hang on, will you?'

She lifted the other receiver. 'Hello.'

'Helen, I've got a Mr Aziz on the phone. Will you speak to him?'

She returned to Laura. 'The plot thickens by the minute. I guess you're busy?'

'That's an understatement. I'm just recording a commentary and then I've got to go out again. A baby's been found dead in its cot and they think it died a whole month ago. I wish Derek could send someone else. I don't think I've got the stomach for it.'

'Oh, my God,' said Helen. 'Poor you. I'll see you later.' She replaced the phone and picked up the other one.

'Sharon, you better put him through.' There was a brief pause.

'Miss Bartlett, good morning.'

'Hello,' Helen said apprehensively.

'Did you get my flowers?'

'They've just arrived. They're beautiful – an extravagant but quite unnecessary gesture.'

'You're wrong. It *was* necessary. I've thought about Thursday a great deal over the weekend, and I wanted to apologise properly.'

'Well Mr Aziz, I accept your apology but, to be quite honest, I think we should agree to share the blame for what happened.'

'Now *you*'re making an extravagant gesture.'

Helen smiled. 'I would have telephoned to thank you, you know.'

'I'm sure you would, but you would have thought about it for a while, wondering if I was making a play for you or if I wasn't being rather too flashy . . . You might even have considered I was being ever so slightly condescending.'

How irritatingly accurate, thought Helen, as she remembered her initial reaction not ten minutes before. 'Well, you might have given me a little time and the benefit of the doubt,' she said quite sharply.

'Yes, I might.' He refused to rise to the bait. 'But I didn't, Miss Bartlett.'

'For God's sake, no one calls me that, apart from the occasional taxi driver.'

'Well,' he said, 'maybe I should continue, since it's quite apt in my case.'

She laughed. 'I'm not sure if I like you or find you stunningly annoying.'

'I couldn't have put it better myself. Shall we start again and give ourselves time to find out?'

There was silence.

'Miss Bar . . . Helen, will you have dinner with me?'

'Not dinner – lunch.'

It was his turn to laugh. 'Quite right. Lunch. How proper. When? Today?'

'I can't today,' she said. It was true because she did not feel prepared but untrue because there was nothing in the diary.

'Tomorrow then.'

'You're very persistent.'

'That's right, I am.'

They discussed where to go and he named a sea-food restaurant in Soho. It was a favourite haunt of hers.

'Shall I pick you up?' he asked.

'No, it's nearer you than me, and we'll never be able to park. I'll get a taxi.'

'You're infuriatingly practical.'

'That's right, I am.'

They both laughed.

'Can you make twelve forty-five?'

'I'll be there,' said Helen.

'I'm looking forward to it,' he said.

'Are you?' Her question belied her confident manner and instantly she regretted it.

He did not appear to notice and answered quietly, 'Very much.'

Helen hung up. How cocksure he was and how smooth. She was strangely excited, yet frightened and angered at the same time. Well, lunch doesn't mean anything, she thought and, with a toss of her head, she attempted to tackle the day's post.

She opened a couple of letters and read them both without absorbing their contents. Her brain was racing on to tomorrow, much as she tried to engage it with today. Defiantly she pulled the little card out of her handbag and read it again: 'I've thought about it. I am sure now that I do owe you an apology.'

She made a sudden decision. Her hair needed cutting, and fresh highlights would be an improvement. She glanced at today's running order. There were no interviews that afternoon, so she dialled the number of her hairdresser.

The next day she made light work of the Jane Fonda routine and sailed into the office telling Sue the letters could wait. She was the life and soul of the ten-thirty meeting, then she busied herself for an hour, making phone calls and answering the mail. On her way to the make-up department she met Laura on the stairs.

'I tried to find you after the programme yesterday,' Helen said. 'You must have shot off.'

'I did,' replied Laura. 'I was tired, and that baby story really got to me.'

'I'm not surprised. Are you OK now?'

Laura nodded. 'Shall we have lunch?'

'No, I can't. I'm sorry – I'm going out.'

Laura was bemused. She understood Helen's depressions very well. She too experienced the sun going behind a cloud, leaving that ghastly sense of desolation and emptiness. They had often discussed it and reasoned that it was probably an occupational and temperamental hazard. The dizzy heights, on the other hand, were not part of Laura's spectrum, but Helen was a creature of both extremes and, for all her professionalism, could not hide her moods from her close friends. Today she was bouncing and blooming. Laura had noticed yesterday that Helen had been to the hairdresser, but that did not account for such a transformation. She was curious but knew that Helen rarely kept anything to herself for long. It was one of the facets of her friend that she liked best; maddening though she might be at times, she was transparently honest.

Meanwhile Helen was preparing with undue care and attention. At three-thirty she was due to speak to a Polish pianist who had recently defected to the West; perhaps she would not have time to do a full make-up when she returned. She sprayed herself with a perfume she had bought on the way back from the hairdresser yesterday. She had not experimented with a new fragrance for ages, but suddenly the time seemed right.

She hummed quietly to herself as she wandered down the corridor.

'Someone's happy,' said Joe, one of the stage crew.

'Hi! Yes, I suppose I am. Are you OK?'

'Mustn't grumble.'

In the quiet of her dressing-room she considered what

to wear. She finally plumped for an old favourite, a translucent dress in navy by Parigi. It was really a summer outfit, but the restaurant was bound to be warm. She added pearl earrings and surveyed the effect in the mirror. Nervously she wondered if she looked too conservative. She glanced at her watch. There was no time to change. She would have to do.

Her taxi drew up at the restaurant at ten to one. For a moment she was sure she must have arrived first. She almost begged the driver to make another tour of the block, like a bride anxious not to appear too anxious by being on time. She need not have worried; Aziz was sitting at a table in the window and raised a hand in greeting as she disembarked.

He rose as she reached the table and shook her hand. 'You look wonderful,' he said. 'What will you have to drink?'

'Perrier, please.'

'You too? The wine waiter's in for a thin time of it.'

She smiled as she sat down. There was a moment's silence.

'I'm sorry,' they both said at once and laughed.

It was a very pleasant lunch. They chatted animatedly, aware that separately and collectively they were on show, yet not resentful of the fact. Independently they selected the same items from the menu; avocado with apricot yoghurt and prawns, followed by turbot grilled in herb butter. They both observed the coincidence but declined to comment upon it. Each learned a little of the other's background but with a leisurely interest that was quite different from the frenzied interrogation they had instigated in the past with other partners, when they had expected the first date would lead to bed and had rushed through certain preliminaries as a gesture towards propriety.

It was almost time to go. The hour and a half had flashed by. Helen found, surprisingly, that she was clinging to the last minutes she could allow herself. She felt absolutely extraordinary: not ill, certainly not drunk, just odd – which was hardly a sufficient symptom to effect an accurate diagnosis. The mirrors around the walls sparkled more than before, imbuing the clientele beside and through them with a greater degree of colour and clarity than seemed reasonable. Everyone appeared excessively animated and she herself felt acutely alive.

He was terribly attractive, of course, and she verified the fact by sneaking one last look at him. Perhaps he was unmoved by her presence; but then, watching him press his full lips to the snow-white napkin, which he did frequently, she caught him playing the same game. He looked up at her from under his dark eyelashes. Their wandering glances met. She fancied her face flushed as he watched her. For the first time she said nothing. He seemed quieter too. He began to finger the rim of his glass with his perfectly manicured hands. She tried to imagine them, clad in surgical gloves, saving somebody's life with breathtaking dexterity. Yes, he was breathtaking, literally, for she found herself short of breath, though in a way that, far from inducing a state of anxiety, was filling her to the brim with happiness.

With a monumental and conscious effort she drew a deep breath. 'I have to go.'

'Yes, I have a busy afternoon too,' he said defensively.

'I'm sure you do,' she said quietly, looking him straight in the eye. He relaxed then, knowing he was not being given the brush-off that, just for an instant, he had suspected.

'I've enjoyed this tremendously,' he said. 'Shall we do it again?'

'I'd like that,' she said. 'Would you let me pay?'

'Certainly not.'

'Share it then – as my apology to you. After all, the flowers must have cost you a fortune.'

He laughed. 'Helen, modern though I may be in some ways, certain things I cannot cope with. One of them is women picking up the tab.'

'That's ridiculous when both people earn good money.'

'We're not going to argue, are we?' he asked, raising an eyebrow.

She smiled. 'We'll discuss it next time.' She put out

her hand. Why was this so difficult? She was generally somewhat theatrical in her greetings and farewells and thought nothing of throwing her arms around comparative strangers. He grasped her hand and suddenly inclined towards her, pulling her gently as he did so and touching his cheek to hers. He turned slightly then and brushed her face with his lips. She blushed, smiled shyly and was gone.

'More coffee, sir?' asked the waitress.

Aziz had been going to ask for his bill but suddenly needed a moment to adjust his feelings before facing his normal world. He sat down. 'Yes, please, and I think I'll have a brandy and a small cigar.' He smiled to himself in his own silent space, protected by his thoughts from the raucous babble of high-powered business and social intercourse all around him. The scent of Helen lingered briefly in the air before being swamped by the other odours pervading the dining-room. He had led a far from celibate existence, and yet he felt as uncertain as if he were an adolescent once more. He knew ahead of time that his secretary, a motherly soul, would tut-tut at him for being unusually late and would not be slow to detect he had broken his golden lunchtime rule of no alcohol.

'Well, what was he like?'

Helen had invited Laura for a drink after the programme. The afternoon had been enjoyable. The interview with the Polish pianist had been stimulating and he had played a Chopin Polonaise like a dream. The programme had gone well and Helen had steered her friend to the social club immediately afterwards. She never minded being on show to her colleagues when she was riding high, though she was not conscious that her choice of drinking location reflected a judgement of her own performance. After some deliberation, and mostly because she was dying to tell someone, Helen had told Laura of the arrival of the flowers yesterday and the luncheon appointment today.

'You're dreaming, Helen, and you haven't answered my question.'

'Oh, sorry. He's nice – very nice,' she said at last.

'That's not what you were saying last Thursday.'

Helen smiled and shrugged her shoulders mischievously 'I changed my mind.'

Laura laughed. 'Life's never dull when you're around anyway. Is this going to be it?'

'Oh, no,' she said too quickly. 'It's just friendly – not at all romantic. I'm sure he doesn't even fancy me.'

'Do you fancy him?'

'Absolutely not!'

Laura took in the glow that was emanating from Helen and smiled at the denial. 'Are you seeing him again, though?'

'Yes.'

'When?'

Helen looked anxious for a second. 'I don't know. He didn't say.'

Her momentary uneasiness was misplaced, as he rang early the next morning.

The pattern of lunches became established. They met frequently, delighting in their new-found friendship and the pleasure with which they anticipated each rendezvous. Privately, though, they both wondered about other consorts. Lunch was innocuous; it was public; it had a time limit. Theirs was a pleasant routine but one that, with courage, was bound to be altered. An innocent question effected the transition.

'What star sign are you, Sam?'

'Scorpio.'

'You must have a birthday soon then?'

He was slightly embarrassed. 'It's next Tuesday, in actual fact.'

'Oh, well, that gives me the perfect chance to buy you lunch for a change.'

'I can't make it – not Tuesday. I'm sorry.'

Helen was cast down by her blunder. Birthdays are spent with wives, girlfriends or families, not with an occasional luncheon date.

He looked in his diary. 'I'm going to Birmingham to

speak at a seminar, but you can buy me dinner if you like. I'll be back by the time you finish the programme.'

How absurd that she should feel such a rush of relief. How amazing that he should want to spend the evening of his birthday, a special occasion, with her. How surprising that no one else had a greater claim.

It was the first time he had picked her up at the studios and his first visit since he had marched out in high dudgeon after their interview. Sam looked vaguely familiar to the security man whose job it was to ask him his business.

'I've come for Miss Bartlett,' said Sam and almost immediately she appeared.

'Goodnight, boys,' she cried as the couple negotiated the doors.

'Is that Helen's new man?' asked the other security man from his seat behind the desk.

'Dunno, Bob. He didn't say.'

'Well, 'course 'e wouldn't say. Be nice, though. Smart sort of a bloke.'

'Bit smooth, if you ask me – not a hair out of place, stitching round the lapels and all that.'

'You're jealous. You'd like to get your leg over a bit of skirt like that, but she's out of your class.'

''Fraid you're right. Cor, I could really give her one, though. Bet she's terrific in the sack.'

'That's a bit disrespectful. You're not supposed to have dirty thoughts about the leading lady, Tony, old son.'

'No harm in dreaming. Be great to have a woman like that just once in your life. You know, just once.'

'I did when I was in the SAS.'

'Oh, Gawd, we don't want to hear all that old shit again. Go up and get your supper.'

'Listen, mate, I've been around. Still, 'spose 'e 'as too. Wonder if 'e's getting it tonight?'

'What, Helen's geezer?' Tony shrugged his shoulders. 'Dunno. They didn't kiss or nothing.'

'Well, she's a lady, isn't she? She 'as to be careful or that Dempster feller'll 'ave 'er in his column again. 'E looked foreign to me.'

'I reckon he must be. Got a funny accent.'

'Well, I just 'ope she'll be OK, that's all. Shall I bring you a bacon roll down?'

'Yeah, go on. I haven't got anybody to keep my figure for, more's the pity.' Tony looked out of the window at the disappearing Mercedes. Some people had all the luck.

Helen and Sam had sat for a moment in the car. Meeting at a different hour made it seem like a first date of which they were both slightly nervous. She searched in her bag and brought out a tiny box which had been gift-wrapped. 'Happy birthday.'

She had agonised over the choice, seeking a stylish memento but deciding against any item that suggested intimacy. She had settled for a little silver bookmark in the shape of a hand.

He coloured slightly under his permanent tan. 'You shouldn't have. How embarrassing.'

'No, it's not. It's your birthday. How old are you anyway?'

'Ten years your senior – forty-five.'

'How did you know I was thirty-five?'

'Ah, I've done my research.'

It was Helen's turn to blush. 'You can open it. It's nothing much.'

He ripped the paper away, switched on the interior light to get a better view, then lifted the lid to find the little hand nestling in cotton wool. 'It's lovely.'

'Do you know what it is?'

'Of course I do. It's a bookmark.'

'Oh, good. I wouldn't have known if it hadn't been labelled in the shop.'

He laughed. 'Well, you probably turn the corners of the pages down. You're far too impatient to go in search of a marker.'

'That'll do – you're getting jolly personal. Take me to Richmond!'

He grinned and kissed her on the cheek before turning off the light and starting the engine.

The choice of restaurant – which was Helen's, since it was her treat – had been difficult too. Again she had steered a middle course. It was too important a meeting to settle for chicken-in-the-basket in a pub, but she was furiously resisting the impulse to overload the evening with ostentation or heavy romantic ambience.

'Where are we going?' he asked as they drove off.

'It's a little place on the river called, rather unoriginally, the Bistro.'

He looked at her by the light of the passing street lamps and grinned again. She felt naked, suspecting he knew in detail all the processes of thought that had gone into making the decision.

After a while he gradually let his hand cross the great divide between their two seats and come to rest palm upwards on her right thigh. She moved her right hand to hold his hand, and for a second, in the twilight, they looked deep into each other's eyes.

When they arrived at the restaurant, he helped her out of the car and, for the first time, put his arm around her as he steered her into the building.

Throughout the meal they savoured the change and promise between them. They talked less than usual, touched more and ate hardly at all. The candlelight enhanced the luminous quality of his eyes. They looked intently into hers. She felt like a willing participant in an experiment on levitation. As he had in the car, he reached for her hand; the feel of him made her glad. He was soft and sensitive, yet strong too, possibly even stronger than she. His mind fascinated her, but his body was making its impact in a less cerebral way. His hair was so much darker and coarser than her own; it was foreign, like him. Strange, then, that she had never felt more at one with anyone in her life before. Those eyes again looked through her into places she did not generally care to expose, and then, lifting her hand, he kissed each finger caressingly, one by one.

Afterwards he drove her back to her flat in Holland Park, remembering, without being told, exactly where it was. They parked in the discreetly lit avenue, and he switched off the car headlights. He let his seat recline, then adjusted hers to the same level and they lay in the darkness, emotionally entwined but without further contact.

She wanted very badly to invite him in but at the same time did not want to disturb the prevailing mood. She suspected he was hoping for the invitation but was reluctant to be the one to suggest it. They talked instead. He told her how he had been sent to Harrow at the tender age of thirteen and what a shock the coldness of the climate and his welcome had been to his system.

'Can I ask you something?' she said.

'Of course.'

'What's your real name? It can't be Sam.'

He laughed. 'Ahmed Sami Aziz. But, you see, being a foreigner I had to have a nickname at school – we all did, come to that. No one could pronounce Ahmed, and they couldn't think how to capitalise on Aziz, so they shortened Sami to Sam. It amused them. I wasn't exactly coloured, but I did come from the African continent, so they figured Sam – short for Sambo, d'you see?'

'That's terrible,' said Helen. 'God, kids can be so cruel.'

'They can, but I survived. In fact, I got to like it – though you can call me Ahmed if you like.'

She laughed. 'No, you're Sam to me, if that's all right.'

They fell silent. They were reluctant to part, yet today had brought about sufficient development in their relationship for them to be hesitant about going beyond that. The tension was tangible. At any moment one of them might take a step too far and invite the other to spend the night.

Helen broke the spell with difficulty. 'I'm going to bed, Sam.' She was relieved to have said it but disappointed with herself.

He sighed. She sensed he felt the same way. 'All right,' he said. 'Have a good night.'

He kissed her then, at first gently and then more insistently, till they realised, separately and together, that it was a question no longer of 'if' but of 'when.'

The phone call woke her. She looked at the clock as she reached for the receiver. It was eight-thirty.

'Did you sleep all right?' His question confirmed the new status of their relationship.

'Very well. Did you get home OK? You hadn't had too much to drink?'

'Everything's fine. That's why I'm ringing, I think. Everything's really fine. Thanks for the best birthday I've ever had.'

'I don't know what to say.'

'Neither do I, which is strange, since neither of us pauses for breath as a rule.' He laughed. 'What I want to say is . . . I'm tingling after last night – I want to see you soon. I want to hold you . . . intimately.' He sounded surprisingly old-fashioned.

'What about lunch tomorrow?'

'No,' he said. 'Dinner tonight. I want to speak to you.'

'Oh, God, that sounds ominous.'

'Helen, stop it.'

'Stop what?'

'You know what. You don't need to be flippant. You don't need to be frightened. That's part of what I have to tell you.'

There was silence.

'Have I offended you?'

'No,' she answered in a small voice. 'No, you haven't. I'm just a bit taken aback.'

'Why?'

'Because I've finally admitted to myself that you seem to know me quite well.'

'I don't, but I'd like to.'

'OK,' she said quietly. 'I'll see you after the programme.'

The same two security men were on duty, and they nodded knowingly at each other when Helen swept past, calling goodnight to both of them, as she launched herself through the revolving doors to the waiting car beyond.

This time there was no birthday, no excuse for her to hold the reins, make the choices, give the directions or proffer the credit card. Sam drove, without saying much, to a pub at Strand on the Green which, she suspected was near his home.

She sat down in an alcove without her usual struggle to be first at the bar to prove she was one of the boys and certainly not mean. He joined her, carrying a bottle of champagne and two rather ordinary wine glasses. He smiled, reading her thoughts. 'Well, I was amazed they had the bubbly – I think we can forgive the lack of crystal.'

He poured out a little, but even that frothed over the top of each glass and dribbled on to the table. 'It's a bit frisky,' he said, 'and I'm nervous.' He finished pouring before either of them spoke again. He handed her one glass, picked up the other and said, 'To us.' They drank.

'Can I ask you something?'

He looked at her indulgently. The phrase was a little habit of hers which he found endearing, for she used it only when she was unsure.

'Yes, anything you like.'

'Are you married?'

'Good God, no. Do you think I'd be pursuing you like this if I were?'

'Is that what you're doing?'

'Hadn't you noticed?'

She smiled. 'Anyway, you still might be – you might have a wife tucked away in Egypt.'

'I haven't.'

'Have you never been married?'

'No. Why?'

'I don't know. I just can't imagine someone like you getting to forty-five and not being. Anyway I once interviewed a psychiatrist who said no one remains unmarried past forty unless they have a problem.'

'Well,' he said, mock seriously, 'far be it from me to quarrel with a fellow victim, but I don't think I have a problem.'

'You've had lots of girlfriends?'

'Lots,' he agreed. His candour was both pleasing and unsettling.

'I'm not surprised. You're an attractive and successful man.'

'I don't see it like that. I'm not successful with women. Well, let's say I am initially, but women don't generally understand my schedule or ambition, and so far whenever anyone has said, "It's the job or me," there's been no contest.'

'That's a bit harsh.'

'Maybe no one's mattered to me enough before.'

She looked at him but ignored the last word. She did not want to feel she was being sweet-talked, that she was responding to a line. She could see quite plainly how easily he could break a heart – and why should hers be an exception? In any case, her heart might never recover if it were broken again.

'You're attractive and successful,' he said.

She shook her head.

'You know you are. I'm sure you're propositioned a great deal.'

'I know lots of men.'

'There you are then,' he said sharply.

He wanted to know about her marriage. It was difficult to talk at first, to put into perspective the months of despair and covering up. She lit a cigarette and looked round the old pub with its panelling, beams and tapestry curtains and upholstery. She thought she would remember this moment for the rest of her life.

He put his hand on hers and leant over to kiss her cheek. 'Don't tell me if you don't want to.'

'I do. It's just difficult.'

'Were you badly hurt?'

'I was – at the time.' Suddenly the floodgates opened. She told him how she had been an actress in a touring production and how she had met Barry when she was in Cardiff. She described their meeting and their marriage and how, subsequently she had given up the theatre and set up a public relations firm. She told him of its success, which had led to her being offered a spot with a regional television company giving advice to people on how to project their businesses or present themselves when it came to job interviews. 'I didn't mean for it all to take off – it just did. At the same time I made sure I was always there when it was important. I was always free for his firm's functions. I walked the dog before I went to work. I baked bread and froze the beans we grew in the garden. I did try to be a good wife.'

'What happened?'

'I was offered the job in London. You won't remember, but there was a nationwide search for the right girl and, unbelievably, I got it. Barry and I discussed the move. He said we'd always be together at weekends – he'd come to me if I couldn't get to Wales – and I thought everything was all right. One day a friend told me he'd been having an affair with his secretary for two years. I couldn't believe it. I thought we had everything, you see: careers, loads of stimulus and a perfect marriage. I expect it was my fault . . .'

'And maybe it wasn't,' said Sam.

'Well, there we are. If I'm honest, I think my pride was hurt more than anything else. I was so desperately trying to be the blueprint of the complete woman.'

'Did you love him?'

'Of course. It wasn't a wild passionate thing – not at all – but we were such good friends I just assumed we'd be together in our old age.'

'Helen, you're the sort of woman who should have passion too.'

'I know, I know. After the divorce I did dreadful things. I had a lot of men. I had passion then but no love. That wasn't right either . . .' She sighed. 'I don't know why I'm telling you all this. It doesn't go with my image.'

'I don't care a damn about the image. I care about you.' He leaned forward and kissed her lovingly on the lips. 'Let me take you somewhere nice to eat.'

'No, don't,' she said. 'It's fine here. It's cosy and quiet, and I'm not very hungry.'

'Well, I'll order some sandwiches,' he said and disappeared.

Helen felt near to tears after her revelations. This man had unlocked thoughts about her past that surprised her. On top of that, her growing interest in him was bewildering. She was excessively aware of his presence and of an opening sensation. More than that, she felt she might depend on him.

She looked around the pub again and realised she had been recognised. A young man hovered. 'It is, isn't it?'

She smiled.

'I couldn't believe it. You – here. I've never met anybody famous before.'

She laughed. 'I'm not famous.'

'You are.' He was indignant. He did not want her to spoil his achievement or deny the stroke of fate that had put him, for a short time, into the orbit of a celebrity. He picked up a beer mat as Sam returned with the sandwiches. She could tell that Sam was anxious not to intrude but that at the same time he was protective and would intervene if the other man outstayed his welcome. 'Could you sign this for me?'

'What's your name?'

'Henry.'

To Henry, she wrote. *Nice to see you. Love, Helen Bartlett.*

'Gosh, thanks,' he said and was gone.

'I'm sorry,' she said to Sam.

'Why? I guess I'll just have to get used to the fact that my lady is loved by most of the population.' The words 'my lady' struck a pleasant yet discordant note.

As they ate the brown-bread sandwiches filled with rare beef and salad she asked, 'Why do you think we hated each other on sight the day we met?'

'I'm not sure,' he said. 'I hadn't seen you on television much myself, but when some of my colleagues knew I was going to be interviewed by you they went on and on about how marvellous you were. It sort of put my back up. It was a bit like being told you must read a particular book or see the latest film. You can never believe it can be that great.'

'I know,' she said. 'Maybe we were just too sensitive of each other's media image. Sorry, terrible phrase, but you know what I mean. I'd only seen you in gossip columns with a succession of women.'

'I think that's the point, Helen, isn't it?' he said. 'A different one for every day of the week. It made you suspect my commitment to my career, and now you're suspicious that I don't really mean what I'm saying to you.'

Helen pushed her plate away.

'You're genuinely not hungry, are you?' He smiled.

'I'm sorry. The food's fine, but I'm not.'

'OK. Let's go.'

In tacit agreement they drove the short distance to his house, which overlooked the river. He led the way and, as if in a dream, she followed him into a cream room whose only feature was a sculpture of a ballet dancer she recognised instantly as the work of Tom Merrifield.

She kicked off her shoes in order to feel the warmth and the luxury of the deep-piled carpet beneath her feet, and then he drew her into a passionate embrace. He pulled her hips towards his as they urgently sought complete contact for the first time. She felt his hardness pressing into her and heard him sigh and groan with utter disbelief and dismay as her closeness and his need for her provoked a premature climax.

'That's never happened to me before in my life,' he said. 'Not even as a teenager.'

She did not know what to say but remembered their conversation in the pub. Perhaps he had a problem after all. She was unsure whether to feel insulted or flattered.

He led her upstairs and into his bedroom, which was blue and subtly lit. He undressed her slowly, kissing each part of her as he uncovered it and rejoicing in her pale skin and slight figure.

She had never thought of herself as frail and, worse, always believed that men found her too capable to want to cherish her. Yet he was muttering endearments – something about looking after her. It was her last coherent thought as she relinquished her usual stance of performing and controlling. Waves of delight flooded through her body as he laid her on the bed while continuing to kiss and caress her. His kisses were everywhere and filled her with an unaccustomed and violent longing. He moved down her body and settled where she longed for his mouth to remain. He licked her with increasing pressure and she moaned with happiness, moving slightly up and down and around and around, beneath his flickering tongue. Suddenly, miraculously, she knew – not thought, but *knew* – she was going to climax. Her whole body stiffened. It was going to happen, and it was all so easy.

She lay, panting, as he moved himself to lie hard on top of her. She loved him then. How wonderful he was. Usually in bed she concentrated on her partner. It made her feel important, worthwhile, but her determined unselfishness generally left her unsatisfied. This was so different.

Now he was ready. She reached down to feel him; he was sticky but solid and large. Maybe he would not be able to take her, she thought, recalling the scene in the lounge. He put his hands under her buttocks, lifted them slightly, then plunged straight into her. She grasped him to her, thinking he might come quickly again and wanting to make it good. He raised himself up and refused to be hurried. His hands and his tongue were never still. He thrust slowly in and out of her. Her breasts hardened against him. If it were not impossible, she could believe it was going to happen again.

'There's no hurry, sweetheart,' he whispered in her ear. 'Love me, relax, ride with me.'

Then he was saying other things that no one had said before. 'Helen, one day, I'm going to come into you like this, higher and higher, slowly and deeply. I'm going to have a great white explosion in you, darling, and together we're going to make a baby.' It had never been a consideration before. It could not be tonight – she was a product of the pill age – but the distant possibility and the sense of belonging, mixed with such potent physical intensity, drove her beyond any frontier of feeling she had reached before. She felt the spasm of his orgasm begin, and as she rose to meet it, the tension and the shuddering and the frenzy engulfed her. She came, noisily, warmly, endlessly . . .

Chapter Four

'Wake up, sleeping beauty. I'm not much of a handsome prince, but I'll have to do.'

Helen shrugged off her slumber with a start. 'What time is it?'

'Seven o'clock.'

'Oh, God, I knew we must be incompatible in one way or another. Why are we up so early?'

'*We*'re not, *I* am, but I didn't want to leave without speaking to you. I'm operating at eight-thirty.'

'Sam, I'm sorry. I never even thought about your schedule. How awful.'

He jumped. 'Awful!' he said. 'Awful is not a word I would have chosen in conjunction with last night. In any case, you couldn't possibly be expected to know my movements.'

'Don't get cross.'

'I'm not cross. I just want you to feel the same way about what's happening as I do. Maybe we should have chosen an occasion when we might have dallied through the whole of the next day, but one can't always plan sensibly with emotions. It's not like organising a timetable.'

'You make me sound aggressively practical,' She sighed. 'Why is everything so tense this morning when it was perfect just a few hours ago?'

'I expect we're nervous – we're probably both terrified of exposing too much too soon. All I am trying to say is that last night was the best, the best ever, and I don't mind being up. I'm quite happy, but I do suggest you go back to sleep. I'll reset the alarm.'

'Do I look terrible then?'

'Helen!'

'Sorry, sorry. You're right, I'm nervous.'

Sam sat down on the bed beside her. He raised her right hand to his lips and kissed the end of each finger before pulling her to him and enveloping her in a great bear hug. 'It was selfish of me to wake you, but I wanted to tell you: I love you, Helen. I love your body and your mind and your spirit.'

'That's most of me, right enough.' She grinned. He kissed her passionately, and she responded to him for all the world as though they had been lovers for ever instead of just a night. 'I love you too. I don't know what's happening. I don't know what we're going to do, but I'm very happy.' They kissed again. 'I read somewhere,' she went on, 'that surgeons aren't supposed to drink or indulge in any sort of hanky-panky before intensive surgery. It makes their hands shake.'

'My darling, I'm trembling all over, but I promise you the patients won't suffer.'

She smiled. 'I should ignore me, I know an awful little about a lot of things.'

'But you store it so well in that pretty head of yours. I hope I finish in time to watch you tonight. I shall think, 'That's my lady, and then . . . I'll have to rush off and take a cold shower!'

She punched him on the shoulder. 'Don't be ridiculous.'

'I'm not. Can we meet later?'

'I'm doing a phone-in after the programme till eight-thirty. Maybe we ought to sleep tonight.'

'We will sleep – as well. You go home and I'll come over to you. I'll bring us a bottle and a take-away.'

'Ah, how wise. Don't trust my cooking, I see.'

'I don't view you in a domestic light, it's true, but, more than that, you'll have had a long day and so will I. Let's just relax.'

'Fine. That sounds great. You'd better go, hadn't you?'

'I had,' he said, then he added quietly, 'Helen, I hope we always feel like this.'

'Me too. It's probably not possible, but . . .'

He put a finger to her lips. 'Don't think about it. Go back to sleep. We'll talk tonight.' He kissed her again, walked to the bedroom door and turned. 'You're very special,' he said. He looked serious for a moment and then, as though drawn by a magnet, moved swiftly back to the bed to sweep her into his arms. He clung to her for several seconds, as if afraid that the next few hours would forge an impossible distance between them. 'See you tonight,' he said unsteadily, as he abruptly tore himself from her and ran down the stairs and out of the house.

Helen looked around the blue bedroom, taking in the mirrored wardrobes, the book shelves and the small television set. It was a room where somebody came to sleep, she decided, not one that the occupant had personalised to any significant degree.

They had made love through the night until finally they had fallen asleep, exhausted, around four. She felt reawakened in a quite spectacular way. For all that parts of her had enjoyed more exercise and attention than they had for many months, she was far from replete. Deep inside her was a longing for more and more and more. It seemed that having been unleashed, her sexuality was taking over and dictating the message loud and clear that it had lain dormant long enough. She picked up Sam's pillow; it smelt of him. She crushed it to her and curled round it as he had curled round her through the night. She tried to sleep, but her mind and body would not be still. Maybe I'm sex mad, she thought, but it was more than that. 'I'm in love,' she said aloud. 'Yesterday I wasn't – at least, I don't think so – but today I am.' She remembered his mention of children and wondered if he had meant it. It was, as he had said, perhaps too much too soon, yet if she allowed a pause for the panic to subside, it felt absolutely, if inexplicably, right.

On his bedside table she found the remote-control panel for the television set, so she switched on the breakfast show. The presenter, a comfortably familiar figure, bridged the enormous gap between this extraordinary morning and all the days that had gone before. She watched the news and the features that followed on fashion, cooking and what the papers said, but she was not in the mood to concentrate.

She decided to explore the house but stopped at the bathroom beside the bedroom. She ran a deep bath and, as she did so, automatically scanned the shelves and cabinet for any signs of a previous female presence. There was none: no cold cream, no bath essence, no cotton wool.

She had meant to soak in the bath but could not relax, so continued with her tour. The room in which he had climaxed so precipitately the night before was as she had remembered it: stylish but without much character – cream walls and ceiling, a very expensive light-coloured carpet and beautifully made brown velvet curtains. The sculpture of the dancer was the focal point, and on trying a combination of the dimmer switches she realised, from the direction of the recessed spots, that this was what Sam intended. It was the first time, outside the Festival Hall where Merrifield often exhibited, that she had seen one of his pieces close up. She had no idea how the sculptor was rated by the *cognoscenti*, but she thought of him as a modern-day Degas. What was it, though, about the little figure that had moved Sam to make some effort in this room, she wondered? Somehow she was glad that he had.

Behind her was a wall covered in book shelves, which she had not noticed the night before. Unlike the bedroom, this was not a light reading room but a professional one, with great tomes like *A Short Practice of Surgery*, which looked anything but short, dominating the space. Surely he had no need to check which incision was to go where?

Apart from the books, the room might have belonged to anyone. It was, she supposed, more masculine than feminine, but it gave little away. Indeed, the only hint that the householder might not be English lay in two drawings of scenes of Egypt by the nineteenth-century Scottish itinerant artist David Roberts, who had been fascinated by Arab countries and their architecture.

She wandered next into the kitchen and smiled suddenly at its similarity to her own. It was white, with gadgets that looked pristine through lack of use. Curiosity got the better of her, so she opened the door of the refrigerator. Her smile turned to laughter as she viewed the lonely contents that could so easily have been hers too: four bottles of wine, a pack of mouldering butter and a vacuum-sealed lump of cheese, long past its sell-by date, lying unopened.

What sort of a man did all this add up to? She shook her head. Not a home-maker, almost certainly a workaholic and definitely an enigma. She had learned all she could and she did not, as yet anyway, feel very much at home. It was time to go.

As soon as she reached the studios Helen made for the dressing-room and changed into a track suit. She applied a smudge of kohl pencil around her eyes and a little blusher to her cheeks. When she entered the newsroom it was still not quite nine.

'You're early,' said Laura.

'I know – I didn't sleep very well.'

'Well, you don't look tired. You look fantastic.'

'I feel fantastic. Come and have coffee in my office. I'll just go to the canteen and get some.'

'What happened?' asked Laura, when they were safely alone.

'What do you mean what happened?'

'You can't fool me. You look like a cat who's been at the cream.'

'You'll have to keep this to yourself.'

'Of course.'

'I've just spent the night with Sam.'

'Aziz?'

'Yes.'

'How was it – as if I needed to ask?'

'Laura, it was sensational. The best thing that has ever happened to me in my whole life.'

'I knew it. When are you seeing him again?'

'Tonight.'

'This is serious.'

'I think it may be.'

*

Helen had believed – somehow it had seemed necessary to believe in order to find fulfilment in her existence – that her celibacy was responsible for her boundless energy. When life is not complicated by allegiance to another, then dedication to a job is total. It was strange that just when, according to her theory and much that she had read in novels, she should have been distracted and dreamy, she was possessed by greater verve and enthusiasm for the work in hand than ever before.

Some years ago she had pioneered an adoption-by-television spot. 'We're not talking about little white babies for infertile couples any more, Derek,' she had explained to her boss, 'but about the best possible families for kids who're in care and shouldn't be. The families might be old or without religion, second-time marriages, single people – you name it.' Derek had been slightly amused at her fire but respectful of the research that had fuelled it. He had given her the go-ahead. Some twenty children later, today was another adoption day. She had worked with this particular couple over a period of four months and now they were ready.

Patricia and Philip were orphans. Their mother had been unmarried and they were the product of two separate liaisons. The family had been watched by the social services for years as the children, plagued by a succession of 'uncles' in the house, had exhibited symptoms of unsociable and neurotic behaviour. The mother finally drank herself to death, thus freeing the children for adoption. Helen, as always, longed to tell the whole story so that the kids would gain all the sympathy they deserved, but she was forbidden to do so.

Philip's great ambition, she had discovered, was to fly in an aeroplane, so she had decided to arrange a flight and film the children in the process. Roy, the film editor, knocked on her door before putting his head round it. 'It's ready for you to see. If you're happy with it, we can go to the dubbing theatre at two.' She sat with Roy at the Steenbeck and watched what they had: the plane taking off, a chat with the children in the air about flying, an interview in the rear of the plane with the social worker, over which they had dropped in several shots of the youngsters' excited faces, and then a more probing talk with both children about the sort of family each would like to find. The sequence ended in a lighter vein with the pilot helping the children down from the plane and presenting each of them with a flying club badge.

'I think that's fine, Roy. I suppose we could have tightened that bit where Philip is so hesitant.'

'I will if you like, but it's very genuine.'

'Yes, and it speaks volumes. I mean, the fact that he can't conjure up the ideal identikit of a mum should suggest to the viewers that he doesn't have much to go on – which is perfectly true, of course, poor little soul.'

'So – two o'clock?'

'Sure. I'll write a couple of commentary sections – it doesn't need much – and I'll record to picture upstairs. Then you're going to pop some music over the exterior flying shots at the beginning, aren't you?'

'Yes, that won't take long. I'll have it down to the studio for you by four.'

For the rest of the day she answered telephone calls and letters and set up future stories. It was a satisfying time and quite as important, in its own way, as the evening to come. She thought about the children as the day progressed. She was going to risk bringing them on the programme because their appearance would certainly add to the appeal of the feature, and she was confident that they were comfortable enough with her to enjoy it. She knew the programme would go well, but she was anxious all the same. Knowing that Sam would be watching, she wanted it to be exceptional. Presenting is totally dependent on rhythm, she thought. When it worked, it was as stimulating as good sex.

Since the children were coming in, she dressed more casually than she might have otherwise in a lavender mohair sweater and pale-grey leather trousers. She walked to the reception area to meet Patricia and Philip.

'You go up to the boardroom now with Jackie,' she said, indicating the duty receptionist, 'and you can watch the beginning of the programme there and have some coke or something. We'll get you brought in during the political spot, which is recorded, and then it's us. I'll introduce the film, we'll all watch it, and then I'll ask you a question each. Next I'll invite people to phone me to talk about you, and then if there's time, you can say goodnight to the viewers. OK?'

'Yes,' said Philip.

'Can I go to the loo again?' asked the little girl.

Helen laughed. 'Of course, but you're not getting nervous, Patsy, are you?'

'I'm not, but my tummy is.'

'Shall I tell you something? My tummy is too, but it'll be all right once we get started. Now, off you go.'

The children raced upstairs with the receptionist, while Helen made her way into the studio. She settled herself at the desk and marked up the scripts.

'Take the phone, will you, Helen?' said the floor manager.

'Sweetheart.' It was Mark, the director.

'Darling, I've told you not to disturb me at work,' she said. They both laughed. It was an old joke.

'Have you done something different with your make-up?'

'No. Why? Do I look dreadful?'

'Not at all. You look absolutely ravishing.'

'Are you trying to tell me I usually look like shit?'

'Yes, you old bag. No, of course not, but you look specially good today.'

'Thanks, Mark.'

'You're welcome. Are the children here?'

'Yes, they'll come in during *Seven Days*.'

'Fine. Enjoy it.'

'I will. Thanks.'

The programme went without a hitch. The children were thrilled to see themselves on film and quite at ease on camera.

'If you had a family, Patsy,' asked Helen, 'what would you most enjoy doing with your mum?'

'I'd like to make cakes,' Patsy said.

'What sort of food do you like best, Philip?'

'Chips,' he answered quickly, and the cameramen laughed. The picture cut to a close-up of Helen.

'Well, it's time for us to go. I'll be taking calls about the children from now until eight-thirty – just give me five minutes to get upstairs. Join me at six tomorrow.' The shot broadened to include one child on each side of her.

'Would you like to say goodnight?' she asked them.

'Goodnight,' said Philip obediently.

But Patsy was enjoying it. 'Yes, goodnight from *Reporting at Six*, especially to everyone at Woodlands Children's Home and Grove Road Middle School.'

'Hey, a presenter in the making!' Helen laughed. 'That's it. Goodnight.'

They were out of time, and the captions were up for a second only, but Helen knew that Patsy's impromptu speech would reap a reward that far outweighed a slightly messy end to the programme.

The children left for the children's home, and Helen grabbed a drink in hospitality before making for the newsroom, which was already buzzing. Three girls were talking on the telephone and scribbling furiously.

'Lots of calls,' said Sharon, who was on the switchboard. 'I've taken some, and so have the others, but one or two people really want to speak to you.'

'OK. When the rush is over, we'll call them back.' The phone rang. 'I'll take it,' said Helen.

The next hour and a half passed quickly, and Helen was so engrossed in what she was doing, and so enjoying the response from some very likely candidates, that thoughts of her own late-evening encounter could not have been further from her mind.

'I'd like to adopt *you* actually,' said the next caller. This was the only hazard: occasionally a nutter got through. Helen was about to put the phone down when she recognised Sam's voice. She laughed.

'You idiot. Where are you?'

'I've just got home.'

'Have you been operating all day?'

'Most of it.'

'You must be exhausted.'
'So must you.'
'Well, my day hasn't been quite the matter of life and death that yours has.'
'I don't know. The adoption will change the children's lives.'
'Oh, you must have missed it.'
'No, I watched at the hospital, in the common room. It was strange having to share you with my colleagues. It went very well. Does it sound chauvinistic to say I was proud of you?'
'I don't think so. Look, I'd better go – do you mind? I just want to gather all the telephone messages together, so I can pass them to the adoption agency. Then I'll come home.'
'Good. I'll join you at about nine-thirty.'
Helen realised that Sharon was looking at her with interest. '*Not* a possible adopter,' she said.
'No, I thought not. New man?'
Helen felt herself blushing as she nodded.
Sharon often operated the switchboard and was quite familiar therefore with the state of Helen's social life at any time. Over the past two years there had been many gentlemen callers who phoned regularly, then less frequently, until Helen would say, 'If so and so phones, just say you can't find me.' And that would be the end of him. Sharon was too busy with her own uproarious social round to be truly concerned with anyone else's, but occasionally she and the other girls commented that it seemed a shame for someone as attractive as Helen to be alone. They had come to the conclusion that she had thoughts only for her career, which was exactly what she wanted them to believe.
'You go.' Helen's voice broke Sharon's train of thought. 'I'll just ring the children's social worker, then I'll be off as well. Tell the others they can go too.'
'If you're sure?'
'Go on. I expect you've got some poor bloke in tow tonight?'
'Got to, haven't you? Especially with pay day so far

away. I'm going to make him buy me a super dinner – I'm ready for it.'

Helen picked up the telephone to ring Alan, the social worker, who, she knew, would be at the children's home with Patsy and Philip. As she did so, she lit up her first cigarette of the day. She told Alan the good news about the telephone response. 'About ninety-five, and probably a third of those are starred as sounding very suitable. So let's hope you find the right family for our two, and maybe a few similar kids will get homes as a result of the programme too.'

Both were aware that the drop-out rate was enormous and that they were still far from the finishing tape. The vetting of applicants was lengthy and intrusive, and many families would find they could not cope with it.

'I've got my fingers crossed anyway,' said Alan. 'Thanks for everything. Oh, the kids want to say goodnight.'

'Helen' – it was Patsy – 'it was funny being on the television. I've got to go to bed, but I'm too excited to sleep. 'Bye.'

Philip was quieter. 'I wonder if my real dad saw it,' he said.

Helen thought quickly. 'Sweetheart, your dad hasn't been in touch since you were a baby. I don't think he'd recognise you now. He wasn't awfully good at being a dad, was he?' There was silence. She went on. 'We'll just have to hope someone else will be.'

'OK,' he said more jauntily. 'G'night.'

'You heard that?' Helen asked when Alan came back to the phone.

'Yeah. I thought he was quiet about something. Don't worry, I'll have a session with him tomorrow and iron a few things out.'

'Fine. Keep in touch, eh?'

'Sure. I'll let you know what happens.'

So the day, the working day, was over and Helen could indulge herself now with thoughts of last night and the evening to come. Her hair needed tidying; she had a habit of running her hands through it when she was on the phone. She renewed her lipstick, added a suggestion of blusher to her cheeks, sprayed on some perfume and was ready.

Inside the Saab, which she adored, Helen adjusted her seat a little and switched on the radio, which was tuned to Radio Three. The familiar frenzied theme of the finale to the fourth movement of Brahms's First Symphony blasted from the quadrophonic system. She turned down the volume slightly and sat soaking in the sound. With a jolt she realised it was nine o'clock and Sam would be at her home in half an hour.

She drove to her flat in record time and looked around. Now that Sam was coming, it seemed unattractive and incomplete. She turned up the central heating, lit a few candles, selected a record by jazz guitarist Martin Taylor and flicked various light switches on and off till she achieved the effect she thought she wanted. Next she checked the bedroom. To her horror she found it in chaos, with the bed unmade. She remembered that she had left late the morning before. What a long time ago that seemed now.

'You're out of breath,' Sam said when she opened the door to him.

'I was making the bed. I'm not very organised, I'm afraid. In fact, I'm probably a bit of a slut.'

He laughed. It broke the ice and enabled her to throw her arms around his neck and kiss him. His arms were full, she noticed. He had a bottle of champagne in one hand and a carrier bag filled with little foil parcels in the other.

'Come on, give me those. Let me get you a drink,' she said, as she closed the front door and led him into the lounge.

'You get the drink and I'll pop the food into the oven,' he said. He kissed her again and went in search of the kitchen. 'That's funny – it's like mine.'

She smiled, remembering her impressions on seeing his kitchen for the first time that morning.

Surprisingly for such new lovers, their meeting tonight had been like that of old, or at least familiar, ones. The pervading sense was one of sweet tenderness, such as exists between elderly married couples who are still very much in love – the sort of cherishing that injects stinging loneliness into those observers without it, happiness for the ageing romance, hunger for such fulfilling delight and joy at the triumph of true love against all the odds.

Suddenly, and quite perceptibly, their tranquillity was disturbed as each sensed a tremendous building up of emotion. The physical tension between them mounted, and as they fell into their first passionate embrace of the evening, they were lost to it and abandoned within it. His hands were stroking and seeking. His mouth never left hers, and she felt that her breasts must explode as she pressed her chest hard into his, anticipating the glorious surrender that they surely must enjoy soon.

He pulled away reluctantly. 'Doctor says you must eat.'

'Oh, Sam.'

'I mean it. You hardly ate a thing last night and, come to think of it, neither of us managed much the night of my birthday either. Was that really only two nights ago?'

She smiled at yet another example of how closely his thoughts mirrored her own. 'Yes – you're forty-five and two days.'

'We could celebrate.'

'We are. OK, let's eat.'

'I'll do it,' he said. 'I want to be sure you're getting enough of everything, and I don't trust you.'

She was glad he was taking charge. For her there was something embarrassing about serving take-away food. It was social eating and yet not quite. She always got very messy dispensing it and somehow felt shy about doing so.

Sam returned with piled plates on two small trays, then he went to fetch his champagne, which was still chilling in the refrigerator.

'You think of everything,' she said.

He grinned, and she thought how boyish he looked and how pleased. 'I like looking after you,' he said. 'I think that's what I want to do.'

Helen's eyes filled with tears.

'Darling, I'm sorry.' The look on his face bore witness to his concern. 'What did I say?'

'I'm probably just tired. I'm certainly overwhelmed. I simply find some things you say almost unbearably touching.'

'If that's the reason you're weeping, I'm pleased,' he said.

Their need for each other could not be put off indefinitely and, despite his earlier insistence that they must eat a good meal, it was not long before they both declared themselves defeated by the amount on their plates. Sam, continuing his ministry, removed the remainder of their meal while she blew out the candles and wandered to the bathroom.

She looked at her image in one of the many mirrors. Her make-up base had long since soaked in or been licked away but, in spite of her tiredness, a glow shone from her eyes, lighting up the thirty-five-year-old face that, until now, had depressed her for its rather too accurate reflection of her age and experience. She stepped out of her leather trousers and divested herself of every other item of clothing. As a gesture towards his presence, she dropped all her garments into the laundry basket – normally she would have left them littering the bathroom floor. She almost threw in her shoes too but then defiantly decided that if he could not cope with some evidence of her daytime life, he was not fit to share her nights.

As she came, naked, into the bedroom, he looked at her, almost as if he were seeing her properly for the first time. She could feel his desire as he pulled her to him. His clothing was rough against her bare skin. She was totally vulnerable in her nudity as he, pressed against her, remained reliable, businesslike and dressed for action. He moaned slightly. With a swift movement he turned her around. He held her close with his left arm, and she felt his right hand unzip his clothing and fumble inside it. She gasped as he pushed inside her and together they fell kneeling and entwined to the edge of the bed. The wooden frame pressed into her chest, while behind and around her he thrust and cried out until finally, spent, he collapsed.

Blue sheets, she noticed. There were blue sheets on her bed which, until now, when her nose and eyes were in close proximity to them, had not registered as the vivid colour of cornflowers.

'Helen, my darling,' he was murmuring as he kissed the back of her neck, 'you must be squashed. Get into bed.'

She obeyed like a child and lay waiting as he undressed rapidly and slid beneath the quilt to join her.

He held her close. 'Did you come?'

Why did men always have to ask that? 'Of course.'

'You didn't. Be honest. I came too quickly. I don't know what's happening to me. I want to take you in love, not lust, for I do love you, but the lust blows my mind.'

Against her better judgement a certain pride was stirring. 'I'm pleased, I think. And, OK, I didn't come. I'm sorry, but I still loved it. Does it matter?'

'Not at all, but it does if you lie to me. Don't ever do that.'

They cuddled in silence. She kissed the beads of perspiration from his brow and hairline as he enfolded her to him. Gradually his caresses became firmer, his kisses more demanding, and again he turned her body away and entered her. Now, though, he took time and care. His left hand fondled her, and his lips and tongue performed a magic act in her left ear. Together they rode for their goal and, as they did so, she became increasingly elated by the realization that the night before had not been a mistake or a miracle. She offered her mind and body to the waves which were tumbling over and around and above them, culminating in a cascade that peaked and frothed and finally ebbed gently away.

How long they lay together, bound by shared passion and melting cohesion, they did not know. He spoke first. 'I never believed,' he said, 'I would ever, could ever, be in love as I am at this moment. God forgive me, I don't want to die, but were I to right now, I couldn't die happier.'

She held him, overflowing with love and gratitude. She had not experienced this bare, unashamed pleasure since she was a child, when she had yet to learn to hold on to such moments, unaware they are all too rare. She knew that she would always remember this split-second of her life but that she would not be able to look back and say, 'I was happy then and I didn't realise it,' for no amount of romantic retrospection could heighten her acute and consummate joy. I am so utterly happy, she thought, and the word 'happy' reverberated around her brain so loudly that she felt he must hear it. Perhaps, in fact, she had spoken it aloud.

'Helen,' he said, 'all anyone could ever hope for is that they might find the person they care for most and complete that person's circle with authentic love. I'd like to believe it's starting.'

She squeezed his arm. It was the last movement of the day.

Chapter Five

It was quite impossible, of course, for a relationship between two such public figures to remain a secret. Both had to attend their fair share of functions and, quite naturally, began to invite each other to fulfil the role of 'partner'. In this way Helen was introduced to the élite of the medical profession, and Sam learned just how long journalistic award ceremonies can last. He also, when time permitted, accompanied her when she kicked off charity football matches or opened Christmas bazaars.

They were referred to as 'constant companions' in the gossip columns, though, since neither of them had recently divorced or discarded another partner, they failed to make the headlines. Without a whiff of scandal, even though they occasionally bopped at one of the in-places, they were regarded as pretty dull material by Fleet Street.

Very few people at the studios commented either; perhaps they were too busy with their own intrigues to realise that Helen's man was lasting the course longer than any former paramour. Derek, for example, alluded to it only once and that was because he could not avoid doing so. During a morning meeting one day word reached them that a heart-and-lung transplant had been carried out on the youngest patient ever. Helen was already privy to the information, since Sam had performed the operation late the night before and had telephoned her to say he would not be joining her as planned.

'I think we should speak to the parents and also to the surgeon,' said Derek. 'It's your sort of thing really, Helen, but we can hardly have you interviewing your own bloke, so I'll send Laura.'

After the meeting, Laura came to find her. 'So, I'm to meet this miracle of perfection at last,' she said.

Helen smiled. 'Haven't you met yet?'

'You know damn well we haven't. You've been keeping him very well hidden.'

'You saw him last Tuesday after you and I'd had a drink and he came to pick me up.'

'Well, yes, a shadowy figure in a distant car.'

'I'm sorry. I never thought – Perhaps you and Ian and Sam and I could have dinner one night.'

'That would be great, but by the time we find a day when he's not performing a transplant, you're not in Bristol, I'm not in John O'Groats and Ian isn't filming in the Philippines, we'll probably be drawing our old-age pensions! Anyway, to come back to today, I'm a trifle anxious, actually, since you had such a rough ride with him when he came here.'

'Oh, God, don't remind me,' Helen said. 'Still' – and a smile spread from her mouth to her eyes – 'it has been worth it. You'll probably fancy him.'

'Yes, and he won't be able to keep his hands off me.' Laura laughed at Helen's shocked face. Helen suddenly saw the joke and laughed too. 'You really have got it bad when you think your own man is so desperately sexy that every woman under ninety-five wants to take him to bed.'

'What's with the age limit?' Helen grinned. 'Anyway, be nice to him. He's been up all night.'

'That's not unusual, is it? It's just a pity he no longer gets any sleep when he's not at the hospital or the clinic!'

'You beast. Do you think it's beginning to show?'

'Well, I don't know about him, but it's not on you. It's sickening, really. You've lost weight, though there's nothing haggard about you. You're swinging from the chandeliers twice nightly. And you look absolutely marvellous. There's no justice.'

'I do feel good,' Helen agreed.

'I know you do, and I'm glad. You deserve it.' Impulsively, Laura kissed Helen's cheek. 'I'd better go. I just hope he's gentle with me.'

'Oh, I think he's revised his opinion about television

people – and our ratings must have gone up. He rarely watched the programme before we met, but now he never misses it. In fact, if he knows he's going to be out, he videos it.'

'My goodness, he's as bad as you. Sweet, though. So you think he'll recognise me?'

'Oh sure. Anyway, I talk about you a lot. He knows who you are.'

With Laura gone, Helen felt deflated. She would have liked to see Sam herself. She had missed him last night. They had fallen into an undiscussed schedule, whereby they stayed some nights of the week at her flat and some at his house. Apart from one occasion when she had been to a function on the south coast which he was unable to attend, and another when he was giving a paper in Manchester, they had not slept apart since the night of his birthday, some six weeks earlier.

Soon it would be Christmas, and she had not yet broached the subject of what they should do. For all his years in Britain, Sam still paid lip service to the Islamic faith so, apart from the rampant commercialism all around them, the season made little impact. He loathed bad weather, however, and said he would never get used to it, while Helen loved cold, crisp days so long as they were dry. Sam liked the trappings of the drop in temperature though: pubs in the country with open log fires, mulled wine and the excuse to indulge in hot, home-made soups and steak-and-kidney pies. Helen found herself forgetting he was Egyptian sometimes; he seemed so English and, as he never tired of pointing out, he had lived far longer in the United Kingdom than he had in his homeland.

The phone rang. 'It's your mother on the line,' said Sharon.

'Oh, you'd better put her through.'

'Helen, how are you? We haven't heard from you for ages.'

'I'm fine, Mummy. I'm sorry – it probably has been weeks.'

'Your father and I were wondering about Christmas. Will you be coming down?'

'That's funny. I was thinking about Christmas not two minutes ago.'

'Well?'

'Um . . . Well, of course I'll be there, some of it anyway. I haven't got round to making any arrangements.'

'You can bring your new fellow if you want. What's he like anyway?'

Helen grinned to herself as the purpose of the call manifested itself. 'How did you know I had a new man?'

'Well, we saw something in one of the papers, as a matter of fact.'

'Mummy! Fancy you reading all that old rubbish.'

'Isn't it true then?'

'Often articles in those sorts of papers aren't.'

'Ahmed Aziz, isn't it?' Her mother pronounced the first syllable like 'arm'.

'Actually, it's sort of pronounced Achmed – "ch", as in the Scottish "loch", with "med" on the end, although the "d" is sort of a cross between a "d" and a "t".'

'How complicated,' said her mother. 'I don't believe I've ever heard it said before.'

'It doesn't matter. Everyone calls him Sam.'

'Oh good. So what does he look like? Is he kind to you?'

'He's very kind to me. But how shall I describe him? Think of Omar Sharif – well, Sam is a shorter, younger version of him. He's got black, crinkly hair, greying at the temples. He's about five foot ten. He's slim apart from a slight roundness in the tummy. He's got a darkish complexion, rather like a dull tan. He's got brilliant white teeth and slightly fleshy lips. I'm not making a very good job of this – he doesn't sound very exciting, I know, but he's wonderful. Come to think about it, Laura's out interviewing him now. If you watch the programme, you'll see him.'

'I'll do that. I think he sounds quite handsome.'

'Well, maybe.' How effectively the choice of words betoken a generation gap. 'Oh, and he's got the deepest, biggest liquid-brown eyes in the world.'

'Yes, well, I can see you're quite taken. Are you getting married?' Her mother always came straight to the point.

'It's early days, Mummy, but it's possible.'

'Ooh, how marvellous! Well, you must bring him down for Christmas.'

'Hang on, I don't know that I will. I haven't asked him yet – he's an Arab, don't forget. He might feel a little out of place.'

'I do think he should make an effort – especially if he's to be our next son-in-law.'

'Mummy, Mummy, don't get carried away. Look, I will talk to him, and I'll call you in a couple of days. I'd better go now. I'm supposed to be working.'

'All right, dear. Take care of yourself.'

Helen felt guilty that she had been deliberately out of communication with her parents, yet the phone call had borne out her reasons. It was natural that they should worry about her and hope she might settle again, but she was not yet ready to be cross-examined about this precious relationship.

The call had unsettled her, so she determinedly threw herself into the papers and the mail. Even so, it seemed an age till Laura returned.

'He thinks the world of you.'

'How do you know?'

'Well, when I introduced myself, he said he was delighted to meet me at last, then immediately asked how you were!'

Helen smiled and looked at her watch. 'That's understandable. We have been apart for about twenty-eight hours.'

Laura laughed. 'Anyway, I must say I was impressed. He's like a god to his staff, and as for the parents of the child, well, he showed me pictures of the baby before the operation . . . so tiny, so ill-looking. Sam let me see him this morning and already he's turning a pretty pink colour. The man's a genius and, better than that, he really cares. Funny, though: I thought he'd be anxious for all the publicity he could get, but once we'd finished, he kept all the other crews waiting while he took me off for coffee.

Mind you, he only wanted to talk about you, so I jolly well told him off.'

'What about?'

'I just said that, apart from a quick drink after work, I never see you now.'

'What did he say to that?'

'He said he supposed he did commandeer your time, but he had years to catch up on.'

'How sweet – did he really?'

'Yes. So I asked him if you and he would like to spend Boxing Day with us. He said you hadn't discussed what was happening at Christmas.'

'That's quite right. We haven't.'

'Why on earth not?'

'I don't know exactly – something to do with his being an Arab, I think. Still, now you've brought up the subject, I might mention it tonight.'

Sam brought flowers when he turned up at Helen's flat that evening. He looked tired when she opened the door, but a smile spread over his entire face, lighting up his eyes, as soon as he saw her. They kissed in the doorway.

'I can't bear to have you out of my sight for so long, Helen,' he said. 'I've had the most wonderful day, really exciting, but I kept counting the hours till I could tell you about it. Of course, I was anticipating getting you into bed, but at the same time I was so looking forward to just talking with you.'

They had never seemed closer than they were that night, and he made love to her later passionately and possessively. The intensity of his need almost frightened her; he seemed to be trying to own every particle of her being.

'What was your husband like in bed?' His question came right out of the blue but confirmed her assessment. She realised it made him as anxious as it did her.

'It was never great.'

'You don't have to say that.'

'I know I don't. To begin with, it was very loving, but . . . Look, I've never told another soul this, but . . . I didn't come with him.'

'What? You're joking. You're not faking with me, are you?'

Helen was stunned. She knew he was struggling with his own powerful feelings, yet there was no excuse for questioning, even momentarily, the extraordinary quality of their love-making.

'I'm sorry. That was a lousy thing to ask.'

'It was,' she said. 'when you couldn't possibly doubt what we have.'

'Do you miss him, though?'

Helen was annoyed, but at the same time she understood that he could not help himself. 'I'll make a cup of tea. I think we should talk this out.'

He nodded, then leapt out of bed to light a cigarette. She watched as he returned and puffed away moodily. He had never smoked in bed before.

Helen took longer in the kitchen than was necessary. She was preparing what she might say as well as giving him some time to collect his thoughts.

When she came back to the bedroom he took the mugs of tea from her, put them on the bedside table and kissed her. 'I'm sorry, Helen. I'm really sorry. I've never been possessive before. Part of me adores what's happening and part of me is terrified.'

Snuggling up to him, she very gently kissed the ends of his lashes before telling him of her early days with Barry – of how she had cared and of her determination to be content with that when their sex life failed to improve. 'Especially when I got into television,' she said, 'I was so aware that it was difficult for him to have a wife in the public eye that I certainly couldn't have told him then that he didn't turn me on in bed. He did to begin with, you see, but when it's never long enough to climax, and when someone never touches you where you're desperate to be touched, in the end, in spite of yourself, you shut off. You stop even hoping. By the time we split up – and, let's face it, he was getting it somewhere else anyway – I had a permanent crick in my neck through hanging over my side of the bed so that nothing made contact, not even our feet. It was terrible. Then, when we decided to get a divorce, he told me he hadn't really fancied me since before we were married because my capability emasculated him.'

With her confession came tears – tears that should have been wept at the time but never had been. Sam held her and rocked her like a baby until the crying stopped, then kissed her tears away. 'All right, I understand, and I'm glad you've told me. I'm sorry it's been so upsetting.'

'I feel better now,' she said, 'in a way.'

They sipped their tea in silence.

'Do you remember,' he asked suddenly, 'that the first night we made love I told you I wanted you to have my child?' She nodded. 'Well,' he went on, 'you never commented on it.'

'You never said it again. I wondered if you'd regretted it.'

'No. I want you to marry me, Helen. I daren't hope that you will, but I have to ask.'

They fell into each other's arms.

'Sam, I love you so much. Please marry me. Please give me your child. And please always voice your thoughts and your fears. I can't stand atmospheres and secrets. I've done all that.'

'I promise,' he said, and, more gently now, they made love again.

Later, lying in the dimly lit room, she mentioned her mother's phone call. 'She wants to invite you for Christmas.'

'Oh, no,' he said quickly. 'I don't think I could cope with that.'

'Why not?'

He explained about some of the Christmases he had experienced in the past and how he had felt out of place.

'You wouldn't feel left out with me.'

'No, probably not, but your mother and father will be looking forward to seeing you, and you should give them your full attention. Of course I'll meet them, but Christmas is too emotive a time for you all. Let's leave it for now.'

She agreed but, despite his earlier promise, she was not at all sure he was articulating everything in his mind.

'Anyway,' he said, 'as the only Arab and bachelor, I usually volunteer to be the duty consultant; it's only fair. We don't have many patients in the hospital, but I carve the turkey at lunch for those who can manage it, and I often have private patients in the clinic, so I pop over there too.'

'I thought you couldn't bear to be away from me.'

'That's true, so I was hoping you'd come back on the morning of Boxing Day. As long as one of the others is prepared to work, I could take some time off and we could do what Laura suggested and join her and her man.'

It had been a long day and an emotional evening. It seemed to Helen that there was some niggling disquiet at the back of her mind that was struggling to emerge as an identifiable idea. 'Do you never feel perhaps you owe it to your own country to go back and practise there? Do you never feel your family would like you to go home?'

'I'm very tired, Helen,' he said. 'Can we have this conversation another time? I'm practically English, as I've told you before, and now I'm going to have an English wife. I love you, and I want to be here with you.'

He curled around her, and the warmth and strength of him soothed her body and mind. It was natural in two such independent characters that there should be some ups and downs, and whatever her abstract anxiety was, it could surely be resolved. She relaxed and slept.

The days raced headlong towards Christmas. Helen was astonished at her reaction to this festive season compared with the last few. Life was hectic. Her days were crammed with personal appearances, recordings and programmes, her nights spent in passionate exchanges, but for all that she was charged with an energy that was invigorating. Somehow she found time to buy extravagant presents for everyone, though the last two years, feeling oppressed by her workload, she had consulted Fortnum's catalogue and selected, within half an hour, gifts for her friends which could be delivered, impersonally, on an appropriate day.

This year nothing was too much trouble. She was replete with good will to all men and women and even found herself, in quiet moments, offering up a prayer of thanksgiving for her good fortune and, indeed, her very life.

On Christmas Eve the programme turned into an old-time music hall and she and the other presenters and reporters donned Victorian costumes and performed for the viewers. Sam was off duty that night and, for the first time since their meeting, came to the studios to watch the programme go out live.

The social club was buzzing when all the participants in the six o'clock show arrived there shortly after seven. 'Best Christmas programme ever,' said Derek, as he always did and, as they always did, everyone agreed. Was not Christmas a time for tradition and ritual?

After a while Helen's friends and acquaintances drifted away, either to drive to ageing parents or to prepare to play Father Christmas to their offspring. When only a handful of revellers remained, Sam took charge and devoted himself to giving them a party. He took them all to supper at a little Indian restaurant, where he ordered for everyone and regaled them with medical stories. It was obvious to Helen they had fallen under his spell.

At the end of the evening he persuaded them to join him in drinking a bottle of champagne. When the cork popped he said, 'As the only Arab in our party, may I wish you every joy this Christmas.' They drank to that, but Sam had not finished. 'May I also propose a toast' – he turned towards Helen – 'to this lovely lady, who is shortly to become my wife.'

There was a moment's silence, then the congratulations flowed not only from their table but also from other diners, who had not been oblivious to the celebrity dining in their midst. Sam and Helen kissed then, and it seemed to her that the lights of the restaurant were spinning all around her. She had consumed a fair amount of wine, but whether she was drunk on alcohol or sheer happiness she did not care.

Back in her flat, she kicked off her shoes and made two cups of decaffeinated coffee. In a few hours she must leave for Bournemouth and the family Christmas, but this was the real celebration. She presented Sam with a Christmas stocking she had bought and filled with ridiculous and inconsequential items: a pair of clockwork feet, a minute jack-in-the-box, a tin shaped like a vintage Bentley and filled with old English confectionery, and a packet of seeds which claimed to contain the necessary ingredients to grow a fur coat. Sam had clearly never received such a gift before, and for Helen it was like watching a child at the first Christmas he is old enough to appreciate. She felt her heart would burst as he unwrapped each nonsensical gift with shrieks of merriment. Next she gave him his proper present, a pair of platinum cufflinks set with cornelians, which had been engraved on the underside with his initials. He took her hand, then kissed her, and she noticed he was very close to tears. They sat for a while, holding and touching and loving. He then excitedly made his presentation, which was a finely woven red wool evening skirt with pointing detail finished in gold thread, a gossamer-fine top with the same gold detail and a huge, fire-red cape with a spider's web embroidered on it in gold and two diamonds worked into it to represent flies caught in the tangle. It was breathtakingly beautiful, and she could not even begin to guess at the cost of it.

'Sam, it's too expensive.'

'Don't you like it?'

'I love it. I've never had anything so lovely. It's just – it's too much.'

'Nothing is too much for you. I want to give you the world, and I'm only just beginning.'

Somewhere she knew she had a recording of carols sung by the choir of King's College, Cambridge. She found it and put it on the sound system, while he uncorked another bottle of champagne. At twelve he solemnly wished her a happy Christmas before picking her up bodily and carrying her to bed.

Her parent's joy at seeing her tempered her happiness with guilt as she consciously tried to slip back into the role of dutiful and single daughter. Everyone else ate too much and slept, so Helen washed up before waking them for the Queen's speech, which had customarily signalled the moment at which they might begin to exchange gifts.

It was all as it ever had been, and yet not quite: phone calls punctuated the day. She had rung the hospital, and he had phoned later, after serving lunch to his patients. He phoned again around six, just before Helen's family settled before the television set for the usual fare of films and variety shows.

Later in the evening, when Helen was washing up again, her mother joined her in the kitchen. The inevitable questions followed about Sam and their relationship and his reason for declining the Christmas invitation. Helen explained as best she could. It was obvious that her mother was hurt and also that she felt left in the dark. Helen wondered if this was the lot of all parents and, for a second, considered whether the children she was hoping for with Sam, would be as careless of her concern as she knew she was being of her mother's.

'It's not that we mind him being an Arab, dear,' her mother was saying. Helen was angered by the implied prejudice, but at least it provided a focal point for her unrest. She felt torn between her past and future, yet she believed they were not irreconcilably at odds.

'Why would you?' she replied.

'Well, I mean, they're from a different culture. I'm sure you can understand our point of view – it would have been easier if you'd picked a nice young British boy.'

'I did that once, remember? It was hardly a success. And "young" is difficult too – there aren't very many young, unattached guys around when you get to thirty-five. There aren't too many men either who can cope with an up-front financially secure workaholic. It does narrow one's choice. And don't forget,' she continued, 'your grandchildren will be Arabs – in part, anyway.'

Her mother dropped the china plate she was drying and burst into tears.

'I'm sorry, Mummy. I am sorry. Don't let's quarrel. It's Christmas.'

'I don't want to quarrel. I just don't know what's going on.'

The phone rang.

'That'll be him again, I suppose. He might as well have come here, since he can't seem to leave you in peace for five minutes.'

Helen kissed her mother on the forehead. She wanted to gather her to her, for was she not regarded as a tactile person? Somehow she could not act in this way with her parents.

She picked up the phone. It was Sam.

'Darling, I'm missing you. How are you?'

Helen, standing at the antique table in the hall beside the drawing-room door that remained resolutely open, felt stilted and awkward. 'I'm fine.'

'You're not. What's wrong? Did I ring at a bad moment?'

'Um – sort of.'

'Helen, I can't bear this. Have you gone off me?'

'No, no, no, no, no. It's just a bit . . . difficult.'

'Ah, you can't talk there.'

'Not really.'

'Isn't there an extension?'

''Fraid not.'

'Can you ring me back later, any time?'

'I don't think so – I'll explain tomorrow. I'll get back early. I'll be at your house by eleven. We're not going to Ian's and Laura's till one, are we?'

'No. Helen, you do love me, don't you?'

'I do – I really do.'

'You see, I never want you to go to bed anywhere in the world where they have a phone without ringing you before you sleep to tell you how much I care for you.'

'You have a knack of saying the nicest things,' she murmured, then, with a look at the open drawing-room door, she drew a defiant, thirty-five-year-old breath. 'Sam, I do love you. I adore you, in fact, and I'm counting the hours till I can be with you.'

He sounded satisfied. 'Sleep well, darling.'

Helen put the phone down and took another deep breath before joining her parents to ask if they would like a drink. They opted for small medium sherries, which she was happy to pour and distribute in order to avail herself of a large brandy. She lit a cigarette too and knew that both actions had been noted with some disapproval.

'Let's play *Trivial Pursuit*,' she said, freshly determined to pay full attention to her family for the final few hours. She reproached herself as they played. Surely, she thought, you can enjoy this and put Sam out of your mind. She persevered and experienced a sensation of watching herself behaving normally and lovingly, while inside she was in torment, going over and over the misunderstanding on the telephone and hating herself for her treatment of her parents in this quiet suburb of Bournemouth. She was alarmed too at her dependence on Sam and his on her, yet, secure in the belief they were to spend their lives together, she persuaded herself that their insularity was permissible.

By the end of the evening she judged she had remedied the situation somewhat. In the kitchen when she and her mother were making hot chocolate she asked, 'Would you like to meet Sam soon, Mummy?'

'Of course. Isn't that what I've been saying to you?'

'Sort of. Why don't you and Daddy come up one Saturday when neither of us is working, and we'll have lunch and go to a matinée?'

'That would be very nice,' said her mother, and on that note Helen felt she could finally, and justifiably, put Christmas Day to bed.

She left the next morning with their good wishes, and her spirits rose as she drove, singing, up the M3. There were few other motorists on the road. Perhaps the rest of mankind was nursing a hangover, or maybe most travellers had already reached where they wanted to be. The roads were slightly slippery, for the night had seen the first snowflakes of the winter – it had almost been a white Christmas after all. The green landscape all around was painfully pretty, embellished as it was by its faint powdering of virgin snow. It was as if the Almighty had sprinkled the world with a dusting of icing sugar from a giant sieve in the sky. She smiled at her culinary analogy and thought how long it was since she had thrown a dinner party. Maybe she would have one and invite her parents.

Surprisingly quickly, she was back at Strand on the Green. Though she had a key, she rang the doorbell. As she heard Sam's movements, she sang 'Once in Royal David's City' through the letter box.

He opened the door and they embraced before he reached into his pocket for a pound coin, which he pressed into her hand. 'A reward for the carol singer,' he said.

'Gosh, thanks. That was easy money. What else could I do for a reward?'

'I'll show you,' he said, taking her hand and leading her upstairs.

'We can't, Sam. We're supposed to be going out for lunch.'

'We can and we will and we'll still go out to lunch.'

Afterwards, lying in bed, he held the underside of his arm to hers. 'Look,' he said, 'different colour, different texture, different cultures, different countries, yet you are the other side of me. All my life I've waited for the right lady. I grew impatient. I didn't think there could be such a person. But at last I found you.' He leant over and kissed the inside of her wrist.

'You waited,' she said.

'In a way,' he replied.

'I wish I had.'

'I know . . . Yesterday one of my young transplant patients had a visit from his wife, who's very pregnant. It was lunchtime, and I thought, this time next year we'll have Christmas Day together and I'll have to pull back your chair further than usual and push it in ever so gently because you'll be enormous with my child.'

As he helped her to her chair at Laura's dining-table, Helen smiled up at him, remembering his words. He smiled back.

'Well, how are you both?' asked Ian. 'Sorry – damn-fool question.'

'Just fine.' Helen knew she was glowing. She could sense and smell Sam all about her.

Laura had gone to enormous trouble over the lunch.

She had cooked a boned goose stuffed with turkey breasts and the blend of dark and light meats was exquisite. It was a while since Helen had been in her friend's flat; it struck her that it had become much more of a home than hitherto. Ian and Laura were quietly comfortable together, she thought. It was true they were both active in, and enthused by, their careers but, consciously or unconsciously, they were building a nest and a future. Helen wondered if they ever sneaked off to bed in the middle of the day. Somehow they were more settled. It was hard to qualify the differences – more mature? Of course, they had known each other longer.

The girls grew more animated as time and the wine flowed. They giggled at the frailties of their colleagues and bitched about their bosses. The men observed them indulgently.

'This isn't supposed to be a company conference,' Ian said quietly at last.

Helen caught in full flood, laughed and took Sam's hand. 'I'm sorry. We'll stop.'

'No, don't,' he said, 'I like career women. I like what makes you tick.'

'I like what makes *you* tick,' Laura joined in. 'I was terribly impressed – ' She laughed. 'I can probably only say this 'cos I'm a bit pissed, but I was terribly impressed the day I did the piece on you. In fact – I don't know if you'd agree – I'd like to do an extended feature, a sort of "Week in the Life of – ".'

Sam blushed. 'Oh, I don't think . . .'

'It's a good idea,' Helen decided.

'I don't think . . . ,' said Sam again.

'Oh, come on, Sam, great publicity. You know your programme needs more money. It could only benefit from it.'

'What about all the less headline-grabbing branches of medicine that are just as deserving?' he asked wickedly.

'You sod.' She laughed. 'Is this where I came in or what?'

'Well, that's settled,' said Laura. 'I've sounded Derek out already, actually.'

'Saints preserve us from organising women,' said Ian. 'We might as well give in – we're surrounded. Have another drink, old boy. Better still, why don't we have a game of backgammon while we leave the girls to sort out our future and theirs?'

Sam threw a look in Helen's direction. She was not sure what it meant. Did he feel uncomfortable with Ian? Did he want to be rescued? Probably not. He had been quite quiet over lunch. Perhaps he was not enjoying himself. Maybe he was not keen on the couple, but they had to be sociable sometimes. After all, the friends she had made since the divorce were important to her; they had seen her through the bad times. Had she not always maintained that she would never again let anyone dictate to or walk all over her, and that anyone new in her life must be able to embrace not only her lifestyle but also the other people who mattered to her? Being in love was wonderful. She had almost forgotten what it felt like. But she had also almost forgotten what anxiety and unrest it automatically brought with it.

He seemed more settled now and, from the determined set of his jaw, she surmised he had every intention of winning. She continued talking and giggling with Laura but, unlike her friend, was hugely aware of the scene in the corner. She relaxed only when she heard Sam's laugh. What a strange man he was. How efficient at work, how romantic with her, and yet how uneasy in a one-to-one encounter with a man he hardly knew.

'Am I an organising woman?' Helen asked later. They were in bed as Boxing Day drew to a close. She wanted to explore everything that had happened at her friends', but it seemed prudent to concentrate on one query at a time.

'Yes,' he answered, but in a perfectly adorable way. 'It's one of the things I like most about you. You're capable but you're loving, efficient but sweet, and I'm very lucky. You leave me space, and I need that. The one thing I can't cope with is a clinging female who expects me to provide her reason for living.'

'I'm suitably warned,' said Helen.

'What? Oh, I wasn't talking about you.'

Helen was puzzled. 'Well,' she said quietly, 'I thought we had a terrific day.'

He smiled. 'We did,' he agreed, enfolding her in his arms, 'as every day is with you.'

Secure again, she kissed him and promptly fell asleep.

Chapter Six

It was nearly as difficult to fill the programme between Christmas and New Year as it was in August. Naturally no one hoped for treacherous weather and the resultant crop of traffic accidents, but without them the news element of the programme was bound to be a bit thin. It was no surprise then when Colin, who was Derek's deputy and at the helm in the editor's absence, announced that they would do fifteen minutes of the next day's programme from a circus on the edge of town. There was little point in booking Post Office lines to transmit the feature live, since Helen would need to anchor the show in the studio.

'Pity, really' said Colin. 'If more people were around, we could have presented half the programme from the circus. We could still do it if we used a couple of the reporters there, but I think the viewers would sooner see Helen riding the elephant or whatever. We'll play it straight and say we recorded it specially earlier in the day.'

Steve, the following day's director, was busy scribbling on the small pad he carried around with him. 'What time will the outside broadcast unit be in place and ready to go?' 'The production office – which is being a bit touchy because it's such short notice, incidentally – says ten o'clock,' said Colin.

'Sod them,' said Steve. 'If there's a scanner available, I can't see what the hassle is – except they've probably had to call in a few irate technicians who're on standby. Anyway, we'll use Helen first, so she can get away. Who's setting it up?'

'Gary.'

'Well, where the hell is he?'

'I'll get him,' said Helen. She returned to the editor's office within seconds, accompanied by the reluctant researcher.

Gary was a newspaper man, as he constantly reminded people. His interest lay in political stories, and he obviously felt he was prostituting his craft by planning a feature on a circus, but, since his colleagues were on leave, there was no alternative. His stance suggested he had the cares of the world on his shoulders; his manner, that he believed himself to be the only person in the company doing an honest day's work. There was no time to indulge him. In any case, he was working overtime indulging himself. He chain-smoked through the meeting and drank two cups of coffee.

'What do you have for us, Gary?' asked Colin.

'Well,' Gary sighed, 'we've got dancing fountains that use God knows how many gallons of water per show. We've got a trapeze artist. Then there's a good talker in the lion tamer – apparently his act's quite unusual. And we've got a clown lined up who's worked in forty countries.'

'We'll start at ten with Helen and the lion chappie,' said the director to Colin, 'and if you can let me have a couple of reporters later, that should sew it up.'

Back in her office, Helen was at a loss as to what to do. There was no post to speak of, and the circus hardly needed any in-depth preparation. She went in search of Laura, who had just returned from shooting a piece on babies born in London and the Home Counties over Christmas. 'Poor little buggers. Two Noels, one Rudolph and one Carol.'

'Oh, God.' Helen laughed. 'Has Rudolph got a red nose?'

'He's red all over, actually. I can't say babies of that age do much for me. Have you got time for coffee?'

'I thought you'd never ask.'

They chatted for a while over the day they had just spent together with their respective men.

'They seemed to get on quite well' said Laura.

'Yes. Sam's funny – sometimes I think he's got no urge

to meet anyone. I've met a few of his colleagues, of course, but no close friends. Perhaps he doesn't have any. It's a miracle he was at the dinner party where we met – and we haven't seen those people since then, come to think of it. Still, when he does get out and make an effort, he's terrific.'

'Someone told me he announced your engagement in the Taj Mahal on Christmas Eve.'

'I think engagement's a rather funny word for us but, yes, he did. Changing the subject, in a way anyway, did you mean what you said about small babies not doing anything for you?'

'Yes . . . no . . . I don't know. Perhaps it's because they belong to other people. Why – do you feel differently?'

'I think so. I never used to even think about them – I'm getting broody, I suppose. Do you and Ian ever talk about getting married?'

'Sometimes, but neither of us is keen. It's me, I think – I can't really imagine life without him, but I can't honestly say I'm desperately in love or anything. I like things as they are. I don't really do much with my freedom but I like to know it's there.'

'I know what you mean. Of course, you're only twenty-nine. I expect I wasn't aware of the pressing passage of time when I was your age.'

'Poor old soul. You were married, though.'

'Yes – just. But, do you know, I never considered having children with Barry. Funny, isn't it?'

'Do you and Sam discuss it?'

'Oh, yes, and he's even keener than I am.'

'Well, when are you getting married?'

'I don't know. This'll probably sound odd, but he refers to our getting married, being married, my being pregnant and our lives with our children, but he never suggests a date. I know it's early days . . .'

'Well, it is, and also maybe he's waiting for you. You're an assertive woman, after all.'

'Not really, and certainly not with him. I don't need to be because he treats me exactly the way I want. Even if he didn't, though, I always feel our relationship couldn't possibly work if I were running it. I know that's not a very modern statement to make, but it's how it is.'

'You're sure he's quite genuine? I don't mean it unkindly, but you don't think he's just in love with the idea?'

'I don't know. I don't think so. You see, I'm quite happy as it is. He's the one who keeps mentioning marriage and children. Do you know, even the first night we slept together he talked about it. I promise you I'm not pressurising him.'

'No, I didn't think you were for a second. I just wonder if he can make the commitment. He is forty-five – why hasn't he done it before?'

'He says he's been too busy and that no one disturbed him sufficiently to make an impact. It's nice to hear, but . . . Oh dear, you've got me worried now. To be quite honest, to begin with I felt swept along – he was much more in love with me than I was with him. But . . . I think I'd die if anything went wrong now.'

Laura looked at her friend anxiously. 'Why should anything go wrong? It's wonderful. It's obviously much more intense than my thing with Ian. Why be pessimistic? He plainly worships the ground you walk on.'

'Maybe it's because it's too wonderful. Maybe I can't quite believe it can last. Maybe I don't believe I deserve it.'

'Well, you do. Forget what I said. You could just get pregnant.'

'No. I told you, I'm not that desperate. I would always wonder if he felt trapped and had married me for that. Anyway, I'm so beastly independent that if I conceived, I'd probably walk out of his life for ever just to prove I wasn't holding a shotgun to his head, so I don't think that's a good idea. I'm still on the pill anyway.'

'Well, why don't you tell Sam you're coming off it just to see if you're ovulating properly and see how he takes it?'

'OK, I might – it's a good idea.'

The door burst open suddenly. It was Gary, the researcher.

'Is this women's talk, or can anyone join in?'

'Oh dear, you found us out. We were just discussing how fanciable you are,' said Helen.

Laura edged behind Gary's not inconsiderable bulk and mouthed, 'May you be forgiven,' as she winked and departed.

The unmistakable and unassailable stench of animal excrement filled her nostrils when she arrived at the circus the following morning. Helen's stomach was never at its best early in the day, and for a moment she had to fight a desperate urge to vomit. But she had done stories in circuses and zoos before, and she knew she would grow accustomed to the smell after a while.

Nothing much seemed to be happening, so she found her way to a tatty café at the back of the big top. Most of the crew, who had finished rigging, were there before her and were wolfing down fried-egg sandwiches and mugs of strong tea.

'Have a sandwich, Helen. Do you a power of good,' said Dave, one of the electricians.

She made a face. 'No, I don't think I could cope with that. Is there a tab or are we paying for our own?'

'Certainly not. Eddie's sorting it at the end.'

Helen ordered a milky coffee and sat down. Steve, the outside broadcast director, joined her shortly afterwards.

'Gary and I had this great idea.'

'What's that then?'

'You do the interview with the lion trainer – '

'I know, we discussed it yesterday.'

' – in the cage with the lions.'

'Fine. Then I'll walk on water,' she said.

They enjoyed this sort of banter all the time.

'I'm serious.'

'Come on, Steve, it's too early to wind me up. I'm not awake yet.'

'I mean it, Helen.'

She realised he did. 'The company wouldn't let me do it.'

'They will, actually. The company secretary's dealing with our insurers now.'

'Is Derek still away?'

'Yes.'

'What does Colin say then?'

'He says, don't get too badly injured because he hasn't got another presenter for six o'clock.'

'Oh, great. I feel truly cherished now. You seem to have thought of everything. Has the lion trainer ever had anyone in the cage before?'

'No, but listen, sweet, I wouldn't ask you if I really thought it was dangerous. It'll make terrific television.'

Of that she had no doubt. 'One take, then. If you fuck up on cameras or anything – tough. I'll do it, but only once.'

'Are you serious?'

'Yes.'

'You're not.'

She sighed. 'Were you serious when you asked me?'

'Yeah – sort of.'

'Well, I'm serious. I'll do it.'

'Listen, Helen, *I* wouldn't do it.'

She laughed. 'You're impossible. Bring the bloke over and I'll talk to him.'

Alfonso dismissed her fears. He would do his act first, he told her, and then come to the edge of the cage and bring her in. 'Just keep your left hand on my right shoulder that's all. I make them very angry in the act, but it's just for show. I've had them all since they were cubs – they adore me.'

'What confidence,' she retorted.

'What are you going to ask?'

'Heavens, I haven't got around to thinking about that. Let's just hope something occurs to me.'

As she walked back to the big top, she passed several of the crew. The word had obviously got around, for she was being weighed up with glances that expressed a mixture of admiration and incredulity.

'Can I have a cigarette?' she asked of no one in particular and was embarrassed by the profusion of brands suddenly made available. 'One'll do.' She laughed.

'Are you sure about this, Helen?' It was one of the cameramen.

'No. Ask me another.'

'Look, love, you don't have to do it. Steve wouldn't.'

'I know. He told me. But I've said I will now.' She looked around. 'Has anyone got a sheet of paper?' The PA obliged. 'I'm just going to write a note to someone, then I'll be ready.'

She sat down in a seat by the ringside. She could see the lions waiting in the rope tunnel as the circus stage crew rolled in the equipment for the act.

Dear Sam,

You'll get this only if I die or am seriously injured. I'm sorry – it was a stupid thing to do. I got seduced by my own importance and the glamour of being the 'have-a-go girl'. I love you. Thanks for everything.

Love, Helen

She folded the paper and gave it to the PA. 'That's in case anything happens to me,' she said.

'Helen, nothing's going to happen.'

For the first time, Helen lost her cool. 'Listen, sweetheart,' she snapped, 'you're not the one who's going to face eight man-eating creatures. I'm about to justify the difference between my salary and yours. Just allow me to be a bit twitchy, OK?'

The PA exchanged glances with the soundman who was waiting to fix a radio mike. It was unlike Helen to play the part of a temperamental celebrity. They watched as she walked around in circles for a couple of minutes, puffing nervously at her cigarette. Then the expression on her face changed, like the sun coming out from behind a cloud; instantly she was all smiles. 'I'm sorry. Let's have the mike, and we'll go.'

It was fortunate that she had not seen the act before she agreed to go into the cage. Alfonso, as he had promised, made the animals appear ferocious in the extreme. The performance lasted eight minutes. Even in the midst of her panic Helen realised it would have to be cut down for the night's programme and wondered if anyone had booked editing time.

The lions were all on their rostra, standing on their hind legs and pawing at the air. Alfonso cracked his whip and they returned to all fours. This was it. He opened the cage door and, in the blinking of an eye, she was inside.

She heard her voice speaking normally while she clung to his shoulder for dear life. 'How long does it take to train animals to this state of excellence?'

He was talking back – so far, so good.

'What do you say to people who feel it's cruel to keep animals in captivity and make them perform for their keep?'

'They don't know what they're talking about. The animals love it, and they are much better cared for here than they ever would be in the wild,' he answered predictably.

One of the lions, a hairy male, snarled as Helen looked at him. He raised his paw and sliced through the air as if he would have liked to bisect her from top to toe. This was not the time to argue with Alfonso. A lioness came down off her perch and walked towards them.

'Lions are essentially lazy,' he was saying. 'This way they're fed and watered, and they don't have to do much about it.' He cracked his whip and, miraculously, the lioness returned to her podium.

'What do they eat in a normal day?'

The lion tamer warmed to his subject.

'Have they been fed today?', She did not register the answer while thinking up the next question, but she hoped fervently that they had been.

Somewhere outside the ring she could see the floor manager, looking much as usual, bearded, slightly bored, with suede shoes and corduroy trousers. She observed the countdown and finished neatly on the zero by saying, 'Thanks for not eating me, chaps,' as she walked backwards to the ring's edge. She backed out of the cage.

'Where's camera three?' shouted Steve outside in the outside-broadcast scanner. 'Cut to camera three. Go for the close-up. God, look at her! She's gone to pieces! Go in tighter.' The camera caught Helen in a quite untypical pose. Her head was in her hands and she was trembling all over. 'Great, great television!' said Steve excitedly. 'Oh, good girl – I love you.' He kissed the air in front of him.

'Nothing's changed since the lions and the Christians, obviously,' muttered the PA to no one in particular.

'OK,' said Steve ignoring his assistant, 'fade. That's it – we've got it. Terrific! I'll go and buy her a drink.'

'Wonderful, Helen,' he said as he reached her. 'Have a cigarette.' Helen nodded. She tried to thank him, but the words would not come. He steadied her hand as he lit her cigarette. She was shaking uncontrollably. He put his arm around her. 'The interview was fine, and you're still alive.'

'That's true . . . Was it really all right? I can't remember what I asked.'

'It was stupendous.'

'I'm sorry – I'm better now. I didn't feel terribly frightened in there. I just felt very strange when I came out.'

'Let's buy you a brandy.'

'Good idea – if we can find a pub that's already open.'

'Sussed that one. Come on.'

Watching the sequence later in the studio, when she was linking in and out of it during the programme, she had to admit it did, as the director had promised, make terrific television. She smiled at her apparent composure in the ring and felt again the engulfing reaction as she watched herself emerging from the cage. 'Well,' she said, live, 'all in a day's work, but I think I'd rather not do it again. That's it from us for tonight. I'm going to have a relaxing evening and weekend, and I hope you have the same. See you Monday. A very good night to you.'

The music came in; the captions were up. It was the end of another working day.

Back in the newsroom, Helen gathered up her diary and papers and was just leaving when the girl on the switchboard, who was a temp, stopped her. 'Do you want to speak to someone called Sam?'

'Yes, sure. I'll take it over here – extension 228. Hi, Sam!'

'Why did you do it?'

'It was great television.'

'It was certainly that. Why on earth didn't you tell me? You said you were going to the circus. You didn't say you were going in the cage with eight lions.'

'I didn't know then.'

'My God, Helen, you're mad.'

'You're right.'

'Are you coming home?'

'Soon.'

'Helen, I don't like you doing this sort of thing.'

The tension of the day erupted, 'For God's sake, Sam, you don't own me. I was doing "This sort of thing" before you ever came on the scene. I'm the best judge of what I can cope with and what I can't. It turned a very mediocre show into compulsive viewing. I'm OK. It was worth the risk.'

'I'm sorry,' he said coldly. 'You're quite right. I obviously have no say in the matter at all.'

'Sam, I'm sorry. I didn't mean to shout. Forgive me – don't let's argue. You're probably right – it was a barmy thing to do, and I certainly wouldn't do it again. Do you still love me?'

He sighed. 'Of course. That's why I got so upset, you idiot. Shall I come and get you? I don't think you should drive now. Let's eat out.'

'OK. I'll be next door.'

As she arrived in the social club she realised she had been exhausted by the events of the day.

'You look all in,' said the controller. 'Have a drink.'

'Thanks, Paul. It has been quite a day. Bloody stupid thing to do, really.'

'Terrific television. You're a good girl – you get better and better.' She smiled and relaxed. This was her world. She was among the people who mattered and understood why she did what she did. By the time Sam arrived she had recovered her equilibrium. She offered a chaste cheek as a greeting. He declined Paul's offer of a drink.

They drove off in silence.

'Where do you want to go?' he asked at last.

'I don't know. Sam, I'm sorry I was so awful on the phone.'

'It's OK. You were quite correct anyway – I don't own you.'

'Maybe that's the trouble.'

They drove on. Parking was difficult, but eventually they found a space in Long Acre. He slipped an arm around her shoulders, and she snuggled up against him.

Once inside the restaurant, he took charge, asking for a table near enough to the piano player to enjoy him but far away enough to be able to converse. He ordered two glasses of *kir royale*, lit them both cigarettes and looked into her eyes. 'Why was today like this when two days ago everything was so marvellous?' he asked.

She sipped her drink and decided to tell the truth. 'Well, today frightened me. I wasn't sure if I was doing the right thing or not, and also . . . some things Laura said yesterday have been playing on my mind.'

'Do you want to tell me about them?'

'Yes and no . . . Sam you know you talk about us being married and having children?'

'Yes.'

'Well, it's not that I'm desperate about it . . .'

'I know that.'

'It's just that you never say when. It's real and yet not quite.'

'Ah,' he said, and now it was his turn to draw deeply on his cigarette and concentrate on the drink before him. 'Let me guess. Laura said that maybe I wasn't as keen as I made out – why had I, at forty-five, never been married? – and maybe I just wanted you for your body and status.'

'That's pretty near the mark.'

He sighed loudly. 'Helen, do you love me?'

'More and more each day.'

'I wonder if your love is strong enough to deal with what I ought to tell you.'

'You're not married after all, are you?'

'No – no, I'm not, but I do have a sort of tie.'

'Go on.'

'I come from a very different culture from your own. Marriages are sometimes arranged, often when children are quite small.' She looked at him, willing him to continue but not at all sure she could cope with it if he did. 'When I was about twenty and on holiday from medical school, my father, whom I adored, told me it was his dearest wish that I should marry the daughter of a great friend of the family.'

'But, Sam, that's antiquated!' she exploded. 'You're practically English – you've said so yourself.'

'Sweetheart . . .' He stopped and took her hand. He pulled her towards him and kissed the top of her head. 'Sweetheart, listen. I'll make it as easy as I can, for both of us. I never cared for her. I did think of myself as English, but it was easier to agree, so we were . . . I don't know . . . betrothed, I suppose. It didn't mean anything to me – I was interested only in my career. In any case, she was just a child of eight. But she – well, she grew up into a typical Egyptian girl, pleasant in a dull sort of way, and she . . . well, she took it seriously.'

Helen nodded, then drank, then nodded again.

The first course arrived: tiny slices of calves' liver on a bed of shredded lettuce mixed with mayonnaise and yoghurt and decorated with strips of smoked ham. They both thanked the young waitress profusely. Sam ordered a bottle of wine. Everything was near enough normal . . . It was difficult to absorb what he was saying. Surely an ancient custom could not possibly have any relevance to them, to their lives, to their future?

He said, 'I had girlfriends, sex, of course. I never honestly considered honouring the arrangement. Then, when I was thirty-two, my father died. I went home. I can't begin to explain the impact his death made on me. I was devastated; it removed a layer. For the first time I had an acute sense of my history and heritage. I felt it fell to me to carry things on, you see. So, in an attempt to glorify his memory, I tried to take an interest in Hamaida.

We spent some time together – always in the company of other people, of course. I tried to like her.'

'What happened?'

One day she somehow engineered it that when I called, all her family were out. There were only servants in the house. She begged me to make love to her. She said she wanted to know what sex was like. She guessed I'd had other women. Maybe she thought she could compete – I don't know. It was not a natural thing for her to do, not with her backgound. She didn't like it much; she was very tense, and I found it difficult to penetrate her. I remember she closed her eyes tightly. I felt she must love me to go through with it, and yet she made me feel so undesirable I almost hated her. I'm sure it hurt, and she was certainly a virgin. She bled all over the place. The whole thing was terrible. There was no passion: it was a cross between rape and masturbation, and I've felt guilty ever since.'

'She didn't get pregnant, did she?'

'No, she didn't. I almost felt it would be just retribution if she did – maybe that would have decided our destiny. She didn't. I was let off the hook. But, you see, in a sense I rendered her unmarriageable – she was damaged goods.'

'But she asked you . . . she's hardly an innocent victim. She can't have it both ways – either she was the virginal Egyptian bride or she wasn't. My God, you're not making all this up are you?'

''Fraid not, Helen. It's all true.'

'So . . . ? Jesus, this is like a tuppeny novelette.'

He ignored her jibe. 'I offered to marry her. It was all arranged. One of my brothers was in France working, another in Italy. I had them flown back. Her house and mine were filled with gifts – gifts that have remained unopened to this day. The night before the wedding one of her brothers came to tell me she didn't want to marry me. Her message was, "I don't want to see you today, tomorrow or ever." '

Helen breathed a sigh of relief. 'Well, that's all right then.' She would have no truck with this superstitious nonsense.

Sam continued, 'I came back to England. I absorbed

myself in work. I was free and yet I knew she cancelled only because I was unkind. I had said I would marry her, but I offered no love and no comfort for the future.'

'That's life, Sam. How does it affect us?'

'Hamaida and I have never discussed the past. Every time I went home I saw her, always in her family's presence. She never said much, just nodded quietly and smiled rather sadly.'

'What a wimp.'

'Helen, don't be unkind. It's not like you. I didn't know you then – I had no viable alternative. Perhaps I even thought one day I'd go back, do what our families had always wanted. Now its different. You're the first woman in my life I've wanted to marry, but I somehow feel before we can – and I know you can't see it – I have to seek permission from my past.'

'You still feel guilty?'

'Yes.'

'Do you ever still feel you might have to end up marrying her to assuage your guilt and honour your father's memory?' It was a shot in the dark. She was almost teasing him, deploying unfamiliar vocabulary in an attempt to jolt him out of this ridiculous notion. She expected him to say, 'No, of course not. Not now.' There was silence. He was serious; he was struggling for breath and suddenly so was she.

'Yes,' he said unhappily, 'yes, I do.'

The room dissolved before her eyes. Realising the enormous impact his words had had on her, he held both her hands tightly, painfully tightly. He relaxed his grip on one hand and picked up her wine glass, holding it to her lips while she drank like a baby. The room steadied. 'Let's get out of here,' she said.

They remained silent until they were in bed in his house. He held her to him, and she sobbed wearily into his hairy chest.

'Helen,' he said at last, 'I will sort this. I can't let you go and I won't. You're right, it *is* antiquated. Nothing and nobody is going to prevent me from spending the rest of my life with you. They can't expect it. I can find happiness only with you – I must have it.'

She was so tired that his voice was coming at her through a tunnel of fatigue.

'That's why I've invited my mother here,' he was saying.

'What?' She was suddenly awake.

'I meant to tell you – I just never found the moment. She'll be here in two days. You'll like her. She's not totally Arab; she's half-French, which makes her much more dominant than she might otherwise have been. I want her to meet you. We'll go to shows together, night clubs, everything. She'll love it here. She always does. She'll love you too, and she'll understand. Everything will be all right.'

Helen blinked in the dimly lit room. 'Where will she stay?'

He sighed. 'Well . . . she'll be here.'

'What about me?'

He sighed again. 'I'll see you as much as ever but . . . she's seventy. We . . . can't sleep together, but it won't be for long.'

Helen felt utterly degraded, a fuck below stairs. Her reasonable side could see what distress any obvious manifestation of their sex life might cause to a morally upright septuagenarian – indeed, she would have found it difficult to sleep with Sam if her parents were under the same roof – but at the same time her emotions were devastated.

For the first night since they had slept together she was too tired to make love, too overcome with the baring of his soul, too disappointed, too isolated.

The atmosphere the next morning was strained. Sam insisted on her eating breakfast. He had bought croissants, Normandy butter, strawberry preserve and honey. She looked at him across the gleaming-white kitchen table, and her heart filled with gladness. He must love her to go to all this trouble, to venture out in his lunch hour and return with a carrier bag full of provisions. It was something most bachelors might do for themselves, but Sam was not most bachelors, and she knew he had run the errand for her alone.

He read her thoughts. 'You could never doubt I love you, Helen, could you?'

'No. I'm sorry I got so upset last night. I'm glad you told me everything – it must have been very difficult. Maybe now everything's in the open I can help.'

'There's nothing for you to do,' he said. 'You are you, you are perfect, you are the woman I love and intend to marry. I have to sort it, that's all, and I'm absolutely determined to walk away from the past and firmly into the present.'

She breathed a sigh of relief; she believed him, she trusted him, and surely fate could not be so cruel as to deny them each other? 'What about the other lady?'

'I don't know. I told you last night, we've never discussed it since. I've hoped over the years that somehow, despite our past, she would marry someone else. But she hasn't, and now she's thirty-two.'

'Younger than me,' observed Helen. 'Young enough.'

'Pretty old in my country, though,' he said, hopelessly.

Since Sam had patients to see at the clinic, Helen was left alone in his house. She skimmed the *Guardian* and *The Times*, poured some more coffee and washed up the breakfast plates. He had not asked her to clear away her presence from the house for his mother's arrival the next day. Probably she should – that would be the more courteous course of action – but the prospect angered her. Their relationship to date had not been constrained or clandestine, and she was offended that it was now being forced into that mould.

She went upstairs to the bedroom and opened the wardrobe door. One pair of leather trousers, two sweaters and a pair of boots were the only indications that she had ever been there. She shrugged her shoulders; she might as well clear them. In the bathroom the evidence was more incriminating.

She ran downstairs to a drawer in the kitchen where she knew she would find a plastic bag; it came from Harrods. At least this was to be an up-market removal.

She crammed it full with all her toiletries and then paused for thought. This was supposedly a temporary measure, but she was suddenly fearful it might prove to be permanent.

The phone rang. She ran to answer it, knowing it would be Sam. 'Darling,' he said, 'all the way over here I kept thinking either I should have told you everything earlier or maybe I should just have struggled with it on my own and sorted it. I don't know. There could never have been a right time, could there?'

'Sam . . . can I ask you something?'

'Of course.'

'You don't think that I should feel that you're as good as married and bow out honourably, do you?' As the words spilled from her she was surprised by them. Until that moment she had not realised she was even thinking along those lines.

'No. Categorically, no. I'm going to make this right. Helen, I want to come home and be with you, but I'll need to hang on a while longer. I lost a patient this morning.'

She was silent for a second. 'I'm sorry,' she said quietly. 'Oh, God, here I am bleating on and . . .'

'I know. It was a routine bypass – I did it yesterday. The guy was poorly, but I didn't expect him to die. Shortly after I got here this morning he just went: no reason, really. It's strange, though. Apart from an ageing sister, whom I'll have to see in a moment, he seemed to be absolutely on his own.'

'Maybe he didn't have sufficient reason to fight.'

'I'll probably dismiss it as that because it'll make me feel better, but it's too simplistic. I'll see the sister in a moment, then I'll write up my report and come home. I wondered if you'd like to go to the National Portrait Gallery to that exhibition of Thirties photography?'

'I'd love it. Shall I come in, to save you driving back?'

'No . . . don't. I want to come home and get out of this suit and also, to be quite honest, I need to hold you. I'll be there as soon as I can. Helen?'

'Yes.'

'I've told you before that I've never been in love with anyone as I am with you. Never forget I love you.'

'I won't. In any case, I intend having you around every day of my life, so you can keep telling me.'

He laughed. 'That's my girl. Stay happy. See you.'

Helen felt reassured, yet restless, in his house without him. She decided to listen to some music. She almost picked out Britten's *War Requiem* but then vehemently rejected it. Perhaps she should have played it for Sam's patient, but she was too afraid for herself. The only end she feared was the possible untimely death of their love affair. She chose Elkie Brooks instead. 'Fool if you think it's over,' sang the singer, and Helen relaxed again.

She was appalled by her mercurial moods and her self-centred preoccupation. She walked to a little wooden box on the coffee table and took out a cigarette. Using it more as a hand prop than a drug, she wandered around the house until she came to a halt in front of the Tom Merrifield sculpture she had noticed on her first visit. It was remarkably fine and evocatively lyrical. The young dancer was poised, caught on the apex of what she thought was called a *posé* turn. It was like one frame of a film, with all the suggestion of a joyous, sweeping movement to follow. Gazing at it and marvelling at its artistry, while indulging one of her other senses with her favourite female singer, she found tranquillity. It was almost a religious moment, and she clung to it in the hope that it might sustain her.

When Sam returned she walked calmly to greet him. He kissed her deeply and lovingly, and they stood together, swaying slightly, almost merging one into the other.

Suddenly he saw her clothes hanging on the hat stand and the large Harrods carrier bag on the floor beneath them. 'What's this?'

'I'm moving out, aren't I?'

'What are you trying to tell me?'

'Nothing. I thought I was doing the right thing. There's not much point in my not sleeping here if there are signs all around the place that I do as a rule.'

'Oh, Helen.' He brushed his hair back off his forehead.

'What a mess. Is it too early to have a drink?'

She smiled mistily. 'Probably not.'

He fixed them both a gin-and-tonic and led her to sit with him on the sofa. He put the drinks down and his kiss, when it came, was light and tender. With the next breath it became possessive. He was all over her. He literally tore the bottom half of her clothing from her body. Then he unzipped his trousers and, kneeling before her on the floor, he entered her violently. He began to sob, and with each thrust he cried, 'Oh, darling – oh, darling – oh, darling.' She was squashed, her neck was bent backwards into the sofa. She was almost suffocating from both her position and his full weight upon her.

He kept up the chant: 'Oh, darling – oh, darling – oh, darling . . .' She sensed him hold back for a second, then felt the full flood of a fountain flowing into her. He shuddered and cried out as if he were in pain and then collapsed.

For one tick of the clock her love, already terrifying for the way it had taken over her life, mushroomed limitlessly. It was more than her, an extravagant, separate, amorphous mass. Mercifully, it overreached itself and split spectacularly into more manageable fragments, allowing predominance to her acute physical discomfort, which seemed a more appropriate representation of their mutual mental turmoil.

She had to move eventually. Sam was totally disoriented; he was sweating and rambling. For a second she thought he was going to have a heart attack: he seemed to be fighting for breath and he was quite incoherent. She persuaded him to lie down on the sofa and she sat, still half-naked, beside him, stroking his brow and encouraging the Sam she knew, understood and depended upon to reappear. At length his gasps for breath subsided into little sighs, which turned into deep breathing, and he slept. She looked at him, this weary man, and realised that no matter what her anxiety was, it could only be a fraction of his. She lay down then beside him, uncomfortably, on the edge of the sofa. She held him in the hope that her warmth and support might somehow lighten his troubled dreams. Then she too, exhausted by the insidious pull of a country a short flight but a time warp away, closed her eyes and sought oblivion.

Chapter Seven

Oblivion lasts only if you're dead, of course, she thought, as she finally sat up and faced Sunday. She had awakened several times in the night and then in the morning had turned over, abandoning herself to the unaccustomed expanse of the whole bed.

At length she had squeezed out every last drop of slumber. Before Sam, when she had spent her life running, this had been her method of recharging her batteries; every so often she had unplugged the phone, hidden the alarm clock and retired to bed with the sole intent of sleeping till she was satiated. It was a ritual reserved for Saturdays-going-into-Sundays, and the following phase comprised spending the next few hours in bed with the papers. Since Sam, she had cancelled their delivery, as she was so rarely there. What a bore! She would have to face the outside world in order to proceed with the routine.

Back home with her pint of milk and copy of every publication she could possibly desire, she opted to stay up and began to read in the kitchen. It was half-past eleven, and Sam was probably on his way to the airport.

Saturday afternoon, what had been left of it after they had wakened, had passed normally, in an abnormal sort of way, with a visit to a gallery and then a perambulation round Camden Town. 'I used to have a flat here,' he had said, 'when I was a registrar. I tried to live on my salary. It was pure affectation and didn't last long: I'd been too spoiled.' It was as if, now he had told her his deepest, darkest secret, he could afford to share lesser ones. 'In truth, my family are so wealthy I need never work again if I didn't want to.' Helen was surprised. She had assumed his house, his car and every other acquisition had been financed by a more than adequate salary. She was pleased she had not known before.

He had wanted to sleep with her; but she had turned him away. Why she hardly knew. She had said he should prepare himself for his mother's visit and that she needed time to think. She suspected she was punishing him – or was it herself?

The papers palled. She took a bath, put a treatment on her hair and a face pack on her face. She shaved her legs and painted her toe nails and it was still only twelve forty-five. She grinned wryly, remembering the vintage *Hancock's Half-Hour* on the subject of Sundays. She plugged in the phone and, after looking up the number, called Deidre. 'Hi.'

'Who's that?'

'Helen.'

'Didn't I used to know you?'

'Don't be like that.'

'How are you?'

'I'm fine. D'you want to play tennis?'

'It's the end of December, Helen.'

'It's still a nice day.'

She walked down the street in search of her Saab, parked forlornly where she had left it several days before. She loved it; it represented something she had achieved for herself, but she rarely drove it nowadays. It seemed to reproach her; it was too special to be relegated to the role of back-up vehicle. It purred into life, and she rediscovered a sense of satisfaction at the feel of the driving wheel in her hands and the power under the bonnet. Being alone wasn't so bad – if it was occasional.

Deidre was waiting. She was a friend from Helen's schooldays and now a consultant paediatrician.

Helen played tennis like a demon. She began shakily but soon had her old chum running round the court, completely outclassed. She was concentrating on the seam of the ball as though her life depended on it, and she killed it time after time with unreturnable volleys.

'That's enough,' gasped Deidre, 'quite enough. Let's go to the canteen.'

They walked from the tennis courts into the hospital, slipping back into easy companionship. Months passed, sometimes years, between meetings but their relationship, always uncomplicated, never altered.

'Are you still seeing the ever-aloof Sam Aziz?'

'Is that what you think of him?'

'Doesn't everybody? If you've found what makes him tick, you're a rare beast. How long have you been together?'

'A couple of months, I suppose.' Helen tried not to be too accurate.

'Well, I tell you, I'm surprised. I always thought he was a completely cold fish.'

'He isn't at all,' Helen denied defensively. 'How do you know him anyway?'

'I don't, but you can't be in medicine and not be aware of him. I always thought he was interested only in the job. Still, you're not much different.'

'What do you mean?'

'Oh, come on, Helen. Remember the old crowd? No, you probably don't. We all get together from time to time. Your name comes up – no one's ever seen you, except on the box. It's just how it is, I suppose, but why do some people sink themselves in their work to the exclusion of everything else? I don't know. It probably makes for success, but does the job do that to people, or do people do that to the job?'

Helen smiled sweetly, changing the subject. 'I'm going to go mad and have the shepherd's pie.'

This isn't East Cheam, it's Holland Park, she reminded herself, as Sunday evening spread uninvitingly before her. Why had she not heard from Sam? Because she kept unplugging the phone, that was why, she supposed. It was easier to know he could not call than wonder why he had not. Suddenly she remembered that the company's ski group was meeting at the social club that evening to discuss their forthcoming trip and, though she was not a member, she decided to join them.

She was greeted with some surprise. ‘Don’t want to come skiing, Helen, do you?’

‘Certainly not. You know me. I’m only interested in indoor sports. I came for a drink, actually.’ She laughed.

‘You old lush.’ It was Ian, Laura’s lover.

‘Hey, good to see you,’ she said. ‘I forgot you’d be here. Thanks for Wednesday, by the way – it was great.’

‘Yes, it was,’ he agreed. ‘Nice to see you. Where’s wonder boy?’

‘Oh, his mother’s arriving today.’

‘I didn’t know she was expected,’ said Laura.

‘Neither did I till Friday night.’

Ian, suspecting the girls might prefer to talk alone, slipped away.

‘Is everything OK?’

‘It’s fine,’ lied Helen. ‘I’d forgotten what it was to have a day and evening to myself. I’m rather enjoying it.’

‘Well, before Sam you rarely had one; you were always out doing PAs. Are you sure you’re all right, though? You look a bit tired and frightfully skinny.’

‘The Duchess of Windsor said, “You can’t be too thin or too rich!” ’

‘Lot of good it did her in the end!’

‘Laura, can I ask you something?’

‘Of course.’

‘I’ll just get you another drink.’

Laura had found a quiet corner by the time Helen returned. ‘God,’ Helen sipped and made a face, ‘this wine doesn’t improve, does it?’

‘What did you want to ask?’

‘I saw Deidre today. You remember her – we went to school together.’

‘Yeah, I know. I met her at a couple of your parties.’

‘Well, would you say I’m aloof? Do I give the impression of being . . . well, self-sufficient and totally wrapped up in the job?’

‘Of course.’

‘I don’t.’

‘’Course you do.’

‘Well, I’m not like that.’

'Aren't you?'

'I don't think so. I don't know what's happening. Was I ever like it, or was I pretending?'

'What's brought on all this self-examination?'

'I don't know. To be honest, everything's *not* quite right, and I don't think I can bear it. I don't know where I am. You know, Laura, I love Sam so much. It isn't easy for me to say that to you, but I do. I'm lost without him, and I don't like it.'

'What's going wrong?'

'I can't really tell you but, you see, he's everything to me. It's the first time it's all come together – love, friendship, passion. I can't do without it.'

'Well, I don't think you have to. Surely you're not nervous just because his mother's coming?'

'No, of course not . . . I don't know.'

'Listen, everything will be fine. Won't she be delighted to see her self-contained son ready to settle? 'Course she will – and, even if she isn't, wait till you present the grandchild. Look, Helen, you've got it bad, but so has he. Don't lose your sense of proportion.'

Walking from the car to her flat, Helen looked around to check if anyone was watching and then kicked a pebble up the street. She ran after it, kicking it again and again and was inordinately annoyed when it rolled down a drain.

In the flat she called her mother. She was not sure why, for she had nothing to say, but she was not feeling aloof and self-sufficient; she was hungry for human contact.

The phone rang. She had forgotten to unplug it after the call.

'Where have you been all day?' he demanded.

'Out, mostly. How's your mother?'

'She's fine. She's in bed now. She was tired.' The conversation continued with neither of them discussing what was really on their minds. 'I've missed you,' he said at last.

'Have you?'

'I have, a lot. It's great to have my mother here. I do love her, although we find it difficult to get close, but I've thought about you so much. I've told her about you, by the way.'

'Oh!'

'Look, I'm not working tomorrow. What are you doing?'

'There's a New Year's Eve programme, but I'm free after that.'

'Good. I'll get my mother to watch you, and then maybe we could all go to the theatre.'

'That's a good idea – it'll make the initial meeting easier if we've got a definite plan. I'll get tickets for something she'd like. I've got a few contacts . . .'

'Helen, you do care for me, don't you?'

'Of course.'

'It's just that you suddenly sound so efficient.'

'Oh, God, not you too.'

'What?'

'It doesn't matter. I do anyway – care, I mean – a lot.'

'Good. Helen . . . always remember that I love you.'

'You said that once before. You almost say it sadly. Why don't you just say, "I love you"?'

'I don't know. It means the same, doesn't it?'

'I'm not sure.'

He appeared to ignore the uncertainty in her voice. 'Will you turn on to your right side now and imagine I'm curled around you?'

She juggled with the phone. 'OK.'

'Can you imagine the feel of me behind you now, stiffening as I hold you?'

She closed her eyes. 'Mmmm.'

'I love you,' he whispered. 'Go to sleep, remembering that.'

The next evening Helen was as nervous as she might have been in a theatre on the first night of an under-rehearsed play. To some extent the comparison in her mind was an appropriate one. You cannot ensure that all the spontaneity that creeps into a New Year's Eve production will be sparkling and funny – all you can do is to stay sober despite the distractions all around the building, knowing that, in this instance, alcohol would not be a help. You cannot rehearse either for an encounter with someone who quite possibly holds the key to your future happiness.

'You look fabulous,' said Laura, coming into the dressing-room they shared after the programme. 'New outfit?'

'Yes.' Helen beamed. 'Sam had it designed for me for Christmas. It's wonderful, isn't it?'

'Amazing. When are you going to meet his mother?'

'Now. I've managed to get us into *Forty-Second Street*. You remember, I did the interview when they opened. They're letting me have the house seats.'

''Bout time you picked up some perks. That's great. His mother'll love it, and I'm sure she'll fall under your spell too. Go and sock it to her. Think of it as another performance.'

In spite of her anxiety Helen found she was humming a chorus from *Kiss Me Kate* as she walked into the theatre. Because of her background she had intimate knowledge of the build-up of tension backstage. She visualised the orchestra drifting into the pit and beginning to tune up, laughing and joking among themselves. She recalled how it felt to be behind the tabs, waiting for the audience to be revealed, and the rush of adrenalin as she encountered them for the first time in the full knowledge that the level of her performance depended upon their response.

'There you are, Helen.'

Her heart gladdened, and her eyes sparkled as they met his. God, he was so magnificent, so – everything. He kissed her and somehow managed to stroke her breast as he steered her to meet his mother. Helen leant against him, desperate for his presence.

Mrs Aziz was dressed entirely in black, apart from a superb silver-mink jacket. She was wearing exquisite jewellery and had very good legs for a woman of seventy. She was stylish and tanned, and had Helen not known differently, she would have placed the older woman as a wealthy southern European. She was tiny, even with three-inch heels, but Helen knew at once she was a force to be reckoned with. Helen took both her hands and kissed her first on one cheek and then on the other. She hoped it was a suitable greeting.

Sam disappeared to order drinks for the interval, leaving Helen unsure how to begin. 'How was your journey?' she asked at last. She wished Sam would come back but relaxed a little as his mother answered in perfect English that it had been pleasant and that she had so enjoyed watching the programme. She then fingered Helen's outfit and said how splendid it was. Helen was delighted and immediately offered the information it was a present from Sam. As she spoke, she wondered if that confession had come too soon. Did it denote a degree of unacceptable intimacy? At least it showed that their common bond had good taste.

The conversation was a little stilted, but not hostile, and Mrs Aziz was quick to thank Helen for arranging the evening. She said she loved the West End theatre and was excited at the prospect of the show. Helen began to unwind as she found she was looking into Sam's eyes – not quite his eyes, as their expression was not yet as warm, but familiar ones none the less. If his mother was like Sam, perhaps all would be well.

She transferred her attention to her lover as he returned and sensed his anxiety level dropping as he found the two women deep in conversation.

In the stalls he directed his mother into the first seat. He put Helen next and himself on the end. Helen would have preferred him to sit in the middle, but at the same time she recognised gratefully, that he was making a statement: she was part of the scenario.

As the lights dimmed, his hand reached for hers and he squeezed it tenderly. Helen responded but could not take her eyes from his mother. As the first notes came from the orchestra pit the old lady's expression lightened into one of happy anticipation, and when the dancing began, with the curtain rising slowly on a stage full of talented, tapping feet, she applauded heartily. Helen breathed out and smiled at Sam in the half light.

'It went much better than I dared to hope,' said Sam. They were sitting in his car outside her flat. They had enjoyed dinner together in a little Covent Garden restaurant and at midnight had joined hands with the other diners to sing 'Auld Lang Syne'. Helen had longed to throw herself into his arms and feel his mouth pressing urgently on hers but, in his mother's company, had to content herself with a kiss on the cheek and a squeeze on the arm. 'Next year,' he had whispered, and she had smiled at him, her spirits lifting.

'Yes, I think your mother had a happy evening,' said Helen.

He reached for her. 'Darling, I love you. It's so important my mother likes you.'

'Is it?'

'Yes, it is. I love her and I hate her, but I can never escape. She's impossible and wonderful. When she writes to me I always look at how she's signed off before I read the rest of the letter, just to see whether I'm in favour or not. I've lived away all my life, and yet I need her love and her approval. Most of the time I don't think I have it.'

'Surely you're exaggerating?'

He shrugged his shoulders in the darkness. 'I don't know. All I do know is, you show me more love than I believed possible. I need you, Helen. Don't give up on me.'

As if I could, she thought in the quietness of her flat, as she went over and over the signs and signals of the evening they had just spent.

As the days passed Helen grew fond of Sam's mother and could not help but be impressed by the way she obviously masterminded the family business, though technically it was run by two of her sons. 'I'm a mixture of Arab and European,' she said once. 'I love Egypt. It's my home. But I have always been too independent to be a good Arab wife in the usual sense. Fortunately, Ahmed – my husband Ahmed, that is – loved me for what I was. He was the most remarkable man. None of his sons measures up to him.'

Helen looked across at Sam and saw that the remark had hurt. It was not her place to comment but, when he failed to do so, she was moved to speak. 'But Sam is a famous surgeon. He gives life to people who otherwise would have no hope – surely you applaud that?'

Mrs Aziz laughed, though without much humour. 'Ah, this Ahmed,' she said, 'he was born to be different. He's always gone his own way. It was my husband's idea he should come to school here. When I saw how he changed – maybe he was always the strange one – I decided not to risk it with the other two. I put my foot down. They went to English schools but in Alexandria, not here.'

'What about the girls?' Helen asked, for she had recently learned that Sam had two sisters.

'They had a governess,' said Mrs Aziz, and that seemed to be that.

Sam was driving Helen back home. 'Well, it hasn't taken long, has it?' he asked bitterly. 'She's been here for less than a fortnight and it's beginning already – the criticisms, the disapproval, the comparisons. I'm sorry I'm not the son she wanted, but I can't really help it.'

Helen could not understand the paradox: the old lady was half-European, yet she seemed determined to suppress that side of herself and certainly did not admire its emergence in the next generation. 'You know, Sam,' said Helen, trying to lessen his hurt and thinking suddenly that all their important discussions these days seemed to take place in the dark interior of his car or hers, 'maybe this isn't such a bad time. Maybe you'll sort out exactly what you feel about your mother, your family, your country, your . . . the lady back home, and maybe, although it's difficult, we should be glad to have this opportunity of taking our relationship back a step.'

'What are you trying to say?' he demanded almost angrily. 'Is there someone else? Don't you want me any more?'

'Sam . . .' She sighed and kissed him. 'Of course I do. I'm trying to be . . . honourable, I think – sensible anyway. Please understand.'

'This is terrible,' he said.

She sighed again. 'It is and yet I'm trying to say it needn't be and maybe it isn't.'

Had he understood? She had tried so hard to explain the development of her thinking but obviously had not found the appropriate words.

The flat, where she had been alone before Sam, reinforced her anxiety. She was alone again, but this time she had tasted paradise, and home was no longer an oasis. There was no point in trying to sleep. She scanned her bookshelves, with their mixture of books she had reviewed, books she might need for research, books she loved and books she ought to read. At last she selected a slim virgin volume by Anita Brookner. In bed she read the first page and then the next; it was like licking a cream cake slowly. She was some way through chapter four when the phone rang.

'Helen.'

'Sam, you should be asleep.'

'So should you.'

'Well, I'm not.'

'Listen, Helen, I've just had a call to say a young man's dying after a road accident in Holland and his parents are willing to donate his organs. You know Laura's doing this piece on me? They've been waiting for a bit of drama like this, so we're all flying to Amsterdam. I'll come back and get straight on with the transplant, which means we'll have to change our plans for tomorrow.'

'Of course, Sam – this is important. Who's going to have the operation?'

'A man from Dublin. They're contacting him now.'

She was so proud of him suddenly. 'Sam, I love you. Go carefully. This couldn't have happened at a better time. Your mother will *have* to see how important your life is here now. I love you, darling – more than you know.'

'God, Helen, if I don't have you to myself again soon, I'll explode.'

'I know. We'll talk tomorrow when you finish. I'll go and sit with your mother till you get through.'

'You don't have to do that.'

'I know. I want to.'

The next day was one of those on which there is not

much news about, so Helen was to interview the author of a book called *Food for the Taking*. 'Are we just chatting, or does he want to do anything practical?' she asked Ron, one of the researchers, at the morning meeting.

'He wants a country-kitchen set because he'll demonstrate some of the dishes. You can discuss the menu when he arrives. He'll be here at two-thirty. He hasn't any television experience, so I don't think we'll risk it live. We'll record at three-thirty.'

The author was much as she had expected, clean-living, clear-skinned, bearded, wearing a big sweater and thong sandals – a caricature of his type, yet she found herself won over by him. He was extremely articulate, and she wondered if he had an eye to the main chance. There was something slightly tongue-in-cheek about his suggestions. 'I'll do squirrel casserole, worm and apple pie, and woodlice and slug dip.'

'Are you joking?'

'No.'

'Would you eat them?'

'Not exactly, but it's all excellent protein.'

'OK, it'll make good television – but I can't promise I'll taste any of it.'

They debated whether they should see the squirrel being prepared and decided against it. They did, however, have some raw slugs and woodlice in a glass jar to show what they looked like before cooking. Who's kidding whom? thought Helen, as they recorded the item. She asked questions about preparation.

'Well, you just skin and gut a squirrel as you would a rabbit.' said the guest.

'Obviously my education is sadly lacking,' she said. 'I've never even eaten rabbit, let alone skinned one, and I must say I prefer to see squirrels running around than in a casserole.'

'They're vermin, though,' said the countryman, which made Helen less inclined than ever to sample the dish. She relented in the end; compared with the lions' cage, this was nothing.

The crawling woodlice and slugs, on the other hand,

offered no temptation, even though she was assured that, once fried, they were crunchy and delicious, and quite delightful when mixed with sour cream and chives. She noticed the floor manager was looking distinctly squeamish and wickedly ended the piece by turning to camera and saying, 'I'm sure all this has gone too quickly for you to write it down, but you can always send in for the recipes or, of course, buy the book, *Food for the Taking*.'

They ended on a close-up of the food, so that they could pick up live on a close-up of her when they put out the item later that day.

'You bitch,' said the floor manager. 'How many people will you put off their tea tonight? As if anyone in their right mind would want the recipes.'

Sam's mother was patently not expecting Helen when she turned up on his doorstep shortly after the programme, but Mrs Aziz recovered quickly. 'How was the squirrel casserole?'

'Don't let's talk about it – I still have the taste in my mouth. Let's have a drink.'

To her surprise, the older woman acquiesced; she rarely drank alcohol. They talked as they drank and Helen was amazed at how often she had to refill their glasses. Perhaps they needed to do this. Perhaps she should broach the subject of Sam and herself while he was away. While she was still considering her move, Mrs Aziz got there before her.

'Are you going to marry Ahmed?'

Helen almost said, 'Who?' before remembering that his mother never referred to him as Sam. 'Why do you ask?'

'Because he's never acted like this before, and he's never come close to marriage either.'

Helen knew that the second statement was untrue. Had his mother wanted the arranged match as much as his father? Was it painful? Had she simply obliterated the past from her mind? She tried to answer casually, 'Don't you think you'd better ask him?'

'I couldn't do that,' said his mother. 'We don't have conversations of that type.'

'Well, I don't think I should answer on his behalf,' said Helen.

'I was nearly twenty-five when he was born,' recalled his mother, ignoring Helen's rebuff. 'I didn't marry till I was twenty-three – that's quite old in our country. My husband was considerably older than that. I admired him so much. I loved him too, but once we had had our children, I never slept with him again. I didn't need that. It was enough to love him as a brother. Maybe there's something wrong with me. I'm not really close to any of my children. It's probably because I find it hard to be tactile – I could never behave with anyone like he does with you. He looks at you, he touches you, you look at him, you embrace. It's really rather disgusting.' She spat out the last word.

Helen was taken aback. She had a fleeting image of Sam as a child and wondered if his mother had ever held him to her. His hunger for love was making more sense by the second.

'Sometimes,' his mother continued, 'I almost feel I've missed out, but when I see how other people mess up their lives with passion and drama – well, I'm glad I'm like me.'

Mercifully, Sam returned from the hospital at that moment. 'What are you two chatting about?'

'Just girl talk,' said Helen quickly. Something akin to a look of gratitude spread over the older woman's face.

Sam looked so weary that she longed to take him in her arms, but the word 'disgusting' had wrought its damage. She pecked him on the cheek and disappeared thankfully to the kitchen, where she rustled up omelettes and salad. In the ensuing uneasy truce she watched the clock and waited for a lull in the conversation so she might escape to her flat to think.

'I'll just phone for a taxi.'

'No,' he said, 'I'll drive you.'

'Oh, no, you won't. It's a rotten night. Stay here and talk to your mother. You've had a long day.'

'No,' he said again, quietly but firmly, 'I'll take you. You'll be OK, Mother, won't you? I won't be long.'

'I shall be perfectly all right. There's a film I want to watch on television. Your television is so much better than ours. Do you know, they even took off *Dallas* in Egypt because it was thought it might turn the peasants into promiscuous capitalists?'

Again, the same measured and vitriolic delivery. 'Disgusting', 'promiscuous'. Helen wanted to run and hide from this uncompromising purity and righteousness. 'Enjoy it, then,' she said weakly. 'I'll see you soon.'

'Will you be here tomorrow?' asked the old lady.

'No – no, I don't think so. I have to drive to Northampton after the show – I'm compèring the second half of a charity concert. I'll be back awfully late.'

'Oh, well, drive carefully.' Mrs Aziz was nothing if not proper. 'And you too, son,' she added.

He looked annoyed but replied quietly, 'Of course.'

Strangely, Sam led her out of the front door to the riverside. It was bitterly cold, and every surface was covered with a film of frost. They walked on till they came to their pub, where he bought them both a brandy.

'Your mother's right to warn you to drive carefully. This is not a night to drive if you don't have to. Let me take a taxi.'

'Helen,' he said curtly, 'I'm enjoying, after a long day, having you all to myself. I don't want to hear any more about it. I'm driving you and that's that.'

She grimaced. 'You don't have to tell me off. I was only trying to be considerate.'

He smiled. 'Sweetheart, I know – I do know. You've been marvellous these last few weeks. You've come out with my mother, been bright and lively, made her feel special. You didn't have to do all that.'

'It hasn't been a chore. I like her, though she frightens me. I think she's a bit mixed up, but I could grow to love her and I certainly admire her.'

'What was she talking about when I came into the room?'

'I don't think I should disclose that – it was surprisingly intimate. I meant what I said, it was woman to woman. She did ask me if we were going to marry.'

'Old busybody.'

'Don't be like that, Sam. A few weeks ago you told me you wanted to resolve the past so you could move into the present. She's taking an interest. That's what you wanted. Don't be unkind.'

'I'm sorry. My mother always did have the ability to make me feel as if I were a schoolboy caught cheating in an exam.'

'Look, in her own way I'm sure she loves you a lot. It may be no bad thing that you'll spend tomorrow evening without me.'

They walked through the pub to the road and then back several hundred yards to where Sam's car was parked outside his house. Inside the vehicle he switched on the engine and the full blast of the heating, then he held her as they warmed up. He kissed her hungrily before moving off in the direction of Holland Park. He drove carefully, for the roads were treacherous, but Helen also gained the definite impression he had no wish to arrive too soon.

After a few hundred yards his left hand stroked her thigh, then moved upwards to fondle her beneath her skirt. He drew to a halt beside the kerb. His movements quickened and she abandoned herself to the overwhelming feelings that were sweeping her body. She climaxed with a little cry. It was not cataclysmic, more like the semi-satisfied delight one experiences on consuming a perfectly presented and delicious *hors d'oeuvre*.

'Good, my darling,' he whispered. 'A nice little come for you. That's to keep you going till we get home.'

She did not protest. She had thoughts briefly for his mother, alone in the house, but their own needs were too urgent to be ignored.

Back in Holland Park they made straight for the bedroom. They wasted no time on stroking or romantic endearments, but undressed hurriedly. In bed he lay full-length on her immediately. She clung to him; they were both cold. She kneaded his buttocks and felt him become tumescent instantly. They made love ferociously. Neither took the other, for their desires were equally matched. She came seconds before him and their cries mingled in two-part harmony in the still of the night. They lay entwined, not speaking and knowing they must not sleep.

'I hate this, don't you?' she asked finally. 'I feel . . . cheap.'

'You're not cheap. Neither am I. This state of affairs can't go on. We're going to get married, Helen – I can't live without you.' With this assurance he leapt from the bed and within seconds was dressed.

'Sam, calm down. Drive carefully.'

His shoulders dropped; his expression quietened. He blew her a kiss from the doorway and was gone.

The next day passed without incident in the office. Certainly there was nothing to compare with the slug and woodlice dip of the day before. She was amused, though, at the number of telephone complaints they had received on the item. Her major concern was the weather. For all that Northampton was a straight run up the motorway, she was alarmed to hear that conditions were hazardous, with long stretches of freezing fog. The weatherman on the programme urged anyone who had no need to travel to stay home that night. She wished she could comply, but her engagement was a longstanding one, and she was not about to disappoint the organisers of the concert.

The public relations department rang to suggest they should book her into an hotel in Northampton.

'Can you get me in easily?' she asked.

'Yes,' said the PR girl. 'Apparently they have loads of cancellations.'

'Well, look, don't bother in that case. I'll keep my options open. I'd sooner come back, but if the weather's really terrible, I'll check myself in.'

On the drive up, despite being an experienced motorist, she became increasingly frightened. She normally loathed being stuck behind large lorries but, on this occasion, stayed a comfortable distance behind one, reckoning that she would have time to stop if the other driver suddenly encountered freezing fog. She thought of Sam and began to pray. 'Oh, God, don't let me die yet.'

Helen did not die but arrived in Northampton just before nine. She changed into her favourite evening dress:

a cream-lace creation by Christina Stambolian. The family who were running the concert burst into her dressing-room when the interval began at nine-fifteen.

'How's my girl?' she asked as she lifted up Samantha, the child who had sparked off years of fund-raising. 'Gosh, you're heavy!'

'Well, I'm ten now.'

'Goodness, so you are.' And Helen looked at the girl's parents, for whom every day had become a bonus.

Samantha had been born with an inoperable hole in the heart and, because of that, her lungs were badly impaired. Faced with such a fateful blow, this very ordinary couple had raised money not only to put their own child on to an intensive nocturnal oxygen programme, but also to help several other children in a similar predicament. Against all the odds, Samantha was surviving. She would always be tinier than she should be, but she was alive. She was also as engaging and as naughty as any other child of her age. Helen turned around to find Samantha stuck into her make-up bag and smearing lipstick all over her little face. 'You couldn't be angry with her,' she said, laughing, but the parents were. Their child might be a walking miracle, but she was not going to be spoiled.

Down to business, Helen asked who was performing in the second half. It was a male-voice choir from Aberfan, which had literally been formed out of the ashes of that devastated mining community. Since the disaster, when a slag heap collapsed, burying most of the infants in the village school, the choir, made up of bereaved fathers, had worked tirelessly up and down the country raising money for children's charities. Helen had performed with them before. This was her balance. Her own life was in turmoil and she saw, through the news, much unhappiness, tragedy and greed, but she also encountered people like this choir and Samantha's parents.

The second half of the concert got under way once Helen had made a short speech about where tonight's money was going. It was a happy evening, and for a while her own troubles and all her anxiety over the inclement weather receded. There was a party afterwards, but as soon as she had swallowed a glass of wine and a sandwich she excused herself on account of the drive to follow, though she had not yet decided whether to wait till morning. On an impulse she sought out the concert hall's manager to ask if she might make a telephone call to London. He left her alone in his office.

'Helen, where are you?'

'Northampton – you know that.'

'Are you still in one piece? The weather's not too bad?'

'It could be better, but don't worry.'

'Are you coming back? Well, what I mean is, could you . . . come back?'

'I hadn't quite decided.'

'Do come if you can.'

'Is something wrong?'

'Yes – yes, there is. My mother and I have had a blazing row.'

Her heart froze. 'Well,' she said, simulating a coolness she did not feel, 'we all argue with our parents sometimes.'

'I never have, not like this. I shouted, I ranted and raved. It was terrible. She's upstairs, packing. She says she's leaving tomorrow.'

'OK, Sam – I'm on my way.'

'Helen, listen . . . listen carefully. Don't drive fast. You should stay really . . . it's just I need you. But go steadily. It doesn't matter how late you arrive.'

The decision was made. She did not even delay to change but simply put on her fur jacket over the flimsy frock. The cold air took her breath away as she stumbled in her high heels over the uneven ground in the car park.

The only advantage of the poor weather conditions was that she had virtually the whole of the M1 to herself. She supposed that if she did drive off the road, no one else would be involved, which was some consolation. The back wheels stepped out every now and then. The road surface was like an ice rink and, despite Sam's warning, she was not driving slowly. From time to time wisps of ghostly fog blinded her. It was a nightmare of a journey, and she needed so much concentration she could not even bear the distraction of her music system.

Soon after midnight she was ringing Sam's doorbell. Without a word he let her in. He shut the door behind them and silently held her in his arms for a moment before leading her to the fire in the lounge and a warming, welcoming brandy.

'What happened?'

'She was a bit off me this morning. She'd gone to bed before I got in last night, but I didn't think too much about it. Tonight I was treated to the full force of her displeasure. Apparently I'm not half the man my father was, I've betrayed my country by not taking my skills there, I've ruined Hamaida's life and I'm denying my heritage by having a close relationship with an English woman. I got angry too – I shouted and completely lost control.'

Helen was absorbing all he had just said. 'I thought,' she said hesitantly, 'I thought she was beginning to like me.'

'Helen, darling, it isn't personal.'

'It feels personal – do you mind? It bloody does!'

She cried then with the built-up tension of the drive to and from Northampton and the uncertainty of the last few weeks. He took out a handkerchief and wiped away her tears, smudging her mascara as he did so. He cuddled her, swaying backwards and forwards in an attempt to lessen the pain.

'You adore your mother, don't you?'

He sighed. 'I do, but I've never been able to please her. Do you know,' he went on, confirming Helen's suspicions of the night before, 'even as a child, I don't remember her hugging me as you are now. The problem is, as I've always said to you, I feel English – but in recent months I've begun to feel more Egyptian and to think that maybe I should be working there. It's not a good time, in a way. There are certain branches of the Islamic faith that are as fundamental and as extreme as anything you've heard of in Iran. They're threatening and growing. For people like my family, they're a terrifying band. I mean, my mother never walks about shrouded with a veil, but it might come to that. I don't know. There's no real trouble yet, but it could happen.'

'Is that one reason why you feel you should go back to Hamaida?' Shots in the dark were becoming commonplace and the subsequent answers, while still as painful, were no longer a surprise.

'I think so, yes.'

Perhaps there was a way, she thought, as the total impact of what might be asked of her, were they to marry, hit her between the eyes. Was it possible she could be called upon to give up her career and go to a strange country? A marriage that accommodated, much as their single lives had, his career here, hers continuing, even if compromised by the demands of motherhood, was one thing. To consider these new options was something else again. Did she love him enough to leave her home and country, as he had? Her heart cried out that as long as she had him, she could cope with anything, but her head advised caution.

'Would it help,' she asked finally, 'if . . . suppose you could resolve the Hamaida thing . . . I gave up everything here and we settled in Egypt?'

Now his eyes filled with tears as he learned, perhaps for the first time, the extent of her obsession. 'My darling,' he said, 'you can't know what you're saying. Egypt is very civilised, but in some ways it was more modern two thousand years ago. I'm sure the plumbing worked better anyway.'

In spite of the gravity of their situation she giggled.

'There'd be no job for you, at least not in television.'

They sat contemplating a life in which she kept house and waited for her lord and master to return to her at the end of each day. Neither was convinced their love could survive such a turnaround. There were two problems now: the girl back home who had remained faithful and still wanted him, and the equally serious matter of where his patriotism lay.

Their love, their fear and their frustration mounted. As he had on the day before his mother's arrival, he took her, as she sat on the edge of the sofa, though as a concession to his mother's sleeping, (or perhaps not) in the room above, he covered Helen's mouth with his hand when she moaned aloud in relief fused with dreadful despair.

Chapter Eight

The lights in her mirror were annoyingly close – dangerously so. They were forcing her attention away from the icy road and her perception of where the curb lay on this freezing, foggy night. She pulled in to allow the pursuer to pass and saw, too late, that he was a policeman.

God, that's all I need, she thought, as the car stopped in front of her. Surely she had not drunk too much, but then she had not eaten either. She wound down her window.

'Bit late to be out and about, madam.' The routine remark bristled with callow smugness.

Helen leapt out of the car. Her heart thumping. 'Yes, it is, officer.'

'Oh – Miss Bartlett,' he said, stepping back less surely.

'Is anything wrong?' she asked more authoratively, praying there were some advantages in being immediately recognisable.

'Oh, no, not really. It's just I think you'd be safer if your fog lamp was on.'

'Heavens, wasn't it? I wasn't thinking. Sorry.' Dare she hope he was going to let her go? In her mind's eye she could already see the newspaper headlines proclaiming to the world that she had been breathalysed and failed.

''Spose you've been out at some function or other.' He indicated her evening dress.

'Yes, in Northampton. Not the best night for it.'

'No. You've probably had a hell of a drive. Tell me where you live, and I'll escort you back.'

Awash with relief, she gave the address and followed him. The going was infinitely easier now. She wondered if she should invite him in for coffee; it was the last thing she wanted. 'Thanks very much,' she said when they finally reached her flat. 'Could I offer you some coffee?'

'No, thanks all the same, but would you just sign this?'

She would have signed away her life at that moment.

Upstairs she fell on the bed. It had been a near thing. She looked at herself in the mirror. What a mess. Her eye make-up had run; her hair was tousled; and her dress was crumpled from the encounter on the sofa and miles on the road.

She was suddenly angry. How dare Sam's mother put her through this? She should have been tucked up in his bed, her rightful place, without risk. How dare the old woman pick a fight with her son, causing him such torment? How dare she wait until the unsuitable, unfavoured girlfriend was risking life and limb on the motorway?

Jesus, it was so unfair. Helen was hurt more than anything and utterly despondent at the realisation the last few weeks had been a charade. She was insanely angry too at the toll it had taken of Sam. How could the old bitch not have seen what a huge effort her son was making? Why could she not have been pleased that he had finally found someone whom he adored, someone who would support him, share his life and give him the love he plainly had never had?

The night was a long one. Helen made pots of tea, smoked cigarette after cigarette and attempted to read. At last the morning came and she could concentrate on the working day.

As usual, the programme provided a focal point. Her spirits rose as she manoeuvred her way through it.

Laura was waiting for her in the club. 'Come on, old thing,' she said. 'You can't fool me – you're fit to drop. What is it?'

'Sam's mother's gone back.'

'Good.'

'Well, yes and no . . . After the most terrible row. She doesn't approve of me at all.'

'So what? She doesn't live here, does she? Forget the old bag.'

Helen wondered whether to divulge more but decided against it. She was aware, though, that her friend was concerned as she took both her hands in hers. 'You hold all the winning cards, Helen. He loves you. You'll see – it'll be all right now you have him to yourself again.'

It was certainly better. They made love ferociously. It was as if he were unable to absorb enough of her after their enforced abstinence. As the weeks wore on, it seemed sometimes as if his mother had never been there and Hamaida did not exist. Helen tried to still her nervousness that they were, in fact, simply becalmed, with the remainder of a difficult course still to be negotiated. Occasionally, bravely, she alluded to the obstacles to their happiness but Sam adamantly refused to discuss them, saying only that the solutions lay within himself. He would kiss her then, almost dispelling her disquiet, as he assured her that he would 'sort it'.

But could he sort it? He was the most capable man she had ever known. She thought she had finally found a partner who was stoical and upon whom she could rely for support, but was that true? Or did she simply wish it were so? Was the fact that she melted at the sight and touch of him significant, or had he happened at a moment when she was ripe for a significant experience? He appeared to be ultimately sturdy and steadfast, so it was a shock when, during a discussion on her forthcoming birthday, a chink in his armour finally appeared.

'Helen, I can't bear this any more. Let's both book leave, go to a Greek island and come back married.' He had a wild look in his eyes, like that of an ensnarled animal who is flailing about hopelessly in search of escape. Which answer was the trap, though, and which offered freedom?

Her impulsive, romantic and gambling nature longed to comply. It did not. Was that good sense and reason, or was it some intangible foreboding that the right answer would prove the wrong option, that he would come to feel she had entangled him or, worse still, that he would retract?

'Suppose,' she said with an artificially level tone, 'suppose we do it and then return to hear that your mother was so incensed at our news, she died of a heart attack without forgiving you.'

'Don't be so melodramatic.'

They fell silent, till he said quietly, 'Helen, you have a wonderful body and a marvellous mind, both of which I find utterly stimulating. You're right – I can't duck this. Our future can never be happy unless I properly resolve the past. I will do it . . . for you, for me, for us, for our children.'

She looked at him, too choked to speak. All her life she had waited to be loved in this all-consuming way. She considered she did not deserve it – for who does? – but she knew she had never had it, not from her mother, her father or her husband. Somehow, unbelievably, she had it now, and if it were to be taken away . . .

'Don't even think about it.' His voice stopped her train of thought.

'You don't know what I was thinking.'

'Maybe not exactly, but I won't let you down, believe me.'

On a bright March morning, full of promise, he woke her with kisses and buck's fizz. Fortunately it was a Saturday. His birthday gift to her was a superb tiny gold wristwatch. Helen knew, without asking, that she had never previously owned an item of such value. She accepted its extravagance as confirmation of his love for her, though she was far more touched by what he said.

'It's delicate, like you.' Again the reassurance that after all her independent years she was viewed as feminine and in need of care. 'I want you,' he continued, 'to learn to take life easier and, whenever you look at this little watch, to remember my words, "Take your time. Take your time." '

Was he asking for time, or was he speaking generally? She did not know and she did not ask, for she was not at all sure he would know the answer himself.

They spent the morning in bed, as lovers do when their needs are totally met by the other, then at midday Sam prepared a light luncheon of smoked salmon, granary bread and strawberries. He was organising everything and was evidently in his element. For Helen it was a strange experience to have a day unravelled, bit by bit, before her. She was not totally comfortable but would not have spoiled Sam's happiness at his own intrigues for anything.

He left her to go back to his own home to check the post and change, but said he would return at three and advised her to put on a dress rather than the trousers she might well have chosen on a Saturday.

In his absence she took a long bath, then made a phone call.

'We haven't met Sam yet,' said her mother.

'I know. I can't really talk when I ring you and he's here; it's just that one or two things have to be sorted out before we can be together, and I don't want to tempt fate by having him meet the family.'

'What sort of things?'

Helen knew she could not tell the Hamaida story, so she confined herself to the difference in their backgrounds and his loyalty to his own family and country.

'What do you mean, his mother doesn't approve of you?' Helen's mother pounced, as Helen had known she would.

'Well, look, Mummy, you weren't keen that he was an Arab, were you? His family isn't keen I'm English.'

'Good heavens, it's not the same thing at all.'

'I think you'll find it is. Why shouldn't it be?'

'Well . . .' Her mother was stumped for an answer. 'Well, I mean, you're a very good catch and . . . these people . . . they have no background.'

In spite of herself, Helen threw back her head and laughed. 'Have you ever heard of the pyramids? Mummy, don't be so beastly colonial. They had a background before we were living in clay huts, or whatever it was we did. Anyway, maybe I shouldn't have told you. I don't want to get into an argument, especially not today, but I felt you were owed some sort of an explanation.'

Sam turned up shortly afterwards, wearing a dark suit. They left almost immediately for what was, to her anyway, an unknown destination. It turned out to be a tea dance at the Waldorf hotel. It was absolutely charming: the potted palms, the quartet that specialised in music from the Thirties and the solicitous waiters. They sat on the edge of the dance floor and watched the rest of the clientele float by. There were Americans, easily identified because they tended to smooch and shuffle. Then there were couples of her parents' age. They were all slightly overweight, though the men, despite their comfortable corpulence, were amazingly light on their feet. Helen supposed, as she nibbled at minute, crustless cucumber sandwiches, that they came from dancing clubs in the suburbs.

After a while Sam invited her to dance. She accepted reluctantly, partly because, while they had bopped occasionally in night clubs, it was a while since she had flexed the ballroom training of her youth, and partly because she had no idea whether or not he could dance. She also realised they would be recognised. He was so dark and she was so fair, they would undoubtedly attract attention; his face was not unknown and hers, of course, would be familiar to most.

Sam danced well and Helen, who never considered she did, found the effortless unity of their movements as sensuous as the sexual act itself.

Normally she would not have eaten more than a couple of sandwiches, let alone the toasted teacakes, muffins with jam and rich, thick Devon cream or the pastries that followed, but today was special and she was living each moment for what it was.

The band changed the mood from the Thirties to a Viennese waltz and Sam insisted they try it. 'Keep your head up,' he said, 'then you won't get giddy.'

She smiled, replete with love for this commanding man who was so full of surprises, and as she did so, he looked, for a second, as if his heart must surely burst. He held her closer and closer. The room was spinning, but she knew he would not stumble. In his arms she was secure and the dizziness was delightful.

They sat down, flushed and giggling, and ordered more

tea. At the same time the band struck up 'Happy Birthday'. Helen was appalled. 'They're all looking now.'

'My darling,' he said, 'of course they are. Every one loves to see an attractive, vibrant woman, and you were born to be noticed even had you not pursued the career you have chosen.'

The waiter arrived at their table bearing a huge arrangement of flowers, whereupon everybody applauded. Blushing, she stood for a moment, bowing and smiling, then quickly sat down. 'How embarrassing, Sam,' she said, though she was pleased all the same. Applause was food and drink to her. She might think she could give it all up tomorrow and live in a foreign country, but could she? The open-ended question was a burden they shared but carried separately.

Helen read the card that had accompanied the flowers: 'This is a very special day. Thank you for making it so. Like the day and the year, you are more than special. All my love, Sam.'

My cup runneth over, she thought.

After the dance they went to the theatre next door to see a Tom Stoppard play, which they adored. They decided against dinner, since neither of them was hungry. On the drive back their never very subdued passion flared into intense desire. He became possessive in his comments and his anticipation of the night they were about to spend together. 'I'm going to fill you with so much good feeling, you'll beg for me to stop, but I won't. I'll go on and on until, at last, you cry out in the night like a cat.'

And so it was.

In the nature of things, anticlimax follows climax as surely as night follows day, but need it have happened so soon? wondered Helen, less than twenty-four hours after the tea dance.

They had spent the night at Helen's flat and then driven to lunch in Chiswick before going back to his house for a relaxing afternoon with the papers. Unexpectedly the telephone rang, and Helen could see Sam, on this, a weekend when he was not on call, flicking through the file in his mind of patients who might be in danger. With a worried look in her direction, he reached for the phone.

There was a pause.

'Hello, Mother.'

Helen mouthed a suggestion to him that she should leave the room. Emphatically he shook his head.

'No, I was out late,' he was saying. 'It was Helen's birthday.'

There was another pause.

'She's fine' – he smiled across at her – 'absolutely fine.'

Helen did leave. She walked upstairs and sat in his bedroom with the door closed. The presentiment of dire consequences, and the certain knowledge that yesterday's joy could not be allowed to continue, became acute. She had no idea what was being said, but she knew fear in those moments, deep, gut terror that she wanted to be appeased. She hungered for the moment he would come to find her, sweep her into his arms and tell her the future was theirs. But, as her appetite grew, so did her conviction that her anxiety could not be assuaged, nor her desires satisfied. She lay on the bed, the scene of so much wonder, and waited.

He came to her, looking stricken, as she had known he must. 'Hamaida's been very ill. She almost died. She's had a complete hysterectomy.'

With a few years of fertility before her, Helen felt for the woman who, even if it were her heart's desire, could not now conceive a child by the man she loved. She was party to Hamaida's trauma, while Hamaida, in all probability, knew nothing of Helen's. How strange, then, that their lives should be so interwoven, that when one of them suffered this blow, the other automatically realised it imposed a similar fate upon her.

Helen crossed her arms and hugged herself as she sat on the bed facing the bleak discovery that only a miracle could make her a mother now.

'Nobody wanted her before,' Sam said, 'but . . .'

Helen took his hands in hers. She wanted to give strength and gain it. She finished the sentence for him: ' . . . No one ever will want her now.'

Over the next few weeks they clung together. Unlike during the weeks before her birthday, they discussed all the problems and possible permutations over and over again. Helen wished she could unburden herself to a third party but felt their situation was too private to share. She was not sure either how she could put into words what she was learning about loving someone from a totally different culture. She contemplated telling Laura but could almost hear her friend saying simplistically that, if he loved her enough, he would stay. Loving her enough was not in question, but only she was privy to that. How could she begin to explain that he was deteriorating before her very eyes with the power struggle inside himself. Though she had loved him for a long time, her love now deepened by the day. He was totally unselfish and honourable, she believed, otherwise there would be no need for options and no pain. She was not, however, aware of what his preparation for any decision might entail.

They were driving from the studios to a little taverna in Camden Town; it was a favourite haunt.

'I'm going to have to go home and speak with her, her family and mine. I'm also going to have to see for myself the state of the hospitals and the predicament of my country.'

She had foreseen thus far. Speaking quietly, she said, 'I think that's a good idea. There's only so much wondering and agonising you can do here. When will you go?'

'May the thirtieth.'

'You can't. That's the day of the Celebrity Gala.' Helen had agreed to appear in a concert in aid of his transplant programme.

'No, it's the day after.'

'By the way,' she said, 'I'm narrating *Tubby the Tuba* with the Royal Marines band as well as compèring the concert; their musical director rang and asked me today.'

'That's nice,' he replied, without knowing why it was nice or what *Tubby the Tuba* was.

'Well, we have a fortnight left then. May I suggest

something? When you're in Egypt, Sam, even if you want to phone me – don't. Concentrate on the situation there.'

'I will,' he said. 'I'd already thought that out. You see, in a way, my love for you mustn't affect the choice. If I am honour-bound to go in that direction, I must, irrespective of you and of us.'

Helen began to cry silently. The pit prop was bending; the roof threatened to cave in.

'For that reason,' he continued, 'I don't think we should make love before I go. I don't want to feel I ever used you. My mind must be free.'

She exploded. 'How can it be free? You can't just eradicate months of loving. You can't just switch it off because it's no longer convenient – or at least, if you can, it wasn't worth anything. What about me? Let's forget your sense of honour for a moment and its hold over your body. If you don't have these requirements, that's fine – for you, but I do. It looks like I may have to live my life without you, and God knows I don't think I can or want to, but Sam, for God's sake, let me at least have you for the time we have left.'

They were almost in Camden Town. He turned down a side street lined with grimy council flats and very little lighting. He stopped the car, switched off the headlights and gathered her to him. He tried to pacify her with kisses, but she was inconsolable.

'If you free me – ' he explained, 'don't you understand? I probably won't be able to free myself, but we'll both know I came to you because it was right and that we did love each other enough to let go.'

It was too philosophical for Helen; her head was pounding and she felt her heart must break. Surely he must need her as much as she needed him? She took his hand and put it to her right breast, holding it there till his fingers relaxed and cupped and squeezed the soft fullness. Any moment now he would caress her, overpower her, drive her back to her place or his and take her. He always had before.

His face remained touching hers. His eyes were closed but tears were escaping from them and Helen could not tell whether her own cheeks were wet with his tears, or hers, or both. They sat together for a long time.

Neither of them was much in the mood for food, but as they grew colder Sam wearily insisted they should try to eat. Helen squinted at herself in her compact mirror, and Sam put on the interior light. She licked a corner of her handkerchief and tried to wipe away the messy flecks of mascara. She applied some powder but was convinced her camouflage would fool nobody. She had been weeping, and she looked as if she had. Sam did not look much better.

The proprietor, who knew them well, made no comment and did not stay to chat after seating them, as he would have done normally. He brought a bottle of Demestica and a bottle of Perrier and retired. They held hands tightly across the table and Helen, even in the pale, flickering candlelight, could see her knuckles shining white. They ate with one hand only, as if afraid to let go of their life-line.

After a while Helen looked around. She perceived that their emotional scene was proving compulsive viewing to their fellow diners and to the staff who had witnessed them on happier days. The tears threatened again and, not for the first time, Helen felt that the job, for all its glamour and excitement, had distinct disadvantages on nights such as this.

Her look froze. An aquarium with two fish swimming in it suddenly caught her eye. One was large and aggressive, the other cowering in fright, it seemed with justification, since its tail was serrated in a manner that nature had never intended. Sam followed her gaze.

'That's cruel,' she said. 'How terrible to have to live in a confined space with another creature who hates you. Where could you escape?' As she spoke, she recognised that her words had, unintentionally, drawn a hideous comparison. She thought of the girl in Egypt. Out of the blue she recalled one of the sayings of the week from an edition of the *Observer*, 'Hell is getting what you thought you wanted.'

Chance would be a fine thing, she thought, but then

she developed the idea further in her mind. If Sam felt trapped by the other relationship, he must, in the end turn back to her. As Laura had said, she held all the winning cards. His devotion was apparent every second of the day. She had to grow up and stop grabbing. She saw herself for a second as a spoiled toddler having a tantrum, stamping her foot hysterically and demanding, 'I want.' It was worse for him, and if only she could be adult enough to agree to his suggestion, he might at least feel that she was the only woman in his life not manipulating him. Maybe then she would be rewarded by his deciding in her favour.

She smiled. 'I'm better now. Could you take me home, do you think?'

He looked puzzled at the change of mood but simply nodded. As he drew up outside the flat Helen's resolve weakened and she longed for him to reverse his plan. Looking at him and touching him, she knew he was on the verge of doing so. His grasp on her thigh sent a message to her secret places, which opened automatically. They were his, for no one else had ever owned them.

She took a deep breath. 'Goodnight, Sam,' she said briskly. She opened the door. He reached for her hand quickly and pulled her back. His lips met hers hungrily. 'Darling.' She sighed unhappily. 'Let's try it your way. Goodnight.'

Inside the flat Helen found she was trembling. She went into the bedroom and switched on her electric blanket, then walked into the kitchen to boil a kettle to fill a hot-water bottle. She felt she needed all the warmth she could get. She removed her make-up with unsteady hands and lay on the bed. She curled around the pillows, rocking against them in a foetal position. She had been born for him, and without his succour she must surely shrivel and die.

The phone rang. 'Helen . . . if I can sort this out, I'll never let you out of my sight and I'll make love to you every day of our lives. If you were here now I'd . . .'

She dropped the phone to the floor. His voice was going

on and on in the distance while she wept in the darkness. Eventually it stopped.

For the next fortnight they pursued this peculiar pattern of behaviour. It was absurd, they agreed, as they cradled each other and cried before separating each night. Helen's only consolation was that he could not stay away. He may not be penetrating her physically, but he was claiming every other portion of her life, and his energy was in no way transferring towards his obligations in Egypt. Alone each night, Helen tossed and turned. She read countless newspapers and magazines and several novels. She had never been so well informed, so tired or so thin.

Through the door of the warming-up room Sam could hear the strains of piano playing. He knocked on the door before entering, expecting to be confronted by a sea of faces.

Helen sat at the piano alone.

'Where's everybody?' he asked.

'I think they took a supper break. They're probably in the coffee shop or the bar.'

'I didn't know you played the piano.'

'I don't now – at least not very well. I'm desperately out of practice.'

'It sounded great to me.'

'When I was twelve, I was sensational. It's just I never got any better!'

'How was the rehearsal?' he asked.

'In the time-honoured tradition of all dress runs, it was diabolical. I missed umpteen cues in *Tubby the Tuba*, and I haven't a clue what I'm going to say all night.'

'Have you time for a drink?'

She looked at the little gold watch he had given her. 'Just about.'

It was a strange evening, for it involved them both to a similar degree. Focusing on the tension surrounding the concert, Helen was able to forget, albeit temporarily, the stress in her own life. They smiled at each other; it was almost like the old days.

Helen was more nervous about facing a group of three

thousand people than she ever was at the prospect of working to at least as many million whom she could not see. Sam ordered smoked-salmon sandwiches and coffee. She felt they must look an odd couple, he already attired in the proper garb for the evening and she in jeans and a big sweater. He looked so distinguished, she thought, in his black tuxedo and brilliantly white pin-tucked evening shirt.

'I have to get ready, Sam,' she said after a while.

'Do you want to be alone for a bit?'

'Yes, I do – just for half an hour. I must get my brain in gear.' She pressed his hand. 'Do you mind?'

'Of course not. I'll go and mingle, but I'll come and find you before it starts.'

In the dressing-room the routine of preparation – making up, teasing out her hair with an electric brush and sticking on her false eyelashes – soothed her mind. It was just another performance, in one sense anyway. At the same time she had high hopes for the success of the evening, for the profile of Sam's programme of work, for the patients whose lives depended upon the fund-raising and for herself. Tomorrow at this time he would be in Egypt, and it was imperative he carried with him the memory of her at her best.

Sam returned. 'You look wonderful,' he said, as he took in every detail of her gold lace and cream taffeta outfit before kissing her gently so as not to smudge her lipstick.

There was a knock on the door and a little man in an oversised maroon dinner jacket stood in the entrance, almost hidden by a huge basket of flowers. Helen went to take them, smiling back at Sam, for of course they came from him. It was almost time and as she looked at her watch, she was momentarily overwhelmed with stage fright. She rushed into Sam's arms, clinging to his steadiness and strength. Then, pushing away all the unwelcome thoughts that flooded her mind at such moments nowadays, she applied herself to the job in hand. 'Go away – I'll see you in the interval. At least I get *Tubby the Tuba* over in the first half. Enjoy it. I'll do my best for you and for everyone who depends on you.'

As she walked on to the platform she instinctively looked up; her old training of playing to the gallery was well ingrained. The applause was tumultuous. It was odd that, despite working every night to far more people than were here, she derived a tremendous sense of affirmation from the packed house before her, whose vibrations told her she was known and liked.

She introduced the Royal Marines, and their musical director took over. Helen was dying for a drink, but if television depended upon split-second timing, so did any sort of musical performance. She paced around backstage, smoking cigarette after cigarette, knowing it was bad for her voice. At last she was on.

The part of the programme she had dreaded worked like a dream. She picked up all the musical cues. It was a heady experience, a mathematical one and also very physical. The singing passages, which she had been most nervous about, went well; the piece was almost at an end. With a broad smile and an expansive gesture that encompassed the whole band, she delivered the last line. A tremendous crescendo surged round her, almost lifting her off her feet. It was wonderfully exhilarating.

Suddenly it was over. The applause was deafening but real. It was the interval, and in her dressing-room she found in a silver bucket the champagne she might have guessed would be there.

Sam appeared in the doorway. 'I know you so well, yet I don't know you at all. You were marvellous.' He crushed her to him proudly.

The remainder of the evening was easy. She drew the winning raffle tickets and compèred the second half with its galaxy of star performers: Peter Skellern, Cleo Laine, John Dankworth, John Williams, Yehudi Menuhin and George Melly. She enjoyed it more and more as the concert progressed. She felt she was just getting the hang of it when it was over.

Sam must have run the four-minute mile, she thought, as he burst into her dressing-room minutes after her return there. 'You're so good at what you do,' he said.

'I haven't been doing what I do,' she answered.

'Maybe not. I know how many viewers you have at six but, seeing a fraction of those actually watching you, I realise how greatly you're loved.'

'Am I?'

He looked straight at her. 'Oh, yes,' he said. 'Yes, you are.'

The Royal Marines' musical director arrived to escort Helen to the green room, and when she and Sam arrived they could barely enter for the crush. Everyone was on a high; the word was that the financial target had been exceeded.

Laura pushed her way through the crowd to Helen. She looked sensational with her thick auburn hair swept to one side and a conglomeration of pearls and Monty Don jewellery adorning her purple evening gown. 'You were terrific,' she said. 'I couldn't have done it . . . I was near Sam,' she added more quietly. 'He had eyes only for you. You have nothing to worry about. He's besotted.'

Helen was delighted to hear it, but nothing altered the fact that within hours he was to be snatched away.

After Laura melted into the crowd, Sam rarely left Helen's side. She was acutely aware of his presence as he lit her cigarette, refilled her glass while holding her wrist, breathed on the back of her neck and constantly slipped his arm around her waist.

'Miss Bartlett,' boomed an elderly, formidable woman, reminiscent of the one who had drummed eight times three into her head when she was in her infant school. 'I'm Mildred Smorthwaite, secretary to Mr Aziz.' She extended her white-gloved hand in Helen's direction. 'We've spoken on the 'phone. Congratulations. You did a remarkable job tonight.'

'Thank you very much. It's nice to meet you at last.'

'I'm pleased to see you, especially here with my boss. He isn't an easy man, you know,' she said more quietly, keeping an eye on Sam, who was in a nearby corner pouring drinks. 'Quite tetchy on occasions, but then gifted people are always difficult. Still, it slots into place now I see you together. You make him very happy.'

Helen sighed. 'I don't know that I do.'

'Oh, yes, there's no doubt about it. He's never behaved like this in the fifteen years I've been with him. He's been a bit quieter the last two weeks, but other than that he's been like a dog with two tails. Don't let him down, that's all. He's so in love with you it would kill him.'

So the dragon had a heart after all.

Helen wanted to take her to one side and explain that it was Sam who was in the process of letting her down, not the other way around. Instead she smiled, and the urge to tell, like the urge to smoke when you are determined to give up, receded with the passing moments and the assistance of a few deep breaths.

Several of Sam's colleagues, some of whom she had met before, came to talk to her. In different ways they broadcast the same message. Sam was hers. He was a changed man since meeting her. The paradox was too great. Helen excused herself and ran back along the corridor to her dressing-room. She sat in solitude with her glass still in her hand, though it was not a practice of hers to drink alone.

There was a knock on the door and Laura entered. The girls looked at each other for an instant before Laura held out her arms and Helen allowed herself to be comforted. 'What's wrong with you two?' Laura asked at last.

'Nothing,' retorted Helen brightly. 'I've just been told by at least five people that we're made for each other.'

'You are, so what's up?'

'He's going back to Egypt tomorrow.'

'Yes, I know. For a holiday, he told me. Why don't you go too?'

'I can't.'

'Of course you can. Just tell Derek and go – they'll have to cope.'

'I can't . . . because Sam doesn't want me to.' Helen breathed deeply.

'Helen, it's time you opened up. I'm probably the closest friend you have apart from Sam – maybe the only one, come to think of it. All the others are more what I'd call acquaintances. I don't want to force myself on you, believe me, but friends share things. I want to help, and

I'm hurt you're excluding me. In fact, I told Ian as much last night. You're in at eight every morning. That's never happened before, not even when you were getting over Barry. You're taking on more and more. You say you're fine, but you look terrible – not on the box, mind, you're too much of a pro for that. You're cracking jokes in the office, but when I catch a glimpse of you when you don't think I'm looking, you seem, well, as if you're in pain. At first I thought you were ill, then I saw Sam one night when he was picking you up, and he looked terrible too. You're still in love, still seeing each other, but, my God, you look dreadful, and I know he's ten years older than you, but now he looks double that. I popped in on him yesterday – I've nearly finished editing my piece on his work – and I couldn't believe the difference between the man I've been watching on the cutting-room screen and the man in reality. Where's all the charm and authority I've come to expect? In short, off-screen you're both a bloody mess.'

'Hey, that's quite a speech, Laura.'

'Helen, stop it or I'll scream.'

'OK – I'm sorry and, deep down, I'm very touched.' Tears welled in her eyes. 'I'm very touched you care.' She sniffed. Laura handed her a tissue. 'Laura,' Helen sniffed again, 'can you keep this to yourself?'

'You know better than to ask, don't you?'

'I'm sorry,' Helen said again. 'Well, a long time ago, years and years actually, Sam was promised, I think that's the term, to a girl back home.'

'Come off it, Helen, that doesn't still happen surely?'

'Well, it did then.'

'But he loves you.'

'I think he does.'

'*Think!* Listen, Helen, I've deliberately spent tonight watching you both. Now, you love him, that's quite apparent. I can see it in your eyes when you look at him or talk about him. But he – he's fanatical. He may be a bit more hot-headed, being an Arab, but he can't take his eyes off you. He tenses the moment any other man so much as talks to you and has to excuse himself from any conversation he's having to get to your side. He's possessive in the extreme. I don't know if it's good or not, but it's like an electric current passing between you. The rest of us are having to stand back in case we get burnt.'

Helen kissed Laura's cheek. 'You are good to me, and if only half of what you say is true, it makes me feel better, but – and this is the big but – it's almost like going out with someone who's married. He's got to resolve it before he can come to me.'

'It's ridiculous,' said Laura.

'It is and it isn't. I can't actually tell you the whole story, which might make more sense. Anyway, it's not terrible like kids dying in Ethiopia, but it is the worst thing that's ever happened to me.'

Laura held her friend's hand tightly. 'I don't understand, but I can see it's important, and I suppose that's why he's going home. Did his mother's visit bring all this to a head?'

'In a way, and a subsequent phone call compounded it. It isn't just the girl, though that's bad enough, heaven knows. He's also got an overdose of guilt about depriving his countrymen of his talent.'

'Saints preserve us!' said Laura. 'He'd never get the facilities back there to do what he's doing here. He's a pioneer; he has to carry on. That's what my film's about – the whole of the medical world depends on him, not just a bunch of lousy peasants.'

'Laura . . .'

'OK, I apologise. That was unfair, but he's brilliant and, quite apart from that, you're my friend and you've been hurt enough. He shouldn't have started it if he couldn't follow through.'

'I don't think either of us realised what we were getting into. Who wrote *The Magnificent Obsession?*' She clicked her fingers in exasperation. 'It doesn't matter, but this is a rather . . . inglorious one. It was like lighting the blue touch paper when we met. Unfortunately, we disregarded the warning to stand well clear.'

Laura kissed Helen suddenly on the top of her head.

'Do you want to come and stay with us while Sam's away?'

Helen looked at Laura with gratitude. 'It's very kind of you. Can I think about it?'

''Course – the offer's there. We better go back; you're the star and you'll be missed.'

It was true. She had been. Helen, though gratified, was chastened by the responsibility and its inherent requirement that she should always keep up appearances.

'What have I done to you?' Sam asked later, when they were heading towards her home in a thunderstorm with the windscreen wipers struggling to reveal the dark, depressing world outside. Helen had her head in her hands as if afraid she might lose it. They stopped outside her flat, and the perpetual question of whether or not they might comfort and console each other had yet to be posed. 'I do care, Helen. Do you know that?'

Drained by the excitement and emotion of the evening, she could only nod. He jerked her head upright, and those terrifyingly dangerous eyes penetrated her skull. Roughly he pulled her to him and kissed her so violently her lips went numb and she felt she was drowning. She fought to get free. 'You're hurting me, Sam.'

'I'm sorry, Helen. I'm sorry, darling, but my love for you is . . .' He searched for an end to his sentence. ' . . . Altitudinous.'

She smiled wearily. 'That's not a word.'

He held her tightly. 'It is now. Could I come in for coffee?'

With one gesture, an imperceptible nod, she could have him. He would love her and hold her through this last night. Her breasts hardened – she felt they might burst out of her flimsy gold chemise. Her womb contracted, and her legs instinctively parted. Yet still she resisted. Maybe he had to experience deprivation to come to his senses. 'No,' she whispered. 'I don't think that's a good idea.'

She got out of the car and took a step towards her front door. She heard a slamming noise behind her a second before he pulled her back to face him. They stood together in their finery, which quickly became sodden. Rain and tears were streaming down her face; there was a salty taste in her mouth; her hair was plastered to her head; and her eyes stung with running mascara.

'Go home, Sam' she shouted as another clap of thunder tore the air. 'Please go and don't ring me, not tonight, not tomorrow and certainly not when you're away.' She blinked in an attempt to clear her blurred vision. 'But every moment from now till we meet again, if ever we do, please remember I'm yours. I was never loved like this before.' She tried to force her mouth into a smile. 'And my love for you is . . . altitudinous too.' With that she turned and, without a backward glance, stumbled up the

Chapter Nine

'You look awful,' said Laura.

'Thanks a lot.'

'What happened after you left?'

'It was very dramatic. A bit like a third-rate movie with a stage hand heaving buckets of water on to us from a great height while the two of us were weeping and declaring undying love and passion to the accompaniment of thunder and lightning. He wanted to stay . . . I wish I'd let him now. He's probably gone away feeling rejected.'

'I don't understand. How could you turn him down last night of all nights?'

'We hadn't been sleeping together for two weeks so that he could focus on Egypt and what he has to do there.'

'Whose idea was that?'

'His.'

'Well, you were just doing what he asked, then.'

'I know, I know, but now he's gone and I might never see him again.'

'Helen, think of how his eyes never left you yesterday evening. Remember what I said, he'll be back. It wouldn't surprise me if he doesn't stick the whole ten days.'

'He will. By tonight he'll be there. They'll manoeuvre him into a corner, and he'll probably find it easier to dismiss me as a pleasant but unreal interlude. You know you said once you're not desperately in love with Ian but you just can't imagine life without him? Perhaps you're better off.'

'Maybe. I'm a different sort of animal from you – you're so extreme. You go down much lower than I ever do, but when you're elated you're so buoyant it makes me exhausted just to watch. I sometimes envy you that.

Anyway, we all have to resolve things in our own way. I think I'm about to have to do it with Ian. I'm not unhappy about it, just unsettled because I think we're reaching a point where a decision will have to be made. It's strange in a way. I think in my case I have to make the choice, but in yours it's totally up to Sam – unless you get tired of waiting. What are you going to do while he's in Egypt?'

'Well, if I can just get through today and tomorrow, I'll collapse at the weekend. I think I'll go and get some fresh air now.'

The phone rang. Helen snatched at it. 'Sharon, I'm going out. Who is it?' Laura heard the surprise in Helen's voice as she said, 'Oh. Well, you'd better put him through.' Laura left.

'Darling, I'm in the lounge at Heathrow. Hang on, let me put some more money in.'

Helen could hear him feeding coins into the pay phone.

'Darling,' he said again, 'I know you said don't phone, but I've been awake all night. I have to know before I go – do you love me?'

'Don't you know?'

'I suppose I do, but just say it.'

'I love you, Sam.'

'Did you get my note?'

'Yes, I did. It came this morning, as you knew it would, just when I was trying to put you out of my mind for ten days. What's the point of my having your address and phone number? You hardly think I'm going to call up for a social chat, do you? Anyway, we said strictly no contact while you're away.'

'I know that's what we said. I just wanted you to have it in case something awful happens.'

'Something awful is happening, but I won't phone you.'

'OK. Keep it for an emergency.' He went on, 'Helen, I don't think I can go. I can't bear to leave you.'

She was willing him to say that England was home and that she was a part of it, but she remembered what Laura had said and recalled the thoughts that had come to her in the taverna in Camden Town. He needed her more than she needed him; she had to be courageous enough to let him go. 'Sam, listen. It wouldn't solve anything. It would only delay our being together. I can't have you if you don't go, you know that. I'm not pushing you away, believe me. In fact, and this isn't meant as pressure, I don't think I can live without you.'

'It isn't pressure. It's what I need to hear.'

'No, it isn't. Already I wish I hadn't said it – you can't be torn in two for ever. You must go to Egypt, and I'll hold my breath till you come back. Sam, I love you more than life itself, but you're a man of honour and I'm trying, perhaps for the first time in my life, to be honourable too.'

There was a pause. Maybe he would still insist upon staying. She could do no more. 'All right,' he said at last, 'I'll go, but will you promise me one thing?'

The tears had sprung now. She could have stopped him; she could have claimed him. What sort of fool was she? 'What?'

'Even if you're very lonely, don't go to bed with anyone else. Is that too much to ask?'

'I have no intention of going to bed with anyone else.'

'Look . . . Oh, hell, hang on, I've got to put more money in.'

She waited.

'Helen, I'm sorry. I shouldn't have asked that of you. It's just that if I knew someone else was having you, I think I'd kill him.'

'There won't be anybody else, Sam, but it's more than fair of me to promise that when you're probably going to bed Hamaida.'

'I am *not*.'

'OK, don't shout. You might – I think we should face up to the possibility. You might, just to see if you could settle for that.'

'Helen, I'm telling you I won't.'

There was silence.

'This is terrible,' he said. 'I've never had such a private conversation in such a public place in my life. Look, Helen, I love you. I'll do what you say. I won't phone you, but I will think about you every second of every minute of every day.'

'Sam, that won't solve anything. Go and, God help me, I don't know how to say this, you know the solution I want, but don't come back without solving it. Look, I can't talk any more. Goodbye.'

She wept then, longing for him, in the lounge at Heathrow, to opt for here, the future and her, to decide that he need not go to Egypt to make his decision. The phone did not ring again. Neither did it ring in the flat, not once, all evening. She could not believe she would sleep, but the struggle to present a good programme against all the odds, the combination of two or three drinks without food and the cumulative effect of the sleepless nights of the last fortnight rendered her physically and mentally immobile. It if were not for the silent phone, she might slumber. With a gesture of defiance she unplugged it. There would be no calls tonight; there could be no calls tonight.

By Saturday morning she was in a state of panic. Perhaps she should take stock – possibly venture out for the day? To test the temperature she decided to go across to the shops. She pulled on a track suit, pushed her feet into ancient moccasins and, as a concession to vanity, added a pair of dark glasses. She ran down the stairs and out of the back door to Holland Park Avenue. She caught sight of herself in a window and hoped no one would recognise her. There was nothing of the celebrity about her now. She bought milk and a newspaper but was disinclined to bother further.

Back in the flat, she made a pot of tea and tried to ignore the mockingly silent telephone in the corner. After her first few positive moves of the day the depression and anxiety were returning with a vengeance. It was half past one in Cairo. He might be lunching with his mother or . . . No, she felt sure he would not have made contact with Hamaida yet.

The phone rang. She started, then rushed towards it, then steadied herself. By the time she answered, she was shaking.

'Helen, it's me.'

'Hello, Laura,' she said, hoping her friend did not detect her disappointment.

'Look, at the risk of sounding bossy, I don't think you should spend the day entirely alone.'

'Neither do I. I think I'll go away.' This was as much a surprise to Helen as it was to Laura, but it suddenly seemed the only solution.

'When?'

'Now, soon . . . I don't know.'

'Don't do anything rash.'

Helen laughed. 'My whole life is falling apart. Maybe it's time to be rash.'

'Where will you go?'

'I wish I knew . . . What about a health farm?'

'It's a good idea. I've half a mind to come with you.'

'Why don't you? You said the other day you had a decision to make.'

'Well, look, I'll spend the weekend with Ian and then we'll see. Do you want to come here?'

'No, you two have so little time alone. I'll ring Derek and see if I can have a few days off, though God knows what he'll say. Have you booked leave already?'

'Yes. I'm not working all next week.'

'Hmm. He may not allow me to be away too, but if he will, I'll go and I'll call you from wherever I am. But are you sure you want to be with me? I'm not exactly at my best.'

'No, you're not, but I want to see you and, to be quite selfish about it, I think you're the only person who can help me sort my life out.'

'I can but try. Look, let me ring Derek while I'm in the mood.'

'Helen?'

'What?'

'Are you all right?'

'Ask me another.' She sighed.

'Helen . . .'

'Don't worry – I'll be fine, I promise. I'll call you.'

Helen lit a cigarette before ringing Derek. It was

unlikely he would accede to her request without argument.

'Derek, I'm sorry to ring you on a Saturday.'

'That's OK. I'm trying to persuade myself I should be working in the garden but I'm not keen, and if I'm talking to you, I've got an excuse.'

Derek lived with his wife and three children in a rather splendid house in Berkshire. He was a rare breed in their business, an unashamed family man.

'Derek, I know this is a lot to ask, but you have said to me several times I ought to take leave, and the company doesn't award you any medals if you don't . . .'

'When do you want to go?'

'What?'

'Look, Helen, I don't know you very well, but I do think you're overdoing it. You look very strained to me.'

His kindness caught her off balance and reduced her to tears. She needed a holiday, she seemed to be losing the battle to control any emotions at all. 'Well, can I go now? I'd be back a week on Monday. I know it's difficult because Laura's away too.'

'Hang on, Helen, I've got a copy of the roster in my study. I've just got to cover myself.'

Helen puffed at her cigarette. Now that the idea had taken root, she could not bear for it to fail.

'It's OK. I'll just bring a different reporter in every day to present the programme. Is there any fashion lined up?'

'Yes. The last in the "High Street" series is supposed to go out on Tuesday, and it's ready. "Medical Matters" is in the can too. Dr Murdoch and I knocked off two last time he was in.'

'Fine. Well, off you go.'

'I hope the reporters don't perform too well.'

Derek laughed. 'You'll talk yourself out of this in a moment. What are you going to do?'

'I think I'll go to a health farm.'

'What about your surgeon?'

Helen tried to sound matter-of-fact. 'He's gone home to see his family in Cairo.'

'Ah,' said Derek, and she could almost hear him putting

ten and ten together. 'Enjoy it,' he said. 'I'd better get into the garden now.'

'Thanks, Derek. Thanks for being so reasonable.'

'That's all right. I'd sooner you were off now than . . . um . . .'

'Have a breakdown, you mean?'

'Yes, I suppose I did mean that. You'd be off much longer then, which would be bloody inconvenient!'

'Don't worry. I'm tougher than that. See you Monday week, and thanks again.'

It was the oppressive silence of the flat that urged her on. A few more phone calls was all it took: a reservation in Leicestershire, a drive to the studios for a couple of tracksuits and bikinis and the ready-packed make-up holdall. A drive from the noise that contrasted so dramatically with the silence of the flat to the quiet of the countryside – at least, it would have been quiet had it not been for Tchaikovsky's 'Rococo Variations' turned up full-blast on the radio to blot out the whirrings in her mind. What was he doing now? Where was he? Was she forgotten?

More music: concentrate on the virtuosity of the cellist. Turn down here – no, there. She must find it soon. She rounded another bend on the wrong side of the road and almost collided with a tractor. Stop the car. Breathe deeply. Be reasonable, always reasonable. Christ, she was pissed off with being reasonable.

She came upon it suddenly: Home Farm, her hideaway.

'Could you park my car and bring my stuff in?' she asked the little lad in long, white gloves. He looked bemused. She pressed a pound coin in his hand. He smiled.

'Good God, Helen Bartlett.' The voice came from a plump face on top of an unflattering powder-blue bath robe, podgier, thinner on top but still recognisable.

'Terry. Long time no see.'

'Yeah. Darling, you're so famous now. I've followed your career, you know. You look wonderful.'

Same old Terry. How could she look wonderful when her life was a shambles?

Sitting in the Jacuzzi, she encountered the first inquisitive viewer. It mattered little. Her presence would be a nine-minute wonder. She moved slightly to allow the powerful jet of water to pummel one thigh, then the other. She let it rise higher. Her spine was in knots; it hurt. It must be doing some good.

There was no requirement to dress for dinner, she discovered. Most people turned up in housecoats. Helen was wearing a pale-turquoise track suit; her long hair was tied back, and she had removed all her make-up except mascara. Terry motioned for her to join him. 'It's ages since we had dinner together, my sweet,' he whispered.

Helen found the melon, chicken cooked in herbs and garlic and salad followed by fresh fruit more than adequate, but Terry complained. 'I'm so sick of this rabbit food, but my new series begins soon. I must lose some weight.' His voice was loud. Unlike Helen, he clearly wanted to be recognised, fêted even. He turned his volume down to a more conspiratorial level as the other diners began to leave. 'I'm glad I've got you to myself. We'll have a drink in the lounge.' They walked through to the bar which served bovril, coffee, slim-line drinks and very dry wine.

'I'll have a diet coke,' said Helen.

'You will not. We'll have some wine – in fact, we'll have champagne. It's only fifteen calories a glass.' Helen suspected that his calculation was optimistic but was not prepared to argue. 'It's the most terrific stroke of luck your turning up. It's been so dull.'

'Terry,' she cautioned, 'I've come to have a rest. I'm not a bundle of laughs right now.'

'But, darling,' he said, gazing deep into her eyes – it was a well-practised technique – 'you don't look as if you need recuperation. You're gorgeous. I often watch you. You're much more attractive than the little girl I deprived of her virtue all those years ago.'

She laughed. 'Oh, you knew I was a virgin, did you?'

'Of course. You were terribly sweet. You were trying so hard to be sophisticated. But it was obvious you'd never gone the whole way before. Anyway you bled all over the place.'

Sam's description of Hamaida rang in her head.

'What's wrong? What did I say?'

She tried to smile. 'It's OK. Somebody just walked over my grave, that's all.'

She had met Terry during her first acting job. It had been a twenty-six week tour of a play that proved not to be a conspicuous success. They had begun in number-one dates like the Newcastle Theatre Royal and the Liverpool Empire, but as news of their notices preceded them they had played out the remainder of the run in less prestigious venues: Whitehaven and Yeovil were two of them, she recalled.

Terry was already in television. He had seemed so suave, and she had been vastly flattered by his attentions. She suspected he had already had most of the women in the company before he asked her out for dinner. He took her to expensive restaurants and made a great deal of fuss over the temperature of the wine. It would strike her as pretentious and pompous now, though she had been impressed at the time. How naive. Eventually they had had sex in a peeling bedroom in Weston-super-Mare. He had known what he was doing; it was not a miserable experience, but she had been a mere diversion, a trifling adventure.

On the last night of the run in Swindon he had sent her flowers, and she had stood on stage with tears streaming down her face, knowing it was his farewell gesture. Had she been in love? Probably not. But hurt? Yes, she had been hurt, for she had given him all she had at the time, and it had not been enough.

Seeing him now, he seemed no longer glamorous but rather seedy, and for the first time she was relieved she had not become Mrs Terry Summerfield the third.

'You've gone very quiet,' he said, as he recharged her glass.

'I was just remembering how you ditched me at the end of the run.'

'Yes. That was a foul thing to do. I wouldn't do it now.'

Helen raised an eyebrow and pursed her lips but said nothing.

Sunday dawned bright and peaceful. Breakfast came in the shape of tea with skimmed milk and a bran biscuit. She had ordered all the Sunday papers and did not leave the shelter of her bed till she and the sheets were black with newsprint. She rang Laura. 'I'm at Home Farm,' she said.

'Where on earth's that?'

'It's in the middle of Leicestershire. They're full at the moment, but they'll have vacancies tomorrow.'

'OK, book me in. I want to get away. It's happened. Ian's asked me to marry him.'

'That's terrific.'

'I suppose so . . .'

'Can you talk?'

'Not really. I'll see you tomorrow.'

Helen went to the aerobics class. She swam. She had a G5 massage, which made her feel she was being hoovered all over. She went to the sauna. She walked in the gardens. She avoided Terry, and when she went to bed alone, she expected to sleep immediately. Instead, every time she turned over, Sam's face appeared before her. His penetrating eyes pierced the gloom, his expression one of stark anguish.

'Oh, God, Sam, do you still love me?'

His image declined to nod its head.

'Dear God,' she said into the stillness, 'please, please don't take him from me. I'm not strong enough. I'll give up the job, go anywhere, do anything but please . . .'

Tears, more tears. Another sodden pillow before sleep that knits up the ravelled sleeve of care.

Laura was not the only newcomer on Monday: the Marvellous Merinda Merrydew also turned up, she of the chat shows, she with the string of notable lovers, she the black jewel of the gossip columns.

'What does she actually do?' asked Laura when they were sitting cosily in the Jacuzzi.

'I don't know exactly. I expect she's an actress, but she's really known for just being famous. She is fabulous, isn't she?'

''Spose so,' said Laura. 'Anyway, your pal Terry's quite smitten.'

'God.' Helen laughed. 'They should suit each other.'

It was promising anyway, thought Helen, as she sipped her tea on her balcony and looked across the putting green to the kidney-shaped outdoor pool. The Marvellous Merinda, in the minutest of bikinis, was sitting on the edge, kicking her legs in the water. Terry was diving – some might have said that was a generous description – in a bid to gain her attention. It reminded Helen of the courtship display of a walrus. She was hardly an expert on wildlife, but it seemed to her she must once have seen a *Survival Special* on the subject, since there was something so familiar about the scenario.

The gravel crunched beneath her window. Helen looked down and saw Laura pacing up and down. She was not aware she was being overlooked and was kicking the ground with each step, making tiny dents in the path as a flurry of small stones took to the air. With her guard down she looked oddly vulnerable, and Helen's heart went out to her friend, who had to decide whether what she was being offered was everything. She decided to risk interrupting Laura's disconsolate constitutional. 'There you are,' she shouted, as though she had just walked out on to the balcony. 'Do you want some tea?'

Laura turned her worried face skywards, squinting against the sun. 'OK. Thanks. Then I thought I'd go for a cycle ride. Will you come with me?'

'Only if you want company.'

'I do.'

'God, I don't know why I don't know what I want,' said Laura. The girls were sitting by the pool sipping diet Cokes. Laura looked wonderful, thought Helen. Her flame-red, curly hair was still luxuriantly sexy even when it was scraped back after her facial. Helen, by comparison, felt she looked pasty, her hair thin and uninteresting when constrained by an elastic band.

'I'm hungry. Aren't you?' asked Laura.

'No, not really.'

'I think it's because we don't get breakfast.'

'Well, there is the bran biscuit, even if it is practically inedible.'

'I don't get one of those.'

''Course you do.'

'I don't.'

'You must do – it's standard.'

'What's it like?'

'Well, square, dry . . .'

'Oh, *that.*' Laura began to laugh. 'I thought it was a cork mat. I put my teacup on it! God knows what we're coming to,' she said between giggles. 'It's ridiculous – here we are, stars of the small screen, having an in-depth conversation about bran biscuits.' Her mood changed suddenly. 'I'm going to tell you something. Perhaps I shouldn't, but I want to. Do you know, Helen I originally made friends with you because I was so jealous I could hardly see straight.'

'Of me? That's impossible.'

'No, not really. I'd been a journalist. I had a track record. You turned up and everyone fawned over you.'

'They didn't.'

'Oh, they did. I was prepared to hate you: I'd have loved to have your job. I deliberately forced myself on you – I'm not sure why. Partly I wanted to overcome my envy and partly, I think, I was hoping to find out something that could have been used as ammunition against you. I feel terrible about it now. Anyway, I found I liked you, and then you were so good at it all. You have a terrific instinct. When I watch you interviewing people, they're always relaxed. I used to think they just liked you and found you attractive, but it's more than that. You intuitively know how to treat them. You're marvellous and you're nice as well.'

'I'd no idea,' said Helen.

'Good. Anyway, I'm certainly not jealous of you now. You still have the job, but I've come to realise how much more difficult it is for someone in your position to have the right relationship. You thought you had it and, God knows, you deserve it, but I would be totally insensitive if I didn't see the problems.'

'In the end,' mused Helen, 'it doesn't matter how successful one is. Two o'clock in the morning comes, irrespective of what you do for a living. I'd given up hope of finding someone to share my life. Then Sam appeared. He persuaded me to love him and I do. But ever since I gave in, I feel he's been beckoning me with one hand and holding me off with the other. I suspect it hasn't ended yet. I love him more than I can say. I can't bear the thought that he won't settle with me. I still hope it'll be OK but deep down, I have this desperate fear I'll lose him and it'll be worse than never having had him. Do you understand?'

'Yes, I think I do.'

'Anyway, enough of all that. Let's sort you out. Ian's asked you to marry him. Aren't you glad?'

'Of course. I love him, and every girl, no matter how career-minded, wants to have the right person to come home to.'

'But . . . ?'

'I don't know. I think I want my freedom. I want the possibility that a multi-millionaire might sweep me off my feet. I want to know that if a phone call comes out of the blue, offering me the job of a lifetime in the States or wherever, I can go.'

'Well, Ian's flexible. If you got that sort of job, he could go too. He probably would; lighting cameramen can make a living anywhere, and it's not as if he wants to keep you in the kitchen, bottling fruit.'

'You're right. I hadn't thought of it like that.'

'Perhaps you think you should wait till someone takes over your life?'

'Maybe.'

'I watched you and Ian at Christmas, and it certainly is different from Sam and me. But do you think it's possible some people love in a gentler, more real, perhaps more lasting way, and that if you have what we have – had – you encapsulate the whole of a lifetime's loving into a fizzling firework? I want it to last, but maybe it can't.

Perhaps it can't translate to real life. What you have may be better. I feel if I lose Sam, all my capacity for loving will go with him. I'll be spoiled for the rest of time. I'll have had the best, and I'll have to make do with that memory for ever. Should you forgo that intensity in order to achieve lifelong love and companionship? I don't know. Am I making sense?' Helen finished lamely.

'Sort of. I'll think about it.'

'Is he saying "Marry me or we finish"?'

'No, of course not.'

'Well, let it drift for a bit.'

'I don't think I can. He always said he wouldn't settle again. I'm aware that he's offering the whole of himself. I can't cast it back at him. In any case, relationships never mark time, do they? It's not possible.'

'No,' agreed Helen, 'it isn't.'

The next two days passed pleasantly enough. The girls rose early and attended aerobics classes. They had treatments to their faces and the rest of their bodies; they took saunas, swam and ate healthy meals. They were amused by a couple who were clearly having a clandestine affair. Good place for it, thought Helen. The lovers rarely joined in the activities, but when they appeared at mealtimes the man invariably ordered a giant steak. Helen and Laura surmised they had worked out their own individual fitness regime!

The girls played tennis; Laura was a better player than Helen's friend Deidre, and the sessions became compulsive. For all their friendship, their type A personalities reared their ugly heads when faced with such personal competition, and each point was vied for to the bitter end. It was strange that they could channel all their tension into an activity that did not really count.

'I brought a video cassette of the rough cut of my feature with me. I'd like to show it to you, if you can bear it.' It was after dinner, a dinner during which the girls had enjoyed the cabaret of Terry trying to ingratiate himself with the Marvellous Merinda.

'Wouldn't you sooner watch it alone?' asked Helen.

'Not really. I've seen it so often, I'm a bit boggled – I'd like your eye on it. I think it's the best thing I've ever done, but I need to know.'

So Home Farm was not to be without Sam's presence after all.

He loomed large on the screen – in his office, with the resolutely proper and upright Miss Smorthwaite; in the wards, showing care for those in his charge. He cradled a tiny blue baby in his arms, coaxing the child's wan little face into a grin. He was seen talking to anxious relatives. There he was again, tired and drawn after the flight to Holland, and now he was in the operating theatre, his own domain. A nurse wiped his brow, sending a stab of unreasonable jealousy to the depths of Helen's own heart.

'I'm deliberately not doing a *Your Life in Their Hands*,' said Laura. 'I haven't included much blood and gore. I thought it was better to concentrate on Sam as the linchpin.'

Helen tried to make constructive comments. There were more than enough bloody pictures for her taste. The patient's skin, painfully pale, was suddenly stained an angry-yellow with iodine; hemmed green sheets were placed round it; then a substance like cling film was applied. A flash of steel, and a swift knife incised the skin, allowing vivid red to contribute its hue to the already Technicolored scene. The picture became a florid, unidentifiable conglomeration to her, but to Sam every part of it must have meaning. A sizzling poker cut through layers of tissue; it seemed to sever and seal, for it appeared to staunch the blood flow somewhat. A huge mechanical saw came into view, neatly slicing through the breast bone. The operation was a curious mixture of brute strength and finesse. Sam's capable hands, those hands that had explored every part of her, were never still. The camera zoomed into a close-up of his eyes above his mask. They were alert and concerned.

'It's fantastic, Laura,' Helen said, as the tape faded to black. 'It's really great. I'm biased, of course, but it's terrific.'

'He can't go home to stay, you know,' said Laura

solemnly. 'It would be like the Pope giving up his position to work as a missionary in a shanty town. Plenty of people can do that. Some have to accept the responsibility of being leaders.'

Helen was relieved to have her instinct spelled out but was too emotional to say so.

During the next day's aerobic class she tried to forget the video, diverting her mind by working her body harder than was necessary. She allowed herself a glance at the rest of the class. There was Terry, sweating more from his lascivious thoughts as he leered at Merinda's rear end than with any real effort; the clandestine couple, who exercised so close to one another they touched constantly; Merinda's braided hair bobbing in time to the music; two elderly, plump ladies gasping for breath; Laura with a faraway look. She caught Helen's eye and grinned.

'Push through. Push through. Harder! Come on . . .'

Helen viewed her crutch with distaste. Toned up she might be, but unused, unwanted . . .

Lying beside Laura, strapped into the Slendertone bands that promised to disperse dramatically such flab as she had, Helen tried to feel glad she was being so responsible to herself. The bored beauticians in pink were waiting for their lunch break. Helen tried to sleep but the alternately contracting and relaxing electronic impulses were too obtrusive. Laura's eyes were closed, so Helen was surprised when she spoke.

'I watched you talking to Terry this morning,' she said.

'Well, you know the history.'

'He's ghastly, isn't he? Do you know, I'm glad I came here.'

'Why's that?'

'Because I think I know what I want now. I can either be single, with all its possibilities, but knowing the risk is I'll become less glamorous, sadder, more tired and played out. I can wait for the big bang which might transform my life, or ruin it, or I can marry Ian. And that's what I'm going to do – I've just decided.'

'Wonderful!' said Helen. 'Let's go and tell him.

Lynette!' she called, 'get us out of these things. We've had enough.'

The girls in pink stopped the current, hardly believing their good luck.

'OK, phone Ian. I'll see you in the bar. I'll order champagne and tell reception you're checking out.'

'Hang on – I'm not sure.'

'Yes, you are. Do it. Do it for both of us. I don't want you here at supper, OK?'

Laura's eyes sparkled. 'Is it the right thing?'

'Yes, it bloody well is. You've got it in your grasp – take it. You can still have your career and, in addition, marriage, babies, someone to go home to. Come on, Laura – there's no choice. Have it, for God's sake. You're miserable here. You think of Ian all the time.'

'I do,' admitted Laura.

'*Quod erat demonstrandum*,' said Helen. 'Go on. I'll be your bridesmaid.'

'Helen, I adore you.'

'Good. Give my love to Ian.'

So they celebrated. Funny place to get drunk, thought Helen, but she did.

Helen was overjoyed for her friend but felt fractious when she had gone. By the law of averages, both situations could not turn out so well. She had tried to concentrate on Laura and put Sam out of her mind. With Laura gone, he claimed centre stage. She took his letter from her bag. Was this an emergency? She sat on her hands to stop herself from lifting the telephone receiver. Had he phoned home? Was he worried about where she'd gone? Should she call to reassure him? 'Stop that,' she said aloud. She had come here to escape the telephone. If she allowed this one to become operational, there would be no peace.

Saunas are supposed to be hot, she thought, as she licked the perspiration from her upper lip. What was the temperature in Egypt? she wondered.

The Marvellous Merinda walked in, disturbing Helen's reverie of her lover's homeland, the land that might become her own. Merinda's adopted prefix was perfectly apt, reflected Helen, as the black girl slipped out of the towel she had been wrapped in. She was glistening with droplets from the shower. Her legs were endless and her breasts high and proud.

'Ah, the little television lady,' drawled Merinda. 'It's nice to meet you at last.'

'And you.' Helen reddened under the other girl's scrutiny. Perhaps it would go unnoticed; she must be the colour of a mottled beetroot already.

The black girl was tweaking her already erect nipples. Helen watched in fascination as they grew bigger and felt her own augment too, though not so spectacularly.

'Christ, I feel horny,' remarked Merinda, somewhat unnecessarily. 'Four days here and no sex – it's more than flesh and blood can stand.' She laughed revealing her perfectly even white teeth.

'Well, there are men around who'd be happy to oblige.'

'Yeah, that poofy old game-show host for one.'

Helen smiled, knowing how Terry would hate to be described in such a derogatory and dismissive way.

'None of the men take my eye, actually,' Merinda said, continuing to look Helen up and down. It was uncomfortably hot. Helen sprang up, out of the door and into the plunge pool in one continuous movement.

As she returned she found Merinda lying languorously on the bottom shelf, so was forced to climb over her to the one above.

'You're very pretty,' purred the actress. 'Great tits, terrific bush.'

Helen's heart was pounding. She was excited and appalled. Perhaps she had misheard.

'Have you ever had sex with a woman?'

'No – no, I haven't,' replied Helen. 'I, um, I didn't know that you . . . well, that you . . . er . . .'

'Were gay?'

'Well, yes.'

'I don't know that I am. I like most things. But you're definitely the most attractive person here. I'd love to lick those little pink nipples of yours. I could really show you a good time.'

'I have a boyfriend,' said Helen, hating herself for the sound of her puritanical schoolgirlish voice.

'So? He's not here, is he? Relax.'

Helen shook her head.

'Oh, well,' said the other girl. 'You've got to try, haven't you? If you change your mind . . .'

Helen shook her head again, grabbed her towel and made to leave.

'Honey child, you don't know what you're missing.'

It seemed to Helen that grown-up, sardonic laughter followed her all the way to her room. Ridiculous to be so upset, but her blushes would not subside. She rang down and ordered dinner, but when it came she only picked at it despite the fact she was not trying to lose weight. She tried to read. She watched the news. She walked round the room and everywhere she turned she saw Merinda's pouting lips, her raised eyebrows, her sculptured torso. What would it be like to kiss her? To lie hard on another woman with two sets of breasts mashed between them? To press the button that would trigger delight in another female? To thrust fingers into that secret hole and feel another's excitement and silky warmth extending and vibrating with mounting passion? What would happen if she succumbed to Merinda's kisses from that soft, ripe mouth and allowed her taut and neglected body to tingle and tighten still more? To join her explosive cries with those of a similar pitch?

Her shriek of surrender shattered the silence. She lay, panting, on the bed; she was on fire, her breasts were bursting. Once was not enough. She leapt up to turn the television sound up high and then lay stroking and loving her own body. Disturbed by her fantasy of the black girl, she conjured up Sam's image, re-running the close-ups in her mind of their most erotic moments. Her cries of release were, to her relief, just as loud, her orgasm just as shattering, her beating heart even harder to quiet.

Next she allowed herself to remember Terry. She had been too inexperienced when she had known him to enjoy him as much as she might today. She pictured his penis. She could see it quite clearly. She had an image then of an identity parade of penises of all her past lovers. Could she put a name to each one without seeing their faces? The idea amused her. She considered calling him and lying outstretched with her legs apart as he walked in. She imagined him taking her immediately as another climax shook her trembling, glowing body.

And now, for the most daring of them all: she who had been brought up in Bournemouth was in bed with all three, being taken, licked, kissed, stroked, torn apart. They were all her slaves, anxious to please. A spasm began in her throat, another in her toes. They raced to their goal, fusing in a giant embrace. The shuddering and throbbing ecstasy came, and she knew nothing more.

Her dreams were full of Sam and Terry and Merinda but, unlike in her daytime imaginings, each spurned her. There were no kisses, no cuddles, no handshakes, no faces. She was running, hoping for a kindly word or some form of contact, but they ran faster, offering only the backs of their heads, refusing to turn.

She woke, frantic, to an empty day and the bleakest of futures. She punched the pillow. 'I'm losing my mind and it's all your fault, Sam. I hate you . . . I love you. I love you, goddamit!' she shouted and burst into tears. She contemplated going home but was not ready to be there alone. She longed to escape, but the health farm had been her bolt hole and now it no longer was. Where in the world could she find refuge? Was she to be condemned to a life on the run?

Swimming up and down the pool, she forced herself to concentrate on her movements. After last night her legs felt as if she had run a marathon. She focused on her strokes, pushing herself on and on in the hope that she could obliterate the desperate ache in her mind and heart. Did Sam care? Had he called? Was he worried? Did it matter? Would he come back married? Each length brought fresh torture. Where would it end?

'Have another drink.'

'I shouldn't, Terry. We've hardly eaten anything for

days and we've had a lot of booze already.' They were in a country pub not far from the health farm.

'Who's counting, baby? You're going home tomorrow anyway.'

'Well, that's true.'

He staggered, rather unsteadily, she noticed, to the bar. They were the object of some interest to the locals; he was enjoying it. It was strange that he seemed so inebriated. Perhaps he was drinking doubles to her singles. He was definitely strident; his account of a very blue joke was clearly audible from the other side of the room. How odd that he had once seemed so fanciable, and how embarrassing that she had welcomed him into her erotic fantasies the night before.

He sat closer. His leg touched hers. They had another drink. There were beads of sweat oozing from his brow and in between the strands of his carefully arranged hair. He groped her knee and suddenly his lips were on hers. Despite her distaste and the whisky on his breath, she returned his kiss. She closed her eyes. I need love . . . I need it now, she thought. 'No matter how lonely you get . . .' Sam's words echoed in her mind. Damn him. He had probably kissed Hamaida. Perhaps they were entwined at this very moment. Perhaps he was loving her, penetrating her. Perhaps this time she was enjoying it. She grabbed at Terry hungrily and pushed her tongue deep into his mouth. But it was the wrong mouth, the wrong man.

She excused herself and ran to the ladies' room. She peered blearily at her drunken image. 'What sort of whore are you?' she demanded of herself.

She walked back as straight as she could and announced she was leaving. 'Goodnight, Terry' she said with as much dignity as she could muster.

'Christ! You're a fucking prick-tease, aren't you? I wish I'd never set eyes on you again. Go to hell!'

She ran to the health farm, stumbling along the dark country lanes that had not struck her as spooky from the comfortable interior of Terry's car. 'I don't deserve anything, least of all Sam. God, I'm a cow.' She was back in the singles scene, the scene she thought she had abandoned for ever. Well, it could be fun but it was strewn with pitfalls, like other women's menopausal husbands, fading stars and drunks in bars. Was that all she could expect? Was it all she was worth? She had thought she was done with it. If Sam would rescue her, she would not have to be a part of it. But she was; he was not here. He had let her down. It was difficult to sleep.

They gave her a packed lunch when she left the health farm, in case she felt faint on the motorway. It was a kind thought. The day was bright and sunny, and her spirits rose as though she were a child going on a picnic.

The flat beckoned but she thought she would leave it for a while, so she drove instead to a cinema in Curzon Street which often showed films she enjoyed. She saw *A Room with a View* and lost herself to its beauty.

Afterwards, in the summer streets of London, she found a replica of the dappled sunlight that had so moved her on the screen. Life was still good. She was rested; she was calm; she was capable. Sam's energy was hers. He could not walk away from the most meaningful experience of his life.

A gentleman of the road lurched up to her, disturbing her reverie. He was smelly and unkempt but not dangerous. 'Got the price of a cuppa, love?'

Why was there always pain in pleasure? Why must her happiness be at the expense of Hamaida's? Why was there homelessness in the midst of affluence and ugliness in the face of loveliness? She sighed; part of life's paradox, she supposed. She smiled at the tramp, who had short, brown stumps in place of teeth, and gave him all the cash she had, about twelve pounds. He hopped away before she could regret her generosity.

Perhaps the man had been a test. He had needed something she could afford to give, so it was right that she should. Sam needed all that she was, and when he had sorted his life out, she would be able to bestow it on him. Tomorrow he would return and tell her all was well. How could she have doubted the outcome? It was time to go home. She could be there now. She was at peace.

Chapter Ten

'How was the rest of it?' Laura popped her head round Helen's door.

'Pretty uneventful. I was propositioned by Merinda, then by Terry.'

'Heavens, they obviously couldn't wait for me to leave. Did you accept?'

'No. Thought about it, though. How's life with you?'

'It's wonderful. I don't know why I got in such a state.'

'Well, it's a big step.'

'Have you heard from Sam?'

'No. He's not due back till today – that's if he comes back.'

The optimism of the previous night had been replaced by pessimism the moment Helen had awakened to Monday and a new week.

After her talk with Laura, Helen went to the ten-thirty planning meeting. It was almost as if she had not been away. At its conclusion Derek called her back. 'How are you now, Helen?'

'I'm fine.'

'Did you have a good rest?'

'Let's say it was different.' She laughed, scooped up the projected programme running order and left.

Sue turned up in her office shortly afterwards, bearing a large, black dustbin liner. 'This is all the post that came last week.'

'I love your filing system,' said Helen drily.

'Yeah, well . . .'

'Have you opened anything?'

'No.'

'OK. Go away – I'll sort through it and we'll deal with it later.'

With Sue gone, she spent a couple of hours sifting through the accumulated backlog. She was happy to be here where she belonged and, though she was anxious for the phone call that would announce Sam's return, she busied herself to allay her fears.

By lunchtime there was still no word from him, and she was beginning to panic about the evening. She had not thought as far as that, but now, if he did not return or contact her, she wondered how she would occupy the empty hours. Filling the week in the health farm had been easy by comparison; there was so much stimulus and she had gone knowing Sam was not a part of it. He was a part of today, however, and now that he had failed, so far, to put in an appearance, she was bereft.

In the afternoon she recorded an item with a former monk who had rejoined the world in order to set up a farming project for homeless boys in India. She became absorbed in the man and his work and was enjoying talking to him after the interview over a pot of tea in the green room.

The phone rang. It was one of the girls from the main switchboard. 'Oh, Helen, the newsroom didn't seem to know where you were. I have a Mr Aziz for you. Do you want to take it?' Helen looked at her interviewee and wondered where in the building she might find privacy. At the same time she was so worried that Sam might ring off that she asked for the call to be put through where she was.

'Helen?'

'Yes. Hello, Sam,' she said, trying to sound casual.

'Are you all right?'

'Yes.'

'I'm back. Can I see you?'

'Of course.'

'Can you talk?'

'Not really.'

'OK I've got tickets for *Cats* – I know you've always

wanted to see it. Can you meet me at the theatre after the programme?'

Her heart was racing. 'That would be very nice.'

'It starts at seven forty-five.'

'I'll try to be there by seven-thirty.'

The programme went well, and Helen could not help but feel satisfied to be back in the driving seat. She met Laura in hospitality afterwards. 'You were great. It's not the same when you're not here.'

'Thanks, Laura. I don't suppose that's true, but I need to hear it none the less.'

After a quick drink she walked to the dressing-room and selected the navy-blue Parigi dress she had worn on their first luncheon date.

As the taxi drew up at the New London, she saw Sam before he saw her. He was anxiously checking every arrival on foot and by car. By the time she had paid the driver he was at her side. He stood back for a second and then swept her into his arms, kissing her passionately. They were surrounded by ticket touts and tourists who were hoping to get into the show. His kiss took her breath away and, oblivious to the crowd on the pavement, she returned it. There was a ripple of applause from the onlookers. They might have failed to get theatre tickets, but they were compensated by a display they had not bargained for.

Blushing slightly, Sam hustled her inside. Seated in the curious auditorium in the round, she asked, 'What happened?'

'I'll tell you later.'

The lights came up like cats' eyes all over the theatre. The music began; it was loud. There was no more time for questions. She leant back in her seat, breathing deeply, grateful to be beside the man she loved but desperate to know her fate. He reached for her hand and squeezed it tightly. She was finding it difficult to breathe.

'Do you feel faint?' he asked when there was a break in the music. She shook her head. 'You do,' he insisted.

'Does it make you feel better if I agree?' she hissed.

'Do you get a kick out of knowing how much you affect me?'

The music began again. His hand stiffened over hers. She knew she had been unkind and that while they were attempting to absorb themselves in this total theatrical experience, they were wounding each other.

The next time there was quiet she whispered, 'Did you ask her to marry you?'

There was a pause. She willed him to answer.

He nodded.

'Did she say yes?'

The music resumed.

He nodded again.

The production was every bit as sensational as she had been promised. In fact, like her situation, it was unreal. The drama in their own lives, however, was occupying most of her attention. She was sitting beside the love of her life; their legs and bodies and arms were touching. She knew he adored her, yet he had just asked another woman to be his wife. The interval came eventually.

'We can't talk here, Helen. Put it out of your mind. Have a drink. Come back with me later.'

She smiled blankly. She sipped the glass of wine he brought her and fought back her tears. She must not weep here, surrounded by the interested glances of people who recognised her. For a second she felt she might lose control totally. She visualised herself running amok, smashing every glass in sight and then racing out of the theatre. Instead she kissed Sam almost platonically and excused herself.

In the privacy of the lavatory she shed a few tears. She emerged and faced herself in the mirror. She repaired her make-up with the intention of re-joining Sam and behaving as though everything were normal. The bells for the second half sounded; she lit a cigarette, not caring that the other stragglers were party to her distress. She felt sick and realised suddenly she was going to vomit. She lurched back into the closet and retched noisily until her stomach was empty, aware in the midst of her sickness that someone in her position should not behave so badly.

As she returned shakily from the ladies' room the bar was almost empty and the unmistakable sounds of a show in full swing were filtering through the heavy double doors.

Sam took one look at the face and the state of the woman he loved. 'I think we'd better catch the second half another day, don't you?' She bit her lip. 'Or did you want to see the rest?' She shook her head. 'Let's go then.'

It was much easier to find a taxi mid-evening than it would have been at the end of the performance. Sam gave the driver his address and cuddled her to stop her shivering, though neither of them spoke till they reached his house.

He poured two brandies.

She spoke first, brushing her hair out of her eyes. 'Tell me what happened.'

'Nothing at first. Where were you, by the way?'

'I asked you not to ring.'

'I know, but in the end I did and you were never there.'

'I went to a health farm.'

'Oh,' he said, gulping at his drink. 'Did you have a good time?'

'Sam . . .'

'OK, it's just that I was frantic. I even rang Laura, but Ian answered.'

'Did he tell you where I was?'

'I didn't speak to him. I felt stupid. I put the phone down.'

'Laura was with me.'

'Oh. Good.'

'Sam, please get on with it.'

He took a deep breath. 'At first I met with my family. I also visited several hospitals.'

'And . . . ?'

'They need someone like me.'

Helen nodded. 'What about Hamaida?'

'We met a few times, with her brothers.'

'Did she say anything?'

'Not much. She never does. She's very quiet – boring, really. She certainly doesn't know the person I've become.'

'But you went back to talk, to straighten things out, to see what had to be done.'

'That's right. So two nights ago we went out . . . just the two of us.'

'And . . . ?'

'She said, "I don't want to spend the rest of my life alone." And I said, which was true, "Neither do I." '

'And then?' Helen prompted.

'She asked if I intended coming home. I said I'd thought about it, and she said she'd always loved me.'

'She doesn't even know you!'

'Helen, sweetheart,' he sighed. 'I'm trying to tell you what happened. Let me finish.'

In answer Helen put her head in her hands.

'She cried and said I'd only ever been interested in medicine and furthering my own career. She said I'd forgotten the needs of my own people.'

'Sounds like moral blackmail to me.'

'Anyway,' he went on, ignoring the accusation, 'there's that and the fact that she isn't marriageable and she cares. There's a stigma attached to being single in our country. She isn't like you, with a career. She told me quite categorically, she doesn't want to die a spinster.'

'She turned you down before. Why was that?'

'I wasn't kind enough, I suppose – I don't know. Anyway, it doesn't matter now.'

'But she's trapping you. She laid the trap all those years ago. All this time you've struggled to keep out of it and now, now that you love me and you've finally found someone you care for, you're punishing yourself by walking back into the very situation you've tried so hard to escape.'

'That's right. Exactly. But I took away her virginity.'

'You told me she begged you to. You said you gave in and that you didn't even enjoy it.'

'That was the truth. I didn't.'

'Was it so terrific for her then?'

'Not in the way you mean, but it was significant. It meant, in her eyes, we belonged to each other. Do you understand?'

Helen nodded. She sat beside him, crying silently. 'God above, I think I could give you up if I felt she really wanted you – but where the hell is she? I know she's been ill recently, but she's never bloody here. Surely if she couldn't live without you, she'd be at your side, appreciating you, supporting what you do.' He held her as the tears flowed. At length she stood up wearily. 'I'll ring for a taxi.'

'No.'

She looked at him uncomprehendingly. 'Why not?'

'Because I love you and I can't let you go like this. Please, Helen, please come to bed with me.' He did not wait for an answer but took her drink from her and led her upstairs to the bedroom, where he undressed her carefully and lovingly. He touched and kissed and owned her, and she was powerless to argue.

She was in the middle of a period, which he could not fail to notice. Afterwards she reached for her handbag and rummaged through its contents till she found a tampon. She was about to go to the bathroom when he stopped her.

'Let me put it in for you, Helen.'

She hesitated. Surely this was a bit sick – it was such a private ritual.

'Helen.'

Drawn back to him, she handed over the little package. He unwrapped it and placed it deep inside her, making more of the operation than it warranted. 'I'll never let you go, Helen,' he said. 'You're mine – the whole of you. Never forget that. No one else must have it.' He caressed her. It was dreadfully wrong and inevitably right.

It was four o'clock when she woke again. Sam was sleeping, holding her tightly. This is the man I love, she thought, and he is engaged to another. She shook him. 'Sam, I love you, but I won't be the dog begging for crumbs under your table. I have to go.' Like her, he was exhausted, and he lay as motionless as though he were dead.

She left the warmth of his bed and dressed hurriedly. She called a taxi and, when it arrived, made her exit without a farewell. In the sanctuary of her own flat she wept. She could not believe she had any tears left, but still they came.

She was disturbed by the persistent buzzing of her doorbell. She looked at the clock; it was seven forty-five. She supposed it was the postman with a recorded delivery or registered package. She put a pillow over her head; he could come back another day. The noise went on and on. Eventually she clambered out of bed and picked up the entry phone. 'Helen, it's Sam.'

As he appeared at her front door he looked pale and tired and frightened. He was carrying a pint of milk. 'The milkman doesn't generally call here,' she said. 'Let me in, Helen.'

She stood back as he entered and closed the door behind him. He put the milk down and clung to her. She felt her tears begin again.

'What are we going to do?' he asked.

'I don't know. I don't know anything.'

'Your eyes are swollen, darling. You can't work like this.'

'I have to work.'

'Is your head aching?'

'Yes.'

'Go back to bed. I'll make you some tea.'

Like a child, she did as she was told. She pulled the quilt right up to her chin. Almost immediately he appeared with a white napkin filled with icecubes. He sat on the edge of the bed and put the pack on her head. He left without saying anything and then returned with two wrung-out tea bags which he placed on her eyes. She lay still, meekly grateful for his ministry. 'You have a great bedside manner,' she said at last. He stroked her hand and disappeared again. A few minutes later she heard the tinkling of china as he carried in a tray of tea. He poured out two cups, removed the tea bags from her eyes and cradled her as he put the first cup to her lips. He was so gentle and caring that it brought fresh tears to her eyes.

'Helen,' he sighed. 'I can cure people who've been left for dead, and now I feel as if I'm destroying the only person I've ever loved. I have to go – I'm operating. Let's talk tonight.'

She nodded, afraid to speak.

'I don't see how you can work today,' he said. 'I don't see how I can either.'

'We both have to – that's all there is to it. Anyway, I'm covering a royal visit,' she said, as though it were quite immaterial.

'Helen,' he said from the doorway, 'please believe one thing. I do care – I care desperately. I love you.' With that he left.

'Helen, you look terrible,' said Derek, when she turned up in the newsroom. 'I don't want to know what's going on in your private life, unless you want to tell me, but a week off wasn't enough. I strongly urge you to take some more time – soon. I'll leave you to sort out when you can go, but you must.'

'All right, Derek. Let me just go and put on some make-up.'

'Are you going to get yourself together in time to do this bloody thing in Regent Street?'

'Of course.'

He raised his eyebrows. 'Jesus, Helen,' he sighed, 'I hope you're right. Here are the passes. Meet the crew in an hour.'

Laura happened to saunter into the make-up department shortly afterwards; Helen got the distinct impression she had been sent by their boss. 'Are you OK?' Helen nodded. 'From where I'm standing I wouldn't say so.' Helen pulled a face. 'Do you want to talk about it?'

'No thanks.'

'Well, you know where I am if you want me.'

Looking in the make-up mirror, Helen wondered where to begin. Her eyes, for all Sam's treatment, were so swollen she could not decide whether the use of cosmetics would camouflage or highlight the problem. She settled for eyedrops, a smudge of grey eye-liner to counteract the redness and a dash of mascara. Next she used a damp sponge to apply some foundation to her blotchy face. It would have to do. She would keep out of the pictures – after all, the viewers would have eyes only for the Princess.

The streets were bustling, the atmosphere electric. It was a novel idea to have the Princess meet underprivileged children from all around the globe in the world's largest toy shop. The crew were waiting, and if they noticed Helen was not looking quite herself, they made no comment.

'Get her arrival, Jamie,' Helen shouted above the hubbub, 'and we'll follow her into the building. If you can get close enough, we'll catch her chatting with the children. If not, we'll vox pop some kids afterwards. I'd better do a commentary on what she's wearing, but I can do that back at base.'

From her vantage point she could easily see the limousine gliding into view. She was surrounded by hordes of excited youngsters waving Union Jacks and chatting happily to the mounted policemen. The car stopped. Two detectives jumped out, and the Princess raised herself from her seat.

The power of the blast knocked Helen to the ground. The players in this decimated pageant froze like particles of dust caught in a beam of light. Suddenly there was uproar – smoke, wailing, screaming. Bits of building and unspeakable horrors of the holocaust flew through the air.

The royal car took off like a rocket and Helen thought she saw the Princess fall back and hit her head.

There was utter confusion. The detectives, so lively a second before, were a contorted mass of bloody tissue. They were probably dead. In her attempt to get to her feet Helen touched a leg and recoiled in disbelief as she saw it was not attached to anybody. A police horse lay writhing and dying with its guts spewing out on to a slab of pavement. For a moment she forgot her report as she tried to comfort a little girl who was disfigured beyond recognition. She cradled the fragments in her arms and sensed the second the child's struggle for life ceased.

A policeman took her arm. 'Leave me alone!' she screeched. 'I've got a job to do.' Where was Jamie? 'What did you get?' she yelled.

'I got it all – I got it all! I never saw pictures like it.' He was wandering around, running his blood-stained hands through his sticky hair.

'Are you hurt?' she asked.

'I don't think so – but I think Charlie may have . . . bought it. He caught the full . . . And where's Cyril?'

The soundman was being sick.

'I must go back,' said Helen. 'This'll make the lunch-time bulletin. I think we were the only crew here, and I was only doing it for the fashion and the children. She surveyed the carnage about her and crumpled. Someone carried her to an ambulance.

Inside the swaying vehicle the sound of sirens was waking her from nothingness to a nightmare. 'Get me out of here!' she shouted to the driver. 'I have to go back to the station.'

'Orders is orders, miss. We're to take you to St Thomas's. We're nearly there.'

Helen saved her strength; she would get a taxi at the hospital. 'You ought to be checked over,' said the quietly spoken nurse in casualty.

'Later,' she shouted.

A taxi drew up. She ran for it.

The building was buzzing.

Helen cut the piece and recorded a commentary. It went out at one. She then began recutting it, with more footage that had come in, for a longer version for six o'clock. She watched a woman on the screen cuddling and weeping over a dead child. It was like watching an actress in a drama.

The rest of the day was a blur. The Chairman, whom she hardly knew, came to congratulate her. She barely spoke to him as she and the film editor sifted the shots, seeking the most graphic, then eliminating them as too gory to be put before the great British public at its tea. The components came together, and she recorded another commentary with quotes on security from the Home Secretary and a run-down of figures of the victims to date.

At last it was done. She sat, a small, shaking figure, in the calm after the storm.

Derek came into view suddenly. 'I'm sending you to hospital, Helen.'

'Oh, no. I've got to do the programme.'

'You're not fit.'

'I *am* bloody fit. Have I let you down? I'm OK.'

'You haven't let us down,' he said calmly, as though she were an overwrought child. 'You were never engaged as a hard-news reporter, but no one could have done it better. However, enough's enough. Laura will link the programme. You must go for a check-up, but perhaps you ought to change first.'

Helen followed his gaze, taking in for the first time the spectacle of her blood-spattered pink suit. She felt like a mawkish latter-day Jacqueline Kennedy. Weariness soaked her body, and now there was a ringing in her ears. 'All right, Derek,' she sighed.

Gary, the researcher, was behind their boss. He could not resist adding his verdict. 'Have to hand it to you, Helen – you're in a different league now. If you don't win an award, there'll be no justice.'

A tasteless vision of herself in an off-the-shoulder blue taffeta gown, smiling and acknowledging the applause at the Royal Television Society ceremony they attended every year, disturbed her thoughts. Derek reprimanded Gary for his gross lack of timing, but Helen was aware his blood was up too.

Disgusted at them all and at the business she was in, she rose slowly from her seat and walked out. The bystanders in the newsroom watched her progress and dropped away in silent appreciation of the fact she had been there and had seen things that the frailty of man cannot cope with. She had a ridiculous sensation of Moses parting the Red Sea. Red . . . red . . . oceans of red.

In the hospital they examined her, pumped her full of

something sedative and left her in a dark room to spend the night.

Laura appeared, all eyes in a white face.

'How many dead now?' Helen asked.

''Bout thirty,' said Laura weakly, 'and dozens and dozens injured – terribly injured.'

'Who could have done it?'

'It was an Arab group,' said Laura, avoiding the anguished eyes of her friend.

Sam chose that moment to enter the room. His face was as white as theirs. No one spoke, so Helen closed her eyes.

When she woke Laura had gone; Sam was holding her hand. 'Helen, I should have been here, but I didn't know. I was operating till seven. Someone said I must be proud of you. I didn't know what they were talking about and then . . . I couldn't find you, and all the time I was thinking of all the terrible things I'm doing to you and how my own kind very nearly finished you off.' Tears were trickling down his face.

For the first time Helen was struck by a sense of her own mortality and she wept too. She spoke first. 'It's nothing to do with you. Arabs aren't all terrorists any more than the Irish are.'

'No,' he whispered, 'but, God, Helen – you might have died and . . .'

'Forget it, Sam.' His mouth met hers and she put her arms round his neck to pull him closer. 'Sam, Sam, don't leave me – ever. Make love to me.'

He straightened up. 'What – here?'

'Yes, here. I want you. I want you now. I want you to show me that bitterness and hatred won't take over the world, that love counts more. Lie down with me.'

'I can't, Helen. It wouldn't be right.'

Inside her head she was screaming. The screams, the sirens and the bells were pummelling her brain. Someone pushed Sam away. Where had all these people come from? Something sharp jabbed into her and the noise stopped.

*

She left the next morning against their advice but promising not to work for a few days.

Back in the studios, she went straight to Make-up and washed her hair. She kept the stream from the jet to a minimum; the water hurt her head. She looked at the stranger in the mirror and, in the absence of her own face, applied cosmetics to the one peering back at her.

'I didn't expect you today, Helen,' said Derek.

'Why ever not?' she asked coldly. 'It was just another job.'

'What did the doctors say?'

'They said I was fine,' she lied.

She sat in her office. Laura appeared. 'I don't think you should be here, Helen.'

'Well, I am and that's that.'

The phone rang. 'Helen, what are you doing there? I'm coming for you right away.'

'No, you're not, Sam. I have things to do. Don't interfere.'

'I'm entitled to interfere. I love you.'

'When you go back to get married, I'll need this job. Go away.'

The pain came back – all of yesterday's events and the impossible hurt that the only person who had ever mattered was not hers. Resolutely she pushed it away.

Everyone was surprised to see her at ten-thirty.

'Today we're beginning our series on speciality acts working in clubs and theatres round the country this summer,' said Ron. 'We've got a knife thrower coming in – the sort of chap who'll never hit the big time but never stops working. We'll record in the afternoon. I wouldn't risk it live.'

'Why wouldn't you risk it live?' asked Helen, remembering the live events of the day before.

'Well,' said Ron, 'this is a bit difficult after all you went through yesterday . . . I was going to ask you to act as his assistant and do the interview while he throws knives at you.'

'OK,' she said.

Several people exchanged glances.

'You don't have to,' said Ron.

'I said I'll do it,' she snapped.

Back in her office Helen mechanically answered the mail. She did not send for Sue; it was easier to draft her letters in longhand than face any more human contact than was absolutely necessary.

At lunchtime she wandered into the canteen, picked up a tuna fish salad and took it back to her own room. She ate without tasting it and skimmed the newspapers at the same time. Her distressed figure, holding the dead child, stared at her from the front page of every one of them.

She tried to gather together all the strands of the last two, unreal days. Why had she been so unkind to Sam? She supposed because he had spurned her twice: once by getting engaged to that wilting, infertile, incapable Egyptian bitch and once by not screwing her senseless when it was all she longed for. She should not want him in a gift, but she did, she did, she did. So – she would fight. If he could not find a solution, she would.

She rang the company's travel agent and almost balked at the cost of her plan, but this was not a moment for parsimony. Her life hung in the balance and so did his. Had Laura not said he must not bury his talents in the desert? And, even if he did, should she not be there?

It was time to meet her guests, the Great Jackerello and the glamorous Gloria. Jackerello was about forty-five. He had a scarf tied gipsy-style around his neck; he was blond and in very good shape. Gloria looked older, though perhaps it was just that the passing years had treated her less kindly. Helen chatted to them in the make-up room, though, being good pros, they did not need much attention. In fact, Gloria, had to be toned down a little for the cameras; her eyelashes in particular were a source of wonder to Helen. Bambi would have died for them.

Once dressed, the make-up made more sense. Jackerello retained his scarf, which was all that adorned the upper half of his body, but below the waist he was poured into a pair of fringed leather trousers which emphasised his neat and very sexy bottom. Gloria wore a sleeveless fringed mini dress with a plunging neckline. Her stomach was a little too rounded, but she was a well-preserved woman. Her legs, in their black fishnets, were shapely and unmarred by varicose veins and her arms were tanned, if a little flabby on the undersides.

The floor manager asked Helen if she was nervous. To please him she said she was, but in truth she was numb. She stood up against the board and the knife thrower, just to get his eye in with a different assistant, threw his first knife. It swiftly embedded its blade by Helen's left ear and continued quivering for a full ten seconds. Suddenly she felt very frightened indeed, but it was too late to duck out now. She had wanted to impress her colleagues with her ability to carry on, no matter what. This seemed the definitive way to do it.

'If you're ready,' said the floor manager, 'we'll go. Start the clock . . . Forty-five seconds.'

'We're just identifying the tape,' she told the Great Jackerello, 'so they pull the right reel off the shelf when it goes out later.'

'Oh,' he said and then, as she looked around the crowded studio floor with its monitors, lights and cables, he continued, 'Clever, innit? And complicated, all this.'

'Not as clever as what you're about to do, I hope . . .'

'Quiet, please,' said the floor manager. The monitor faded to black. He waved his arm and Helen was away.

'How do you become a knife thrower?' she asked.

'It's in my blood,' he said.

'I hope that's an inappropriate choice of word,' she said. 'Have you ever injured anybody?'

'Oh, yes,' he said nonchalantly. 'My wife Gloria's been to hospital several times. Just little grazes, mind, nothing serious.'

'All right,' said Helen. 'Well, I'd sooner Gloria did the act than me, but just to get the feel of it I'll start it off for her. Where do I stand, and what do I do?'

He put her up against the board and told her not to move.

'I wouldn't dream of it,' she said.

'You will, though. Everyone does. You'll flinch, but

you won't realise it. Doesn't matter, though. I know what you'll do and I'll throw in a way that compensates for it.'

'I just hope I react predictably then.'

The knife whizzed past her right ear at tremendous speed and lodged itself into the board. She gasped and tried to think of the next question. The second knife found its place by her left ear. She felt hemmed in and still she could not speak. He threw one more knife and she found her voice. 'Stop!' she cried, 'I've been a guinea pig long enough. I've found out what it feels like and it's terrible. Let's bring in Gloria to take over.'

'Cut to camera two and go in tight on Helen. She's gone a very funny colour,' said the director in the box.

Back on the studio floor, Helen watched as the glamorous Gloria smiled while knives outlined her body. Jackerello answered all the questions, and the interview turned out quite light-heartedly. Time was up; she asked the artist to throw one more knife and the director cut to a close-up of it as it stuck into the board only an inch away from his worthy assistant. The studio froze; the floor manager put his finger to his lips. After ten seconds, as the cameras faded, he said, 'OK, everyone, relax. We'll just wait for a clear.'

'What's a clear?' asked Jackerello.

'Well, there are two reasons we might have to go again. One is if they didn't like the content, they hadn't got the right shots, or they didn't like my questions, and the other is if there were a technical fault on the tape. That's what they're checking now. I hope it's all right because I wouldn't want to do it again.

'That's a clear,' said the floor manager, as the sound men moved in swiftly to unmike Helen and the guests. 'Back at five-thirty, everyone.'

Helen had tea with the knife throwers and promised them she would mention where they were performing for the summer when they cut to her live after the recorded close-up of the last knife.

'Bloody nerve-racking, this television business, I think,' said the Great Jackerello.

'It's nothing compared with what you do . . . or Gloria, come to that.'

'You get used to it.' Gloria spoke for the first time. 'Bit monotonous sometimes. I find meself working out what I'm cooking for supper while he's doing it.'

'You don't!' he said indignantly.

'I do,' she replied in a bored voice.

Sam was in reception after the show. Without a word he hustled her outside and into his car, where he kissed her possessively. 'Have you got some sort of fucking death wish?'

Tears stung her eyes; perhaps she had.

'Helen, for God's sake.' He was breathing deeply, trying to calm his anger. 'Yesterday you were nearly killed by accident and today you might well have been killed by design.'

'It's a funny old business I'm in, isn't it?' she said flippantly.

Driving along the Embankment, she sneaked a look at him. She knew he had noticed; the stern set of his jaw relaxed. He was so beautiful and so vital to her. She reached over and stroked his left thigh. His eyes transmitted a look so full of love that she tingled all over. Could there be worse to come? Maybe, but surely the gods could not separate them in the end. They could try but she . . . she would not allow it.

The Italian restaurant was crowded, and they were quickly drawn into its convivial Mediterranean ambience.

After dinner he suggested they should talk and offered her the choice of staying where they were or going home.

'Let's try here. It might prevent me from getting too emotional. Let's both attempt to keep level-headed. As I see it, Sam, and I'm trying to see straight, the only problem I have is that I'm totally loopy for love of you. You, on the other hand, have loads of problems. I want you to write them down now. We'll make a list and then we'll see what you've found.' He nodded. She squeezed his hand as she observed his face, pinched and white in the candlelight. 'Right. Put down: (1) Hamaida; (2) country; (3) mother; (4) father; (5) career; (6) honour.'

He followed her instructions.

She opened the discussion. 'How strong is the pull of your country?'

'Fairly and growing. I do believe they have a right to expect I'll return with my skills.'

'How important is Hamaida to you?'

'I'm sorry for her.'

'Do you love her?'

'No. Let me explain, Helen. Arabs on the whole don't put their women on pedestals. We tend, in my sort of class anyway, to marry them, give them children, provide them with prosperity and servants and expect them just to be there. I'm over-simplyfying it, but basically that's how it is.'

'Do you love me like an Englishman then?'

'I don't know. It's the English part of me that met you. I love you like a man possessed – God knows where nationality comes into it.'

'If we were married, would you treat me as a typical Arab wife?'

'Never.'

'Let me ask you this then: would honour be served if you went back, married Hamaida, set her up financially and left again to come and live with me? I don't need to be married to you. Would that satisfy her need for status, show respect to your father's memory and keep your mother happy?'

'I don't know, Helen. Not my mother certainly, the rest possibly, but it wouldn't solve my dilemma about working there.'

'No, I see that.' Helen looked around the thronging restaurant. At the next table sat a woman in the last stages of pregnancy. She bore her huge stomach as proudly as a trophy, and her male companion attended to her every whim with pride.

'Look, Helen, can we continue this at home? I want you to myself. I need to hold you.'

She nodded. 'Let me get the bill for once,' she said.

'No! I've told you before . . .'

'OK, OK, you Tarzan, me give in.'

They both laughed. Some things were still normal.

He did not ask which house they should go to but drove instinctively to his own. Inside the dimly lit lounge she stood for a moment looking at the little sculpture of the dancer.

'Did you see that woman?'

'Which woman?' asked Helen, pretending not to know.

'The pregnant woman at the next table. That should have been you, Helen.' He reached for her and she felt for a moment all might be well. He did love her – he could not let her go.

They stood bound by their joint passion and Helen moved her hand lower till she found the growing swelling of his desire. She stroked him and he closed his eyes, then, taking her arms with both hands, he put her away from him and sat her on the sofa. 'Look, love,' he said, 'I went back to sort this. I obviously haven't. I took you two nights ago because I needed you so much, but I shouldn't have done. Then yesterday I nearly lost you for ever. It's time for decisions not . . . I can't make love to you.'

She was as stunned as if he had slapped her round the face. 'All right,' she said viciously, 'I'll buy a vibrator.'

'Helen, that's crude.'

'Look, I don't have to apologise for my sexuality. You awakened something in me – I can't just lock it all away again.' She strode away from him and lit a cigarette. She turned. He looked so forlorn she drew a deep breath and said more kindly, 'Would you consider talking to someone else? I'm too close to help.'

'I don't really have any special friends,' he said sadly. 'Well, there is one. He's a surgeon in Paris. But other than that . . .'

'I meant professionally.'

'A psychiatrist? Helen, I'm not mad.'

'I'm not suggesting you are, but you are under an intolerable strain. It would be a responsible thing to do.'

'The answer lies within me,' he said in a tone that

brooked no further argument. He was at once every inch the invincible Arab.

She tried a different tack. 'You have divorce in your country. Could you go back and marry her, get divorced, look after her financially, wait a couple of years and then let me come out and join you?'

'Darling, I don't know. You've never been there. I don't know that you could settle.'

'I don't know either. There's another option, if you can ignore the feeling you should work in Egypt, you could marry her there but live here and we could still have our baby. You could visit her a couple of times a year or something.'

'Darling, angel.' He took her hand and kissed it. 'I love you. You want to make the whole world better. But, sweetheart, don't offer any more. You're demeaning yourself. You told me you wouldn't accept the crumbs from under the table.'

She took a deep breath. 'I know and I shouldn't . . . but I love you.'

Tears, tears and more tears.

There was nothing for it: her plan had to be activated. She had, perhaps unconsciously, wondered if her harshness today, coupled with the drama of yesterday, might have elicited the response they both wanted. Could she still love him despite his indecision in the face of the past forty-eight hours? She almost wished she were free of it but she was not, so it behoved her to make one final attempt. She would trust her instinct. She would go to Egypt.

Chapter Eleven

Winging her way to Sam's own country, Helen remembered with acute pain, undulled by the passage of time, the occasion of their last meeting. She went over and over the events of that night and of the days that followed.

She had refused to see Sam and had even one night, as she went automatically to take her contraceptive pill, flushed the whole packet down the lavatory. Why load her body full of chemicals when her sex life, and indeed everything else, was at an end? She had talked herself into believing there was no future, yet she could not accept it. That was why she was going to Egypt, was it not? To try to change things.

Superstitiously, though, she had told Laura the romance was at an end. If publicly she allowed no hope, there might be some. She knew Laura did not believe she had finished with Sam. 'Why are you going to Egypt then? You'll think about him all the time.'

'I probably will, but I'll get it out of my system.'

'You're barmy, Helen.'

An increasingly worrying thought hit home. 'I'm not going mad, though, am I? I'm not behaving . . . strangely?'

''Course not. You're the sanest person I know.'

Helen was not entirely convinced.

Sam telephoned every day, twice a day sometimes. 'You can't go there.'

'I can and I am.'

'I want to take you.'

'Fine – come with me.'

'I can't. You know that. Not now.'

'That's that then. I need a holiday; everybody says so. It'll be warm and I'll feel better.'

The calls went on, telling her all she longed to hear about his love but still manifesting his complete inability to see a way out. She had no choice but to fly away.

At Cairo airport she looked for the guide she had been promised would meet them. She spotted him holding up the name of her tour company and, for the first time, was able to isolate the plane passengers she might never see again from those gathering with her.

They smiled nervously at each other. Helen was not unaware that she had been recognised by most of them and she immediately felt they were wondering why she had come alone. There seemed to be something about women travelling solo that evoked sympathy rather than admiration. No one ever seemed to think, how courageous of that girl, who undoubtedly has many friends, to come away on holiday on her own; rather, how odd that someone in her position has no one with whom to travel.

On the coach ride into Cairo, Helen began to weigh up her companions. There was an irrascible Scottish retired army officer who had, as he announced to one and all, been here in the war. He tried out his pidgin Arabic on the driver, who seemed singularly unimpressed. Helen was comforted to discover there were three other single people, all in their thirties and, in addition, a youngish couple from the North who promised to be fun. She was here on a mission, but it was gratifying to find she would have some company.

The guide announced that his name was Ahmed. It would have to be, thought Helen with a sigh. He pointed out one or two landmarks of interest, including a massive statue of Rameses the Second, but mostly he let them look and chat. He indicated that tomorrow they would begin their education in earnest; tonight they could relax.

In the lobby at the Rameses Hilton they grouped together, waiting for their rooms to be allocated. One of the single men was to be next to Helen. he offered his hand. 'I know who you are,' he said. 'I'm Jonathan Seabrook.

I'm in television too – the other side, actually. I'm a designer.'

'I'm delighted to meet you, Jonathan,' she replied.

'As we're both travelling alone, I wonder if you'd care to have dinner?'

She hesitated. 'I'm not very good company at the moment and I'm a bit tired. I thought I'd have a sandwich in my room.'

'I only meant something light in the coffee shop.' He smiled. 'I'm rather tired myself.'

'I'm sorry. I didn't mean to sound ungracious. Of course, let's do that. I'll meet you in an hour; once I've had a bath I'll be much more sociable.'

Inside her room, which was huge, with two double beds, she suddenly felt very much alone. She was in Sam's homeland but that fact had hardly impinged upon her yet. She might have been anywhere in the world. The air-conditioning protected her from the temperature outside, and from her window the Nile looked much like any other river.

After bathing and washing her hair she felt much more human. She selected a light-weight pink dress and sandals and applied the minimum of make-up. Right on cue, Jonathan knocked on her door.

'Would you like a gin-and-tonic?' he asked.

'I think I'd die for it.'

In his room, which was identical to her own, he broke open his bottle of duty-free gin.

'I've been here before,' he said. 'Not on a tour like this, but on business. The Egyptians are funny. They pretend to be more liberal than the rest of the Arab world, so they don't condemn alcohol officially; they just make sure you can't get hold of it too easily, and when you do it's ruinously expensive.'

After a club sandwich in the coffee shop, which again had little of Egypt about it, Jonathan suggested a drink in the piano bar.

The barman, called Ahmed, was utterly charming and insisted on exercising his English. 'I went to English school,' he said. 'Many of us did before 1956. We love you.'

It seemed a propitious start. The view was magnificent, the company uncomplicated and Helen felt her confidence growing. 'I wonder where everyone else is?' she asked Jonathan.

'Darling,' he said in a theatrical rather than romantic way, 'they don't have our stamina. They've probably gone to bed.'

'What do you make of them all?'

'Joanna, the girl with the floral dress, is a PRO in the fashion industry. The couple from Manchester are called Steve and Rosie – they're OK. And the short, fair-haired chap is a psychiatrist, Freddie Longhurst. You might have heard of him – he does quite a lot of telly and radio.'

'What about the army man and his wife?'

'They'll be all right as long as he doesn't lecture us too much on Cairo, past and present.'

'You're wicked.' She grinned.

They had a couple of exorbitantly priced cocktails to the accompaniment of the Western piano music and then, at eleven, Helen bowed out to go to bed. 'What time do we meet tomorrow?'

'Eight-thirty,' said Jonathan.

'Oh, that's not too bad. I heard some of the tours begin at three.'

'Well, when we get further south you'll be amazed how hot it gets. You couldn't cope with being out in the middle of the day.'

'I'm glad you've taken me under your wing, Jonathan,' she said, and she meant it.

'My pleasure,' he said. 'See you in the morning.'

While she was in company, she was the Helen the world knew. Back in her room, her longing for Sam hit her like a hurricane. What on earth was she doing in his country without him? The phone rang. She expected it to be Jonathan, inquiring whether she had negotiated the lift and hotel corridors without incident.

'Miss Bartlett?' asked the hotel operator.

'Yes.'

'I have a call for you.'

'Hello?'

'Sam! How did you find me?'

'Ah, well, I knew which company you'd travelled with. It only took a couple of telephone calls and a bit of detective work. How do you like my country?'

'I've hardly seen it yet. We begin properly tomorrow.'

'Are there any nice people on the tour?'

'Yes, very nice. One in particular, Jonathan – he's a television designer.'

'Oh,' he said coldly. 'I see.'

'Sam, stop that. You don't really think I've come here to have a holiday romance, do you?'

'No, I suppose I don't. What's he like?'

'Very charming, very dapper. Might be gay.'

'Oh, good,' Sam said quickly.

'Sam, you're impossible. You're the one who's engaged to someone else.'

'I know . . . Helen?'

'Yes.'

'Do you remember when we met, after the interview, at the Harrisons' dinner party?'

'How could I forget?'

'I'm not totally insensitive – I wasn't, even then. I knew how upset you were, yet you kept the whole dinner party swinging till you got tired suddenly.'

'Or drunk suddenly.'

'Well, whatever – I was terribly impressed by your bravery.'

'That's a nice thing to say.'

'Well, I'm even more impressed now. I don't deserve you. I know you love me and I can't believe my luck. I know I'm treating you badly, but I want you to know that I love you – I love your body, I love your mind and I love your courage.'

'Sam, I came here to . . . well, one of the reasons was to get myself together. Please don't go on.'

'I had to tell you.'

'I'm glad you did, but you do deserve me and I hope . . .'

'I know. Look, I'm going to do something positive.'

'Oh, God.'

'Wait a moment, listen. I'm going to fly to Paris at the weekend to speak to Jeremy.'

'Who's Jeremy?'

'He's my oldest friend. He's a surgeon.'

'Oh, yes, you mentioned him.'

'You said I should talk to someone else and I suddenly realised it's the only thing you've ever asked of me. You're the one person in my life who never pressurises me – it's the least I can do. You'll be on the boat for the weekend anyway, so you'll be out of contact.'

'You seem to know a lot about it.'

'I don't mean to check up on you. I just wanted you to know I am trying.'

She sighed. 'How's your day been?'

'Great as far as the job goes. A patient I was sure would die is suddenly picking up.'

'Maybe things are getting better.'

'Maybe they are. I love you, Helen.'

'I love you too.'

Eight o'clock in the morning came all too soon; it was, of course, only six at home. Inspired with the hope that Sam was determined to straighten out his life, she had slept well for the first time for weeks, and though she was excited at the prospect of seeing Cairo, she longed to continue sleeping.

After breakfast Ahmed arrived, all smiles, to begin his task. A mini-coach was waiting to convey them to the Citadel, a vast place. For the first time Helen began to appreciate the various periods of history in this country. It was also much more Arabic than her liaison with Sam had suggested. When singing broke out from the minarets, calling the faithful to prayer, she was astounded to see perfectly ordinary people, shoppers, bus drivers and market stall-holders, drop to their knees quite unselfconsciously and prostrate themselves in, what she presumed, was the direction of Mecca. Although she had known such things went on, witnessing them was a profound shock to her system.

They went next to the Cairo Museum, which was a huge affair. They were told they had one and a half hours in which to see it. Helen was reminded of a visit to Paris. She had been meandering round the Louvre when the doors had crashed open, revealing a coach-load of Americans who demanded noisily to be directed to the *Mona Lisa*. Once there, they snapped the picture with a blaze of flashlights and departed as quickly as they had come, leaving the more casual visitors with the impression that they had been flattened by a tornado.

Helen tried vainly to absorb all the information that was buffeting her, for if – she should not allow herself the thought – if all went well, her children would be part of this heritage. The high spot was the treasure of Tutankhamun. It stretched over a whole floor and Ahmed bid them take notice so that when they visited the tomb, which apparently was tiny, they could compare its size with the cornucopia it had held to itself for so many centuries. 'It is only,' said Ahmed, 'because he was such an inferior king that his tomb remained intact; those of the prominent figures were plundered and most of their bounty lost.'

There were two hours for lunch and Helen decided to break away. Alone, the city seemed frightening. First, at the doors of the museum, she was pestered to change money.

'Dollars?' asked a succession of poor but traditional-looking Arabs. 'No,' she answered.

'English?'

She nodded.

'You wish to change money? Good rate.'

'How much?' she asked, and was astonished to be offered much more favourable terms than those of the official dealers. She changed fifty pounds, aware that perhaps, in this bartering country, she should have pressed for more, but proud at the same time that she had coped so well on her own.

Although the hotel was near by, it took a while to reach it. The traffic and the fumes that arose from it were oppressive in the blistering heat. Cairo was seemingly undergoing extensive modernisation. As she walked she vowed never again to complain at roadworks or the rush hour in London: this was chaos such as she had never experienced. She had supposed that the sight of Europeans was a common one in this cosmopolitan capital, so was surprised at the many comments during her short journey.

'You English?'

'Yes.'

'Beautiful lady, welcome.'

Little children too went out of their way to smile, speak English and generally ingratiate themselves with her. Perhaps the tourist drive was a subject on the schools' curriculum.

As she reached the hotel, fifteen minutes later, it occurred to her that she had not considered she might be mugged; there had not been one threatening moment. Of course, theft is forbidden in Arab culture, but she had not realised the whole population adhered to the rules so well. She had planned to explore the city further during her lunch break but she decided instead to rest. She summed up the morning. These people were not so strange. Home, though – could this be home? So far she had encountered only the working and out-of-work classes. The hierarchy, however, families like Sam's or Hamaida's, would undoubtedly be a different matter.

She ordered a litre of mineral water and a sandwich and then lay down on the bed. Almost immediately the room-service waiter arrived, bearing what she had ordered plus a bottle of champagne in a silver bucket. 'There seems to be some mistake,' she said. 'I didn't ask for that.'

'Compliments of Mr Aziz,' he said. It seemed the man in her life, who declared he could not be with her, was determined to trespass on her space so constantly that she could not, even had she wanted to, put him out of her mind.

'Don't open it now,' she said. 'I'll never catch up with my sightseeing party.'

'Whatever you say, madam,' agreed the waiter, flashing her a smile that revealed perfectly white teeth. He reminded her momentarily of Sam. She tipped him and noticed that the name on his badge was George. He was the first Arab she had met who was not called Ahmed.

Jonathan was looking anxious as she rejoined the party. 'I wasn't sure I should let you go off on your own,' he said.

'Well, I came to find out certain things, and I can't do it surrounded by Brits.'

For the next two hours the coach took them into Old Cairo, and here the level of poverty was much more obvious. Ahmed was saying, 'We look after our own people; in our religion we are responsible for each other. When we have, we share it.' Helen felt the system must be breaking down somewhere; there were bedraggled and under-nourished beggars everywhere she looked.

They stopped at an old Coptic church, St Sergius, reputedly built on the site where the Holy Family found refuge on their flight into Egypt. Helen asked more questions than most. How many Coptic Christians were there? Did they live in harmony with the Arabs? Was the form of their religion nearer Catholicism or Orthodoxy?

'Darling,' interrupted Jonathan, 'are you doing research for a programme?'

Helen laughed somewhat shamefacedly. 'Just a habit, I guess.'

She bought a couple of books and a copper, silver and brass plate of the Holy Family and, as she did so, wondered if she were trying to curry favour with the Almighty, should he exist.

On the way back to the hotel the party was caught for a full hour and a half in a traffic jam. Unlike in Paris or Rome, and despite the heat, the natives rarely sounded their horns. They seemed to accept it as the norm; perhaps, indeed, it was. In the coach, which was not air-conditioned, they began to wilt. Only Jonathan was lively and determined to make plans for the evening. He rounded up the four singles and the young couple and suggested they go out on the town that night. 'After all,' he said, 'we didn't come here to eat club sandwiches in an American hotel. I'll ask Ahmed where one goes to eat ethnic,' and off he went to the front of the bus. The Scotsman, who was listening in, advised the revellers-to-be that they should not, on any account, eat the salad.

Jonathan returned cock-a-hoop. 'OK, I've got the name of a place. We'll meet in reception at eight.'

Helen checked her watch; she was anxious not to be a party pooper but knew she could use a couple of hours' sleep before going out. She would have time, but only just.

'Let's get dressed up,' said Rosie.

'What do you think?' asked Joanna of Helen.

'Oh, do let's,' said Rosie again.

Helen smiled. 'Why not? We'll go mad.' Remembering the champagne, she invited the other five to share it before their outing, and they split up with promises to assemble in Helen's room at seven-thirty.

Helen did sleep. The heat had got to her and she felt like a sponge which had soaked up more than its full capacity. When she woke she realised she was quite exhilarated at the prospect of going out on the town. She washed her hair and let it dry naturally. She also put on her full war paint and decided upon an outrageous sequin sweater which she had packed without holding out much hope of finding an occasion to wear it.

'Helen, this must have cost you a fortune,' said Steve as he expertly uncorked her champagne.

'It was a present,' she said.

'I knew it – you have an Arab lover. That's why you disappeared so mysteriously at lunchtime,' said Rosie.

'Something like that.' She smiled.

'Don't you go out with that heart surgeon?' asked Joanna. 'I'm sure I saw something in the papers.'

What price anonymity? thought Helen. 'Yes,' she answered.

'I suppose you're meeting his family?'

'Something like that,' said Helen again, uneasily remembering her plan. 'Now, let's get you all a glass.'

For such a diverse group, thrown together entirely by chance, they mixed well. Joanna was beautifully dressed in a little black number with black shoes and tights and a single strand of pearls. Rosie was in black too, with sequins decorating the bodice of her dress; she was plumper than the other two women but younger and her good humour was infectious. She lived with Steve and was studying to be a social worker. Freddie observed rather than spoke, though Helen thought he would be worth drawing out later. It did not take long for the six to demolish the bottle of champagne, so Jonathan shepherded them to the two taxis he had organised. He negotiated the price before they left the hotel and they were off.

At the restaurant they discovered they were distinctly over-dressed but because a large number of locals were eating there, which gave it a stamp of approval in their eyes, they decided to remain. 'Sod it.' Jonathan laughed. 'we're foreign to them; they probably expect us to be off the wall.'

The waiter, a skinny, cross-eyed individual in a long Arab robe and turban, approached them with roughly typed menus.

'What shall we drink?' asked Jonathan. 'Could we see your wine list?'

'We have white and we have red,' said the Arab.

'Oh.' Jonathan was deflated for a second only. 'Well, two bottles of each, I should think.'

'And some mineral water,' said Helen.

They ate bread and an assortment of dips, most of which seemed to be based on lentils, then they tackled a variety of meat dishes: tiny chickens and pigeons that had obviously dropped dead of malnutrition. 'I don't think we need worry about any hidden lead shot,' said Freddy sardonically. Helen laughed. She wondered if they were all going to be terriby ill and ate more sparingly than the rest.

The waiter brought salad. 'Don't eat the salad,' they chorused, mimicking the Scotsman.

It was an entertaining evening, all the more so because it was unexpected. There was only one brand of wine and none of them would have countenanced it back home, but since there was no alternative, they began to develop a taste for it. The effect was intoxicating enough and it would perhaps have the added virtue of pickling anything undesirable they might consume.

Back in the hotel Jonathan was insistent they should sample the piano bar that he and Helen had discovered the night before. The upper-crust Egyptians indulged this noisy group, surprised to find they were English rather than American, and everybody bought everybody else drinks. Jonathan, who was drinking very heavily, decided to give them a turn on the piano, and the pianist, who was not enjoying much of a hearing, let him have his way. He struggled through *Für Elise*, which he had obviously learned at school and probably not played since then, and then lauched into 'As with gladness men of old'. Helen was not sure a Christian carol was politic and decided, since it was midnight, to leave them to it. Joanna opted out with her, though the others stayed.

Back in her hotel room Helen kicked off her shoes and stepped out of her black taffeta skirt. The phone rang almost immediately. It was Sam.

'You were out late.' She presumed he had tried to call earlier.

'Yes. A group of us went to a restaurant and then ended up in the piano bar. We had a lovely evening. The rest are still going strong.'

'Are you alone?'

'Of course.'

'I'm sorry. Do you miss me?'

'Yes,' she said honestly, 'I do, but I am enjoying it. I saw so much more today and so far your countrymen are extremely hospitable.'

'They'll love you,' he said. 'They'll think, with your colouring, you're a princess. Wait till you get further south – they'll be offering a thousand camels for you.'

'Gosh, that's a lot.'

'You haven't seen the camels!'

Lying in bed later, Helen felt more optimistic than she had for a long time. Maybe this trip had been a good idea from all sorts of angles.

*

‘Ahmed!’ shouted an imperious voice from the back of the bus, ‘if you don’t give us a coffee break soon I’m going to be very sick all over your coach.’

Everyone laughed. It was the first utterance of the day from Jonathan. He had been the last to clamber aboard that morning and had looked distressingly green around the gills. Apparently the soirée had gone on in his room after the piano bar closed. Helen was surprised she had slept through it, for it seemed that several late-night drinkers had accepted Jonathan’s invitation to prolong the party.

‘What time did you leave?’ she asked Freddie, with whom she was sitting for the first time.

‘Around four.’

‘Well, you don’t look bad on it.’

‘Ah, well, (a) I’m a hardened drinker and (b) I took it more slowly than the rest.’

They journeyed on in silence; he was obviously a man of few words.

Ahmed, clearly worried about his coach, did make a coffee stop. It was literally in the desert and had nothing of a motorway café about it, being a mere stall manned by two painfully thin Arabs. Most of the party chose soft drinks, but Jonathan and Helen insisted upon coffee. When it came it was of the Turkish variety, strong and sweet and absolutely what Jonathan needed. Helen felt it gave her a shot in the arm too. Whatever else this trip might be, it was certainly not restful. Already that morning they had been to Memphis and now they were *en route* to Sakkara.

Back in the coach she watched as the countryside slipped by. If Cairo seemed foreign and unfamiliar, a veritable chasm opened up once they left that city. There were little pocket farms alongside the Nile and she saw oxen bearing yokes with buckets at either end. Later she caught a glimpse of a donkey walking around in circles pushing some machinery. She supposed it was something to do with irrigation.

She began to understand why this land must exert such a strong pull on the man she loved. It was tribal; it was proud; but much of it was in dire need. She wondered, in the event of Sam's returning, if the poor would ever get near him. She supposed it was more likely he would end up educating other surgeons. He could be like a pebble in a pond whose ripples spread ever outwards. She had a vision of what might be achieved and wondered again if she could give up everything back home in order to come here and help.

Sakkara compounded her feelings for the country, overshadowed as it was by the Step Pyramid, the oldest in existence, dating from around 3000 BC. It made the Tower of London look positively modern, and here, surprisingly, there were no turnstiles to be negotiated. It amazed her that the Egyptians were quite happy for visitors to walk up and touch this ancient monument. She thought of the preparations back home for tonight's programme; they seemed almost inconsequential in the face of this eternal history and never-ending landscape. The desert was spellbinding and its effect on her, as on so many in the past, was deeply disturbing.

Back in the hotel she was unable to shake off the mood. Excusing herself from the group, for they were all to meet again at three the next morning in order to fly to Abu Simbel, she sought peace in her own room. She wanted to speak to Sam about her impressions, but they were not, as yet, totally formed. He would ring, she supposed, and, persuading herself that she would prefer not to have her sleep interrupted, she asked the operator not to put through any calls.

She tossed and turned. The real purpose of her visit could not be delayed indefinitely. She had wanted to know what a woman's place was in this country. So far she had no clear picture. She got up suddenly; yes, the note Sam had sent before he came to Egypt was still there at the back of her wallet. There's no point phoning now, she thought. I'll do it after the boat trip.

She went back to bed. Sam would not approve, of that she was sure, but it was her life too. What was Hamaida really like? Perhaps she was buoyant, flirtatious and fun. But, if so, why had he not married her? Helen remembered Sam's mother and her abrupt departure. She also recalled the night they had spoken woman to woman. Which of these females held the key? Where was the real pressure coming from? Was the Egyptian girl really important or simply an excuse to prevent Sam's commitment to her? Questions, questions, questions. She was about to fall asleep when the telephone rang to tell her to wake up.

The rest of the party looked as tired as she felt. It was the middle of the night and none of them was chatty. They identified their luggage, for when they returned to Cairo it would be to a different hotel.

At Aswan, where they would end up, they were forced to leave the plane, relinquish their tickets, walk around a terminal building, which was little more than a shack, pick up a fresh boarding card and re-enter the plane, which, during their brief and ludicrous perambulation, had mysteriously filled up with other travellers. Her previous seat was occupied and, with very poor grace, she settled into another, just in front of Freddie. He leant forward, 'You don't seem quite yourself today. Is it because it's early?'

'Probably.'

'Well, I'm a good listener, you know.'

'I don't want to be psychoanalysed, thank you very much.'

'That's a little harsh.'

'I'm sorry, but I can't be kind all the time.'

'No, I suppose not,' he agreed. 'Look, this stretch only takes about half an hour I think, but I should close your eyes and try to sleep. You'll feel better.'

She did not argue.

Although it was still earlier than she might usually have had breakfast, Helen could sense from the rising heat that they were now in a region with a very different climate from that of Cairo. It was plain that by midday the temperature would be intolerable.

Helen walked with Freddie. Jonathan and Joanna were just behind. 'This better be worth it,' moaned Joanna, 'that's all I can say. God, what a schedule!' Following them came Steve and Rosie. Rosie was suffering and was walking with her head resting on Steve's shoulder, which must have been uncomfortable for both of them. The party rounded a corner and stopped, open-mouthed. Joanna spoke first. 'It's worth it.'

The massive grandeur of the Nubian Temple of Rameses the Second, with its gigantic and awesome seated figures, three complete and one smashed, on guard outside, was a stupendous sight. They ventured inside and, later, into the smaller temple dedicated to the Goddess of Love, Hathor, but, wonderful though their mysteries were within, nothing compared with the breath-taking spectacle of that first moment. They learned of the temples' original construction and then of how, in the 1960s when they were threatened by the rising waters of Lake Nassar during the construction of the high Aswan Dam, the world's engineers had combined their talents to move the whole edifice. All the sandstone had been injected with synthetic resin and cut by hand into over a thousand huge blocks before being shifted to a new site up and away from the waters that would have submerged them. Helen felt gladdened that miracles still happen, for the relocation and preservation of such a wonder seemed as marvellous, in its own way, as the initial building.

It was a happier group that took the flight back to Aswan. Perhaps the overwhelming immensity of what they had seen minimised any problems each might have. They were to stay at the Aswan Oberoi Hotel and, for a couple of days, could stop rushing around. Before long they were all lying under huge parasols by the side of the pool, sipping drinks and behaving as tourists might in any sun spot.

Most of them slept for the afternoon and made the trip to Aswan proper only when Jonathan decided to organise another tasting of the local cuisine. The streets were dirty and dusty, and if the restaurant in Cairo had qualified for two stars, this, unquestionably, would have been zero-rated. There were no menus at all and the whole interior was in urgent need of a spring clean.

'Two white and two red!' ordered Jonathan with authority.

'So sorry,' came the response, 'soft drinks only.'

'Hmm, soft drinks only,' repeated Freddie sarcastically. 'Can anyone think of three more chilling words in the whole of the English language?'

The food was not unlike that of the place in Cairo. They all avoided the salad, and Helen also waived the dubious pleasure of the roughly shapen meatballs with deep finger-nail imprints.

The streets they had walked the night before were totally different in broad daylight. The market was in full swing and the further they walked, the fewer tourists they saw; perhaps for the first time they were encountering something approaching work-a-day Egyptian life. They had been told by Ahmed they must barter. Most were unsure how to go about it, but Rosie picked it up quickly. Helen stood in mute admiration as the younger girl haggled to halve the cost of several metres of superb Egyptian cotton. Helen settled for some musky essential oils and henna. In all probability she had paid over the odds, but the price was still a fraction of what it would have been in England.

Soon it was too hot to shop further, and they spent the remainder of the day resting in their own rooms or lying by the pool sipping mineral water and eating the ubiquitous club sandwiches. At least it was not a boozy holiday. With the dent a small drink made in their spending money, Helen wondered if a trip to Egypt might prove more efficacious for problem drinkers than countless meetings of Alcoholics Anonymous.

'Darling, I had no idea you had such well-developed biceps.' It was Jonathan, of course. Having settled on the river boat and unpacked their luggage, the tour party had taken to the Nile in traditional yachts called feluccas. They had visited Kitchener Island, an abundance of greenery and exotica, and were now on their way back to the boat which was to be their base for the next few days. Helen had been told the Nile was green and greasy, but it did not seem so. As the sun set all around them the sight was magnificent. The felucca was making very slow progress by sail, and eventually the boat owner, who looked all of ten years old, decided to use the oars.

'Would you like someone to help you?' Helen had asked.

'Thank you, madam,' he had replied hastily, and thus it was that Helen found herself rowing the assembled party.

'You want Egyptian husband?' asked her fellow oarsman. 'We run business together.'

Helen started at the first question before recovering her equilibrium and smiling but shaking her head at the little man. She noticed Freddie watching her quizzically; for some reason she felt uncomfortably exposed.

'I would help out,' said Jonathan, 'but it's my back.'

Freddie said nothing but Steve, after Helen had proved herself, insisted he take over.

The next four days were a mixture of concentrated culture and leisurely afternoons spent lying on the upper deck, shrouded by parasols, watching the Nile glide silently by. Each day they left the boat in the cool of the early desert morning and by the time they returned, replete with another history lesson, the sun was literally burning bright. It was strange, thought Helen, as they assessed the various periods, how the finest art seemed to be the earliest. She was appalled that so many beautiful carvings has been violated by the early Christians; the faces and the feet of all the figures of the gods had been rubbed away in an attempt to render them impotent. Why was there always fear of a different culture, and why did that fear so often erupt in force? Helen thought of Sam's mother turning against her, and of the wanton destruction of the scene in Regent Street, and wondered if the world would ever change.

On their last night on board, moored at Luxor, Rosie announced they must all go shopping one last time.

'Surely it's too late,' said Helen, for dusk was falling.

'No, I checked,' said Rosie.

They humoured her and exercised their bartering skills

yet again. 'I'm just getting the hang of this when we're on the point of going home,' said Helen.

'You might be back, of course,' said Freddie, breaking his silence for once.

Jonathan was negotiating for rugs and leather goods. The others left him to it, though wondered how he proposed to get his purchases home. Rosie was bargaining too. She had told them she loved shopping anywhere and was, courtesy of Steve's money, getting her necessary fix.

Dinner on the boat that night was a superb buffet; it was the best meal of the holiday so far. Afterwards Ahmed suggested they all go for a drink at the Old Winter Palace Hotel. They hired two horse-drawn carriages, and Ahmed persuaded the drivers to agree to a ridiculously cheap rate to take them there and back.

The hotel had obviously been grand, and Helen could imagine European dowagers in the Twenties and Thirties whiling away their winters there. It was a cross between a tribute to the British Raj and one of the old and peeling hotels in British coastal resorts. Jonathan was elated with his market transaction. 'I'm having it all shipped back,' he said. 'I'm going to design an Egyptian room in my flat. It will be absolutely wonderful.' He bought drinks for everyone. Ahmed bought the next round. Helen wondered at his presence when he could easily be off duty. At first she assumed, uncharitably, that he was simply ensuring a large tip when they finally bade him farewell, but then she began to notice he was particularly attentive to Joanna. Now she thought back, the two had been seen together quite often during the past few days. Maybe he, a strict Moslem, was enjoying a taste of Western freedom; he was certainly drinking, which generally he did not. Joanna's reasons must be somewhat different. She claimed to have an elderly, wealthy husband. Maybe this was part of the deal; she could take single holidays and spice her absence with a touch of younger extra-curricular activity so long as she was discreet. It was strange what women, even modern, capable and independent women, would settle for.

When they returned to the boat Helen decided to go

straight to bed. Unusually, Freddie suggested seeing her to her cabin. He said little, but at her door, surprisingly, kissed her on the cheek.

The next morning they visited the Valley of the Kings. They had been promised it was the high spot, and so it proved to be. When Helen remembered the unending treasures from the tomb of Tutankhamun in the Cairo Museum she could not believe that all she had seen could once have been housed in such a small space. In common with the rest of them, Helen marvelled at the vibrant colour of the carvings and sceptically felt someone with an eye to the tourist trade must have come at dead of night and performed a touch-up job with a paint brush.

Emerging, blinking against the sun, she was amused rather than annoyed to hear, 'Helen Bartlett! Fancy you being here! We watch you every night. We come from Edgware.' She chatted to the couple, and just as their intervention was becoming intrusive, Freddie appeared at her elbow to steer her away.

It was an anticlimactic party that sat in the dusty transit lounge at Luxor airport. The four days on the boat had left their mark on all of them, and none appeared particularly thrilled at the prospect of a final day and a half in Cairo.

Someone said, 'I think I'd prefer to be going home now.' The others nodded in agreement. So would I, thought Helen, but I still have something to do.

They were eventually settled in the Mena House Hotel in Giza. Helen did not know if there were plans for any of them to meet up that night but she decided, no matter what, she would spend the evening alone. She could see one of the pyramids from her window. It drew her eye time and time again. Helen felt almost as if she were being hypnotised and wondered whether she would indeed return to this curious country with which she had begun a love affair. As she looked around her room, she saw for the first time a large arrangement of flowers; this was certainly a very up-market hotel. She glanced at the room-service menu and decided she would finally risk the salad. Surely here they knew to wash it in mineral water, or maybe their own system was safe.

Her meal arrived: spicey chicken, salad, olives, bread and a half-bottle of wine. It was very good. Halfway through eating it the phone rang. 'Darling, how are you? Did you get my flowers?'

'Oh! Oh, yes, I did. They're beautiful. Thank you very much. How are you?'

'Much better. I've been longing to get hold of you. I had a great weekend in Paris, except that poor Jeremy's going through it. His wife's just left him. But he was very helpful. I told him everything . . . well, almost, and he put a different perspective on it all. I've written to Hamaida to see if she would accept some sort of financial support. I still don't know if I should go home and work, but I'll settle one thing at a time.'

Helen's barometer zoomed from low to ecstatic.

'How do you like my country?'

'I love it. Sometimes it's exasperating, but especially sailing down the Nile I really felt at home.'

'Good,' he said, then added, 'Helen, you know I love you.'

'Yes.'

'Well, as I've told you, I'm taking steps to sort everything, but would you bear with me while I do? Maybe we shouldn't meet for a while.'

Helen felt that the last few months had been a succession of emotional swings and roundabouts. One minute she was on a carousel, the next thrown off, with nothing for it but to watch the rest of mankind go merrily round. 'Whatever you think,' she answered quietly and put the phone down. The solution was no nearer, not really, but could she affect it?

The next morning the group visited the pyramids and the Sphinx. They queued for admittance to the Great Pyramid but, once inside on the tiny, cramped stairway, with the pushing and pulling of people of every nationality, Helen felt unbearably claustrophobic and left the rest of the party to return to the outside world. Once there, she was surrounded by Arabs in sandals and flapping gowns, all of whom had something to sell.

'No, thank you,' she said, which was a mistake, for

once she had spoken, they were encouraged, even though her answer had been in the negative.

'You wish Egyptian husband? I give one thousand camels for you.'

She almost laughed, remembering Sam's prediction. 'No. Go away.' They did not. She was not frightened of being robbed, but she was threatened by their invasion of her space and privacy. 'Go away,' she said again. No one moved. 'OK,' she said angrily, 'I'll go.'

'Where you go?'

'I'm going back to my hotel.'

'I walk with you.'

'No!' she screamed. 'I was really enjoying being here but you've ruined it. All I wanted was to be left alone.'

They looked uncomprehendingly at her. She walked away but it was not until she was halfway down the hill that the last of the vendors finally gave up.

Back in her room she wept with frustration. There was a knock on her door. Wearily she went to answer it. It was Freddie. 'What are you doing back here?'

'I had a bad scene up there – they wouldn't leave me alone.'

'Well, we're all going to the Papyrus Institute now.'

'You go. I'm not going anywhere.'

'Oh, yes, you are,' he said. 'You're going to get your ten out of ten and a gold star like the rest of us. You'd better wash your face,' he added without sympathy. Meekly she walked into the bathroom and complied.

The Institute was fascinating. The whole process was explained, and they watched the reeds being laid, criss-crossed and later rolled to mesh the layers together. 'Papyrus, real papyrus, not the banana-skin imitations you see everywhere, lasts three thousand years,' said the young Egyptian, as he encouraged them to walk around and buy samples.

'You can write your essay now,' whispered Freddie and, forgetting her earlier trauma, she smiled at him. 'We have the afternoon "at leisure", as they say in the trade,' he said. 'Come back and we'll have a drink and some lunch – just the two of us.'

He took her hand, which was as surprising as last night's kiss had been.

They sat in a lounge in the hotel and Freddie ordered campari-and-soda for both of them. Because she felt on guard at his sudden attention, she asked him several questions. She looked at him as she did so, taking in his baggy cotton suit with the sleeves fashionably rolled up. He was just a little too short, portly and old to look trendy, but it was a meritorious attempt. 'Are you married?' she asked, after several less impertinent questions.

'Getting out of it.'

'Oh.'

'It's OK. I can talk about it. Sally, my wife, left the proverbial note behind the clock and disappeared from our Suffolk cottage, taking my yellow Labrador dog with her. I missed the dog. I probably deserved it. Later she sent for all the furniture.'

'That wasn't very nice.'

'No, it wasn't, but I don't think I was the best of husbands.'

'Is there any chance you could get back together again?'

'Doubt it, so that's why I'm running. Why are you?'

'I'm not running.'

'Oh, yes, you are. People who come on this sort of holiday in their thirties, alone, fall into certain categories.'

'OK, if you're so clever, what are they?'

'Well, for a start they have to be relatively well off.'

She looked at the tab for their two drinks and smiled. 'That's true.'

'Secondly, they're either here because they've accepted their solo state and are quite happy with it, like Jonathan, or they're like you and me, trying to prove they can function on their own and appear fun to the rest of the world. Trouble is, we're constantly pulled back to the realities of what we've left behind. So if this thing with your bloke doesn't turn out . . .'

'I don't know what you're talking about.'

'I think you do. I've watched you. You're a very attractive and efficient lady. You're also kind, but you're certainly sad.' Helen's eyes filled with tears. He reached for her hand. 'I'm sorry. I didn't mean to upset you. My wife always said I was too blunt.'

'It's OK. Let's have another drink.'

He signalled to the waiter. 'Maybe I could call you when we get back.'

'Surely that wouldn't solve anything? Don't people have to put something properly behind them before grabbing the first bit of driftwood that floats by?'

'Well, I've been called a lot of things . . .'

'You know what I mean. You're a psychiatrist, after all.'

'It doesn't always help in one's own case. Let's just start by having a meal some time.'

'I don't know.'

'You have to eat. Anyway,' he went on, 'whatever your problem – I suppose it's something to do with his family or yours not approving the match – I'm sure he'll get it right. He'd be mad to let a woman like you go.'

Back in the hotel room Helen packed hurriedly. Then she dialled a number 'Do you speak English?' she asked the Egyptian who answered the telephone.

'A little.'

'I wish,' she said loudly and slowly – oh, God, how typically British she was being – 'to speak to Mrs Aziz.'

The girl must have understood. 'Madame, Aziz. You wait.'

'Hello,' said a voice Helen recognised.

'Mrs um Madame Aziz, it's Helen Bartlett.'

'Helen,' said the other woman with very little warmth, 'how are you?'

'I'm fine. Look, I know it's a lot to ask, but I wonder if I could come to see you?'

'Where on earth are you?'

'In Giza.'

'My dear, have you come specially to see me?'

'Yes, I think perhaps I have.'

'When would you like to come?'

Helen took a deep breath. 'Actually, now.'

There was a long pause. 'All right, Helen. I'll see you in fifteen minutes.'

It was done.

The hotel porter fixed a rate with the taxi driver and Helen was on her way. She forced herself to take notice of the passing streets as she rode towards one of the most decisive meetings of her life. The journey to some extent reminded her of the taxi ride on the night of the Harrisons' dinner party. Then too she had travelled from a fairly run-down area to a more opulent one.

They were soon in a suburb that reminded Helen more of a tour of the movie stars' houses in Beverly Hills than the gentility of St John's Wood. The driver stopped in front of a veritable palace.

'You wait,' said Helen, praying he had some English.

'OK, princess.' He smiled.

The house was Moorish on the outside but the interior was a mixture of Arab and European influence. Much of it was white and marble, but the drapes and pictures were probably French. Helen had never been inside such an elegant dwelling in her life. Her high heels tapped loudly on the sparkling white Italian tiles.

Madame Aziz sat on an antique sofa. She was the queen of this domain. She rose imperiously. 'A little mint tea, Helen.' She offered one cheek, then the other, to be kissed. Helen had almost been tempted to kiss her hand.

'That would be very nice.'

Helen sipped the unfamiliar brew gratefully; she was very hot, though the house was expensively and efficiently air-conditioned. This is Sam's past, she thought. How can I compete with it? Her mind traversed a continent or two to her own little friendly flat in Holland Park. How basic it must have seemed to him.

'What brings you to Egypt, Helen?'

Helen looked at the older woman. She could play games now, or she could offer everything, deal her final hand in the hope of winning. Honest by nature, she had no alternative but to risk all. 'I came – ' She coughed and started again. 'I came to get away and to have a holiday. That's the official reason anyway, but I really came to talk to you.'

'Go on.' Sam's mother's stance gave every indication of being implacable.

'You once spoke very honestly to me, and I want to do the same. By the way, Sam doesn't know I'm here, and I'd prefer it if you didn't tell him. I want to tell you he's everything in the world to me. I love him, I need him and I promise you I'd cherish him for ever. I want to ask whether you could ever accept me as his wife.'

'Have one of these sweetmeats. They're very good.' Helen sighed but took one none the less. 'Helen, I appreciate your openess. I like you very much, but it's not possible. You're not one of us. Ahmed is promised to another. His place is here. He should work in his own country, and he should marry.'

'He can't give you grandchildren if he marries Hamaida.'

'Ah,' said the old lady, 'I see you know more than I thought, but it doesn't matter. My husband wanted it. Sam, as you call him, has ruined Hamaida's life.' For a second Helen wondered if Madame Aziz knew that Sam had taken the Egyptian girl's virginity. 'She has waited for him, you know, more years than I care to remember.'

'Well,' Helen interrupted, 'he proposed once.'

'I don't want to talk about it.' Helen had never been faced with such intransigence. 'She is – ' Madame Aziz had the floor – 'a lovely and dutiful Arab girl.'

Helen came back at her. 'I'm sure she is, but I don't believe she loves him as I do. I want to meet her. I think we should speak.'

'As it happens, she takes tea with me most afternoons. She'll be here any minute. You can stay or you can go.' The inflection remained uncompromising.

Helen felt she was an extra in a Bette Davis movie. She tried to speak. She almost took flight, but curiosity got the better of her. This was what she had travelled so far for.

'Very well, stay, but I must ask you not to intimate to Hamaida anything of your close relationship with my son. She's not been well, you know. We mustn't upset her.'

Oh, no, thought Helen, we mustn't upset Hamaida. Bugger Hamaida. I'll ask her what I damn well like.

The two women sipped their tea in silence.

A smile spread over Sam's mother's face suddenly. She said something in Arabic, then, 'We will speak English because of our English visitor.' She was icily polite. 'I met Helen when I visited Ahmed. She is in television.'

Helen turned to look at her rival. She was small, thin, very dark. Her hair was immaculate, her nails manicured and painted, her smile sweet rather than happy, her eyes round but sad.

'I'm so pleased to meet you, Helen' said the dark girl in heavily accented English. 'I've never been to your country, but I hope to go shortly. Do you know my fiancé?'

Helen stared at the other girl. There was such a lump in her throat she could hardly speak. 'A little,' she croaked. She looked towards Madame Aziz for comfort. The woman with Sam's eyes nodded almost imperceptibly. 'Um, Madame Aziz says you've been ill. I'm sorry.'

'Yes, I have, but I'm better now. I look forward to my wedding. It will be a new start. I shall grow strong planning our house and our future.'

Helen's questions refused to articulate themselves.

Was Sam Hamaida's entire *raison d'être?* It seemed so, but he was hers too. They perceived it differently, that was all. How could she ask now if this frail female would give up a dream? She, who was deemed so eminently capable, had no right to deny this dull girl her only feeble ambition in life. She thought of Sam's letter and realised it would cause desperate pain. She had wanted to find out and now she had. Yet surely there was some sympathy? His mother's obdurate refusal to meet her eyes again stopped her in her tracks. She was the outsider; she could never belong. Helen heard her voice say, 'I wish you happiness. Forgive me – I must go.'

Somebody must have shown her out. Somebody must have put her in the taxi. Had she paid the driver?

She was sitting in her hotel room. It was dark outside.

Her chest was locked in a vice. She could not move. The phone was ringing. Had it just begun? Maybe, Well, let it. It stopped. Now there was banging on her door. Well, that would go away too. Was it tomorrow? Was she late for the plane? No, it was tonight.

'Helen! Helen! Come on, for God's sake!'

She walked to the door in a trance and struggled with the lock; at last it opened. Freddie was there. 'What's wrong with you? You look ghastly. Have you been drinking?'

She shook her head. 'Actually . . .' She began to laugh. 'I have. I had mint tea, lots of mint tea.' It was suddenly terribly funny. She covered her mouth to suppress her laughter, but it really was very amusing. The laughter burst out.

'Helen, stop it!'

'I can't.' She laughed. 'It was really awfully good mint tea.' Her mouth was wide open; something caught in her chest and all at once tears poured down her cheeks. She sobbed and gasped for breath.

He held her then. Had she been able to see, she would have noticed his usual sneering expression had been replaced by one of genuine concern. He rocked her backwards and forwards.

'Oh, Sam,' she murmured.

'It isn't Sam,' he said, angrily pushing her on to the bed.

She heard him pick up the phone. Everything was confusing and a long way away. 'You'll have to go on,' he was saying. 'Don't argue, Jonathan, Helen's not very well. I'll try and bring her along later.'

'Where are we going later?' she asked in a simple little voice.

'Helen.' He sat her up sharply and grabbed her by the shoulders.

'You're hurting me.'

'Good. Look at me – I'm Freddie, remember?'

''Course I remember. What are you talking about?' she asked in a more normal voice.

'Oh, God, Helen. Look, we were all supposed to be

going out to eat. Are you up to it?' She looked at him. Her lower lip trembled as more tears spilled from her eyes. 'No, you're not really. Have you . . . Look, I hate to ask you . . . you're not on anything, are you?'

'I don't know what you mean.'

'Drugs.' She shook her head. 'Helen, wait here.'

Where did he think she was going?

Moments later he returned with a glass of water and two little white pills.

'I don't take pills.'

'You do now. And, for the second time today, wash your face.'

'I ought to change.'

'Yes, well, carry on.'

'Go away then.'

'Helen, I'm a doctor. Just get on with it.'

She slipped out of her sun dress. She was wearing nothing else. 'What should I put on, do you think?' she asked blankly.

He pulled a little cotton two-piece from her suitcase. 'This'll do.'

Somebody's face stared at her from the mirror. Automatically she cleaned the streaked make-up from it and applied some more. She brushed her hair.

'Good girl,' he said, when she returned from the bathroom. 'Those pills will calm you down. Just don't drink too much, OK?'

She nodded.

She let him hurry her from the hotel, and as soon as they reached the restaurant, she snapped back into her public persona.

'Are you all right?' the others chorused.

'Yes, I'm fine. I think I got too much sun.' She looked to Freddie for reassurance. He smiled.

Everyone else was in festive mood and knocking back quantities of Egyptian wine while vowing never again to touch the stuff. Helen sipped slowly but tried to join in eating some of the food. Everything was, as she had said, fine. Life would go on. Not as it had been but . . .

All six swapped addresses and phone numbers. It

reminded Helen of the end of a theatre run, when actors promise eternal friendship and cry into their beer, only to come across a tear-stained slip of paper with a name and address on it weeks later and have to search the memory hard for a face that fitted the details.

Back in the hotel Freddie accompanied Helen to her room and phoned down for a nightcap. He gestured towards the flowers. 'From the man, I suppose?'

'Yes.'

He grunted. 'I was proud of you tonight,' he said.

'You were very kind to me earlier. I appreciate it.'

'Do you want to tell me what happened?'

'No, thank you. I just did something that . . . that I knew was a recipe for disaster but, well, it was no help to find out I was right.'

'I'll go.' He stood up. 'I think you'd better sleep.'

Helen rose, weakly, for his goodnight kiss, which suddenly became a passionate one. She resisted for a second, then found herself not only responding but enjoying it.

'He's a lucky man, your fellow. I might just hang around for a bit . . .'

'We're both rather emotional here, don't you think?' she said as steadily as she could.

'What a mixture – a beautiful *and* level-headed woman. Very rare.' He grinned. 'Your man will move heaven and earth for you if he's got any sense.'

Strange. Perhaps it no longer mattered what Sam felt. It was obvious to her now that he was not the master of his own destiny. She spoke slowly. 'It's over, Freddie. It's really over.'

'I wonder,' he said from the doorway. 'I'd like to think so, but I bet you anything you like he'll be waiting at the airport tomorrow morning. You'll see.'

Chapter Twelve

Despite her disbelief in Freddie's prediction, Helen's heart was racing as she surveyed the sea of faces anxious to meet their loved ones. She had sat with Freddie on the flight, though he had said little. He was just behind her as they emerged from customs. 'Told you,' he said, almost before Helen had reacted to Sam's waving figure.

She turned to Freddie and offered her hand. 'Thanks for everything.'

'Don't thank me,' he said. 'I'll be in touch.'

Helen held herself remote from the embrace she longed for. She forced her mind back to Sam's illustriously superior mother and the pallid fiancée making her pedestrian plans. 'You're not one of us,' Madame Aziz had said. That was certainly true. But was Sam? Despite her official acceptance that all was lost, he was here. The final chapter had not been written.

'Aren't you glad to see me?' he asked, looking thin, tired and frightened. He had never been loved. He never would be by those decorous females who were at that moment plotting his life till death parted him from it.

'Glad, Sam? Of course I'm glad.' And gladness released itself into every tissue of her body. She felt like one of his patients when the blood supply is connected to a new heart; her blue coldness was diffused suddenly with pink warmth.

'Who was that guy?' asked Sam, once she was safely stowed in the Mercedes. 'Was it Jonathan?'

'You've got a good memory.' She laughed. 'No, it was Freddie, actually.'

'What does he do?'

'He's a sort of media psychiatrist.'

'Hmm, pretty high-flown trip then, with the three of you working in television.'

'It was great,' she said, without appearing to notice Sam's petulance. 'Wonderful country, good company and lots to see.'

Should she go on and tell him all that had transpired yesterday? She wanted to, for she hated secrets, but she knew her actions would be construed as interference. In any case, having faced the fact that she could not win, she was having second thoughts; yesterday seemed a dream and today did not.

He drove her back to his house and only then did she dare say, 'What happened to the idea that we shouldn't meet for a time?'

'I thought again. It isn't only women who are allowed to change their minds.' He smiled. 'I'm doing all I can. I needed to see you. I hoped you felt the same. I wondered if you could stay here for the weekend . . . as my friend.'

Helen, back in the role she despised of accepting whatever comfort came her way, was bound to accept. The alternative was an empty flat and no work until Monday, longing and hoping for a phone call that might or might not come. 'I'll try if you'll try,' she said. It was a strange two days, for though their desire for each other was intense, and his at least was physically assessable, they did not make love.

In the office on Monday Laura burst in on Helen a few moments after her arrival. 'I've something to tell you.'

'You got married,' said Helen.

'How did you guess?'

'I didn't. I was just being flippant. At least . . . I don't know. Maybe there's something different. When?'

'Saturday.'

'You rotter. That was the day I got back. Why didn't you invite me?'

'We didn't invite anybody. Right up till the last moment I think we both thought one of us would call it off.'

'Are you happy?'

'Blissfully – boringly, perhaps.'

'I couldn't be more delighted,' said Helen, and she meant it, though she was filled with envy at the fruition of a relationship that made no pretence of being as vital as her own.

'What happened to you?' asked Laura.

'I can't go into it now. Do you want to have a drink when we finish, or isn't that allowed now you're legal?'

''Course it is. Anyway he's away, filming.'

'Did you meet anyone?' asked Laura in the club that night.

'Lots of people.'

'You know what I mean.'

'Well, there was Jonathan, who was decidedly asexual, and there was Freddie.'

'Let's concentrate on Freddie. What was he like?'

'Short, fair, a bit plump, about forty, a psychiatrist who dabbles in our business, getting divorced.'

'And . . . ?'

'Well, towards the end he seemed very keen on me. More than that, he was very kind.'

'Good. Did you go to bed with him?'

'Certainly not.'

'Are you a born-again virgin or something? Why on earth not?'

'Well, I thought he might have the small man's problem.'

'Oh, chip on the shoulder, you mean?'

'No. Small prick.'

Laura laughed. 'You're disgusting. Anyway, it doesn't always follow.'

'No,' said Helen, remembering, 'no it doesn't. But you know what I mean,' she continued. 'Is there, after all, anything more disappointing? You know when you read in magazines that size doesn't matter, well, who are they kidding? Do you think these things are always written by men?'

'Maybe. I really hadn't thought about it.'

'Well, think about it. What's best?'

'Long,' said Laura.

'And fat,' Helen finished for her.

Laura put her hand to her mouth and giggled.

'Well, am I right?'

'Yes . . . yes, you are.'

'OK, what's next best?'

'Long and thin, I suppose.'

'I don't think so. Shorter is OK, as long as it's still substantial, then long and thin. But short and thin is definitely out.'

'You seem to have made quite a study.'

'Well, at least I know what I don't want.'

'Is that really why you didn't go to bed with Freddie?'

'No, of course not. I didn't go to bed with him because I don't think you can get over one thing by latching on to another. Anyway, God help me, I'm still in love with Sam.'

'What's happening there?'

'Well, having rung me in Egypt to say we shouldn't meet for a bit, he was at the airport. We had a comfortable weekend. I even slept there. But no sex.'

'Is he normal?'

'Oh, yes, he's normal.'

'No, I mean . . . Helen, there does seem to be more trauma in this relationship than joy.'

'I know, but I'm just beginning to understand what his background is all about.' She paused and was on the verge of describing the peculiar tea party at the end of her visit when Laura spoke again.

'Are you seeing him tonight?'

'No. I told him I need some time to be alone.'

'Do you want to be alone?'

'Not a lot.'

'Neither do I. Let's go and get a curry.'

Back home, soaking in the bath, Helen thought of her friend's advice that evening. With her new status Laura seemed suddenly a cut above her in achievement and confidence. She had advised, 'Don't be so available. If you look at what happens every time you go away or make a stand, you'll see he comes running. If you still want him, just make sure he has to work at it.'

Helen tried to sound off-hand when Sam called. She

watched herself in the mirror as he spoke. She flushed with pleasure as he told her he loved her, but she manoeuvred her face into a stern expression in response. He was not unaware she was being less than forthcoming. 'Why am I getting the cold shoulder?'

'Because we're in a state of limbo. You keep telling me you're sorting everything. I'm staying away till you do. You partly want to see me,' she went on, 'and yet you don't, and you certainly don't want to make love. Why don't we do our own thing and not meet till the weekend?'

'What do you mean, "do our own thing"? What are you going to do?'

'What are *you* going to do?'

'Well, work . . . I don't know.'

'I don't know either, but I'm not about to jump into bed with anyone else, if that's what you're asking.'

'Helen, you're distancing yourself from me.'

'Yes, I am. It's my only protection.'

'Will you meet me on Friday? Jeremy's coming over.'

'Maybe it would be better if you have some time together alone.'

'For Christ's sake, Helen, enough's enough. Stop punishing me. I want you to be there. I want to show you off.'

Did he mean it to sound that proprietorial? 'OK, Sam. Pick me up after the programme.'

'Helen, I do care. I do love you.'

Drawing herself up to her full height, she replied, 'I'm glad,' and forced herself not to tell him she loved him too and for ever.

The next day Helen was due to record a medical feature. The programme's resident doctor, Ken Murdoch, turned up in time for lunch.

'I did what you asked. The hospital delivered the you-know-what,' she said to him conspiratorially.

'Good girl. Good production values, eh?' Dr Murdoch was proud of his command of television terms.

'Derek won't like it, though,' she said.

'Probably not. Still, it does illustrate the point.'

'Yes,' she agreed, 'and he's always telling me I might as well work in radio if I don't find good visuals.'

On the studio floor they set up shots for the feature.

'Can you pick up the phone at the newsdesk?' said the floor manager.

'Helen, it's Derek. What *is* that?'

'What's what?'

'You know perfectly well what I mean – that . . . thing in the glass bowl.'

'It's a placenta, fresh from the hospital. I had the baby born specially.'

'You can't use it. It's hideous.'

'Oh, Derek, don't be so . . . male. It's good television, as you would say.'

'Well, what's the point of it?'

'The subject's post-natal depression, as you know. The placenta is loaded with progesterone. The woman carries it for nine months and suddenly it's gone, so to speak. Most experts believe the condition is caused by the hormonal change.'

'Well, why doesn't every woman get it?'

'See, you're getting interested now. That's what I'm hoping to bring out.'

'OK, you win, but no close-ups. You can refer to it, but I'm going to tell Mark to keep his distance.'

The floor manager started the clock.

'Animals don't get post-natal depression, as far as we know,' said Helen, when he cued her. 'Is it because they eat their afterbirths?'

'Well,' said Ken, 'I don't wish to put people off their tea but, as you can see, this is a placenta. It's packed full of really good things – in fact, they often find their way into cosmetics because of their hormonal content. So once the woman has given birth, she loses all this very suddenly, and some women react to it badly. Maybe you're right about eating it. I did hear of a woman in Hampstead who fried hers up with some onions, but that's by the by. Now, why do some women get it and others not? There does seem to be a correlation here between women who suffer PMT and post-natal depression . . .'

Ken expounded the latest theory and Helen finished by giving the post-natal depression association's address.

'I think you went too far,' said Derek when Helen returned to the newsroom.

'We'll see,' she said. 'If you do get any rude phone calls, I bet they'll all be from men. We're giving information the average woman needs, and you know our audience profile better than I do. We're not talking about the As and Bs, who are capable of finding out if there's a support group for their particular malady or whose old men play golf with the local doctor . . .'

'I know you mean well, Helen, and that the viewers like what you do. I'm just saying I think you might have gone a bit over the top. We'll see when it goes out tonight. I've a good mind to make you stay and take the phone calls after the programme.'

All her firm intentions wavered as she reached home. Ian was back, and Laura's domestic happiness was so evident that Helen had hesitated to suggest that they should have more than a quick drink after the programme. Why should marrying the man have changed her friend so obviously when she had lived with him for ages? And did she really want this enclosed commitment for herself?

She rang her mother; she rang Deidre to fix a tennis game for the next evening; and she longed to call Sam but she did not. She poured herself one drink and then another. She recognised she was on a slippery slope, drinking alone, but it blurred the edges of her uncertainty and pain.

Sam called her. He too was drinking alone. He felt torn in two, he said. She maintained her cool. Perhaps it was the only thing he understood. Hamaida was cool, cold, frigid probably, and he was going back to her.

Freddie phoned. He did not allude to any warm feelings he might have, though he did invite her for dinner. She declined.

The next two days passed slowly. She focused on her job; she played tennis; and she berated herself for her weakness as she mentally ticked off the hours till she could meet Sam.

Then Laura had her first row as a married woman and appeared at Helen's flat at half-past eleven. She was distraught. 'I knew we shouldn't have got married. I knew this would happen.'

'You've had rows before. Why is this so terrible?'

'Because we're married,' Laura wailed.

'That's ridiculous,' said Helen. 'You're the same people. It's only a worse row than usual if it really *is* a worse row than usual, not because it's a pretty typical one that you think is worse just because you've tied the knot. What happened, anyway?'

'I stayed late at the club. I went to meet you.'

'I didn't think you'd be there, so I played tennis.'

'Well, Ian was supposed to be out. Anyway, I got back a bit tipsy, and he was already in. We both got cross, so I threw a dinner plate at him, and he threw a jar of marmalade at the wall. It was a hell of a mess.'

Helen laughed. Laura looked at her angrily. 'I'm sorry, sweetheart,' said Helen. 'It just sounds so awfully Tennessee Williams.'

'That's nothing – we often throw things.' Laura smiled suddenly. 'I suppose you're right. It's no worse than usual but . . . do you think he thinks we shouldn't row now we're married?'

'I don't know. Let's ask him.'

'We're not ringing him.'

'We are because, quite apart from everything else, he's probably worried sick about where you are.'

'I doubt that,' said Laura, though she made no effort to stop Helen from picking up the phone.

'Hi, Ian, it's Helen. I've got Laura here.'

'Put her on.'

Without a word Helen held out the receiver to Laura before tiptoeing out of the lounge to the kitchen.

Two minutes later Laura rushed in, her eyes shining. 'Thanks, Helen. I'm going home.'

'Anytime.'

'Well, at least we've got our first married quarrel out of the way.'

Helen laughed. 'Off you go. Get straight to bed and enjoy it. Have one for me.'

'I'm sorry, Helen. Is it still awful?'

'I'm surviving, but around this time of night, quite apart from wanting him to solve everything because I love him, I'm just desperate to be poked. I know that's dreadful but it's how it is.'

It was very difficult to concentrate on the work before her on Friday. She was nervous about meeting Jeremy, afraid that he might not like her and might therefore cast his vote in favour of Egypt. She wanted to be everything wanted of her, but most of all she wanted Sam, and though she was prepared to go to any lengths, she was becoming less and less sure what those lengths were.

The programme went well, which was gratifying since she was certain Sam would have encouraged Jeremy to watch it. Afterwards she and Laura went to the club.

'Hey, the friend's terrific-looking,' said Laura. She was facing the door as the two men came in. Jeremy was taller than Sam. He had steely grey hair and piercing blue eyes, Helen noticed, as they greeted each other for the first time. They shook hands. His were soft but his handshake was firm. Unusually, Sam kissed her full on the lips; he generally behaved much more discreetly on her territory. She thought it unfair of him to stake his claim so vehemently when, in all probability, he could not honour it, but she was filled with enormous joy none the less.

Helen signed her guests in and bought everyone a drink. Ian appeared unexpectedly and Helen was amused to see Laura colour slightly. Her eyes shone. She was patently deliriously in love, no matter how she tried to deny it. She had never looked more beautiful. Had Sam noticed? Could this example of marital bliss create the longing for it in him that it already had in her?

With the catalyst of an interested third party, Helen and Sam recaptured much of the romance and simplicity of their early days, as they ate in a restaurant overlooking the river that night. He kissed her frequently, stroked her bare arms and was the very model of an attentive consort.

Helen's only anxiety was that he was acting a part for Jeremy in an attempt to divert attention from the seriousness of the situation. Was he assuming a role so as to persuade his friend that his troubles were not so great and to prevent any introspective discussion? Was he trying, in his own way, not to lose face? Had he really opened his heart and bared his soul to his oldest friend?

They had certainly talked, Helen discovered, when Sam had excused himself to visit the lavatory. Jeremy leant across the table and took her hand. 'You're absolutely delightful. Sam made me watch the programme. You're terrific – everything he said you were and more. I know you've had terrible problems with him, but do stick it out. I've never seen him like this. He's so much in love with you, I think he'd die if he lost you.'

Helen said nothing, but she smiled at this comparative stranger. Jeremy was not unlike Sam. Maybe that was why she felt so much at ease. Each was at the top of his profession. They both had perfectly manicured, soft hands and were immaculately groomed, with the solvency to support their sense of style. The only differences were those of colouring and accent because Jeremy, for all his years in Paris, was British to the core.

Sam returned and was immediately followed by a waiter bearing a bottle of Bollinger in a silver bucket. 'Helen,' he said quietly, once the waiter had left, 'I've put you through so much. I hate myself. I would just say, and it's a reason, not an excuse, I haven't been able to help it.'

She kissed him.

'Right, you two,' said Jeremy, raising his glass, 'a toast to your happiness. I'm not going to let you get this wrong. You're in love and you're made for each other – it's as simple as that.'

'It isn't,' said Helen, springing to Sam's defence. 'It isn't at all. You know the story, you know about Hamaida and you probably know Sam's mother.'

'Well, I don't know her, though we have met. But, Sam, old boy, you simply can't let all that stand in your way. Why don't you just get married and be done with it?'

'Helen wouldn't have it.'

'Heavens, you're as bad as he is.'

'Jeremy,' she said seriously, 'if this is going to be for ever, we have to get it right.'

'You're a remarkable lady,' said Jeremy. 'That's why Sam should hold on to you. Listen, I'm talking from experience. I've been a louse and a cad. My wife is French. I thought French women understood that men have affairs. Well, she understood all right, but she suddenly decided not to tolerate it. Then I realised, too late, that none of the other women had ever been important, which is pretty ironic. Sam,' he urged, 'don't muck this up, or you'll regret it for ever.'

Helen turned to Sam. 'Does Jeremy know the whole story about Hamaida?'

'If you mean do I know he "robbed her of her virginity", or whatever nonsensical phrase he used, yes, I do. I understand,' he said lowering his voice, 'that this means more in your culture, but even so, are you really going to let one mistake ruin your life? It seems to me she's a conniving little minx who deserved what was or wasn't coming to her.'

Helen privately thought Jeremy had overstepped the mark, but Sam said nothing.

Back home, for Sam had ordered a taxi to go to his address, Jeremy, who was obviously a man of tact, declared he was exhausted and made for the spare room.

'Well?' said Helen. 'How do you feel after the lecture?'

'The English side, the boy who went to school with Jeremy, agrees with him totally. It's just . . .'

'I know,' she said, 'but we've probably talked enough for one night.'

'Come to bed,' he said.

Once there, she offered no resistance when he began to make love to her. Fleetingly she wondered if he would regret it afterwards, but her mind and her body were locked into the forthcoming experience, and she could not have stopped him even had she wanted to. It was as good as it had ever been, better perhaps because of their recent abstention. Neither of them slept much, and Helen lost count of how many times she climaxed. She considered heaven must be like this, one prolonged orgasm, for if paradise were perfection, she had sampled it here on earth.

Over dinner on Saturday night Helen described her day. She had been speaking at a seminar entitled 'Women in a Man's World'. They laughed as she entertained them with wicked parodies of the other speakers, who had seemed to feel their brief was simply to slag off the entire male species. 'There was a camera person,' she said, 'big woman, raw-boned, crew-cut, possibly gay. She said she could do anything a man could do and better. Well, good luck to her, but she's the exception. Most women like being women and we like men around us. Ours is a greater struggle because we want everything – good job, power and financial security – but we still want to play a feminine role. We want to be wives and mothers as well, and we're not sure how to cope with it. Is it any surprise men don't either?'

'Wow! Did you say all that?' asked Sam.

'More or less.'

'I bet they liked you better than the camera person.'

Helen grinned. 'They did, actually, especially when I told them about my fight for the placenta.'

Jeremy insisted on being filled in on the story and, in spite of being a gynaecologist, both he and Sam agreed with Derek. It was too strong.

'You're impossible,' she said. 'That's what women like me are up against.' And she swept off in search of the ladies' room. When she returned Jeremy stood up and apologised. Sam stood up too. 'Are you really angry?'

She smiled. 'I was, but it's over now.'

On the Sunday morning Jeremy brought tea in bed to the lovers. Helen was a little taken aback, for she was sitting up, reading the papers, with nothing on. Jeremy did not seem to notice, but Sam hurriedly threw her a bathrobe, indicating with his eyes he would prefer that she were covered up.

'Now, what are we going to do today?' asked Jeremy. 'I'm enjoying myself so much I shan't go back till tomorrow morning.'

'Well, you and Helen can plan it,' said Sam. 'I've just got to pop into the clinic for a while. Maybe we could drive out to the country and have lunch.'

'Let's go to Brighton,' said Jeremy. 'I haven't been there since I was a child.' And so, even before Sam left the house, the day was mapped out before them.

Helen pottered into the kitchen to make coffee. She was still wearing Sam's bath robe, which was ridiculously large on her. Jeremy wandered in dressed in the casual gear beloved of English gentlemen, a superbly cut tweed jacket and cavalry twill trousers. Helen was glad he had added a tweed tie rather than a cravat; otherwise he would have reminded her too closely of her first boyfriends in Bournemouth.

'I meant what I said the other day, Helen,' he said. 'You're a remarkable girl. Sam's very lucky. He won't let you down in the end. He's very stubborn. He's always got what he wanted in the long run, and he certainly wants you. You obviously have a great time in the sack.'

'How do you know? Has he told you?'

'My dear girl, for the last two nights I have been lying awake, next door to you feeling more randy by the second.'

'Oh,' she said, blushing.

'What an English rose you are,' he said. 'Look, Helen, it might get worse before it gets better but, believe me, you're meant to be together. It's going to work out. In the meantime I'm going to give you my phone number, so if you need a friend, you're just to ring. And I'll take yours, if you don't mind – I might need a friend too.'

'Sorry,' she said. 'I think both Sam and I forget you're having a bad time yourself.'

'Mine's of my own making, though – that's the worst of it. I might just come back and settle here.'

'So through your misfortune you're reacting exactly the same way as Sam. There's something about a crisis that seems to send people scurrying for their own patch.'

'It's totally different,' he said.

'I'm not sure. Are you getting a divorce?'

'No, she's a Catholic. She doesn't believe in it. Anyway,

I'm still hoping she'll come back, though she says she won't.'

In Brighton they behaved like a trio of teenagers. They ate hamburgers in a café, played the machines on one of the piers and, later, walked around the Regency Pavilion, which they had all last visited on school trips. They were in light-hearted mood and Helen, looking at Jeremy, thought for a moment that this was the nearest she had ever come to having an older brother. She said as much.

Sam laughed and said, 'I'm not sure he sees you as a sister.'

'Shut up,' said Jeremy, but he laughed too.

Helen joined in, though she was not quite sure what the joke was.

The next morning they went their separate ways. Sam left first because he was operating.

Jeremy saw Helen to her car. 'I'll be back soon. Don't worry.'

'I'm not – not at the moment anyway. I'm on cloud nine. You've been such a help.' And, standing on tiptoe, she kissed him on the cheek before jumping into her car and heading for the studios.

'You look better,' said Laura when the girls met up.

'I am. We've all had the most wonderful weekend. Sam and I are back to normal. Let's hope it lasts, but it's terrific for now. Laura, I'm so in love with that man I can't think straight. After the meeting I'm going to pop out and buy myself something to wear tonight to celebrate. We're going to that visiting ballet company at the Coliseum, then we're having supper at the Pelican and then . . . who knows?' She smiled broadly.

Helen took one last look at herself in the mirror. She had put on today's purchase, a beautiful, drop-waisted heavy silk lavender dress by Caroline Charles. The shade complemented her colouring perfectly. She looked good and she knew it. She ran down the stairs to where she knew Sam would be waiting, her high heels announcing her arrival before she came into view. Something about his demeanour halted her in her tracks. He was not the same man who had waved farewell so gaily just a few hours before. Perhaps he had lost a patient; that always depressed him.

He did not kiss her. 'Do you mind if we forget the ballet and go home?' he asked.

'No,' she said, though she was bitterly disappointed. 'Of course not. What's wrong?'

'I'll tell you later.'

Back in his house he poured two very large brandies. He gave one to her as she sat tensely on the sofa. He walked away and stood at the fireplace, facing the wall. 'There's no easy way to tell you what I have to say – not easy for you and not easy for me – so, please, just listen. When I finished operating today two men were waiting to see me: Hamaida's brothers. She received my letter and then, apparently, told them, for the first time, what transpired all those years ago. I suppose that was her right: she was upset, I expect. They were as angry as if I'd raped her – maybe they believe I did – and as if it had happened yesterday. They told me I had insulted their sister, their family and my father's memory. In days gone by, I suppose our tribes would have waged war over it. So,' he concluded, his voice as unemotional as if he were delivering a prepared paper, 'I've given in my notice. I'm going back on October the third, and on October the tenth I shall do my duty and . . . marry their sister.'

Chapter Thirteen

'Errr! Errr!' It was three o'clock in the morning and Helen was standing at the bathroom mirror, poking a furred tongue at her hostile image. 'When are you going to stop playing Russian roulette with your life?' she demanded of the hollow-eyed wreck before her. She pinched the skin around her jaw line, which seemed flabbier than that of a few weeks ago. Her face reminded her of the pale, puffy countenance of a chief executive's wife who drinks the hours away till her straying husband, the only source of interest in her life, comes home. 'The only difference,' she said to the mirror, 'is that no man wants to come home to you.'

She drank the iced orange juice she had fetched from the kitchen when she had wakened from her uneasy sleep. She gulped it down in one breath, like a victim of the Ethiopian famine who has not tasted liquid for days. She was still thirsty, so returned to the kitchen, where she drank three full tumblers of Perrier water before staggering, unsteadily, back to bed.

Lying there, with the room swimming before her, she said, 'Oh, God,' into the stillness. She stopped herself. God did not enter into it. There could be no God. She hated him, though, if he did exist, and she hated Freddie, with whom she had spent the evening, because he was not Sam. She hated Jeremy because her fall had been all the more humiliating following his unshakeable confidence that she would win in the end. But, most of all, she hated herself.

The last few weeks were a period she would have preferred to forget. She had struggled through each day delivering, she hoped, what was required by the company but, once past the deadline of the programme, had dedicated herself to drinking to oblivion. She had accepted every invitation proffered, but when there was none she had drunk till closing time in the company bar. She was becoming a bore and, unfortunately, she had the perception to realise it. At last she fell into an unsatisfying sleep.

The telephone rang. She struggled out of her unhappy dreams and glanced at the clock. It was nine o'clock, time to get up. 'Hello,' she said aggressively.

'Miss Bartlett?'

'Yup.'

'It's Mildred Smorthwaite.'

'Oh, yes. How are you?' she asked, not caring.

'I'm fine. How are you?'

'Pass,' said Helen, knowing she should make more of an effort but unwilling to do so.

'I'm ringing before my boss, Mr Aziz, gets in.'

'Yes.' It was an uncompromising assent.

The older woman sighed audibly. 'You're my last resort. Can you do anything?'

'About what?'

'About . . . him.'

'Why?'

'I think he must be ill. He's forgetting appointments, he's . . . well, I don't know how to describe it.'

'I shouldn't worry. You'll soon have a new boss, won't you? He's resigned.'

'That's true, but the whole NHS transplant programme might collapse.'

'I don't know what you mean.'

'Well, he never drew a salary from his Health Service work, only from the clinic.'

'I didn't know that.'

'If he goes, leave alone for a moment how many people will die, the entire system might grind to a halt and a lot of people, myself included, will be out of a job.'

'That's terrible,' said Helen, 'but what can I do?'

'Well,' said Miss Smorthwaite, 'I . . . I gather you're no longer together, but . . . please, think of what you've done. I'm sure you have your reasons, but do you know how lost he is without you?'

'You don't understand,' said Helen. 'I haven't given *him* up, he did it to *me*. He's going home. That's what he wants.'

'He's got a funny way of showing it then. Please talk to him.'

'I'd like to help,' said Helen, 'but you don't know what you're asking. Anyway, we're not in communication.'

'Well, at the risk of even more trouble, I'm going to tell him I phoned you. By the way, you sound terrible. You sound like he looks.'

'Thanks a lot.'

'Helen – may I call you that? – I don't know what the problems are, but surely they can be resolved? He was so happy with you. He's a broken man.'

'Goddammit,' said Helen, 'he's doing it to himself. It's out of my hands. Goodbye.'

Helen was even more disquieted than usual when she went into work. Laura came looking for her but, as had been her pattern over the last few weeks, Helen told her she was too busy to have coffee. She hated herself again when Laura withdrew, but she could not help the fact that her friend's stable situation served only to aggravate her own unhappiness.

Sue came in. 'Do you want to do any letters?'

'No,' said Helen, 'but I will. I'll draft out what I want to say in longhand. I'll bring them through.' She did not want any prying, or even any compassionate, eyes in her office, watching her.

Sue returned to the other copytypists. 'I think Helen is getting worse,' she said to no one in particular. No one in particular could offer any comforting words.

After the programme Helen went to the social club, as had become her routine. She was into her third or fourth drink when the steward came to tell her she was wanted on the telephone. 'Who is it?' she asked.

'I don't know. He wouldn't say.'

It was less trouble to take it. 'Hello.'

'Helen, it's me.'

'Sam, why have you called me here?'

'I want to speak to you. I'm coming over.'

'No, you're not. Don't you dare come here. I won't have it.'

'OK. Come here.'

'No.'

'Helen, I beg you . . . I have to see you.'

She sighed. 'All right. I'll have to get a taxi. I've drunk too much to drive.'

He opened the door but said nothing. Helen stared at the man who was responsible for the best and the worst of her life. He moved towards her and suddenly they were in each other's arms, clinging together as though they were the only couple left after World War III.

'You still don't understand, do you?' It was Saturday morning, and the erstwhile lovers had wakened to find themselves curled round each other like four-week-old puppies in a basket. The night before they had talked till their combined exhaustion had enabled them to sleep. Sam had surfaced first, telling Helen he must go into the clinic to see a patient. She had lain in bed for a few minutes and then, as in happier times, and because she could not stay away, joined him in the bathroom. He was lying immersed in the tub and she, perched on the edge of it, remembered the past when most of their days had begun thus, with discussions about their immediate schedules or their hopes for the future.

A tear rolled down her cheek, a tear that dissolved the distance between them. He kissed her tenderly and carried her back to bed, then, putting a huge towel under his wet body and hair, he lay beside her. 'You still don't understand,' he said again.

'I understand all too well.'

'You haven't accepted it, though.'

'I have, I have,' she said, sniffing through her tears. 'I didn't call you. You called me. I was . . . getting on with it. I have accepted it. If I thought there was any hope, I wouldn't be so miserable.'

'I want you to be happy.'

'That's ridiculous. Are you happy?'

'That's not the point.'

'I think it is. I can't be happy. I love you. I want to be with you. I want to have your children. It's natural to grieve at the end of an affair.'

He probably considered 'affair' a cheap and inappropriate word. 'Helen,' he said, 'you know I care, don't you?' There was silence. 'Don't you?'

'I don't know what I know.' His mouth pressed hard on hers; it took her breath away. When at last he drew back she said, 'I'm sorry. I didn't mean to play games.'

He held her then tightly and still more tightly. 'Don't you know,' he said. 'I spend every waking hour thinking of you? Don't you know the regrets I have? Haven't I shown you in every conceivable way how much I care for you?' His tongue began circling her ear. His lips grazed her cheek, and then his tongue hovered at the entrance to her lips. She must keep them closed. She must reject him now, for both of them; if she capitulated, they would be more enmeshed than ever. 'I want you more and more. I fancied you the day we met, almost a year ago. I did, I promise you, like mad. But I adore you now, Helen, and I'm desperate to prove it to you.'

His hands caressed her shoulders and fingered her right breast. Her nipple hardened under his touch, and her breathing quickened. His tongue, failing to gain admission to her mouth, sought refuge in her ear; it was loud but so good. He tried to kiss her again, and she permitted the tips of their tongues to meet, to touch, to play. Suddenly she relaxed; his tongue forced its way past her teeth and his hand was travelling lower, finding her moist and wanting. They looked at each other as they heard and felt her involuntary readiness. He moved his hand and took hers, placing it where he needed her. The palm of her hand formed a cradle over him. She felt him stirring but hesitated before yielding to the urge to stroke this body and this man who was more than life itself. His fondling was quicker now, and she echoed his movements. They looked down at his growing desire, and then away, and back to search deep into each other's eyes.

Believing that if they made love conventionally, his guilt would overwhelm them both, she moved down to take his tumescent organ in her mouth. She licked and kissed him, confident as he writhed beneath her that his pent-up passion would spill on to her tongue, achieving a more acceptable solution. He pushed her away, rolled over and quickly entered her. She gasped: why did it have to be so marvellous? Why did he have to feel it was wrong? He filled every inch of her as he began thrusting slowly and deliberately. Just as deliberately he suddenly withdrew. He was breathing hard. 'Helen, will you take me? Will you let me come inside you?' Her mind and her body were at odds with each other. While she longed for the logical conclusion, she was terrified of its aftermath.

'Sam, how can I turn you away? I love you. I adore you. I just can't cope with what you might say when it's over.' She took him in her hand again, and the decision was made. He groaned and reached for a silk handkerchief under the pillow. His seed spurted into it, and they watched the sandy-coloured square turn a deepening brown with the impotence of their encounter.

Her own frustration overcame her and, sensing it, he kissed her all over till his lips found their throbbing goal, He tongued her, but she had thoughts only for the whole of him plumbing her insides. She looked down at the shock of his dark hair between her white thighs and only then succumbed to his expert caresses and her own fantasy of his vital body depositing the essence of life not uselessly into a handkerchief, but high and deep inside her . . .

'Well, all the neighbours are up now,' he said. She came round to find him propped up on one elbow, grinning at her.

'I'm not noisy,' she said, covered with embarrassment.

'Oh, no?' he said. 'I wonder, then, why the people in the next house are craning out of their window to get a better view.'

They laughed and kissed again but the prevailing mood remained tense.

'I want you to get out and about,' he said. 'You need to forget me.'

'I'm doing my best,' she said. 'I've had dinner with lots of people in the last few weeks.'

'Have you slept with anyone?' he asked angrily.

'Sam, stop torturing yourself.'

'You're great in bed. You should keep at it.'

'Are you going to get your rocks off imagining me being pawed all over by somebody else? Is it a solution to leap on to every Tom, Dick or Harry who might fancy a quick screw?'

'I don't know,' he said unhappily. 'I don't know anything.'

'Neither,' she said, taking his hand, 'do I.'

'We'll talk about it when I get back,' he said.

Helen sighed, wondering what there was left to talk about, but she said nothing.

Once he had gone she felt uncomfortably restless in his house. It had been a haven, a nest. They had never discussed where they would live after their marriage, but she had supposed it would be here. She stood in front of the Merrifield sculpture, hoping it would work its usual magic, but instead it made her cry. She pulled a strand of hair round to her nose and sniffed at it. As she had suspected, she smelt revoltingly of cigarettes, but this did not deter her from lighting another. She must pull herself together: surely she had more backbone than this. What was the point of hanging around Sam for the weekend when, even though he had been desperate to see her, he had not for a second suggested altering his long-term plans? She ran a bath and lay in it till the phone rang, forcing her to leave its warmth and safety.

'Darling, it's me.'

'Have you seen your patient?'

'No. I'm just going to. I rang you first to check you were all right.'

'I'm fine. I'm going to disappear in a moment.'

'Where to?'

'Um . . .' Helen searched her mind for inspiration. 'Norfolk!' she said triumphantly.

'Why there?'

'Because that's where we used to go for holidays when I was little.'

'Helen, for God's sake, at least wait till I get back.'

'I can't promise,' she said, putting the phone down.

Helen dressed herself in yesterday's clothes and tried to read. She smoked another cigarette, fiddled with the radio and then just sat, thinking of nothing in particular. She should go. There was no point in waiting.

'Don't split from me like this,' he cried, as he hurtled through the door.

'I'm not,' she said wearily. 'I just can't be here, not today. This house, you, everything . . . It was all so special. Maybe tomorrow will be better,' she said, as she wiped away yet more inevitable tears.

He poured her a brandy. 'What have I done to you?' he asked.

She studied him. Her eyes were fixed, but her brain and mouth would not collaborate to find an answer. She sipped her drink; it slipped down too easily. He took the glass to refill it, but she stopped him, knowing that if he succeeded in pouring two measures down her throat, he would be in a stronger position to insist she did not drive anywhere.

'Will you come and see me tomorrow?' he asked.

'Perhaps,' she said.

'Let me drive you home.'

'No, thank you. I'm going to walk, and when I get tired of that, I'll pick up a taxi. I do love you, Sam, but I must go.'

Sam sat fingering her brandy glass. It was a while before he could bring himself to pick up the fragments of his own day.

Helen walked by the river for a while and then hailed a cab, hoping the driver would not be talkative. Back in her flat, she washed her hair and dried it quickly with the hairdryer. She applied some mascara, appraising her appearance at the same time; the debauched living of the last few weeks had certainly taken its toll.

In her bedroom she slid open the doors of her built-in wardrobe and saw at once the lavender dress. It lay, as it had for weeks now, in a crumpled heap by her numerous pairs of shoes, a symbol of her bitterly crushed hopes. Hopes that she had known, since her meeting with Hamaida, could never be realised, but hopes that, even with that realisation, had been shocked to be so utterly annihilated.

As if in a dream, she wandered round and round her apartment. She sat for a while. Nothing made sense. Her flat, her job, her life – what were they without him? She walked to the drawer beside her bed and searched through the contents. There were a few blue pills, some white ones, some Paracetemol. She arranged them on her dressing table in a neat pattern. Were they a deadly enough cocktail?

The sun was shining through the windows. She saw the headlines: 'Star in suicide drama'. She should call someone for help, but there could be no help. There was no fight left in her – just a hideously bleak calm. I don't exactly want to die – I just want to stop, she thought. Mechanically she gathered the pills together and put them into her handbag.

Through the car windows it appeared that life for some was going on normally, but she was cocooned from the teeming pace of Ladbroke Grove and the districts that followed. A red light flashed. Yes, cars run on petrol, Helen. She was forced to stop.

Even before he saw the name on her credit card, the cashier was eyeing Helen with more than the usual interest he reserved for solo attractive women in sprauncy cars. 'It is, isn't it?' he asked.

She nodded.

'You do get up to some crazy things,' he was saying. 'What about that knife thrower and the day you went into the lions' cage? Sooner you than me. Still, I 'spect you make a lot of money.'

'It's all a myth that we're paid a fortune, you know,' she said, slowly trying to drag herself back to the real world.

'Is that a fact?' he replied, totally unconvinced.

She smiled weakly, signed the grubby scrap of paper he thrust in front of her, collected her receipt and left.

The car found its own way. 'There you are,' she said aloud. 'You must be all right.'

The next time her brain connected with her eyes she was in the curiously flat landscape dominated by sky and dotted with pink cottages that spelled East Anglia. At last she came upon the little unpretentious town of Cromer and inevitably made for the once grand hotel where she had stayed as a child.

Heads turned.

'Oh, I just felt like a day away from London,' she said simply. 'Do you have a room free?'

'Certainly, Miss Bartlett,' said the young receptionist, who could hardly wait to get rid of Helen so she could ring everyone she knew to tell them she had met a celebrity.

In the unaccustomed stillness Helen came to. She was in Cromer. Why was she in Cromer? She got out her pills. I suppose I didn't run anybody over on the way, she thought.

She went out for a while and wandered by the sea. She was wearing dark glasses and was able to wend her way without the usual interruptions. Looking out over the beach, she saw groups of little children running excitedly in and out of the waves, their bodies browning in the sun and glistening with sea spray and sweat. Family dogs were romping around in ever-decreasing circles. How easily pleased dogs are, she thought. She gradually re-established a link with the outside world. I think you're all right after all, she said to herself reassuringly.

She noticed a youngish man with a handkerchief, knotted at the four corners, covering his head. His wife was unfashionably dressed too, and they were helping their only child, a little girl, to make a sandcastle. It was like replaying film clips of her life, and Helen was suddenly filled with a fearful nostalgia for the innocence and sweetness of childhood. But was it that, or was it an appalling sense of loss at what was being denied her? It seemed certain that Sam would go and, with him, her dreams. She would never feel the same again, never marry and never experience the joys of motherhood, unless . . .

Nothing that had happened in the last few days could have made her pregnant, but she remembered again the impassioned love-making of the weekend of Jeremy's visit. It was more than five and a half weeks since she had menstruated, but it had not occurred to her until now. She tried to wish herself back into the automatic pilot that had brought her here, but real feelings were pressing for recognition. I couldn't possibly be, she thought, and with the certainty came a wave of tortuous despair and sadness. Blinking away the tears behind her dark glasses, she returned to the hotel, where she ordered a tray of tea and some sandwiches.

In the faded, chintzy bedroom the incongruity of her situation suddenly hit her. Perhaps she would end up not only without Sam but lonely and old and eccentric. Maybe she was eccentric already – a weekend in Cromer was not exactly what her viewers might envisage for her. She imagined herself here at seventy, with a walking frame and egg all down her jumper, talking about the early days in television in exchange for the odd drink. She wondered if she would learn to say, 'When I was a gel . . .' She smiled, if a trifle ironically, as her tea tray arrived.

She looked at the white sandwiches nestling in their doily. She did not think she was hungry, but the benefits of the sea air were beginning to tell, and she found, as she nibbled at the first sandwich, that her appetite was returning. It dawned on her too that, apart from her earlier medicinal brandy, she had not had a drink or a cigarette since leaving Sam.

The thought of him introduced a degree of stress into this little room. She considered ringing but decided against it. She was just beginning to feel stronger, and renewed contact could put her back where she had started. I will try to be more sensible, she promised herself, as she picked up another sandwich. If she was pregnant, an abstemious regime must be embarked upon immediately. Thinking back over her drunken forays of the last few weeks, and trying for a second to count how many cigarettes she might have smoked, she thought of the foetus she could be carrying. That would be the ultimate punishment: not just to have Sam's child after he had gone, but for it to be born handicapped because of her excesses during its first few weeks in her womb. It was too awful to contemplate. She began to weep again and, knowing she was incapable of clear thinking, she stripped off and lay naked on the top of the single bed, crying till she slept.

The flapping of the curtains at the little open windows woke her. She was slightly chilled, for a cool early evening breeze had got up while she had slept.

She had a side view of the sea, overlooking a patchwork of roofs with pantiles, broken tiles and no tiles at all. The beach was quieter now. She supposed people had left or had gone back to eat in their lodgings. The evening extended before her, so she decided to go out. It was strange to be so directionless.

Walking down the ramp from the hotel to the promenade, she was jostled by families with teenage boys who were eating soggy, flaccid chips out of trays with their fingers. The smell sickened her. Someone muttered, 'It looks like whassername off the tele.' Helen walked on, unsure whether or not her cover had been blown. She saw posters advertising 'Seaside Special: The Last Authentic end-of-the-pier Show'. It was due to start at eight-fifteen; it was now ten past. The evening was solved.

Someone had marketed a great idea – that this was a show with a preservation order stuck on it. It was doing remarkably good business, and it brought to mind a television documentary she had read about but not seen. She fancied it had featured this very production. The power of the box never ceased to amaze her.

It was surprisingly good entertainment of the type she might have enjoyed with her parents in the late Fifties, though probably the beautifully made, glittering leotards of the dancing girls were cut higher on the leg than in days gone by. 'Roamin' in the gloamin',' she sang along with the rest of the audience. The singer had built his act on the theme 'Around the World in Song'. 'There'll be a welcome in the hillsides,' they sang. Were there any Welsh there? 'And when Irish Eyes are smiling': at this she broke down and wept, even though she did not know any Irishmen. Where was the Helen Bartlett the world knew? On the end of a pier in north Norfolk and seriously questioning her sanity.

After the show she walked quickly through the busy, brightly lit bar. Her mascara had probably run, and she did not want to be recognised. She stood for a while, watching the tumbling waves that were edged in the reflected coloured lights of the pier. The tide would come in and go out again, no matter what. 'No man is an atheist when confronted by the ocean.' She was sure somebody at some time must have said that. The movement of the sea was hypnotic. It had a look about it of rich, black, icy velvet. Velvet generally suggested warmth but not here. For a second she wondered what it would feel like to walk into the waves until their coldness consumed her. 'Oh, God,' she said, 'forgive me. I know I'm being dreadful. Don't you care at all?' The moment of crisis was averted and she walked on.

Back in the hotel she asked for a glass of warm milk. It appeared there was only one ancient retainer on duty, a courteous, bald-headed porter in a faded maroon jacket. Helen thought it unfair to make him trudge up to her room, so she waited in the lounge. Again she was taken back in time to the holiday when she had been eight. Milk had not been a bedtime drink of hers for years; she had asked for it almost without thinking, perhaps in association with this particular building.

The old gentleman returned with a tray bearing a silver coffee jug full of milk, a glass and a spoon. 'Put the spoon in the glass before you pour in the milk, madam,' he advised, 'then it won't crack.'

It was all so wonderfully old-world, and again she felt almost like a child as she took note of the instructions.

In her room, while sipping the warm and comforting liquid, she debated again whether or not to call Sam. At the moment he did not loom large here, but once she had spoken to him, it would be a different story. She thought of how anxious he would be, but perhaps a generous helping of anxiety might encourage him to sort his priorities. He had sorted them, however; there was no point in assuming he had made a bad or temporary decision just because he had not ruled in her favour. The numbness came back. She looked mistily across the room to where the pattern of pills was arranged. She was too tired to fetch them. They would still be there in the morning, when her legs might work again. Perhaps she could sleep now – or was she sleeping already?

Helen woke to a sunny Sunday. She felt quite normal. She lay still, waiting for the peculiar sensations of yesterday to swamp her, but they did not. Gingerly she sat up. The room was real. She put a foot on the floor; it was firm. The pain was there, but more like a receding headache than an acute migraine. She would test her improvement outside. The air was invigorating and she felt better than she had for a long time. Her appetite too returned with a vengeance. Ignoring the gazes of the other hotel residents, she ordered tea and two poached eggs on brown toast. There were so many simple pleasures in life she had been too busy and tormented to sample of late, and poached eggs was undoubtedly one of them.

She toyed with the thought of staying in Cromer but her catharsis was complete. She was alive and able now to put everything in perspective. She could even allow contact with Sam.

There were recriminations, of course. She should have phoned. She should never have gone. She dismissed them. 'I only came back to say I'm better and I can cope with us just being friends,' she said and smiled the smile he found so utterly captivating.

'Let's go to the pub,' he said. 'If we hurry, we could have a late lunch.'

'All right, but I shall get fat because I had breakfast.'

'Sweetheart,' he observed, 'there's more fat on a French fry!'

Back in his house they read the Sunday papers and then

the restlessness began, the restlessness she thought had gone, the restlessness, in their sophistication and civilisation, they must submerge in order to enjoy a platonic friendship; the restlessness that rears its head between two lovers whose tension demands expression in love-making. She moved first, to stand behind the armchair in which he was sitting. She kissed the back of his neck and he took her left hand and held its warm softness to his cheek. Sensations of comfort and love oscillated between them.

'Come to bed,' he said at last.

She nodded.

They lay together, hardly daring to move. The phone rang; it was on her side of the bed and she reached for it automatically. He prevented her.

'Are you expecting a call from Egypt?'

'It's possible.'

'I'll go to the bathroom and you can take it.'

'No!' he pulled her back. 'Stay here. We're not in. Leave it alone.'

'Suppose it's an emergency at the hospital or the clinic?'

'They'll ring again.'

'You must answer it, Sam.'

'I won't!' She never argued when he employed that tone. He held her while the ringing continued. Finally it stopped, but the damage had been done; it seemed to Helen that every time she acquired some tranquillity it was immediately and brutally destroyed. He kissed her gently and hugged her to him, and this action thawed her emotions. The tears flowed. 'Don't cry, my sweet,' he said. 'Please don't cry. You know how much I love you.'

'Yes . . . I believe I do.'

'Helen,' he said more strongly, 'Whatever happens, I want you to go to your grave in the certain knowledge that no matter who has loved you in the past, your parents, your husband, other lovers, and . . . no matter who loves you in the future, I love you, more than the sum total of them all.'

She said nothing.

'Say something,' he said.

'I can't, Sam – don't ask. I just can't.'

He turned away from her. She thought he might sleep but suddenly she felt his hand reach out to fondle her. It was as if his face were turned to what he must do in the East but his body could not help responding to what he knew and loved in the West. He turned to her and kissed her deeply, then rotated her body and quickly pushed himself into her while he continued to reach around to maintain the rhythm and pressure of his caress. She was frightened, for she felt he was acting against his better judgement, but instinctively she reacted to him as her compulsive longing asserted itself. There were no whispered words of endearment but each of them rode together to their peak and the release it must bring. She was on one of those swingboats that had been an attraction at the fairgrounds in her youth. The hope grew into a certainty that at any moment she would topple over the edge of delight and experience the rapid succession of little pulses, like smiles, deep inside her. The warm, prickly sensation began to spread upwards from the soles of her feet.

'Oh, Christ! Oh, no, Sam – oh, my God, no!' For at that second she was to abandon herself to ecstasy he pulled himself out of her abruptly and aggressively.

This was the moment she descended to the pit of degradation. Nothing that had gone before, nothing in all the months of turmoil, compared with this. She felt like a prostitute whose client turns away at the eleventh stroke, filled with repugnance and shame. She lay rigid and defiled for a few minutes then rose, rescued all her scattered clothing from the floor and went to take a bath in an attempt to eradicate the episode from her body and her mind. She spent a long time alone and did not leave the humid heat of the bathroom until she had dressed.

Sam looked at her. 'I don't suppose there's any point in my saying I'm sorry, but I am . . . desperately.'

'No, there's no point, Sam, no point at all. There's nothing more to be said.'

Driving through the sunny evening streets to her own flat, the unreal emptiness returned. Death must be like this: the end of everything. She considered driving on and on for ever and ever. No one would find her. Or perhaps she could crash into a wall and wake from this nightmare for a searing second before she died.

Some time later she realised that she had no idea where she was. She stopped the car. She was shaking and felt as afraid as if she had stumbled into an alien land. So she was losing her mind after all. She searched for her atlas of Greater London and forced herself to concentrate on it until she memorised her route home. Her legs would hardly hold her as she staggered into her flat. She shut the door behind her and leant on it for support, then with a monumental effort lurched into the bedroom, where she threw herself on to the bed and slept.

Some hours later the doorbell buzzed. She slipped into her dressing-gown and reached for the entry phone. Perhaps all the suffering was worth it after all – perhaps Sam had come to his senses.

'Hello.'

'Helen, it's Freddie.'

'What do you want?'

'That's not very friendly.'

'No, it isn't.'

'Let me in, Helen.'

She pressed the button that would release the catch on the front door and went to her own door to wait for him.

Freddie took one look at her. 'You need a drink,' he said.

'I was going to give up.'

'I don't think this is the time.'

He poured brandy for her and a scotch for himself. 'Do you want to tell me?'

She shook her head.

'If you're not careful, you're going to make yourself very ill,' he said.

She said nothing. He took her hand. She sat passively while he talked and from time to time recharged their glasses. The dazed dreaming had taken hold again and she could not bring herself out of it. Freddie embraced her. It was not unpleasant. He was not Sam, but he was solid and kind and here. He did seem to be here. He slipped his hand into her robe and, cupping one of her breasts, bent to kiss it. He untied the belt around her waist; she was outside herself watching this man uncovering her for the first time. He began to stroke her, which brought her back to reality. She sat up. 'Just what do you think you're doing?'

'Ah . . . a reaction.'

'Get out of my flat, Freddie,' she said quietly.

'Helen, I'm sorry. I thought maybe you needed to be loved.'

'Well, I do, but not by you . . . I've done with all that anyway. I've just given it up for ever. Now,' she said, her voice steadily rising, 'I asked you to get the hell out of here.'

'Don't get hysterical. I don't think I should leave you like this.'

'I don't care a tuppenny fuck what you think. Get out, Freddie, just get out!'

He backed off the sofa. 'OK, if that's what you want. Calm down, Helen. I'm going.'

Finding herself alone again, she looked at the half-filled brandy glass before her and, with great deliberation, walked to the kitchen and poured its contents down the sink. She was not going to be destroyed by this man, that man, the demon drink or cigarettes. From now on she would be reliant on nothing and nobody. She took another bath and then, before retiring, dug out the Jane Fonda video cassette. Tomorrow she would begin a fresh campaign. She would turn herself into super-woman – super-cool, super-efficient, super-self-sufficient.

'Have I got a goodie for you today!' said Derek with a laugh at the next morning meeting.

'Oh, yes?' she queried.

'Mr Danger from Denmark.'

'Who on earth's that?'

'He does an act in Clacton, and the punters are either walking out or staying and being very sick.'

'What does he do?'

'He sticks daggers into himself to the tune of "The Ride of the Valkyries".'

'This isn't April the first, is it?'

'No, I'm serious.'

'It's ridiculous, Derek. At the moment he's frightening hundreds of people at a time and we're going to give him the chance to terrify millions. Where's the sense in that?'

'It'll make terrific television.'

'Oh, my God, where have I heard that before? Look, I'd just like it put on record that I think it's bloody irresponsible.' And with that she swept out.

They were due to record at eleven-thirty, so she went downstairs to the make-up department. If the powers that be deemed this speciality act suitable for the viewers, so be it. On her way Helen passed through reception. 'There are flowers for you, Helen,' said the receptionist. 'I had them put in your dressing room.'

'That's very kind of you,' she said and made a quick detour to see whom they might be from. While she was persuading herself she wanted no further contact with Sam, she was shaking with anticipation that they might be from him.

They were from Freddie. 'Sorry,' read the card, 'I took advantage of a situation. You're beautiful even when you're tearful but you're terrifying when you're angry. Love, Freddie.'

Well, that's that, she thought.

In the make-up room she made the best of a bad job. Her skin was blotchy from weeks of heavy drinking and continual crying. The phone rang. 'There are flowers for you in reception, Helen,' said the make-up girl who took the message.

'There can't be. I've had them.'

'Well, that's what she said.'

'OK,' said Helen. 'Thanks.' She wandered back to the front desk with her hair in heated rollers. There were more flowers; these were even more splendid than the first. Perhaps Freddie was genuinely fond of her after all.

In the dressing-room she unpinned the little envelope and took out the card. 'A million apologies to the only love of my life from "the other side of you",' it said. She pressed the card to her chest. Tears threatened again. How could so much love go so badly wrong?

Mr Danger from Denmark was about six foot six in both directions; he was dressed like Tarzan in the movies. She wondered how good he was at his act, for on close scrutiny his body appeared to be a mass of scars. She offered her hand, which was lost in the giant paw held out to her.

'I've heard what you do,' she said. 'I'm not sure I'm feeling strong enough. But what'll happen is, you'll do a brisk ten-second warm-up, I'll walk in and we'll talk briefly while you begin your act, and then we'll bring up the music, I'll walk out of shot and you can finish.'

He nodded. She supposed he spoke English. He picked up the tools of his trade, a cross between knives and enormous hatpins, and followed her into the studio. He rehearsed the end of his act to the throbbing music, so that the cameras could get their positions.

'Excuse me,' said one very green-looking cameraman, as he rushed from the studio. There was a hiatus. Helen waited confidently for someone to call a halt to the proceedings. No one did, and some minutes later a relief cameraman appeared and quickly made a note of his shots.

'OK, we'll put a clock on it,' said the floor manager. 'When I give you a cue,' he said to Mr Danger, 'you go into your warm-up.' The big man nodded. The clock reached minus three, the monitor faded to black, the floor manager dropped his arm and, as the picture came up, the guest gave a blood-curdling cry, plunged a pin into his left arm and then wiggled it backwards and forwards until it reached home.

Helen walked in. 'I understand people are frightened by your act, and I think I can see why.'

'I'm unique,' he said.

'I wouldn't dispute that,' she answered, as he plunged another instrument into his right arm. 'Do you always stick these weapons into precisely the same holes?'

'Oh, no,' he said and, taking a long, thin pin, he pierced one cheek and pushed the sharp end through his mouth and out of the other side.

Helen felt dizzy. She breathed deeply. Without realizing it, she covered her face with her hands; she peered between her fingers and, despite the fact she had a minute to go on the interview, she wound it up by saying, 'I think we'll bring in your music now and just watch the rest of it. Thanks for joining us.' She walked out of shot and up to the other end of the studio, where she drank two glasses of water. Wagner must be turning in his grave, she thought, as the music swelled to another crescendo. She kept her eyes averted from the scene and caught the look of one of the sound men who shook his head slowly. It was over at last.

'We'll just wait for a clear,' said the floor manager.

'Well, I'll tell you something,' said Helen, finding her voice. 'We're not doing it again.'

'Hear, hear!' said the cameramen.

Helen looked at Mr Danger and saw threads of blood appearing in the areas from which he was removing the daggers. 'Would you like a drink?' she asked, determined to be sociable.

'That would be most kind,' he said in his heavy Scandanavian accent.

They went to the green room, and the large gin-and-tonics arrived. Helen began to giggle. She tried to smother it, thinking he would be offended, but the more she tried to suppress her laughter, the more it burst out. She was looking at his dimples, which on inspection proved to be holes, and she could not wait for him to take his first sip, imagining the gin spraying out from both sides of his face like a trick performed by a clown.

Nothing of the sort happened; it was all very disappointing. 'What else do you do in your act?'

He put his glass down and looked into her eyes. 'I hypnotise women. I love beautiful women.'

Helen swayed slightly; for a second she was suspended. His eyes bore into her. She shook her head vigorously. 'I didn't ask for an encore – I think you've done quite enough already. We only paid you for one act. Thanks for coming. I have to go. I'll get one of the girls to look after you.'

He smiled. 'OK, little lady.'

In the newsroom Derek was waiting. 'Wonderful stuff, wonderful! The best television I've ever seen. You were great. You really looked horrified.'

'I was.'

'Yes, well, anyway, it was smashing . . . But, look, don't be annoyed . . . it was far too horrific to transmit at six. It'll never go out, I'm afraid.'

'And when Derek, that's my boss, said "It'll never go out, I'm afraid," I thought I'd kill him.'

'It sounds frightful.' Jeremy laughed on his end of the line in Paris. 'Anyway, the reason I phoned – and I don't want to upset you – is, what on earth's gone wrong with you and Sam? I've tried to ring him several times at work. The dragon, what's her name, Smorthwaite, always says he's busy, so tonight I waited until ten o'clock and rang him at home. He was polite but very distant.'

'Oh. But was he all right, do you think?'

'I don't know. I thought you might throw some light on the matter.'

'Jeremy, our relationship has completely disintegrated. I don't know how much I should tell you but . . . Remember the day you went back?'

'Yes. I thought you promised to call if you were in trouble.'

'I did, but . . .'

'Never mind, Helen. What happened?'

'That very day two of Hamaida's brothers went to see Sam and he met me that night. He told me he'd resigned and he was leaving for home on October the third and on October the tenth he was going to do his duty, I think he said, and . . . marry their sister.'

'Oh, my God, Helen. I'm so sorry. I wish you'd called.'

'Well, instead I went on a bender. I was in such a state I couldn't contact anyone. I was drunk every night for three weeks. Then last weekend we got together at his instigation . . . I can't tell you what happened, but it was terrible, really, the worst. The only good thing is I've taken stock this week. I've been very boring – I've come home after the programme every night, I haven't had a drink at all and I've stopped smoking. I am trying not to be a wimp.'

'Helen, you're not a wimp. You're a very brave lady. Look, I think I'd better come over next weekend.'

'Well, don't do it for me. I'm OK.'

'Helen, I think you should still stick in there. He might not go home, or maybe he will, but it'll never work. He'll be back.'

'Jeremy, stop it. I've been through all of that in my mind. To save my sanity I've simply had to believe it's completely over. Anyway, how are you coping?'

'Better than I thought I would. I'll tell you next weekend. I'll ring you when I get in.'

'Fine . . . Jeremy?'

'Yes.'

'Could I ask you something?'

'Of course.'

'Is it possible to get pregnant less than a month after you stop taking the contraceptive pill?'

'It's possible, but most people have to try for quite a while.'

'That's what I thought.'

'Helen, what are you saying?'

'I've . . . I've got a . . . friend in that position. I just thought, you being a consultant gynaecologist, I'd check for her.'

'I see,' he said.

The phone rang again almost immediately. It was Sam. 'You've been on the phone for ages,' he said accusingly.

'Yes,' she said. 'Jeremy rang.'

'Did you tell him everything?'

'No. I told him you were going to get married but I obviously didn't go into any of the lurid details of last weekend.'

'He rang me too.'

'He told me. He's worried about you.'

'He doesn't need to be.'

'Fine.'

'I was just thinking, Helen, about the weekend he was here and how great it was.'

'It was,' she agreed quietly.

'Helen . . .' She heard him take a deep breath. 'Helen, let me make love to you . . . just once more. Last weekend was terrible. There's no point in going on about it, but I'm lying here with the most massive erection – please come over. Let the last time be . . . well, as good as it's ever been.'

'No, Sam. I'm sorry.'

'Listen,' he said, 'it's Friday, the ninth of August. Two months tomorrow I'm supposed to marry somebody else, God help me. In less than two months I'll be leaving here, maybe for ever. Please, Helen, I want to give you something to remember. If you could see me now, you wouldn't be able to resist.' He sounded boyish and teasing but was utterly serious beneath the banter.

Hating herself, she said, 'All right. I'm coming.'

Because of her ban on alcohol, at least she was fit to drive, though it was past midnight – but was she wise? If they made love wonderfully, it would be harder than ever to put him out of her life, and if it proved to be another disaster, she was not sure that this time she could survive. She wanted to turn back but could not.

He must have heard the car draw up, for he was at the front door as she rang the bell. He kissed her even before he closed it, then his right hand began a slow caress around her body. He kissed her breasts through the track suit she had donned so swiftly back home.

Upstairs in his bedroom he removed her clothing hurriedly; he was in a frenzy. She gave into his every move, but something was wrong.

'Damn,' he said. 'Damn, damn, damn. I was so ready for you before you came and now look at it.'

'It doesn't matter, Sam. You're obviously overwrought. Lie down. It'll be all right, you'll see. There's no hurry.' Her fingers coaxed him expertly, but nothing stirred. At last she gave up.

'This is the most demoralising thing that's ever happened to me,' he said. 'I wanted so badly to give it to you, Helen, like I used to, hard and . . . I just wanted . . .' He burst into tears. 'I am so sorry, Helen, really sorry.'

'It doesn't matter,' she said, with tears streaming down her face as she struggled back into her track suit. 'It's nobody's fault.' She ran from the house and drove off at speed. 'It doesn't matter,' she said again into the darkness. 'It really doesn't matter. Nothing matters . . . nothing at all.'

Chapter Fourteen

A sledge-hammer, that was what it was, a sledge-hammer buried deep in her abdomen like the ice pick that had, she seemed to remember, ended up in the brain of Trotsky, thus terminating his existence. She tried to ignore it for a second and to focus her attention on all the unhurting bits of her. Did she feel ill? Not terribly. It must be muscular then. She was pleased with her diagnosis; she did not host and produce the medical feature for nothing.

The pain had awakened her; it was still early. She cast her mind back over the week. Was it really only seven days since she had last seen Sam? It was. Mind you, he had been on the telephone every day, twice a day sometimes. In the last week she had thrown herself into a strenuous fitness regime. She performed to the Jane Fonda tape in the mornings and again in the evenings and she had joined a health club to fill in the odd lunchtime when she was not busy. She was feeling fitter and, more than that, was beginning to feel proud of herself for regaining control of her life. She was keeping busy at work and determinedly cheerful. She had recalled that, when viewers cast her in the role of agony aunt by writing to her with details of their loveless marriages or broken hearts, she had always exhorted them to be positive – to learn a language or take up karate. Was she not being positive? She was. It was nobody's business that she wept when she was alone. No one knew about that, not even Sam, and in her occupied daylight hours she almost forgot it herself.

Freddie was the only one who had tried to probe. She had been surprised to hear from him again. There was no place for him in her life, and she had told him so. Moreover, she had no wish for his analytical techniques to be deployed in her direction, even if they came free gratis and for nothing, so she was efficiently bright with him too. 'I liked you better when you were real,' he said angrily the last time he had telephoned. For a second she had almost lost control of her act. She wavered but it was obviously a psychiatric ploy that she had the good sense to resist. She would not let him near. No one was to come near, and in that way she would render herself impervious to any further hurt. She might never, she supposed, ever, in her heart of hearts, be truly happy again, but she would sacrifice that extreme in order to eliminate the other.

This spasm seemed to be gripping her for a long time. It was eight-thirty. She picked up the telephone by her bed and called the office. 'Samantha, it's Helen.'

'Hello. You're ringing early. I'm only just in.'

'Is Derek there yet?'

'Just. He's on the phone to one of the units – there's been a bad crash on a contraflow system on the M1.'

'Not *again*. Well, you'd better not disturb him. Just say I don't think I'll be in for a while. There's something wrong with my stomach – I've probably strained a muscle.'

'Are you all right?'

'I don't know. I'll ring later.'

Helen considered her next step; this really was a ridiculous predicament. It was like a music-hall joke about an old boy stuck in a compromising posture with lumbago. She braced herself against the pain and swung her legs out of bed. She took a deep breath, for now she felt very ill indeed. She tried to stand, but the stabbing sensation was too intense and the room began to swim before her. She put her hand to her head and realised she was perspiring, though her body was shivering. She fell back on the bed.

The phone rang. 'Good morning, sweetheart.' It was Sam.

'Hello, Sam,'

'What's wrong?' he asked.

The concern in his voice caught her off guard. 'I seem to have twisted something in my tummy.'

'What do you mean?'

'Just that. I can't move. I know it sounds melodramatic, but I really can't move. I tried to stand. I can't.'

'Oh God,' he said.

'Keep calm.'

'I should be saying that to you.'

She laughed. 'Ooh, that hurt.'

'I'll call your doctor.'

'No, you won't. I'll call him. I expect you're busy.'

'Well, I am about to get scrubbed up but . . .'

'But nothing. I'll cope. I'll call him now. I'll phone you later.' She put the phone down to prevent further argument and to stem her need to say, 'Yes, please alter your plans. Be here. Take charge. Look after me.'

She rang the surgery; it was engaged. She rang again and again and again. Eventually the line was free and she got through to the harassed receptionist. 'It's Helen Bartlett here.'

'Oh, Miss Bartlett, how are you?'

Damn-fool question, thought Helen. She had visited the doctor only occasionally, once when she had laryngitis and then, of course, for repeat prescriptions of her contraceptive pill. A thought struck her with the same force as had the pain earlier. 'That's why I'm ringing. I'm very uncomfortable and I can't move.'

'I think you'd better get yourself down here right away,' said the girl helpfully.

In spite of herself Helen smiled. 'I'll do my best – I'll get a taxi.'

'Fine,' said the receptionist cheerfully. 'I'll see if Dr Brookbank can fit you in.'

Helen called the taxi company. Fighting waves of nausea, she pulled on a track suit and slipped her feet into a pair of sandals. On her hands and knees she reached the door to her own flat and then negotiated the stairs down to the main entrance by edging herself slowly, a step at a time, on her bottom. She would have liked assistance, yet, perversely, she was pleased to be spared the indignity of being discovered by any of the other occupants.

The taxi driver rang the bell and, gritting her teeth, she pulled back the heavy front door. 'Miss Bartlett,' said the taxi driver, catching her as she almost fainted, 'you do look queer.' Helen said nothing for she could not. He half carried her to the cab and half carried her from it into the waiting-room when they arrived. She realised suddenly that she had come out without money. 'That's OK,' he said. 'Have it on us.'

The receptionist grinned at Helen as she edged herself into a chair. She tried to breathe deeply. There was a mother and her child who, every now and again, pretended to be an ambulance, accompanied by suitably strident sound effects. Obviously she should concentrate on the pain in order not to lose her patience. The mother was a viewer in all probability.

She was supposed to be going to the launch of one of the major girlie calendars, for yesterday she had interviewed the photographer who had taken this year's raunchy pictures and two of the girls who had appeared in them. Helen considered she might have stood up to their younger and more curvaceous beauty had she been on form, but decided, even after the doctor had given her a shot to get her on her feet to do today's programme, she would duck out of the gathering of the world's most beautiful people. She smiled as she remembered the girls, Melanie from Alabama who thought that 'nood mardlin' would get her into the movies, and Suzanne from Romford, who had missed her dog while posing on the sun-drenched beaches of Jamaica. 'E's ever so intelligent,' Suzanne had said in the interview, and Helen had had to bite her tongue to stop herself from saying, 'How would *you* know?'

The little boy had finished being an ambulance, she noticed. He was now a fire engine. Mercifully the receptionist interrupted her thoughts and announced that the doctor would see her. Helen stood up and the room went black.

When she came round, she was in the surgery. She was

lying nude from the waist down, but she did not feel like a model in a prestigious calendar. The doctor pressed down hard on the offending pain and then removed his hands with a sudden jerk. Helen cried out as the quivering continued for several seconds. 'Now, my dear,' he said, 'presumably you're with Bupa?'

Helen nodded.

'You have regular private gynaecological checks too, don't you?'

'Yes, with Sebastian Turnbell,' she whispered.

'We'll ring him and we'll also get an ambulance.'

'Surely that's not necessary,' she said, reasserting her independence.

'I'm afraid it is.'

The doctor gave the receptionist a number Helen knew well; Sebastian operated at the same clinic as Sam. As the woman left to make the telephone calls, the doctor closed the door. Thinking she was alone, Helen allowed a tear or two to escape.

'Could you be pregnant?' he asked bluntly, out of sight.

'It's unlikely,' she said.

'But possible?'

She nodded.

'I'm sorry to say I think you may have an ectopic pregnancy. Do you know what that is?'

'I think so . . . It's when it's growing in the Fallopian tube, isn't it?'

'That's right.'

'Will they have to operate?'

'I should save the questions for the surgeon,' he said unhelpfully.

After that everything happened very quickly. She was carried out on a stretcher to the waiting ambulance, and the next thing she knew she was being wheeled into a room and slid on to a bed. Someone punctured her left arm and set up a drip. This is madness, she thought. I'm never ill.

Sebastian, a clean-faced, greying man in a well-cut suit loomed before her. 'Well, well, Helen,' he said, for he knew her both from her annual consultation and from the odd medical function she had attended with Sam. 'When did you have your last period?'

'I can't remember . . .' She was normally so precise. 'Probably seven weeks ago.'

'Have you had a pregnancy test?'

'No. I'd only just come off the pill, and, um, I'd had a lot of . . . emotional upset. I didn't think . . .'

'Well, it might be an ovarian cyst, but my gut feeling tells me it's not.'

'Does it mean I'll lose the baby if there is one?'

'Oh, yes I'm afraid so, but I'll take a look first. You'll have to sign a form, though, Helen. Who's your next of kin?'

'I thought it was . . . Oh, God, I don't know – put the company down.' She burst into tears.

'Don't worry,' he said. 'Does Sam know you're here?'

'No, but he . . . he rang this morning. He knew I didn't feel well. But, Sebastian, you mustn't tell him what it might be. We're no longer together.'

'I thought as much. I heard he'd resigned, and he hasn't seemed himself lately. Still, we'll talk about that later. Is he the father?'

She nodded. 'Nevertheless, you mustn't tell him: it wouldn't help.'

'All right,' he said, and patted the hand that was not attached to the drip.

'Sebastian?'

'Yes?'

'Please . . . save my baby if there is one . . . if you can, and please . . . leave as many of my bits intact as possible.' She was deeply upset now.

'Helen, all I can promise is that I'll look after you. I'm going to give you an injection. It'll make you very drowsy. Things won't seem so bad.'

Helen flinched as the needle went in and shortly afterwards there was only blackness for the second time that day.

She was thrashing about on the bed. There was a warm stickiness beneath her; her throat felt as though it were packed with cut glass; and there was a smouldering pain somewhere low down in her body. There were blurred figures before her and, though she could hear them, she could not convey her feelings back. She was thinking hard, please help me, give me a drink of water, where the hell is Sam?, but she was not sure if she was voicing her thoughts. She started shaking her head from side to side.

'It's a pity she's come round so quickly.'

Someone else said, 'It's typical of her.'

'Well, she's profoundly distressed. I think I'd better give her something.'

Helen felt like a trussed and tranquillised tiger on a veterinary operating bench. She submitted to the indignity of being rolled over and having a needle plunged into her backside because there was no life left in her. The whole sequence, alternatively, might be a dream. A feeling like reaching the summit of a roller-coaster began in her toes and swept in a curve through her body, engulfing her brain. Then there was nothing.

When she came round again the room seemed more real. She tried to speak. 'I . . .' Her voiced cracked.

'Helen,' said the voice that came from the seated figure holding her hand.

'Sam?'

'He'll be here soon. It's Jeremy.' He bent over and kissed her cheek and then offered a beaker of water in which there was a bent drinking straw. She gulped at it but he steadied her. 'Helen, go easy or you'll be sick.'

She sipped again. 'My mouth,' she said, 'tastes like the inside of a vacuum cleaner.'

She heard the smile in his voice. 'I know, pet, but put up with it for a while longer. Just one more sip.'

Helen made the best of it and closed her eyes.

'I'll come back tomorrow,' said Jeremy, as Sebastian entered. She wanted to ask where Sam was or whether he cared but felt too drained to articulate the questions.

Sebastian closed the door so that they were alone. 'Who was that?'

'Jeremy Woollard. He's a friend of Sam's.'

'Oh – practises in Paris, doesn't he? He's written some very good papers.'

'Probably. Well, what did you do to me?'

'It was what I . . . what we thought. I had to remove your right Fallopian tube and, while I was at it, I took away your right ovary, which wasn't in great shape either.'

'Was all that absolutely necessary?'

'Helen, you would have died if I hadn't operated. It's a very serious complication.'

'So . . . my baby?' She began to cry.

He patted her hand. 'You're not too old to have another – your left side is functioning. It'll be more difficult to get pregnant, but not impossible.'

'I forgot,' she said wearily. 'It doesn't really matter.' Tears streamed down her face.

'Helen,' said Sebastian, 'I know you're upset, but I also think you're exhausted mentally and physically. I'm going to give you something to make you sleep now.'

'Why not?' she said. She was beginning to feel like a pin cushion.

Some time later her hand made contact with blood beneath the sheets, though she was too dopey to determine whether it was seeping through the surgical dressing covering her wound or flooding from her vagina. She pressed the bell that was attached by a safety pin to her pillow.

Two nurses and a houseman ministered to her nether regions. They were whispering but she thought she caught the word 'surgery' before she slipped into sleep.

'She's not been at all well,' a nurse was explaining in her doorway. 'She was haemorrhaging earlier, but it stopped in the end. She's had two pints of blood and we're just keeping an eye on her now.'

'I must see her,' said a familiar voice. 'I won't stay long.'

It was dark outside; Helen supposed it must be quite late. Sam stood in the doorway. He looked haggard and pale. 'Darling, I'm never with you when it counts,' he said. 'I'm sorry. I should have been here, but I've literally been in the theatre since nine this morning.'

'What time is it now?' she asked weakly.

'Half past ten.'

'You must be tired,' she said, trying to form her mouth into a smile.

'What happened? I managed to see Jeremy – he's waiting for me now – but he didn't know anything, or if he did, he wasn't saying.'

'I had an ovary taken away – some sort of cyst, I think.'

Sam looked puzzled. Through the haze of drugs and pain she perceived he did not believe her, but maybe he believed that she believed she had spoken the truth.

'I'll go and let you sleep. Thank God Jeremy's here.'

'Go carefully, my little love,' she whispered into the room rather than to him. His face was suddenly in front of her and he gave her the tenderest of kisses. She thought he was crying but perhaps the tears were her own. Stay here and make love to me, she thought, but it had been useless before and she was useless now . . .

Sebastian visited her bright and early the next morning. It was Saturday, but he obviously thought his private patients were worth a visit. Helen was grateful but guilty, thinking of those who could not afford to pay for such attentive treatment.

'When can I go back to work?' she asked.

'Oh, heavens, she's got her voice back.' He smiled. 'Not for a while – we're not by any means out of the woods yet. Don't you realise how serious this is?'

'Oh, I realise,' she said, though her mind led to her unborn child and was not concerned so much for her own well-being.

'You'll be here at least ten days.'

'Oh, my God.'

'Listen, Helen, you'll just have to accept it.'

The room began to fill with flowers – from Sam, from Jeremy, from the company, from Derek, from Laura. By lunchtime it was embarrassing.

Laura telephoned. 'Helen, I'm so sorry. What happened?'

'The official version is I had an ovarian cyst.'

'Will you tell me the actual version when I come to see you?'

'Sure, but leave it for a while. I don't feel very well yet.'

Helen used her remote-control panel to switch on her television set. A news bulletin was just beginning. 'There is still no trace of four-year old Cindy Patterson, who disappeared while playing outside her home in Notting Hill Gate at around eleven yesterday morning.' A picture of an adorable black toddler flashed on to the screen. 'Fears are growing for her safety.' The picture dissolved into a short clip of the distraught mother pleading for her child's return.

Helen's heart went out to the mother. How strange that at the very time she was having her own baby cut from her, this other woman should have lost her viable and energetic four-year-old. Oh, God, she thought, you took my baby, you took the child in Regent Street – what sort of a God are you? Surely you don't need this one too? She began to cry.

Various people, Sam included, came to see her but she was too depressed to speak. Sebastian returned and prescribed some heavy sedation. 'Obviously you must grieve, Helen,' he said, 'but you'll impede your physical recovery if you're too upset. It's for your own good.' She did not argue, for she had relinguished any form of control. 'I'm also putting a ban on visitors,' said Sebastian.

'Good,' she answered.

Saturday passed and most of Sunday. She was lying, motionless, with the television set off, her supper tray untouched and the papers unopened beside her. Jeremy crept in. 'I've had to jump through hoops with Turnbell just to have five minutes, but I'm going back in the morning and I had to see you.'

She looked at him with eyes as heavy as her heart.

'It was an ectopic pregnancy wasn't it?' he pressed.

'No, it was an ovarian cyst.'

'Helen, don't insult me. Don't you think I know my own job? Listen, have you ever asked – begged – Sam not to go home but to stay?'

'I don't think so . . . not in so many words.'

'You should – he's devastated. He loves you. He doesn't want to go back. Helen, you must tell him about the baby. You must ask him to stay.'

'I can't. If he doesn't want me enough, I won't grovel.'

'It's not grovelling. He needs to be saved from a terrible fate and, quite apart from that, medically he'll be wasted. Please try.'

It was a long-playing gramophone record. 'I really don't feel very well, Jeremy. Do you mind going?'

He sighed. 'All right, but I'll ring you and I'll be back in a fortnight. Helen . . . ,' he began again with a desperate sadness in his voice.

'Goodbye, Jeremy,' she said calmly.

The days in the clinic passed gradually. Helen did what she was told. She took a bath when the nurses encouraged her; she submitted to Sebastian's physical examinations; and she made some attempt to eat. The only commitment she made for herself was to watch the news. There was still no sign of the little black girl, Cindy, and Helen's mind was inextricably linked with her fate.

Sam came to see her every day. He held her hand but neither of them said much.

Sebastian was sitting with her a week after the operation. 'Do you want to tell me?' he asked.

'Tell you what?' she responded blankly.

'Helen, you've been through a lot. You were hurt in Regent Street as well. It's not surprising you're . . .' He looked embarrassed. 'Would you see a psychiatrist? You're fit enough, physically, to go home soon, but I'm not happy about your state of mind.'

'When can I go?'

'Sunday, I should think.'

'That's good.'

'You didn't answer my question, and I don't think you should be on your own at home.'

'I want to be alone. Anyway, I know a psychiatrist – Freddie Longhurst. I'll call him if I need him.'

'But will you know?' asked Sebastian as he left, looking worried.

When Sam came in the next day she told him she would be going home on the following one. He offered to collect her.

'Thanks,' she said and that was all.

Helen felt far less steady on her feet when the fresh air hit her while walking the few steps from the clinic to Sam's car. He was so caring, so solicitous, as he guided her up the steps to the front door and then up the flight of stairs to her own flat. Inside she stopped with surprise, for the furniture in the lounge had been moved around to accommodate the baby grand piano by the bay windows that was gleaming in the sunlight.

'What – ?' she began.

He kissed her gently. 'A coming-home present,' he said.

Now was the moment, now when his kindness both gladdened and saddened her. 'Sam,' she said, 'is there any possibility that if I asked you, pleaded with you, to stay with me, you'd give up the idea of going back to Egypt?'

He looked stricken.

'No,' she said. 'I thought not. Could you make me a cup of tea?'

'I did ask him,' she said to Jeremy, who was phoning from Sam's house.

'Can I come over tomorrow?'

'Yes, but don't tell Sam. I don't want to see him.'

'When did you have the conversation with him?'

'It wasn't much of a conversation . . . When I came out of the hospital a week ago tomorrow.'

'Have you seen him since?'

'No.'

'He's very upset.'

'I'm sorry. What can I do? Do you know, they still haven't found that little girl yet. She must be alive, it's the only thing that makes any sense – '

'Helen, I don't know what you're talking about. What little girl?'

'Surely you know.' She sighed with irritation. 'I'm going to bed. I'll see you tomorrow.'

The next day, while she was waiting for Jeremy, the

phone rang twice. She was touched by the concern of her friends but removed from it. She felt entirely tranquil; she had no hopes, no desires, no secrets. Perhaps she would feel more alive when she returned to work. She supposed she could still function in the accepted way in front of the cameras; television had, for a while, become as unreal and unfamiliar to her as it was to the average viewer. She was planning to return in a week, for she was rested, but how she felt about it she hardly knew. She had no feelings except one: she was desperate for Cindy Patterson to be found alive. She made a date with every news bulletin and read every newspaper reference to her.

The first call was from Laura. 'Helen, you've put me off long enough. You've obviously been very ill, but surely I could see you soon?'

'Sure . . . I'm sorry. What about tomorrow?'

'Fine. I'll be round after work. What was wrong with you, by the way?'

'I'll tell you tomorrow.'

The other call came from Freddie, who had been ringing every other day since her return. He had seemed upset that he had not known she was in the clinic and that she had not told him. His first call on her return had reflected his sense of rejection. 'I know you've been ill, but only because they said so on your programme.'

She had told him she had a little gynaecological problem.

Today he said, 'I insist on seeing you, Helen.'

Might as well be hung for a sheep as a lamb, she thought. Everyone seemed determined to turn her sanctuary into Clapham Junction. 'Tuesday?'

'I'll be there – around six.'

'Fine,' she said, though nothing was.

Jeremy arrived. 'What little girl?' he asked, as he had on the phone.

'Cindy Patterson, the little black girl who disappeared just up the road from here on the day of my operation.'

'Oh, yes. I think I read something in the papers.'

'Something!' she said witheringly.

He developed a theory about the projection of her grief

on to this child but kept it to himself. He looked searchingly at her. 'How are you?' he asked.

'Rested.' She smiled, though the smile stopped short of her eyes.

They talked for a while, but Helen felt as though she were encased in glass. It was of little consequence – perhaps, indeed, it was desirable.

'I'm worried about you, Helen,' he said at last.

'You don't need to be.'

He spoke more loudly. Even through her partition she could see he was getting exasperated, though obviously it could have nothing to do with her. 'Helen.' He held her hands and, pulling her to him, kissed her on the mouth. 'I have something to tell you.'

She forced herself to try to look interested.

'I've thought about you a lot,' he went on. 'A lot – do you hear? I've tried to bring you and Sam together and finally I have to admit it's not working. I could shake you both – you're so in love, it's bloody ridiculous – but, well, I too have feelings for you and they're growing. I won't intrude before and unless Sam goes, but if he does, I want to see you – for me.'

Was he being kind? How could anyone fancy, even like, the empty shell she had become? It was probably a trick. Or was it? She felt an emotion stirring. It was difficult to identify, so she settled for confusion. 'I don't think you should have said all that.'

'Probably not. It's too soon and you're still very shocked.'

'Am I? Is that what it is?' Her voice was cracking.

'Ring me any time you want. I'll phone you from time to time but I won't be back, not till we see what happens.'

'We know what's going to happen.'

'Do we?' he asked, and with that he kissed the top of her head and let himself out.

Helen intended to tell Laura everything but that changed when they came face to face. 'You look wonderful,' said Helen, struggling to come out of her torpor.

'Thanks. I feel wonderful. You'll never guess what.'

'No,' agreed Helen quietly, 'I probably won't.'

'I'm pregnant.'

Pain, very real pain, fought to manifest itself, to live, to strangle her.

'Are you pleased?' pressed Laura.

'More than I can say,' said Helen calmly. 'Are you?'

'I'm so thrilled I don't sleep at night.'

'That's terrific,' said Helen flatly.

'What *was* wrong with you, Helen?'

'I told you,' she replied.

'You said there were complications.'

'I was probably being melodramatic. It was an ovarian cyst. The only complication was I had to have an ovary removed and a Fallopian tube.'

'Oh?' queried Laura.

'That's all, honestly. I just seem to have made a song and dance about it. I've been very ill, but it was probably . . . I think I was tired, you know.'

'Sure,' said Laura.

'I'm fine now. I'm just – Look, thank you for coming, but do you mind if I go to bed now?' asked Helen, like a little child who is bored with a grown-ups' party.

'To be quite honest, I was relieved,' Laura told Freddie when she finally traced his number. 'It was like talking to someone who wasn't quite there. Do you think she's having some sort of breakdown?'

There was no news of Cindy Patterson on either the one o'clock or the five forty-five bulletin on Tuesday; worse than that, she was not even mentioned.

Freddie arrived. She saw him take in the untidiness of the flat and, as she looked around, the state of her environment made an impression on her for the first time for days. Papers were strewn everywhere, and the kitchen was full of empty mineral water bottles and dirty teacups.

'Don't you have a cleaning lady?' asked Freddie sharply.

'I gave her a holiday. I didn't want her fussing while I was at home.'

'Are you eating?'

'Of course,' she lied.

He said nothing, but went to her drinks table and poured two large brandies.

'I don't drink any more,' she said.

'Helen, for heaven's sake, one drink won't hurt. You're not an alcoholic.'

'How do you know?'

'Because I treat them – it's part of my business. You do have a . . . dependency problem, but it's not as simple as drink. After your marriage it was the job, then it was Sam, then it was your job, then it was drink, then it was the job again, coupled with the keep-fit regime. You're not an alcoholic. Look, we'll prove it. We'll both have one, but only one, and then we'll go out and eat.'

Helen took the drink and sipped it. 'I don't want to go out.'

'Have you been beyond the front door since you came home?'

She shook her head.

'Helen,' he said very gently, 'you're not very well, you know. I can't treat you because I'm emotionally involved, but will you see a friend of mine?'

She shook her head again. 'I'm OK.'

'You're *not* OK. I had a phone call from a friend of yours today – Laura. She was very worried.'

'It's kind of you all, but I can cope. Look, I'm not much fun and I'm awfully tired. Please go away.'

The police issued an identikit picture of a relative of Cindy Patterson's. They said they wanted to eliminate him from their inquiries. As yet there was no sign of the child. Everyone believed she must be dead – everyone except the child's mother and Helen Bartlett.

Helen took to playing her piano. She was learning the Mozart A minor sonata. The plaintive theme of the first movement unlocked her coldness, and the odd hot tear escaped from the prison in her head to roll to freedom down her cheeks and on to the black and white keys.

Sam rang, her mother rang, Sebastian rang, Derek rang, Jeremy rang, Freddie rang, Laura rang. Sometimes it seemed there were endless bells in her head. Freddie said something about letting herself feel loved – what a ridiculous notion. She was polite but unforthcoming.

'I'm going back to work on Monday,' she said to each of them in turn, who then, predictably, replied, 'Are you sure you're fit?', to which she gave the stock answer, 'Yes, I'm well rested . . . I'm fine now.'

When Monday came she felt unsure and certainly a little unsteady on her feet. She put make-up on for the first time since her illness and, also for the first time, was horrified at how thin her face had become.

There were vast quantities of mail and she spent the day quietly in her office. She ate alone there at lunchtime and gradually made a dent in the backlog. There was nothing to be recorded in the afternoon, so she stayed in the newsroom area later than usual before going to the make-up department.

'Are you sure you're well enough to be back?' asked Marcia, the make-up artist.

'Yes, I'm fine, thanks. Can I have a hair wash?'

It was soothing to have someone else wash her hair again and Helen, back in the routine she knew so well, began to feel more normal, even slightly excited at the prospect of presenting the programme.

All went according to plan. No machines broke down and there were no live interviews. It was, in fact, a pretty dull edition, though she was not complaining; she felt she was being eased back gently.

They were on the last recorded item when a piece of paper was handed to her. The director spoke in her ear. 'Have you got the newsflash?'

She nodded at the camera.

'OK, we've begged an extra twenty seconds from Presentation. When we come out of this, read it, say a quick good night and we'll come out – no music.'

'You know what you're doing?' asked the floor manager, who had listened in to the same instruction.

'Yes,' she said quite normally, despite the hideous chill that was spreading through her body.

'Ten seconds . . . ,' said the floor manager. 'Coming to you.'

'Tom Kelly reporting,' she back referenced, 'and we end with a piece of news that's just come in. "A body has been found in a ditch near Little Slaughter in the Cotswolds. First reports indicate that it is of a toddler, who was found bound and gagged. It is believed to have lain there for several weeks. Police say it is too early to positively identify the body, though there is speculation it may be that of the missing London four-year-old, Cindy Patterson." ' Helen looked up from the papers and into camera. 'A very sad note on which to end. See you tomorrow, Good night.'

Somehow she must have got into her car and driven home, for that was where she found herself. It was nine o'clock and there was someone for her at the front door. She wandered to the entry phone.

'Helen, it's Sam.'

She pressed the button and waited for him. When he appeared she crumbled; she threw herself into his arms and wept. Through her sobs she repeated the words 'our baby' over and over again. It was an incantation. Helen was too distressed to witness the alarm in Sam's face, but she was aware of his presence holding her while she cried. Finally he persuaded her to lie down. Eventually the sobs died away.

'Jeremy said something to me about how concerned you were about the little girl. I thought you were upset when I saw the programme, but I didn't realise . . . Helen, it's not like you to get so emotional over a news story.'

'I was sure she would live, and then the child in Regent Street, and . . . our baby needn't have died in vain, don't you see?'

'Helen, what are you talking about?'

'It wasn't an ovarian cyst.'

'Oh.' He sighed. 'I don't think I ever believed it was, but I pushed the other possibilities out of my mind.'

'It was an ectopic pregnancy,' she finished clinically.

Sam's eyes filled with tears. 'I wish it had lived,' he said, 'then there would have been some evidence of our love but . . . how would you have coped? How would I have coped halfway across the world, with my only child growing up here?'

'I didn't get pregnant deliberately, but it was conceived in love that weekend Jeremy first came over. I wasn't taking my pill because we'd stopped making love. But I killed it; it's my fault . . . I didn't even know I was pregnant, but when I was so upset over losing you, I smoked and drank it to death. I've been punished now and quite rightly . . . I was given the chance to keep a piece of you, but I destroyed it.'

'Who says so?'

'It stands to reason.'

'Listen to me, Helen. You didn't do anything – it was an accident of nature. When the two parts of us came together it was in the wrong place, that's all.'

She listened to his choice of words and realised how carefully he had selected them. 'Yes, the wrong place and the wrong time . . . Could it be, if we're not allowed each other in this life, that we might be in the next?'

'I'm sure of it,' he said, his voice breaking with emotion. 'Helen, we'll always be friends.'

She shook her head. 'We won't be, Sam. Don't let's pretend. Can you imagine calling me from Cairo after you're married, saying, "Hi, Helen," and me saying, "Hi, Sam, how's the wife?" Oh, no. It's just not possible.'

He pressed his lips hungrily on hers and, though she fought against responding to him initially, her instinct took over. 'Helen, Helen, Helen,' he murmured into her hair.

She tried to smile as she pulled away. 'A month tomorrow you marry someone else. I'm pleased and happy to see you today, but I can't bear to see you again. I love you, Sam. I'll always love you, but . . .'

He squeezed her hand.

'If I had been pregnant . . . normally,' she went on, 'I wouldn't have told you. I wouldn't have used it as a weapon to try to get you to stay. But I would have loved to have your baby . . .' The tears flowed again.

'I know. Jeremy says you're a remarkable woman. He's right.'

'I'm going to play you a piece of music, and then I want you to go.'

She sat at the keyboard and swiftly played through a couple of pages of densely packed notes.

'That was beautiful,' he said. 'What was it called?'

She left the piano stool and walked with him to the door. 'It's one of the Bach two-part inventions.'

'What's a two-part invention?'

'It's . . . a short piece of counterpoint for two hands.'

'Or two players?' he asked.

She nodded. He held her gaze in the doorway. It was as if a silent, unseen spider were spinning a web of mutual love, pain and despair to hold them for ever in the moment. Would it bind them through eternity, or would it disintegrate as soon as he turned or she closed the door?

'Always remember that I love you,' he said, finally turning away and walking out of her life.

Chapter Fifteen

In her dream a bee was buzzing around some flowers. She was wandering by the river with Sam. As she emerged from this happiness of bygone days, the buzzing continued. Helen had slept later than usual; it was eight-thirty and the noise of the bee was actually emanating from her entry phone. As she reached for it her stomach contracted with the realisation of today's date. D day. Departure day for Sam. 'Yes?' she said.

'It's Streamline Taxis here,' said a voice. 'I have a package for you.' She slipped into her dressing gown and ran down the stairs to the main front door. It was more than a package; it was a tea chest. 'I'll take it up for you,' said the driver.

'Thanks very much.' She raced ahead to find her purse so that she might tip this obliging delivery man.

Helen stared at the chest but no clue immediately came to mind as to what it might contain. She emptied out armfuls of polystyrene squiggles and found a substantial object wrapped in newspaper, which she quickly uncovered. It was the little dancer, the Merrifield sculpture she had loved for so long, though she could not recall ever having mentioned the fact to Sam. Attached to the figure was a tiny card on a string. 'Always remember that I love you,' it read.

Suddenly the feeling was back, the feeling she had fought against and pretended was extinct. She ran to pick up the telephone. The dialling tone was loud in her ear; she listened, mesmerised by it for a moment, then deliberately replaced the receiver and walked away. I am so sad, she thought. I was off my head a few weeks ago, I see that now. I'm better, but I am so very sad . . .

She had not been in her office long when Laura appeared, bearing two cups of coffee. 'I thought you might be a bit upset.' It was kind of her friend to remember.

Helen nodded. 'I expect after today it'll be better.'

'Well,' said Laura, 'You're already much more together than you were a few weeks ago. I don't mind telling you now, I thought you were going mad.'

'I thought I was too,' Helen said quietly.

'Maybe he'll come back.'

'Maybe,' said Helen, 'but I have to believe he won't.'

'I hate to say this, Helen, but I've always thought, perhaps I've even said, I wonder if he's just one of those men who can never commit.'

Helen shook her head. 'Don't ever say that to me again. It's possible, of course, but for my self-respect and my sanity I have to believe that what we had was real. I have to believe he loved me, otherwise a year of my life has been built on unreal foundations. I have to believe that it was the trauma of at last finding a woman he wanted to marry that provoked the crisis. I may be deluded, but I have to hold on to these things. Incidentally, he sent me the little Merrifield sculpture this morning, the one I told you about. That was sweet, wasn't it?'

'It was,' agreed Laura. 'Any message?'

'A little card, not even signed, which said, "Always remember that I love you." '

'Then I'm sure he does. Drink your coffee.'

Helen sipped it slowly.

'That bloody battle-axe of a mother,' said Laura, 'I could ring her neck. I think if she hadn't been around, everything would have been all right.'

'You can't blame her, Laura.' Helen sighed. 'I've thought about it a lot. It's a bit presumptuous of us sitting here, thirty-five years younger than that lady, writing off all she cares for, all she believes in. Who's to say, just because we're modern and cosmopolitan, that we're right and she's wrong? More than that,' she went on, 'it's tribal. Sam said that once. It is a matter of honour and of heritage: one can't fly in the face of that.'

'You're taking this very well,' said Laura.

'Not really. I'm screaming inside. It seems that the moment I finally unclenched my grip on my own destiny and allowed him to look after me, he began to prise away my fingers, one by one, from the rock I was told was so secure. I don't think I'll ever get over it.'

Around one o'clock Derek came looking for her. 'I want you to interview Arnie Franks.'

'Fine,' said Helen. 'Who is he?'

'Your mother would remember.'

'Well, that doesn't help me.'

'He was a band singer in his day. Came from Barnsley or somewhere like it, but he made it big in the States. He's passing through town on his way up north to do a farewell tour.'

'Not much point if no one knows who the hell he is.'

'Some will. Perhaps he just wants to get back to his roots. I don't know if he can still sing even – he must be older than God – but we've got to do him. One of today's items has gone down the pan, and there's a hole in the programme at the moment.'

'OK. What time's he coming in?'

'He's not. He hasn't got time. You're to meet him at the Pan-Am Clipper Club lounge in Terminal Three at Heathrow at two fifteen.'

Helen panicked. 'Oh, no, Derek. I can't go.'

'Why not?'

'Well . . . I mean . . . what about the programme?'

'Look, just knock off a quick interview. Get him to sing to you if possible. You'll have it in the can by three, back here by four. Loads of time.'

'Can't somebody else do it?'

'Come on, Helen, don't give me a hard time. They can't. I haven't got anybody. Anyway, it's your sort of thing.'

'All right Derek, I'm sorry.'

Fate had not finished with her yet, she surmised, as she motored out to Heathrow. She had never before interviewed anybody at Heathrow. Why today of all days? She had no idea of the time of Sam's flight; perhaps he had left the country already. Again misery threatened to destroy the calm she had built up during the past few weeks. She had tried to put Sam out of her mind. There had been no contact. She had seen Freddie a couple of times and Jeremy had called her, but neither could replace Sam. She believed no one ever could, but she had gone on living, one moment at a time, refusing to yield to the desolate notion that death was the only solution.

October the third and, with the whirling of the wind, the first leaves of autumn were falling. She recalled the night she and Sam had driven back from the dinner party and how she had almost slipped on the wet, rotting foliage in the gutter as she had emerged, unsteadily, from his car.

There had been an interview with a nutritionist once. Helen had almost forgotten it. The woman's words came back to her: 'Often we have to do without our favourite things, for the very items we are addicted to are those to which we are allergic.' Was Sam an allergy as well as an addiction? It was difficult to say, but she acknowledged, perhaps for the first time, how detrimental the past year had been to her health, in spite of the fact that she longed to live it all again and to continue doing so. 'Oh, Sam,' she said over the music from the car radio, 'how can you leave me when there is so much love? How can you go?' But he had.

The crew were waiting for her by the open-plan newsagent's near the Clipper Club lounge. 'Have you met the singer?' she asked Mike, the cameraman. 'Yes, and his objectionable PR man. You'd think his client was a cross between Tony Bennett and Frank Sinatra the way he's going on.'

Helen sighed. Hype on the one hand and a disgruntled crew on the other were not a recipe for success.

She went to the lounge with the cameraman. It was full of passengers with the deathly pallor that accompanies jet lag and the resigned acceptance that your life and luggage are in somebody else's hands. The television was blaring from the far end, and Arnie Franks stood looking aggrieved that no one was fawning over him.

Barnsley did not spring to mind as his obvious birthplace. His hair, augmented by a weaving technique, was faded blonde. He had a tan and perfectly capped teeth. He was also wearing rather too many gold rings.

'Mr Franks.' Helen greeted him warmly. His eyes lit up in response to her recognition. 'I'm Helen Bartlett. I'll be doing the interview, but I'd like to suggest we do it outside. It'll give more of a sense of urgency – you rushing off to get another plane and all that. And this' – she made a sweeping gesture at the assortment of untidy bodies and used coffee cups – 'is not ideal.'

'I'm yours to command.' He smiled.

'OK Mike,' she turned to the cameraman, 'can you set up outside, near where we met by the telephones?'

'Yes, sure,' he said. He liked Helen; she was efficient. And, unlike her, he would be finished for the day once they completed the task in hand.

Helen chatted to Arnie until his PR man, Jerry Shroder, came back. He had been checking on the flight to Manchester and did not seem at all pleased that Helen was treating his client in a familiar rather than a deferential manner. The cameraman returned and beckoned them.

'This won't take long, will it?' said the PR man, trying to regain command of the situation.

'No.' Helen smiled sweetly. 'But if you don't have the time . . .'

'We have the time,' he said quickly. 'By the way,' he asked nonchalantly, 'how many viewers do you have?'

'We're watched by an average of twelve million.'

'We definitely have the time,' said Arnie.

As they positioned themselves, Helen looked up at the monitor above them. Her heart missed a beat when she saw the flashing 'last call' symbol beside flight MS778 to Cairo. Beyond them were jostling crowds exiting through the departure gate at right angles to where they were standing. She hoped with every fibre that she would see Sam one more time, yet she hoped just as intensely that he had arrived early with nothing to do and had long since passed through this section.

'Are you ready, my dear?' asked Arnie.

'Oh . . . yes. I'm sorry.'

The electrician switched on a couple of lamps. Helen was so used to them she was oblivious to their brightness. Passers-by, however were drawn to the scene by their unfamiliar flare like moths around a flame.

Helen launched into her questions. Even if Sam had not left, he had no way of knowing she was here, so he would never see her. 'How long is it since you were in England, Mr Franks?'

'Well, let me see now, I guess it's all of twenty years.'

'Really? And where will you be playing?'

'Manchester, Leeds, Newcastle . . .' The list went on. Helen tried to keep her mind on the job.

'What would you say was the song that made you most famous?'

'Oh, there were so many,' he said, 'but on my tour' – he fielded the question expertly – 'I'll have something for everybody.'

Suddenly she saw him. He was a mere twenty yards away. Other travellers kept blocking her view and the crowd around her was moving in, interested to see television at work and to establish the identity of the ageing interviewee. He put his dispatch case down to search for his documents, and she observed the moment he became aware of the strong lights to his right. He turned, picked up his case and stared uncomprehendingly. Someone walked in front of him and then he reappeared.

'Helen!' She saw him say her name, though the noise all around was too great for her to hear it. He took a few steps towards her. 'Excuse me,' she said and pushed her way through the people. 'Helen!' he said again, and he stretched his free hand towards her though he was being buffeted by travellers intent on barging through the gate to their waiting flights. She took a few more steps and stopped. She willed him to come to her. He could . . . he could . . . He could move through the madding crowd and take her in his arms. He could still declare his intention to stay. She closed her eyes for a second and when she reopened them there was an even greater sea of faces between them. He looked at her and as she returned his gaze she saw tears fill his eyes and then spill down his pale face.

'Don't give up on me, Sam,' she cried mentally. 'There aren't many males man enough to handle me. You can.'

He stood fixed to the spot as signals flashed back and forth between their anxious eyes.

'For God's sake, Sam, move. This is your last chance.'

He was motionless.

She turned from him and immediately regretted it; she looked back to give him the benefit of the doubt.

Slowly he shook his head. 'I love you,' he mouthed, as he began to walk away. He took a few steps, then looked back at her with the haunted look of a man mounting the scaffold. 'I love you,' he mouthed again, and then resolutely walked on and disappeared under the big yellow departures sign.

Helen stood for a moment or two, feeling as though all the blood had drained from her body.

'We really must get on,' said Jerry Shroder, tugging at her elbow.

'I'm sorry,' she said, as she rejoined the group, 'I thought I saw someone I knew.'

'Are you all right, baby?' asked Mike.

'I'm fine. Sorry to have interrupted things. Can you pan off a passer-by or something to give me a cutting point?'

'OK, running,' said Mike.

'Well, Mr Franks, many of your fans will catch up with you on tour, but for those who won't, how about a quick burst of song?'

'Sure,' said Arnie, taking centre-stage. He reached for Helen's hand and stared deep into her eyes. 'But I miss you,' he crooned in his husky, over-generous vibrato, 'most of all, my darling, when autumn leaves start to fall.'

There was a pause; Helen edged herself back out of the shot. She saw Mike tighten to a close-up of the singer. She caught the cameraman's eye, slowly raised her head, then nodded.

'OK,' she whispered. 'Cut!'